Iron Lake Burning

Copyright © 2003 by Marty Duncan
All rights reserved.
No part of this book may be reproduced, stored in a
retrieval system, or transmitted by any means,
electronic, mechanical, photocopying, recording,
or otherwise, without written permission
from the author.
Cover Illustration by Rachael Jaster, © 2003

Published by BookSurge, LLC
North Charleston, South Carolina
Library of Congress Control Number: 2004104080

ISBN: 1-59109-870-X
This book is printed on acid free paper.

MARTY DUNCAN

IRON LAKE BURNING

A NOVEL

Imprint Books, Inc.
2003

Iron Lake Burning

TABLE OF CONTENTS

1. A Rainbow Certain	1
2. There's Always Optimism	13
3. Broken Arrow	25
4. Dangerous Chemicals	37
5. First and Goal	47
6. Intimidation	53
7. Losing Control	65
8. Waiting on da' Big Guy	75
9. Shoelaces and Sarcasm	83
10. Football on a Frosty Night	93
11. An Early Skirmish	101
12. 'Roll with the Punches'	111
13. A Seductive Mirage	119
14. Flames Across the Street	127
15. In the Swamp	137
16. Iron Circle	147
17. Drawing the Line	157
18. To Love Controversy	167
19. Crossing the Line	179
20. Hand of a Friend	185
21. Iron Lake Board Guilty	199
22. 'Hell doth Freeze Over'	211
23. Retaliation	219
24. Little John and Robin	233
25. We will Know Them by Their Limping	241
26. Graduation Day	253
27. Consequences	263
28. A Little Awareness, Almost No Change	269
About the Author	277

Order Additional Copies of *Iron Lake Burning*
Directly from the publisher (on line) at www.BookSurge.com
Read two chapters of Marty's other novels at www.omagadh.com

Gold...then Iron When a disgraced Japanese Army officer tries to recover a priceless religious artifact for his emperor, James Harant (Office of Naval Intelligence) is forced to balance his growing love for Heather Mackay against his duty to defeat the Colonel's *Code of Bushido.*

Kelsey: a Civil War Tale When Patrick Harant joined the 6th Minnesota Volunteers, Kelsey O'Neill knew he felt compelled to serve the Union. She was left to defend herself on the frontier. (**Due to be published in 2004**)

There are two people to whom this book is dedicated. They were young and loving and caring before the anger and hatred and distrust in Iron Lake came into their lives and the lives of their parents.
They were there during five tough years, years when we did not discuss what was happening to their father at his job. Those were five years when we clung together and held each other tight, and that is why this book is dedicated to Derek Andrew Duncan and to Darcy Lee Duncan Helder.

And Dedicated To...
All those parents and grandparents who supported 'our' children by their attendance at games, conferences, and concerts; parents who volunteered to make cookies and pumpkin bread for bake sales; parents who supported the school's administrators even when we seemed to be 'officious' and 'stuffed shirts'.
Dedicated also to the public superintendents who accepted minimal salary for maximum responsibilities and spent their careers in service to children. They were the superintendents who worked to make the world a better place.

These People Helped:
My friend and Lead Teacher at Marble Elementary, Donna Anderson; another friend and Media Generalist at Vandyke Elementary, Bonnie Gelle; long time friends and readers, Gerald and Mary Jane Young; and of course, my long time friend Carolynn Lee Swensrud Duncan.

CHAPTER ONE
A Rainbow Certain

"Life is a vale of tears," his Gramma Louise said to Tom Harant when he was eight years old. Somehow, he thought she meant a veil of tears and regret...a misty mythic veil of regrets that each man and woman must somehow meet and defeat during their lives. It was only later, when he came to think about his years in Iron Lake, that he remembered her words.

"Life is a valley, all right," he once said to no one in particular.

During the week he was in the hospital, Tom Harant remembered little of the doctor who told him to go home and chop wood. For the first three days, the drugs kept him in a vegetative state...he could remember sitting on his bed for one entire day. The last four days were equally hard to remember. There were two counseling sessions. However, the patient Tom Harant was not in for drug treatment, so the counselors seemed to take little interest. He remembered telling a doctor at the Golden Valley Center about the stress of working in a fish bowl. The doctor told him to chop wood twice a week. That was the sum total of what Tom Harant, Superintendent of the Iron Lake Schools, remembered about the week his wife put him in the hospital for stress.

The unfortunate thing was he couldn't forget what he really needed to forget...the seven months before, during and after the Iron Lake strike. He desperately wanted to forget the weeks in August 1990 when the School Board was debating whether to risk a strike. He would have preferred to be somewhere else when the fire occurred, or when the Board held a public meeting with 600 angry parents in attendance. He wanted to forget the illegal actions of the School Board (which he *somehow* was supposed to prevent). And then to get the telegram from the Department of Defense, telling him that his son Mark was injured in the Gulf War. Those seven months piled stress upon more stress until Tom Harant was almost beside himself. At least, he thought, I am a new man...32 pounds lighter than when school opened back in September.

That was one advantage of working in a fish bowl with lots of angry neighbors, as he explained to his good friend Wrecker Kline. Tom was whistling in the woods to a choir of deaf trees. Wrecker and his wife Mary Jo were sitting in Tom's breezeway for a late snack after a baseball game (Iron Lake 7, Tivoli High 1).

"Don't do it," Wrecker said adamantly. "You'll ruin your chances for a new contract." Wrecker was a nickname, from his days playing college football. He was wearing his traditional black sweatshirt with 'Notre Dame' printed across the chest. Wrecker was a large man with large hands, and a happy-go-lucky demeanor.

Wrecker looked at Crystal…he knew Tom's wife would worry about the prospects of having to move again. She was sitting with her fingers clasped, her head down, looking at the kitchen table. Wrecker saw the top of her blond hair…and he saw her head jump once. She reached for the coffee cup in front of her, out of a need to do something, anything to get Wrecker to look elsewhere.

"Explain it to him, Wreck. You know how stubborn he can be." She said these words quietly. Crystal was lifting her cup, knowing she wouldn't have to say anything more. She glanced sideways, trying to look at Tom without actually looking at him. Her husband was staring at Wrecker, trying to force a smile onto his face. *'It's such a nice face,'* she thought, *'you don't deserve him.'*

Crystal was proud, and at the same time possessive, about her man. He had what a neighbor described as a pleasant face, eyes of a blue that turned azure when Tom wore a blue dress shirt. His brown hair was worn short, in a fashion that he called 'Drill Sergeant' short. 'Wall street conservative,' Crystal liked to call it. Tom's bushy eyebrows and straight nose tended to make his appearance somewhat stern but Crystal knew that inwardly, Tom was an affable teddy bear who cared about people and their kids.

"Mr. Wrecker Kline,…I'm not trying to shovel 'manure' here. I think my tenure at Iron Lake is about over," added Tom when he winked at Mary Jo. She had that 'Oh, brother, here we go with this old argument' on her face. Wrecker's wife had a pleasant face, with thin eyebrows and soft cheekbones. She was everybody's picture of compatibility and always knew what Wrecker was thinking. For the baseball game, she had worn a white blouse under a solid red blazer, the traditional red and white of Iron Lake.

Mary Jo laughed and reached across the table to pat Crystal on the arm. Crystal's lips separated in a wide smile but it was a smile of determined stoicism. Crystal knew that Wreck couldn't change Tom's mind. These two men had been arguing about this subject for months.

"You need to put it behind you, Tom."

"And do what? What should I do about the sleepless nights...the pacing around the house...the sounds I hear in the quiet of the night...the screams of teachers on the line...the sirens during the fire...the threats that were made...you tell me," he said emphasizing the words *"darn it"*.

"Try to forget the strike, Tom. You're not helping Crystal and you're not helping yourself by remembering."

"Don't you think," Tom said, "I've tried to forget?"

Tom got up from the kitchen table and walked over to the cabinet above the refrigerator. He took out a bottle of E&J Brandy, and poured himself a stiff shot. Then he buried the brandy under ice and diet cola. He brought the drink back to the table, and sat down. Crystal was looking at him, with that expression on her face.

"On a week night?" she said. "Aren't you going to offer some to Wreck?"

"Yes, I guess I am," he said getting to his feet. He knew that Mary Jo wouldn't drink anything stronger than wine, and then she limited herself to one glass per night. Wrecker and Tom, on the other hand, seemed to enjoy drinking together...each knew that what was said in Tom's kitchen stayed in Tom's kitchen. Wrecker was a minister of the Evangelical Lutheran Church in America. He claimed the ELCA was a great homogenous group of Lutheran churches that specialized in missions to the heathens in Africa. Tom took Wrecker with a grain of salt, and knew that confidentiality was a two-way street. Wrecker had shared some of his secrets with Tom and Crystal. Tom knew that Wrecker could be trusted, and added,

"Percy says...write the book, tell the story and let the rest be damned." He said this while pouring Wrecker a double shot of brandy. "But then you know Percy...damn the torpedoes...full speed ahead."

"That's our Percy," Wrecker added. Everyone around the table knew Perseus Smith as an assertive yet obstinate member of the Board of Directors, who invariably let everyone know exactly where he stood on any subject. Mary Jo laughed when she remembered the night Percy came to the spaghetti feed at the church, dressed like a French nobleman, with frilly cuffs and a lacy shirt. Percy was going to talk to an American Legion group about the right to hold an opinion.

"Who is he angry with this month?" Crystal asked, expecting either Tom or Wrecker to know the answer.

"The federal government. Some highly placed doctor says there is no evidence that 'Agent Orange' has caused lung cancer or leukemia." Tom knew all about Percy's anger. Percy was a Vietnam Vet, married to a 'long-suffering' yet patient woman. During the stretch break at Thursday's Board meeting, Percy harangued Tom about the government's failure to support the medical claims of Vietnam veterans.

"So Percy says write it. He probably thinks writing it will help you to calm down?" said Wrecker, expecting an argument.

"That's enough...from both of you," said Crystal as she stood up. She moved to the oven and pulled the door open. With a heavy mitten on one hand, she removed a flat pan that held eight apple turnovers. She placed the pan on a cutting board, and proceeded to open a package of white frosting. With her back to the other three, she added,

"We don't need to relive the strike, do we?" She nipped off a corner of the white frosting and squeezed it onto the apple turnovers. When they were ready, she turned toward the table. Her husband was sitting... looking into the murky cola of his drink...staring at the swirling colors, trying desperately to see the future. Wrecker and Mary Jo were looking at her. She thought the scene reminded her of a Norman Rockwell painting...friends gathered around the table in her Early American kitchen.

*****

The kitchen was anything but Early American. It was almost the way they had found it. Maple cabinets above the sink. Maple cabinets including a pantry and a broom closet went along one wall. The former owner removed a bedroom wall and created an eating nook with a picture window that looked into their huge back yard. Tom and Crystal had purchased the owner's maple dining set...with eight Early American chairs...they were the only things 'Early American' in the room.

The kitchen was carpeted with bright blue, a shimmering blue outdoor carpet. The previous owner had found the carpet on sale at a warehouse, and bought it without asking his wife. He purchased so much of it that blue carpet covered the kitchen floor, the breezeway into the garage, and the master bedroom. While Tom was negotiating the price for the house, the owner's wife confided to Crystal that she wouldn't miss the 'aqua-velvet' carpet, as she called it. Crystal smiled and said nothing...she knew that Tom had fallen in love with the trees that shadowed and swayed above the house.

Tom's trees, as she came to call them, were part of a tree nursery. When the nursery went out of business, an astute businessman had saved the trees that ran down the property lines. Each lot had thirty and thirty-five foot Norway pines or twelve foot White pines running along the edge of the property. As Tom discovered later, on a quiet night sitting in the breezeway, you could hear the murmur of voices among the pines, a quiet shushing sound that Tom described as the music of the trees. He found the breezeway was the perfect place to sit while reading a Ludlum or MacLean novel late at night.

It was Tom's house, more than it was Crystal's. In the first year, he painted the entire house by hand, slate gray with white trim. In the second year, he trimmed the trees higher, and manicured the lawn. In the third year Tom scraped each window, replacing old putty with new and painting the windows slowly and carefully. The previous owner had built a fountain by pouring cement into a hole. Unfortunately the fountain tilted after it was built. The water sloshed out of the pool on the low side. Tom tackled the long neglected fountain and managed to get a pump to throw water six feet straight up. He had to refill the fountain every five hours, but he enjoyed the task.

Sitting in the breezeway, on a quiet summer night, Tom decided that everything was just about perfect. His father, who rarely said one word of praise to anyone, had complimented Tom for fixing the fountain. Frank had posed by the fountain, with Tom's son Mark, who was home from a tour of duty aboard the USS George Philip (FFG-12), a guided missile frigate. Mark was 26 years old, during that long, lazy summer when Tom and his Step-dad took time to talk to each other. That was the summer before the Iron Lake teacher's strike—the same summer before a forceful dictator named Saddem Hussein invaded Kuwait.

*****

"You want me to forget the strike. I can't. Just as I can't forget my father and his pain. Or the pain of some of the people here in Iron Lake." Tom drank from his brandy…at first, a sip…then a swallow. He stood up and stepped back from the table. He looked at 'the Ramblin' Wreck from Bechyn Tech' and watched while his buddy Wreck raised his glass in a salute. No words passed between them.

Crystal came up beside Tom and placed her hand under his arm. She squeezed his arm. Tom raised his glass to Wreck and said,

"May the sun always shine,

Upon your window pane," before his friend Wrecker added,

"May a rainbow be certain

To follow each rain."

The two men had a tendency to become maudlin when they drank brandy. The two women thought they understood their men. Crystal and Mary Jo were down-to-earth ladies, sworn to support their men while getting their children through high school, and with luck, college. Tom's dedication to his school district meant that Crystal rarely raised a word of concern. What happened in Iron Lake troubled her. Moreover, she knew that Tom carried a large amount of guilt for the teacher's strike in 1990, and for not visiting his father who was dying with bone cancer that fall.

"The rain seems to follow me around," Tom said quietly. "I'm not chopping enough wood," he added and laughed. Mary Jo had a puzzled look on her face. Tom had not told a soul about the psychiatrist's prescription. After all, who would want to know that their School Superintendent had been to see a psychiatrist during the Iron Lake strike? Such a revelation would have diminished the faith people held in Tom. He was smart enough to know that such a revelation would lead to questions about his competency.

"I have this dream, Wreck. Can you imagine this?" Tom walked to the table and sat down. "I'm running through this field, trying to reach the trees at the border of the field. Someone is chasing me. I can't see who it is and I don't know why I'm running. I burst into the trees and I circle around to my right. Through the dark I see three men…they are carrying shotguns."

"Are you sure they are after you?" asked Mary Jo, loudly.

"Yes," said Tom, with determination.

"It's a nightmare, Tom." His friend Wreck had a puzzled look on his face and was about to stop Tom's comment.

"I can't see the faces of the three men," Tom added.

"It's a dream, Tom."

"Yes, it is. But why am I running?"

"Can you be leading them, instead of them chasing you?" Crystal seemed to have this momentary flash of insight. "Maybe they aren't after you. Maybe you were leading them?

"I feel a lot of dread…almost as if I know my end is coming."

"Is that all bad?" asked his friend Wrecker.

"No…it's not all bad. There must be an end to my work here in Iron Lake. It would feel good to get rid of the bastards and leave."

There was a small gasp at his shoulder. He turned to look into Crystal's blue eyes. He could see the worry and the fear, deep in her blue eyes. "I don't want to tell you this…but," he continued. Both her hands circled his arm. He could feel them tightening on his arm.

"There was a rumor," said Wreck.

"And you didn't tell me?" stated Crystal with a glare at Tom.

"Would it have made any difference?"

"No."

"What did they do?" asked the Wreck, leading Tom into telling them what they knew they didn't want to hear.

"They voted Four to Two to ask me to resign." Tom turned and put his left hand over Crystal's hands. He could see tears welling up into her eyes. A drop of water squeezed out of her left eye and ran toward her chin. 'At least our kids are out of high school,' he thought to himself.

"Which four?" asked Wreck.

"Cratt, Trivic, Arnie and Glacial Linda. She always follows Cratt's lead."

"Can the vote be reversed?"

"One of the four of them would have to move to rescind the original motion. Or Percy or Fitzsimmons would have to move to rescind and hope no one remembers Robert's Rules."

"Even then, it would require two of the original four to vote to rescind and rehire you," the Wreck said, casually.

"Not likely," Tom said quietly. He was still looking into Crystal's eyes. He knew she was hurt. They had put so much of themselves into this school district. Church choir, the local Cable Commission, Economic

Development, and Sunday morning coffees out at the resort on Iron Lake.

*****

Caramel rolls and coffee were the tradition at Bulrush Bay Resort, on the north shore of the lake. On Sunday mornings, a small group of traditionalists came together at 'Bulrush' for the rolls and the conversation. It was an opportunity, as Tom Harant believed, to meet with the 'movers and shakers' of Spencer County...the businessmen and leaders of the county. The men brought their wives dressed in their Sunday best and two groups formed, the men to discuss politics and the women to talk about their children.

Bulrush Resort was a campground and boat rental on Iron Lake, just off the county highway that ran around the lake. Walking from the lot, the new visitor was always impressed by the huge bony skulls and jaws of monster Northern Pike that were nailed to the power poles by the marina. Some of the skulls, from 30-pound Northern Pike, were bigger than a child's head. In summer the marina held the boats of the faithful who motored across the lake to Bulrush Bay. In the winter, snowmobiles would be lined up on the shore. It was here on a Sunday morning in early June that Tom Harant began to wonder about Connie Cratt.

Tom was standing outside the restaurant, looking at the marina, when Cratt walked up with two bottles of beer.

"It's a little early in the day, isn't it?" Tom asked.

"You went to church, didn't you?"

"Well, yes." Tom reached out and took the bottle that Cratt offered. He lifted it to his lips and swallowed a third of the bottle. In the back of his mind, Tom knew he shouldn't add to his waistline. Mr. Cratt, however, was a member of Tom's board.

"Nice morning, what?" Connie was wearing a white shirt with a plain brown tie. His suit coat was probably in his car. He reached up and scratched the back of his head and then took a swallow from his beer.

"Too much politics, in there," Cratt continued. "They're all talking about the fall elections...the mid-terms they call them. Hell, ain't nobody give a damn about the mid-year elections, 'cept maybe his Honor the so-called County Commissioner."

Tom was looking at Cratt, trying to figure where the conversation was going. Connie had a 'standard' face if there was such a thing. Bushy eyebrows above brown eyes, over a straight nose that protected an equally bushy mustache. Connie seemed to be a little warm. He wiped sweat off his forehead. He reached up and pulled his tie down, loosening the button at the collar of his shirt.

"Well..." Tom ventured. "You know some people...they love to discuss politics. They're probably just frustrated men who wanted to run for office but their wives said no."

Cratt laughed. He looked at Tom, wondering how much he could tell the local school superintendent. Then he took another swig of his beer. "I've decided to run..." he began, while looking at his beer bottle. Then he added, "for state president of my union."

It was a cool morning. Tom felt a shiver along the backs of his arms, or was it a premonition of disaster? He asked Cratt if he saw a conflict of interest.

"Hell, no. The Amalgamated Sheet and Metal Workers of America are an AFL-CIO union. We're damn proud of who we are. But we do no business with the state, and certainly we do no business with the Iron Lake Schools."

"Will you stay on the school board?" Tom was afraid that Cratt would want to continue on the board, raising questions about Cratt's loyalties, just when the School Board was entering negotiations. It was June of 1990...six months before the Iron Lake strike.

"Hell...I don't suppose you could get a strong Republican to take my place," laughed Connie. "Most of the men in Iron Lake are wimps..."

Inwardly, Tom cringed. He had never heard anyone refer to his neighbors as 'wimps' and he looked around to see if anyone was in hearing distance. A small breeze blew a few dead leaves across the grass and into the lake. Two of the boats at the dock knocked into each other. To the south beyond the lake, dark clouds were forming.

"And that applies to your so-called teacher's union. They don't know what a union is. They are just a group of over-paid pansies...flaming commies as far as I can tell...I'll whip them into shape this fall."

He raised his bottle and finished the beer. They were standing in the shade when a dog walked quietly past. The dog meandered over to one of the power poles with the skulls of northerns. It raised its hind leg and wet the pole. As it was finishing, the dog looked up and saw the empty eyes of a northern skull staring back. It yelped, and ran off for a short way.

Tom chuckled. Cratt looked at him, as if to ask why he was laughing. Tom didn't reply. He stood and looked at the man, one of six who shared the power on the Iron Lake school board.

"But you're just one of six, Connie. You can't run the Board."

"With three more votes, I will run it."

"Why would you want to?" Tom asked.

"So the rest of the state can see how I can stand up to these blood sucking teachers and their liberal leaders...that Don Diamonte, in his fancy building across the street from the State Capital...Christ, Almighty. The Minnesota Education Association isn't a real union, not like the Federation of Teachers, the MFT."

He handed the empty bottle to Tom, telling him to send his wife out...that they were heading for home. Afterwards, driving back into Iron Lake, Tom wanted to tell his wife about Cratt's comments. Something kept him from speaking. He thought about the dog that was scared by a skull and shivered. He had only been on the job at Iron Lake for one year...and he wondered if Iron Lake would turn into a 'valley of tears'. He saw leaves blowing across the street...sure sign of an early fall.

*****

Standing in his kitchen three years later, he saw gentle tears in his wife's eyes. He knew she was feeling bad for him, for all they had been through during and after the strike...dealing with *the shadow* of Connie Cratt that cast a pall across their lives and the lives of Iron Lake teachers. Now, to have the board ask for his resignation...in what amounted to a betrayal.

Three years after the strike, Tom was not ready to quit. His friend Wrecker told him not to tell the story. If anything, Tom felt the story needed to be told. He wanted people to see Connie Cratt as he really was: a vindictive man trying to live up to his father's reputation as a union organizer.

"It's your guilt, isn't it?" she said one day when she had the courage to challenge him. He didn't respond. He was looking out the window at a rain cloud approaching from the southwest...it was raining in that corner of Iron Lake. He knew the storm would blow over in about fifteen minutes, leaving the corn and soybean fields damp with the rain they needed. The farmers called these storms 'million dollar rains' for the value they added. He could sit afterward in his breezeway and look in the direction of the retreating storm. He would marvel at the blue sky that followed the rain. Some days, feeling blue, he wondered if it would ever be his turn to feel the joy of a rainbow.

Ten years later, in Fairmont, Minnesota Tom said to himself, *'I should tell this story. It's the real story of Iron Lake.'* The year was 2002, ten years after the strike. Tom and Crystal were in Fairmont, his third school district. His kids were grown, and 'well launched'. That was how he described Corrine who was called Cookie by her Dad, and Carl…and his oldest, Mark who was now a Lt. Commander in 'Today's Navy'.

"It's the story of how four people ruined themselves, of how a fire led to a death, and how people deluded themselves, thinking they could control four members of a school board who set out deliberately to bring down a union."

That was how Tom described the story, how it felt in his gut. Crystal knew that Tom, more than anyone else, still carried guilt about the strike, still thought there was more he should have done during that tumultuous year. She knew, when he felt blue, that he was searching for the joy of a rainbow.

CHAPTER TWO
There's Always Optimism

In this world there are two types of school superintendents, Tom was fond of saying. There are the young and idealistic who want to set the world on fire. And there are the other type, older and cynical... the superintendents who are content to let the younger teachers 'lead the charge' towards a better school system. In 1990, Tom Harant was a realist who knew that the School Superintendent couldn't win every battle with the school board. Nevertheless, he was forty-seven years old, and still looked forward to improving one or two programs for his kids. He still believed that if you explained the need to a school board, in a majority of times, the board would agree with the superintendent.

Tom was an optimist who believed the schools *could* be improved. He had a difficult time understanding the attitude of his predecessor.

"When I met Arley Green a year ago, he seemed tired," Tom told the audience in his breezeway one night. It was election night in May 1990. The Iron Lake voters had voted 1210 to 690 to approve an excess levy of $65,000 per annum. Crystal was serving iced tea with plum wine to their guests Percy and Eileen. Percy was the Vietnam veteran on the board. Eileen worked as an Early Childhood teacher. They wanted children, but Eileen had recently said she already had one child to take care of...her Percy.

Tom's third guest that Election Night was Corrine, also called Cookie. She had just finished her first year of teaching at Iron Lake. Corrine had walked over from her bungalow two blocks away.

"How long did he work here?" Corrine asked. She was wearing a light cotton dress of pale yellow and a dark blue windbreaker. Tom smiled at her, knowing that his entire family was proud that Cookie became a teacher.

"Thirty-five years, or so I've been told," said Tom.

"Why was he tired?"

"That's not what I meant."

"Not tired?"

"No, more like he just didn't care. He had done his stint, borrowed the money the school needed, and left the district in debt. He didn't care." Tom saw 'Cookie' looking at him and realized that she idolized her father. A stone turned in his stomach. Her blue eyes seemed to be laughing at him but he knew better. Her lips had formed into a half-smile, telling Tom that she was interested in whatever Tom had to say.

"There's a story they tell about Arley," Tom added.

"Tell your daughter," Percy broke in. He was sitting back in the yellow wicker chair, admiring his iced tea. Percy was on the board two years earlier when the board fired Arley Green.

"Well, it seems Billy Washburn was sitting in the last row of chairs in the board room, daydreaming. He noticed Arley looking at him and Billy moved his head. There was no reaction from Arley."

"He was asleep, with both eyes half closed." Percy had been sitting next to Arley when he heard a soft rumble. "It was one of those marathon meetings you hear about." Percy had touched Arley's arm and he woke up, momentarily.

"He fell asleep, again, with his head propped up on his fist." Tom laughed, picturing the scene. For the superintendent to fall asleep, someone had to be talking an issue to death.

"According to Mr. Washburn, Arnold Murkiwasser was talking about how the custodians need to use more paint in the summer. Arnie was going on and on about paint and its value for school morale."

"Listening to Arnie talk is about as exciting as watching paint dry," added Percy. His wife Eileen perked up, and laughed. Arnie Murkiwasser owned a paint and home decorating store in Iron Lake.

"He's the same way in his store," she said stridently.

"Well, anyway, seems like Connie Cratt decided to shake up Arley. He sticks in a motion to fire the superintendent. The motion passed four to two. And they went on with the agenda."

"And ten minutes later," Percy said, eagerly racing through the story, "Arley gets up and leaves for the men's room. He slept through the entire motion."

Then Percy added, "So, while he's gone, Curt Fitzsimmons, who hates Cratt's guts, makes a motion to rehire the superintendent and give him a $3,000 raise." To Corrine, Percy explained that Fitzsimmons runs the largest hog operation in Spencer County, feeding one hundred sows and producing eight hundred piglets every five months. Mr. Fitzsimmons distrusts Connie Cratt and believes every employee is entitled to be treated fairly.

"So, what happened?" asked Corrine.

"Well, Glacinda Fallow had gone to the lady's room, leaving five members. Patty Trivic changed her vote and the motion carried three to two."

"And the superintendent?"

"No one told him, figuring he could read it in the minutes."

"That's the point of my story," Tom added.

"What is?"

"That he just didn't care" Tom was trying to make the story illustrate the cynicism he found in some of his fellow superintendents.

"Next day, Billy Washburn, I mean Mr. Washburn," he said looking at Corrine, who worked for Washburn, "takes the minutes to Arley's office and congratulates him. Arley says 'What for?' And Mr. Washburn says, 'for getting fired and a $3000 raise while you were visiting the men's room, and you didn't know it."

There was dead silence for a long minute. No one said anything. Corrine knew that her Dad liked to tell stories with a punch line. Crystal, who knew her husband, finally asked,

"And what did Arley say?"

"He said, 'that's nice'. That's all he said." Tom chuckled.

*****

A dark four-door sedan drove slowly past Tom's house. Tom heard the motor but paid little attention. Corrine was telling Percy and Eileen Smith about her first year as an Art teacher. Crystal had gone into the kitchen to retrieve Tom's bottle of brandy. Tom had proposed that they have a toast to the Iron Lake schools. After all, he noted, the voters had said yes to the $65,000 annual levy by a landslide.

Tom could hear the car turning around at the end of the block. It was a half-hour to mid-night on a quiet Tuesday night in May. Tom guessed some high school boy was bringing his neighbor's daughter home. The car slowed in front of Tom's and when it was even with the breezeway, stopped. The streetlight reflected off the car's hood…it was a

Ford sedan. A light breeze moved through the trees, and rustled pages of a magazine in Tom's breezeway. The driver got out of his car, stood back from it and swung his arm, slamming the car door.

The man took four steps onto Tom's lawn. He stopped under one of the Norway pines that guarded Tom's house. With the street light behind him, the people in the breezeway saw a black outline, but little more. Tom stood up just as Crystal re-appeared from the kitchen.

"What is it?" she asked, putting the brandy on the table between Percy and his wife.

"Someone wants to talk to me, I guess." He moved toward the door out to the front lawn. The man under the tree had not moved.

"Can I help you?" Tom said rather loudly.

"Want to talk to you, Mister Harant," came back the reply.

"I'll come to you." By this time, Percy was standing behind Tom, asking why Tom was going into the yard. "He wants to talk to me and I don't want him coming any further."

Tom pushed the screen door open and walked into the yard. Percy stood inside the breezeway where the man could see him. The three women watched Tom walk out to the pine trees. The man had not moved. As he approached, Tom said,

"Pretty late at night for a visit isn't it?"

"Guess so," the man answered.

"And you are?..."

The man stood quietly, not moving. His right hand suddenly came up and he smacked it into his left palm. He stood looking at Tom and his right hand slowly retreated until he put it into the windbreaker he was wearing. He leaned toward Tom and a whiff of whiskey passed by Tom's nose.

"George Fallow, I raise chickens east of town. My wife is on your *so-called* Board of Education." The emphasis he placed on *so-called* turned the words into a sneer.

"And what do you want?" asked Tom.

"Piece of advice, Mr. Harant?"

"You giving out advice, Mr. Fallow?" Tom felt defensive, being attacked at his own home by a man he had met once before, at a school district picnic. The man was about Tom's height, at four inches taller than six feet. He was perhaps 50 to 60 pounds heavier with bulky shoulders and the arms of a farmer.

"I'm here to tell you to watch out," said Fallow quietly. "You may think you have this here town fooled, but we know what you are."

"And what is that?"

"Some fancy salesman, that's who."

"Are you talking about tonight's election?"

"Yes, I am."

"I only told people why they should vote yes."

"You hoodwinked a lot of people."

"Is this your opinion, or your wife's opinion?" It occurred to Tom to wonder if Glacinda Fallow felt the same, that Tom was distorting the need for the $65,000 increase in the local levy. Glacinda and Cratt both voted against running the levy referendum...but they kept their mouths shut during the campaign.

"Speaking for myself."

"Well, your neighbors voted for it."

"And raised my taxes."

"That's how majority rule works."

"And raised my taxes. Connie says all of this tax increase is going into larger salaries for the teachers. Is that true?"

"Depends on what happens in negotiations."

"So...it is true, isn't it?"

"That we will probably increase teacher's salaries...yes, I suppose it is."

"More money for them teachers," said Fallow with no enthusiasm. While he was saying this, Fallow reached into a back pocket and pulled out a small glass bottle. He unscrewed the top and offered some to Tom. When Tom refused, Fallow took a long hard swallow of the contents. The smell of whiskey again floated past Tom's nose.

"Majority rule, Mr. Fallow. That's how it works." The hour and the man were beginning to wear thin. Tom took a step backward. "If you have nothing else, you've said what you came to say, haven't you?"

"Just you watch out!" Mr. Fallow was replacing the bottle in his back pocket. "My wife Linda says you are an okay guy. But Connie thinks you're some kind of slick salesman."

"Good night, Mr. Fallow."

"Same to you, Mr. Harant." The man turned toward his car. Tom crossed the yard and was opening the breezeway door when he heard the car motor start up. To the four blank faces he encountered in the breezeway, he said simply that the man wanted to express his displeasure with how the election turned out.

Crystal had poured cola into Tom's brandy. She stood up and gave the glass to Tom. She looked at Tom and he patted her arm.

"Nothing to worry about, my love."

"Let's hope not." Crystal turned away from Tom and began collecting the glasses. It was a signal that the gathering was over. Eileen pulled her light shawl over her shoulders and pulled Percy towards the door. Corrine followed them out, mumbling something about getting some sleep before another school day.

When Crystal came back onto the breezeway, Tom was looking out the window, staring at the Norway pines in the front yard.

"Was it nothing, Tom?"

"I don't know. That was Mr. Fallow, Glacinda's husband. Sounds to me like Cratt has been stirring up some ugly opinions, where the teachers are concerned." Tom knew all about ugly opinions. Cratt reminded him of a lynch mob leader who was willing to lead until someone with a fist or a pistol stood up to him.

*****

Tom was taking a required class in college, Speech 101, when he first heard about ugly opinions. At Marquette University in the 1960's, undergraduates were required to learn how to speak in public and how to build an oral argument for any position. Audiences learned to identify ugly opinions. These were arguments without solid foundation that amounted to personal attacks. After becoming a superintendent, Tom learned that it didn't matter if you had good, solid rational reasons for making a proposal. The emotional fervor of a parent or a taxpayer could sometimes outweigh rational arguments.

"Sometimes I just don't understand the school board," he said quietly to Crystal. They were sitting on the breezeway, enjoying the euphoria after the levy referendum passed.

"What did they do?"

"They approved a bus pickup at the ice arena."

"Is that bad?"

"I told the mother who started the rebellion that she was less than a mile from the elementary school. Her five-year-old will not qualify for bus aid."

"So you told the board not to do it?"

"Yes," he said, looking out across their back yard. Tom had turned the fountain on earlier. The sound of the splashing, late at night, was restful.

"So, what's the whole story?"

"The mother gathered up a petition from all the mothers up there in Conroy Addition, near the ice arena. They came…or many of them came…to the board meeting to plead for the 'safety of our children'."

"That sounds like a good cause."

"Very emotional. They did not want to admit that their children have been walking to the elementary school for the past twenty years without an accident."

Tom reached over to Crystal's arm and patted it lightly. She looked up at him knowing he would do as the School Board ordered. His role was to implement the decisions of the Board. He smiled at her, and she smiled back.

"Still, it hurts to have the Board ignore my recommendation. The Director of Transportation told the Board how much the extra bussing would cost. Did they pay attention? They listened and then ignored his advice."

Tom got up and walked to the back breezeway door. He found the switch for the fountain and turned it off. To his right, a full moon was throwing silver flashes across the back yard. The leaves on the triple birch were flashing as they shimmered in the late night breeze. A bat came flashing by, searching for insects. From a block away, Tom could hear a 'Hoot' owl calling to its mate, while it hunted flying squirrels. He heard Crystal picking up the glasses off the table and knew it was time for bed.

"We had a card from Carl."

"Oh?"

"Nothing serious. He needs more pocket cash."

"Figures. Why else would he write?"

Tom picked up one last glass from the table and followed Crystal into the kitchen. Their son Carl was in his second year at Marquette University in Milwaukee. He had chosen Marquette because it was much closer than Notre Dame, and slightly less costly.

*****

Tom had faced that same decision in the spring of 1961. Just about the time that Alan Shepard made his historic first flight aboard the Mercury capsule, Tom was preparing to graduate from Faribault High School and choosing a college. Minnesota's leader of the Democratic-Farmer-Labor party, Senator Hubert Humphrey had nominated him for the Naval Academy. Something about the long years and arduous summer training sessions at Annapolis turned Tom away from Annapolis. He never had any money of his own and working during the summer months was mandatory. At least work seemed mandatory to Tom.

He chose Marquette when the Navy offered him a full ride scholarship in the Naval Reserve Officer Training Corps (NROTC). Marquette was closer, and he could work in the summer. Tom's Aunt Jane, out in New Jersey, would add to the kitty with the $1,000 Tom needed to supplement his Navy scholarship. He enrolled in Marquette, telling his friends that there were girls at this college. As if that made a difference. It was years later before he admitted to himself that during his two years at Marquette, he was afraid of girls and 'mostly uneducated' where females were concerned.

His one obsession, in those years, was to buy a car. He worked at Faribo Canning that first summer after graduation, and the second summer. Then he found a job in Milwaukee, stocking shelves at a liquor store. His job included protecting the owner. Aaron Burt wanted Tom and his 6'4" of bulk to protect the store if questionable people came in. If they were wearing long coats, Aaron wanted Tom to come up front and watch the customer. Aaron told Tom to make sure his liquor didn't disappear into those long coats. That's exactly what Tom did. But his grades dropped dramatically during his second year at Marquette.

The $50 'beer money' the Navy gave him, plus what he was earning from Aaron Burt almost guaranteed that Tom would get into academic probation. When he did his platoon leader assigned him to weekend study sessions that he attended with religious fervor. He dedicated himself to mastering calculus but the mysteries somehow floated over Tom's head. Years later, he recalled the Christmas take-home test his sadistic Physics instructor had given the class. He tried to study the textbook all during Christmas break while trying to unravel the mysteries of the 'period of an arc' at sea level and three miles down a mine. When he should have been studying, Tom and his friend Richard were at a movie or in Richard's kitchen drinking whiskey sours and arguing philosophy. Richard had discovered Kirkegaard and Kant. The physics test came back with a 'D' on it. In March of his second year, Tom was caught with his briefcase containing liquor in his dorm room. The university suspended him and he went home to Minnesota.

*****

His trip home closed the book on Marquette. Tom was told to report for reserve duty at Wold Chamberlin Airfield in St. Paul. The Navy told him they didn't need him. He stayed home in Faribault, looking for work. His buddies graduated from Marquette University in 1965 and 1966. They went on to service in Vietnam in the two years before the Tet Offensive. Thirty years later Tom realized he was carrying 'survivor's guilt' for not serving.

It had been a difficult two years at Marquette. While the other boys in his group had girlfriends and bragged about their conquests, Tom couldn't find the courage to ask a girl for a date. He had little pocket change and was embarrassed about the state of his clothes. Girls were a mystery. In his second year, Tom started weekly visits to Callahan's Bar on 13th street. He was tall enough to bluff his way in. No one asked for a Wisconsin ID. It was during his second year that he developed an infatuation with his roommate's girl, Patty.

Miss Patricia Cellario was a dark-haired, dark-eyed beauty from a mysterious world of northwest Chicago. She came from an Italian suburb, as did her boyfriend Bob. Patty had a beautiful face, soft cheekbones and long black eyelashes. She was what was known, in those days, as a Latin Bombshell. She had attended a private high school for 'upper-class' girls and her girlfriends wanted desperately to have fun. Patty was a mystery…demure, quiet, and reserved. She was trying to find her way in a confusing world.

Their last night together, Tom took Patty to their favorite pizza shop, and they shared a small bottle of wine. It was a night drawn with indelible ink. Tom would remember the strains of 'their' song, Nat King Cole's version of 'Misty' played on the jukebox. He would remember with crystal clarity and sad regret the next two hours, parked on a side street. The words from 'Misty' kept rumbling through his mind "…I'm as helpless as a kitten up a tree." He remembered wanting desperately to kiss Patty, while she sat next to him, sighing. She was patient and said nothing. In the end, he had no courage. He never kissed her.

*****

Months later, after making pool tables in LeCenter for three months, Tom was allowed to buy his first car, a 1950 Ford sedan. He had lost the Navy scholarship, embarrassed his family and tried desperately to pretend that it meant nothing to him. It was one of those incidents that Tom, with his strong willed determination, filed away for future reference. He wrote one letter to Patty in Chicago and she sent one letter when she was in Mexico. In the back of his mind, he knew he had been 'way too timid' with Patty. He somehow knew that he might never see her again…and he filed Marquette into the back of his mind.

"Sometimes," he admitted to Crystal, "I miss some of the people I met at Marquette. They were special to me."

"Do you want to go back?"

"Someday, at least to look up Patty and Bob and Ted and see how they survived the past 25 years."

"But you can't go back."

Tom looked out over the back yard, with its quiet calm. Crystal walked over and touched him on the arm. And he added, "Yes, I know."

*****

Perseus Alexis Smith had both hands hooked under the edge of the long table in front of him. He was standing, glaring at Robert Barnes, the lead negotiator for the teachers. A small group of ten teachers was sitting behind Barnes, providing moral support. Three school board members were sitting to the right and left of Percy Smith. Two other board members were standing to the back of the room, talking quietly with Arley Green, the superintendent.

It was three years before Tom Harant arrived, the year the teachers claimed that the School Board didn't respect their efforts, and the Board's proposal of a 3.2 percent increase was too small. February had rolled around, and Percy Smith had convinced the Board to increase its offer to 4.5 percent.

"But it's not enough. Our neighbors in Urholt just offered 4.8 percent. If we accept your offer, we will be laughingstocks for settling too early."

Percy was looking at a man who invariably managed to get Percy 'rather riled up' as observers noted. Barnes was wearing his large 'Teachers Care' button on the lapel of his brown suit jacket. His brown-rimmed glasses were partially down his nose...he looked like a professor dressing down a recalcitrant student. Some members of his team actually thought he was trying to 'get under' Percy's skin.

"I know all about the dimes," Percy stated bluntly.

"The Urholt teachers can take their opinion and stuff it. We sent the dimes back." Robert Barnes was still furious. The teachers at Urholt had sent $10.00 in dimes, to imply that Iron Lake teachers would settle for a dime when they ought to hold out for a dollar.

"Is the Board..." but Barnes stopped in mid-sentence. For a man who was known in Iron Lake as 'Bluster Barnes', he had been relatively polite during this negotiation session. "Are you going to increase your offer?" The veins in his neck were bulging. His face was starting to turn red. He stood and glared at Percy. The board members at the table were looking down at a sheet of paper, on which Conrad Cratt had written 'Drop the offer to 3.6 percent. They don't want to negotiate'.

"It's been suggested," said Percy softly, "that we lower our offer to 3.6 percent."

There was a moment's quiet, before Barnes exploded. He picked up the Board's written proposal and threw it at Percy. It hit the floor with a plop and slid up to Percy's right foot. He looked down at the crumpled pages, then back at Barnes. "You don't want to negotiate. All you want to do is squeeze and squeeze and squeeze," Percy said.

"Well, make us an offer we can take back," shouted Barnes. There was silence throughout the auditorium. The two board members at the back of the stage were walking toward the front. Superintendent Green was beginning to shake his head, almost as if he were chastising Barnes for his outburst.

"Damn you, Barnes..." Percy began to say. His shoulders were slumped as he grabbed the back of the long table. He heaved and the table flew upward, turning slowly as it fell into the space in front of Barnes. Papers continued to fly and float and scatter across the area between the two men.

His audience was dumb-founded. No one said a word. Connie Cratt started laughing, and the teachers walked out *en masse*. The contract was settled at the next session. Four years later, when they went into the next round of negotiations with their new superintendent named Harant, Cratt told the story while Percy Smith sat and watched.

"I only have one thing to say, Tom."

"Go ahead, Mr. Smith."

"I'll support you on almost everything. Especially if it's good for kids." Percy went on to issue a warning and said, "The Iron Lake teachers are out for blood. They settled for less than Urholt and it has rankled them for years."

Tom looked at Percy, considering his words. He thought back to a conversation he had downtown with a farmer. The farmer warned him that Percy Smith was obstinate. 'He's been to Vietnam…infantry. He ain't afraid of them teachers you got up there on the hill'.

Tom had responded that he appreciated the man's opinion. Listening to Cratt's story, Tom wondered. Would Percy let his animosity toward the teachers override his better judgment? The Board members standing around the meeting room laughed. Barnes started to snicker, and Percy smiled. Tom watched them laugh, and wondered if this group would be laughing in November.

CHAPTER THREE
Broken Arrow

There were no members of the press present on that warm evening when the negotiators for the Iron Lake schools met for what was to be their last 'almost cordial' session. Not that the press couldn't be present. In Minnesota, the press and the public are allowed to attend negotiation sessions. But in most of the small cities of 'Greater Minnesota,' there are no members of the public, or the press, for that matter, with the patience to sit and listen to grown adults who are failing to talk 'common sense,' and who are saying the same things tonight that were said last week and the week before.

In the Boardroom that warm night, the language devolved from typical 'short hand' expressions into gestures and symbolism. The participants knew that something momentous had occurred but they were not quite sure that they could believe their eyes. What did it mean?

The Boardroom was a typical classroom where once elementary children played and read books and learned math. The room had a counter, storage cabinets and a sink at one end. In front of the counter, a long table was set up, with two black leatherette chairs on each side, and a single chair at the head. The blackboards were gone, the walls covered with vinyl wallpaper. A large Springfield school clock hung prominently (and noisily) on the wall.

The session began when the superintendent declared his neutrality. Tom Harant entered from his office, wearing his typical dark blue suit. He sat at the end of the long table. In previous meetings, Mr. Harant advised the school board members and sat on their side of the table. In this meeting, however, he was conspicuously sitting at the head of the table, between the two sides.

"My role," he said to both sides, "is to act as a resource person." Tom, who professed to be Irish, smiled at the people at the table. In his white shirt with a blue tie, he seemed rather conservative. His smile and the twinkle in his eye would have convinced most adults that here was a man who meant well, but was easily misunderstood. At this meeting, most of the adults ignored his presence.

To Tom's left sat Patty Trivic, fussing with her notebook. She had worn a pale yellow summer dress and her brown hair was pulled back from her face into a ponytail. She was rubbing an insect bite on her cheek while she turned pages in her notebook. Patty was particularly obsessive about taking notes and she was reviewing last week's notes when the clock on the wall clanked another minute.

Robert Barnes sat to Tom's right, smoothing his wind-blown hair with one hand while the fingers of his left hand drummed a beat on the table. He had chosen to ride his 'Harley' to town, because his motorcycle always made him feel taller than his actual height of five feet six inches. He felt stronger when he got off his 'hog'! A short man, Barnes had steely gray eyes that tended to bore through people from under his bushy eyebrows. 'Bluster' Barnes was also known as 'Bluster Be Damned' for his frequent threats, exaggerations that he failed to carry out. Behind Barnes, and away from the table, sat Sylvan Plant and Sandy LeBoef, two teachers who were moral support for 'Bluster' Barnes.

Tom Harant looked up when the last member of the Board team arrived. Connie Cratt, a six-year veteran on the Board was wearing a brown sports jacket over a blazing red tie, topped off with a brilliant white cowboy hat. He walked to the middle of the table and stopped, looking down at 'Bluster Barnes'. The two men looked at each other but Cratt seemed to be challenging Barnes, reminding Barnes that Cratt was in charge. He stood for a moment. It seemed to Tom Harant that Cratt was waiting for someone to admire his hat.

"New hat?" asked Barnes, finally breaking the silence.

Connie Cratt didn't answer. He took the hat off and held it in his left hand. With his right hand, he straightened his brown hair. It was slightly damp, causing those who noticed to believe he came to the meeting directly from a shower.

" I just got out of the fields thirty minutes ago," was his gruff response. Connie Cratt's face wore the dark stain of many hours in the sun and the darker ridges caused by too many years on a farm. His face displayed years of struggling to maintain a living on a slipshod farm while putting three children through the Iron Lake schools. Cratt held a day job as a mechanic for Spencer County. His wife Sharon worked as a receptionist for a dentist in Cherry Grove, the next town east of Iron Lake.

Together, Connie and Sharon Cratt were struggling to find the money to help their daughter Karen who was a freshman at Bemidji State. Over the past ten years, Cratt had grown to distrust and dislike the teachers at Iron Lake. *'What have they done,* he was fond of saying, *'to prove they have earned a salary increase? Anything at all?'*

He turned to his left and began to toss his hat onto the counter behind the board table. Then he stopped and turned back toward Bluster Barnes. He plopped his hat into the center of the table, directly in front of Barnes.

"Everybody here should know…" said Cratt with a smile, "who is the good guy at this table."

"So you wore a white hat?" asked Barnes.

"Yes, that's about it." He sat down across from Barnes and next to Patty Trivic. Mrs. Trivic watched Cratt's performance while she held her place in her notebook. She opened her notebook and pointed at a page. Cratt leaned toward Patty and glanced at the page of notes. While he was looking, he couldn't ignore the scooped neckline of her dress. He glanced to his right appraising her breasts then studied the notes where Patty was pointing.

He straightened up and looked at Barnes. "So, where are we?" Then Cratt turned to the superintendent Tom Harant and asked, "Did we make the last offer?"

"The Board made the last offer," Harant said quietly. His shirt was strangling his neck and he tried to loosen his collar by running a finger inside the collar. From Tom's point of view, it seemed obvious that Cratt was reinforcing his point. Cratt and Trivic were waiting for a counter-offer from the teachers.

"Patience," said Bluster Barnes. He was feeling stubborn but confident in his position. "We all need a little patience." He watched as Connie Cratt stood up and moved to the coffee pot that was holding lemonade and ice. The pot was a 30-cup aluminum brewer, collecting moisture on its sides.

Robert Barnes sat with placid expression and glanced at Cratt by the sink. He looked out the window at the school's Century Elm, standing sedately in the early evening sun. *'Be like the elm,'* his friends had advised him *'...strong and silent'*. Barnes was anything but calm, although his face showed little emotion. His stomach churned through each negotiations session. This meeting was no different...except his union leaders had given him specific instructions for tonight.

Barnes ran his fingers through his brown hair. His eyes reflected the clarity of the pale blue sky. *'Like an observer at a chess match,'* his face displayed calm detachment. His right hand tugged on the collar of his light blue and white plaid shirt, for a moment. Somehow, Bluster Barnes felt out of place, despite leading the negotiating team through eight difficult contract talks over sixteen years. He quickly wrote a note and handed it to Sylvan Plant who stood up and left the room.

Cratt was carrying a Styrofoam cup back to his chair when Barnes glanced at the school's CEO, Tom Harant. Mr. Harant's eyebrows were raised, as if he was asking a question. Barnes saw the expression and turned to his rear. Behind him, Sandy LeBoef (also called 'Beefy') was leaning back with his legs stretched out, a manila envelope resting on his rotund stomach. He lifted the envelope and passed it forward to Barnes.

From the envelope Barnes extracted three sheets of paper, containing the teacher's reply. He passed the papers to Mr. Harant, who in turn gave them to Trivic and Cratt.

Cratt read the paper for about fifteen seconds, then crumpled it into a ball and threw it on the table between himself and Barnes.

"You have no patience, Mr. Cratt," said Barnes to the Board's chief negotiator. "You've been here before, Connie. We all want to settle this contract."

"Oh...do we?" snarled Cratt in reply. He leaned forward in his black swivel chair, looking at the shorter man. His intense brown eyes glared at Barnes, while his white shirt struggled to restrain the veins in his neck.

"You don't know how difficult it was to get the board to make its last offer of $4200 per teacher." Cratt was famous for his lack of patience, like a politician on Election Night. "And your counter-offer is a flat statement that you do not intend to come down from $5200 per teacher?"

Connie picked up the crumpled ball of paper and threw it over his shoulder. The paper ball arrowed off the wall and came to rest in the sink next to the sweating coffee pot with the lemonade.

Warm air seemed to flow through the room. The one air conditioner was struggling to make a difference. The room still retained much of the day's heat. In better years, when enrollment was higher, the room had once been a classroom with black and white floor tiles. An enterprising custodian, however, had installed beige carpet to soften 'any noises' in the room next to the superintendent's office. Three long tables along one side and eight black leatherette chairs made the room a focus for public meetings.

Sylvan Plant came back into the room with a white motorcycle helmet. He placed it on the table next to Cratt's cowboy hat. The two hats sat on the table while Barnes smiled at Cratt. Patty Trivic broke the stalemate. She laughed and said,

"Well, boys, looks like you have parity on the board table." Tom Harant laughed to himself. Behind Barnes, his assistants Plant and LeBoef smiled. Cratt and Barnes continued to look at each other, without saying a word.

Outside the school building, shadows lengthened as the sun fell in the west. The majestic Century Elm stood nearby throwing shadows across the grass much as it had for over one hundred years. A blaze green cicada, high in the tree, chattered like a rapid machinegun, drilling the silence with a staccato 'brrrip'. The heat and humidity of middle August in Iron Lake seemed almost to slow time, like molasses on a cool pancake.

*****

Iron Lake in mid-summer is a quiet place, a small town on the way to almost nowhere. It's a town on the road west to South Dakota...a town on the road east to the Twin Cities. Iron Lake is a town like hundreds of others where the grocery store closes at eight in the evening. The bank and the drugstore both close at five. The town has two essential stores... both hardware stores that stay open past closing if they know someone is dashing into town from the country. On this quiet night in August, the 'Municipal' had three pickups and two cars parked in front. There were, it seemed, people with a thirst who helped the local liquor store and its pull-tab operation to maintain an acceptable profit level.

The main feature of the town, of course, was Iron Lake, a good fishing hole of around 1200 acres, two miles long by one-half mile wide, with cabins and houses abutting each other "elbow to elbow" around the lakeshore. Iron Lake was a good fishing hole if you knew where early settlers had dumped rock in the 1870's. The rock piles seemed to produce the best results and each year, a near record Northern Pike was caught 'just off the rocks' as the locals said. Two resorts, Albers Shady Acres (with the small cabins) and Bulrush Bay Resort and Lodge drew heat-weary visitors from the Minneapolis area.

An attraction in town was the 'Municipal' pit stop, if you were thirsty. To motorists, Iron Lake was a spot on the road where drivers slowed briefly until they were past the town's blinking yellow light on Minnesota Hwy 30. The town had three churches and a downtown featuring an Econofoods, a drugstore, a bank, two dentists, two hardware stores and the local 'church' where nearly everyone congregated on Friday night, the Municipal Liquor Store. The town was rarely in the news and its residents preferred their anonymity.

During the Depression 1930's the local dairy farmers trucked their milk and dumped it on the railroad tracks in Iron Lake…to protest the railroad's heavy-handed shipping rates. A few head of useless milk cows were killed. The newspapers in far-off Minneapolis described the futility of the milk producer strike. Four decades later the old timers still gather for coffee in the RX Drug store and occasionally they argue about a time when their wasted efforts failed to convince the railroad owners in far-away Chicago.

These same curmudgeons of the coffee table had been noticeably shocked when Iron Lake teachers went out on strike in 1985. Nevertheless, two days of sub-zero cold forced a quick end to the '85 *Strike*. The teachers got another $100 added onto their salary schedules and they were satisfied. Down at the RX Drugstore, however, the old-time pundits were angry and vowed in future they would not allow themselves to be pushed around by a gang of *intellectual tyrants*. To these veterans of the 'coffee debates', the people up the street with the college degrees were effete intellectuals who didn't know what it was to work with their hands.

The year 1985 was the year the Coffee Gang wrote a letter to the Iron Lake *Cynic*, known for its biting editorials. The Gang 'informed' the citizenry far and wide that they were going to keep an eye on the local teachers, who obviously didn't *'care a tinker's damn*' for the children of Iron Lake. In a month, however, everybody quietly and conveniently forgot about the Coffee Gang.

Five years later, neither the Coffee Gang nor the *Cynic's* staff was paying any attention to the progress of negotiations. After all, nothing happened in the summer. School was out. No one talked seriously during the summer months. Nevertheless, in Iron Lake in 1990, while no one worried, it was superintendent Tom Harant who noticed the ratcheting of aggressive language at the table.

*****

Barnes continued to wait for Cratt to react. One of the teachers behind him passed a note. He leaned back to read it.

"You have our position," he said directly to Connie Cratt, "or you did until you threw it in the sink."

"Fifty-two hundred per teacher is too much," answered Cratt. He looked at his creamy-white hat sitting on the table. "You want to be the good guy…put on my hat…or tell us how many teachers we have to lay-off to meet your demands."

Barnes reached for the hat with his right hand. He almost touched it before sliding his hand to his three ring binder, sitting open in front of him. He wanted to remind Mr. Cratt there were twenty-three items of language unresolved but something kept him quiet. *'Get the money resolved, first'* an old time bargainer once told him.

"You know," Barnes said finally. "We maintain that satisfied teachers create a happier school. We can't be satisfied…" he paused for effect "…*with less than the state average increase.*"

"Well, then you aren't going to be satisfied," said Cratt coldly, without flicking a facial muscle. "Why don't you say something I don't know?"

"Such as what?"

"How about a counter-offer?"

"You have it. Fifty-two hundred dollars per teacher."

"We made the last offer. Your position hasn't moved in two weeks." Cratt picked up his pen and placed it in the pocket of his white shirt. Looking sideways at Patty Trivic, Cratt motioned with his head towards the Superintendent's Office.

Cratt looked at the superintendent who was sitting quietly watching this scenario play itself out. "Do you have anything to add?" challenged Cratt, staring directly at Tom Harant. Tom's eyes involuntarily moved to Cratt's right hand, where a knuckle was rapping a pattern on the table.

"No," said the superintendent, just as Cratt and Trivic began to stand up. Patty was collecting all the loose papers, indicating they were moving into another room to caucus as a team. Cratt led the way into Tom's office. Patty came in and began to close the door just as Connie Cratt threw a barb through the still open door, "Good guy, indeed!"

Cratt sat on one of the hard plastic chairs of Mr. Harant's sparsely furnished office. Patty Trivic put her notebook on Mr. Harant's desk and sat down. Tom was opening a window when she said, "What do you think, Tom?"

Harant looked at the *'Dream Catcher'* of black feathers and tan string with white beads that hung in his window. James Arthur Whitecloud had given the 'catcher' to Tom last May, right after graduation rehearsal. He said the 'catcher' would keep angry thoughts from entering through the window near Tom's old wooden desk. *The 'catcher' is failing to do its job*, Tom thought. He wondered if the 'catcher' could help the adults to find 'words less abrasive.'

"What do I think? Barnes is very intense. His fingers are shaking," Tom said slowly. "Something's wrong."

"What do you mean?" asked Cratt.

"I don't know, exactly. It's almost as if Barnes doesn't want you to increase the Board's offer."

"That's baloney," said Cratt. He was never one to mince words. In front of another board member, he wanted to project the image of control. He crossed his legs and looked at his highly polished boots. Connie smiled to himself, thinking that for once in his life, people were listening to every word.

"We're at $4200. The teacher's proposal asked the Board to show its good faith by adding $200 more. But the district can't *afford any more*, can we?" Cratt growled at Harant.

The tenor of his voice was low and guttural. Behind Tom, Patty Trivic's jaw dropped, slightly. She had never heard a board member talk this way to the superintendent. Tom was standing in the window, enjoying a slight breeze. The breeze caused the *'Dream Catcher'* to twist and turn. Tom watched it for a moment, thinking.

"They want you to return to the table with no increase. It feels like a fever is running..." Tom paused a moment.

"Say what?" asked Mrs. Trivic.

"A blood fever. Like at Wounded Knee. A lust for blood. I think our teachers have that same fever. Their negotiators want to push the school district into a strike." Tom Harant was known as a man who read extensively, trying to make up for his own lack of attention in history class. Rumors across the state said that other superintendents were seeing strange behavior at the bargaining table.

Trivic sat quietly, watching Connie Cratt. Tom Harant began to write a memo about the progress of negotiations. Cratt picked a piece of lint off his trousers and flicked it toward the wastebasket.

"Then we'll increase the offer by $200 per teacher," Connie said through clenched teeth. "Then Barnes can go back and report that the Board changed its position."

"Ah, well…" Mrs. Trivic seemed to be saying. Her hand came up and pushed a loose strand of hair behind her ear. She fussed with her dress for a moment, smoothing the material, before looking at Tom Harant. "$4400 is a long way from what they want?" she seemed to ask.

"True," said Tom. He chuckled while visualizing Bluster's face if Connie Cratt were to increase the Board's offer. Then he added, "He wants you to refuse. He wants an excuse. He wants you to break the peace arrow."

"The what?" said Cratt.

"The peace arrow. The Dakota tribes," continued Tom, "kept peace arrows. When they went to war, they first broke the peace arrow and sent it to their enemies."

"Your $200 offer might force Barnes to act. That's what Tom is saying," added Mrs. Trivic. "Is that right?"

Tom was silent for a moment. Then he told Cratt that Barnes was planning to walk out of the negotiations session. Tom had a 'friend' who had warned him two hours before the session began.

Cratt smiled. In retrospect, some days later, Tom Harant began to wonder if Cratt's smile had been a foreshadowing of what happened next.

*****

The Boardroom felt hot and imponderable, like a locker room with bad ventilation. Connie Cratt stretched his back until he was looking down on Robert Barnes, across the table from Cratt. Barnes smiled back at Cratt, blinking occasionally and drumming his fingers on the table. Connie told Barnes and the rest of the room about the peace arrow and how he was determined not to break the peace. Then he began to increase the Board's offer.

The air in the room seemed to crackle with electricity. Barnes reacted by sliding both of his hands under the sides of his notebook.

Cratt raised one hand and looked at it, drawing the attention of the other adults. "We will add $100 to the salary for the first year…"

The book in Barnes' hand slammed shut like the crack of a .306 Remington deer rifle. Barnes began to stand and picked up his motorcycle helmet. Behind him, the two teachers stood up and moved toward the door. Barnes looked down at Cratt, whose face was a blank. Mr. Harant's jaw had dropped. Patty Trivic was staring at 'Bluster' Barnes.

"I'm not finished," said Cratt, with determination.

Barnes turned toward the door.

"I said I'm not finished," said Cratt, louder this time.

Barnes turned at the door and looked at Mrs. Trivic and Mr. Harant before settling on Connie Cratt. He pointed at Cratt's white hat. "Put on your white hat, Connie. It might fool a few people."

Cratt watched Barnes in silence. In a quiet moment, the old classroom clock mechanism snapped off the end of another minute. Barnes turned and left the room. His footsteps were heard moving down the hall.

Patty Trivic looked at Tom Harant, the school's superintendent, and asked, "What am I going to report?"

"Tell the rest of the Board that they walked out on us."

"Do you think they will strike?" she asked, frowning.

"We can only hope that cooler heads will prevail," said Tom.

"Let'em go," added Cratt, "they don't know what a real strike is." He reached out and picked up his cowboy hat.

In the silence, Tom watched Cratt smile while he put on his hat. Cratt was leaving, walking away from Trivic and Tom. He turned at the door and ran his hand along the brim of his hat, echoing a gesture by a man who was supremely happy. Then Cratt turned and left Tom sitting with Patty Trivic.

Tom felt at a loss to know what to do. Could anyone convince the teachers not to strike when the Board might be stubborn and unyielding?

He looked at the clock when another clank of the mechanism marked another minute gone. Mrs. Trivic closed her notebook. "An interesting session, *I think?*"

Tom Harant was thinking about Barnes sudden reaction to the offer by the Board. He didn't hear Mrs. Trivic's question and didn't know the answer.

Outside the building, the three teachers paused to talk by the Century Elm. A breeze ruffled through the grass. To the west, a red sun cast dark shadows across the lake. Somewhere down the tracks north of Iron Lake, a train mourned its passage through another small town.

CHAPTER FOUR
Dangerous Chemicals

The world was quiet with expectation in the morning. A slight damp covered the grass while a slim fog stood quietly on the bay below the red brick building. In the cedar tree next to the entrance, two grackles were conducting an argument with a red squirrel. A man was walking up the sidewalk, smiling. His approach drove the squirrel to abandon its claim on the trunk of the cedar tree. It dashed across the sidewalk and up the trunk of a tall pine tree, hiding on the far side of the tree. The man barely noticed the squirrel, absorbed as he was in the white fluffs that crossed the dome of his mind.

The man stopped on the steps into the two-story red brick building. He turned to survey his domain. To the south, a long building of tan brick and glass housed the Iron Lake Elementary School. To the north, an agglomeration of buildings, large and small, outlined the gymnasium, boiler rooms, science wing and main structure of the Iron Lake High School. Directly in front of the man, a row of small white houses defined themselves with dark green shutters and gray asphalt shingles. The man had more than once wondered if these were 'Sears' houses, purchased from the catalog for $525 plus $30 delivery. He looked at the cement stack near the boiler room of the high school, and frowned. It was seventy feet tall, of poured concrete, standing unused for forty years. It was a blister on the man's horizon.

"We oughta tear it down," he said to himself while he opened the glass door of the office building. He turned and entered the hall outside his office, dodging a small woman who was trying to exit the building. He watched her leave and turned toward the reception area of his office.

"Mrs. Kneiss is upset," said Judy, from behind her desk. "But that's not unusual, is it?"

The man smiled at Judy, knowing that her expertise was personnel management. She typed the contracts with the unions and she knew the language and the interpretations. In the opinion of Tom Harant, her boss, there was no finer expert to run the details of the school district. Judy started working for the school superintendent when she was eighteen. She was approaching thirty-six years in the superintendent's office and Mr. Harant was her seventh CEO.

"Will Mrs. Kneiss file a grievance?" asked Tom.

"Not likely."

"Why was she here?"

"She wanted my interpretation. Personal and emergency leave is for members of the immediate family. This was a third cousin she had not seen for fifteen years." Judy pushed her blond hair away from her face, and smiled at Mr. Harant. He smiled in return; affirming her interpretation of the 'quagmire' called Personal Leave.

"Typical way to start a 'Kneiss' day," added Tom.

"Or not so Kneiss," added Judy, groaning at their mutual puns. Her blue eyes crinkled a little and the corners of her mouth turned upward. She touched her pugnacious nose with one finger and held it there. To Tom Harant, it appeared that she was signaling for quiet. Out of the corner of his eye, he saw a man approaching the open door. Tom turned toward the man.

"Morning, Percy."

"Morning, yourself," responded the bulldog as he pushed past Tom and walked into Tom's office without being invited. Percy was wearing a suit and that meant that he was probably on his way to a meeting of the County Commissioners. Percy's eyebrows were pulled together into a frown.

"This doesn't look good," said Tom to Judy. He turned and followed Percy into his office, putting his briefcase on the corner of his desk. Then Tom walked back to his door and closed it. Percy thanked him, for closing the door.

"You're upset about something, Percy."

"You got that right, Tom." He was standing in front of Tom's desk, making no move to sit down. His dress shirt seemed a little tight around the collar. He was wearing a light blue shirt and a tie with wide stripes. 'A power tie', as he called it. Percy watched Tom maneuver behind his desk. Tom seemed to be moving slowly and deliberately and gradually sitting down.

"What's up?" asked Tom.

"We are a target of the MEA," stated Percy with a blank expression on his face.

"Oh, really?"

"A teacher in Cherry Grove called, last night. My cousin Matt Verity. He says the Minnesota Education Association is itching to make an example out of the Iron Lake schools, at the first possible moment."

"Why would they want to do that?"

"One or two strikes at the beginning of October will put pressure on all the other school districts."

"Ah, that makes…" Tom was thinking out loud. "Sense, maybe." His shirt collar felt a little tight. Tom ran a finger around the inside of his collar. When he reached the button in front, he unbuttoned the collar and loosened his tie. He joined his hands in his lap and steepled his thumbs. *'A bit early in the day to be loosening my collar?"* He looked up at Percy and tried to smile. "This is serious, isn't it?"

"If it's true," added Percy.

"How can we find out?" Tom looked worried.

"You can't."

"Because," said Tom slowly. He scratched the left side of his head, ruffling his brown hair. Then he sat straight up, stretching his back muscles. "They will claim that there is no strike, until it actually happens."

"You got it right," said Percy.

"So what do we do?" asked Tom. He was beginning to recognize the enormity of what could happen if the Iron Lake teachers went out on strike. School would be disrupted. Kids would be on the streets instead of in school. Parents would be upset. The town fathers would be unhappy with the bad publicity. The Chamber President would be 'beyond' herself. Enormous pressure would fall on the Board of Directors to make an immediate settlement.

Percy glanced around for a chair. He moved to his right, grabbed an executive chair by its arm and pulled it in front of Tom's desk. After he sat down, he looked at Tom, expectantly. Tom was looking out the window at two fishermen in a boat. They were slowly trawling through Bulrush Bay, just below Tom's office.

Tom raised his head and pointed at the fishermen with his nose. "Water's too warm in August," he said with a laugh. "Good fish go deep in the summer." He glanced at Percy and then down at his desk. A pink slip informed him that Connie Cratt wanted to see Tom about 9:00 a.m.

"We keep this to ourselves," said Percy.

"And do nothing?"

"Not exactly," Percy responded. "You have been informed of a threat. You have to prepare to deal with it." Percy raised a hand and brushed a piece of lint off the lapel of his jacket. He was watching Tom, waiting.

"A Strike Plan," said Tom with doubt in his voice. His stomach was turning flips, just at the thought of deciding how to handle strikers. In his mind, he could see a picket line at the front entry to the parking lot. And he saw angry teachers waving fists and placards at cars that were trying to enter the parking lot.

"But it has to be tough," added Percy. "No pansy plans to coddle the teachers. If they go out, they're out."

"Are you sure?" asked Tom.

"It's like a war. You have to be tough and forceful and blunt and obnoxious to get the other side to negotiate." Percy was sure of himself. He had watched the North Vietnamese dither and delay, postpone and prevaricate. The peace talks in Paris, France dragged on for twelve months before the United States eventually caved in and planned to 'withdraw' from South Vietnam.

*****

"Man, you are blunt," said the seaman at the side of the boat. His commander, Percy Smith was standing behind the .30 caliber rapid-fire gun at the stern of the 'Riverine Forces' PBR (Patrol Boat River). He held the gun steady on the water buffalo that was standing on the shore. Next to the buffalo, two Vietnamese in black pajamas were pleading for the life of their buffalo.

"They say don't shoot. They were forced to haul the cargo," added the ARVN liaison officer from the shore, where he had been interrogating the two peasants. A half hour earlier, Smith's patrol boat caught the two peasants and their buffalo in mid-stream, crossing the Dong Nai River. The cargo packs contained small packages wrapped in duct tape. With a knife and a taste on his tongue, Lieutenant (Junior Grade) Percy Smith decided they were hauling unrefined poppy paste, the raw material for heroin or cocaine.

"That's buffalo manure," he said. "And you know it." The ARVN soldier began to back away from the two peasants. They looked at him, then at Lt.(jg) Smith behind his gun. Percy raised a hand and waved them to move away from the buffalo. They took two steps, hesitating and looking at their great black behemoth.

A 'Brrrip' shattered the silence with forceful hammers on the eardrums. The sound went across the river and returned in an echo. Steel-jacketed bullets from the .30 caliber gun ripped through the neck of the water buffalo. Its head began a slow descent toward the ground. The muzzle of the buffalo plowed into the muddy track of the river crossing. The neck was still attached to the body of the buffalo and it stood its ground dumbly, spraying blood in all directions, not knowing it was dead.

"That's what I call blunt," said Lt.(jg) Smith, with loud authority. Looking at the ARVN soldier, he waved him back on board the Riverine boat. He pulled out a pack of cigarettes, and acting like the Marlboro man, prepared to ride his PBR off down the river.

*****

"Tough, forceful and blunt!" Tom Harant thought to himself, thinking about Percy Smith's comments an hour ago. He looked up and realized Connie Cratt was almost into Tom's office. Tom began to stand up.

"Sit, dammit!" Cratt was in his usual agitated state. He was wearing jeans and a white cotton shirt. Tom presumed that Cratt was probably on a coffee break.

"Ok, Connie."

"And listen a minute." Connie sat in the chair that Percy had used an hour earlier.

"I have a neighbor who teaches Fifth Grade in the Middle School, Sylvan Plant. He's that lump of wood that sits behind 'Bluster' Barnes and eggs him on. Same guy that borrowed my tractor and didn't check the oil. Damn thing cost me $800 to repair."

"And?" asked Tom.

"He stopped by this morning. He says, and I quote, 'You thought you were going to impress us with another $100 increase to the salary schedule. Well, I guess we showed you who's gonna be boss in this round of talks,' or something like that." Connie leaned forward, which forced his enormous stomach to bulge outward. His shirt strained at the buttons. He was waiting for a response from Tom Harant.

Tom didn't feel like arguing with the man. He sat and waited.

"This is between you and me," added Mr. Cratt. "I'll do what I can to get the contract settled, *but* I am not about to be pushed around."

"I understand that," said Tom.

Cratt jumped to his feet and walked across the office. He glanced at the books on Harant's bookshelf. He spun back to Tom. "You know I am going to run for State President of my union, don't you?

"Yes, you told me."

"There will be press people watching me if the Iron Lake teachers are so stupid that they go out on strike."

"I am sure the press will watch all of us."

Cratt said nothing for a moment. He looked around Tom's office, then out the window at Bulrush Bay. The sun was throwing yellow bands through the windows, giving Tom's office a warm look. Just at that moment, a black grackle crashed into the window. It fell to the ground outside Tom's office. Cratt walked over to the window and watched the bird recover. In a few moments it had its bearings and flew away.

He turned and looked at Tom Plaine. "Don't expect me to be some kind of nice guy if the teachers strike. I will be just plain mean. I don't owe these people anything. Hell, everybody knows that the Iron Lake Education Association ain't a real union."

"You will be blunt, I expect," said Tom quietly.

"And I'm just as good as they are," added Cratt. He hadn't told anybody that he was writing a book. A secretary in the national office of Amalgamated Steel Workers was providing him with research material. His office was in an old house just across the street from the superintendent's office.

Tom wondered what he meant by 'just as good'. "We are all equal under the law," said Tom, somewhat lamely. He didn't know where this conversation was going.

"You know about my house across the street. I'm using the first floor as an office, compiling material on unions and their leaders, especially Philip Murray who ran the Steelworkers in the 1940's. I'm writing a book."

There was dead silence for a half-minute. Tom Harant was flustered. He looked Connie Cratt in the eyes, *but* he couldn't see any laughter. Tom had to take him at his word.

"That's great, Connie. How far along are you?"

"I'm 'bout half done." Connie looked at Tom, wondering if he needed to help Tom believe that he, a steelworker and mechanic could write a book. "I have insured the manuscript for $100,000."

"Well, I'll be damned," said Tom.

"That old house, you never know. The wiring is not the best," said Cratt and he seemed to be smiling to himself.

"Yes, I would be careful," added Tom.

"Meanwhile…about the teachers." Cratt walked over to Tom's office door. He touched the doorframe and looked back at Tom. "You should record everything that is going on, beginning with last night's meeting. Record that they walked out on us, while I was trying to improve the Board's offer. Keep detailed records."

After Connie left to return to work, Tom sat at his desk thinking about the morning. The clear blue sky and the white fluffs stumbling across the dome of heaven. Percy and his anger. The grackle that hit the window. Connie and his revelation about a book. Judy came in with his phone messages and he thanked her. He asked if she had ever heard of insuring a manuscript. *"No,"* she said with a blank expression on her face.

*****

Conifer B. Cratt (also known as 'Connie') learned to control his anger in the naval barracks at the Naval Training Station, San Diego, when his drill instructor shouted in his face, "What kind of name for a man is Connie?" His D.I. believed in belittling the new recruits, at least for the first two weeks. Connie found that if he jammed his fingers into his palms the pain would help him focus his anger. He also learned to lean forward, almost as if he was going to attack in response. The members of Training Platoon #1579 sympathized and could see his anger. The D.I. was on his case each and every day…until Connie shouted out, "Sir, my name is Conifer, Sir!"

Which made everything fine for two days. Then his D.I. Rudy Martinez checked his personnel file and discovered that Connie had an unusual middle name. The next day while he was dressing him down, Martinez asked, so everybody could hear, "Do you want to balsam, fat boy?" Connie looked down at Martinez, but said nothing. Unfortunately for Connie, he made friends with a recruit named Johnson, also from Minnesota. He told him quietly how his mother loved country-western music. When Johnson said 'so, what?' Connie admitted that he was named for a lyric, *'I pine for you and balsam.'*

Moreover, Johnson couldn't keep his mouth shut. It was all over the platoon. When a recruit from Texas made a remark, Connie decked him with a right uppercut, for which he received three days in the brig. When he came out of the brig, he brought a ton of anger with him. He resented the constant badgering by his drill instructor and thoroughly hated the name 'Balsam'. In his first fitness report, his D.I. remarked that Connie carried a 'residual anger' toward persons with authority. When Connie graduated from 'Boot Camp', he was assigned to the San Diego motor pool to learn mechanics.

Two years later, he married Marjorie Johnson, the sister of his buddy Bill Johnson. They settled down in a small bungalow within a trolley car ride to the Naval Base. One year later, their boy Byron James was born. Connie was beginning to talk about a second child when his wife suddenly deserted him. She sent a note from Tijuana, Mexico informing him that she was living with a Navy Petty Officer, and not to try to find her. When his enlistment was up, Connie moved Byron and himself back to Minnesota where he found a job working at the Murkiwasser Paint Factory in Iron Lake.

Unlike many fathers, Connie took an interest in Byron's education when his boy started First Grade. He liked helping the boy with his reading; sometimes they would play 'Battleship' when they should have been working on math lessons. His boy grew up and Connie got a job as a mechanic with Spencer County. When Byron was 12, Connie fixed up a scooter for his birthday. For his thirteenth, Connie presented him with a rebuilt Harley Davidson. But Connie felt cheated. He never got to serve aboard a ship. His wife deserted him and to Connie it seemed that he would never be more than a mechanic.

It was about this time that Connie put money down on a farm to the east of Iron Lake. That same year he began to think about running for the school board. He began to realize that he could 'push back' against the women who were making Byron work so hard, if he was their boss. Who knew what could happen? There were some women who admired powerful people. He became active with the Metal Workers Local within Spencer County. In 1987 he was elected President of MWL Local #313 and in 1988, he was appointed to the regional bargaining council. He felt like he was a man in a hurry to receive recognition for his stalwart activities on behalf of the 'rank and file' of his union. Moreover, he began to feel like a man who could push back when the women in his life tried to push him around.

*****

Late in the afternoon, the Chemistry teacher Mr. Wayne Williams walked into Tom's office, carrying a pile of papers. He gave them to Tom, explaining that he had completed the inventory of the chemicals. He also presented Tom with a list of dangerous items that he wanted to have destroyed by the county.

"You know what those are, don't you?"

"No, I don't," admitted Tom.

"Those are the chemical components for making 'lysergic acid' and we are not about to make LSD in my chemistry lab." Dressed in jeans and a ratty cut-off sweatshirt, Williams did not look like a scientist. A swatch of brown hair was sticking up and there were smudges of dust on his face. He had the clear eyes of a dedicated professional, matched with an enormous smile. "You remember LSD, don't you?"

"That's great, I think." Tom sat and looked at the list. He was wondering about the really dangerous items that could cause a fire.

"Didn't you talk to me last spring about chemicals that could start a flash fire if they were mishandled?" Tom distinctly remembered telling this teacher to get rid of those chemicals.

"I have reviewed my schedule of experiments. The hazardous chemicals are locked in a fireproof storage vault and I am the only person allowed to use them."

"What about the chances of fire?"

"The sulfur-phosphorus-water experiment to which you are referring will only be conducted outside, away from the building." Tom was surprised at the man's reaction. It seemed to Tom that this teacher was on the defensive. Tom was trying to do his job and Mr. Williams seemed to take offense. Tom told him to file a report when the 'LSD' chemicals had been removed from the building.

In April of the following year, Tom reviewed the August inventory list with a list compiled in February. It was then that he found the inconsistency that pointed to a possible cause of arson…a fire that led to the death of George Fallow, the husband of the agent who coincidentally sold the insurance on Connie Cratt's manuscript.

*****

Tom opened the file drawer of his desk, the deep drawer that held the hanging files of current projects. He rummaged around in the back and found an old notebook with 30 blank pages. He placed the notebook on the desk in front of him and opened it to the first page. He entered the date, August 26, 1990 and recorded the actions of the previous night. Included in his notes were comments about Cratt's 'so-called' book and Tom's instructions to the Chemistry teacher, Mr. Wayne Williams.

CHAPTER FIVE
First and Goal!

Lights were turned on in the towers. Rain was falling past the lights, making brilliant white streaks as the drops fell towards the ground. In the stands the stalwart among the fans held umbrellas. Some were holding plastic bags in an attempt to shelter from the rain. Along the near sideline, football players in red and white uniforms were yelling at their teammates on the field. On the other side, players in the silver and blue of the Cherry Grove Schools were yelling equally loudly at their mates. The downs marker indicated second down. Cherry Grove had the ball on the twenty-four yard line of the Iron Lake Panthers.

It was raining at noon when the groundskeeper came to mark the lines on the field. He made sure that Mr. Harant understood this. The rain made it difficult to put down chalk and some of the chalk was washed away before the game began. Mr. Harant told the groundskeeper not to worry; the fans knew he did his best in a difficult situation. The rain continued all afternoon and the field turned to mud with scattered water pools. Early in the game, one player was tackled and buried face down into the wet mud. He jumped up sputtering, claiming he could have drowned.

Iron Lake's football field is built in an unusual location. At first glance, it appears to be a small peninsula that juts into the lake, less than two blocks from the high school. The field itself is close to the level of the lake. Iron Lake veterans claim the field has always been too wet, being that close to the water table. But the old timers know the truth…the peninsula was a dumping ground for broken concrete that is allowing water to seep into the ground below the playing surface. About once a year, the Board of Education held a half-hearted discussion about replacing the old football field. The discussion ended in futility. The Football Boosters love the old wet field with its damp grass. The letter-winners among the Boosters cherish the site. According to tradition the team jogs two blocks to the field, passing among long lines of fans and cheerleaders and band members.

Tom Harant watched two men in the silver and blue of Cherry Grove walking back into the football field from the direction of the parking lot. He surmised that the two men had been out to their pickup truck for a couple of beers. They stopped near Tom and one of the men glared at Tom.

"You, the superintendent, aren't you?" asked the closer of the two.

"Yes, I am," answered Tom, with an expression of curiosity on his face.

"When are you going to get a new field?" asked the man loudly. He was trying to watch Tom and watch his football team at the same time. "We would have two more touchdowns by now but your field is crappy."

"We oughta protest," said the other man.

On the field, the Cherry Grove quarterback snapped the ball, took two steps backward and started to slip. He managed to hand off to the fullback who began to run toward the left side of the line. It didn't appear that he could get much traction. He cleared the line of scrimmage but an Iron Lake linebacker dove into him and they went sliding across the wet grass.

"See what I mean?" The man hesitated. "Do you?"

"We both do," said another man, approaching from the visitor's sideline. A tan fedora was keeping the rain out of his face. He was wearing a dress shirt and tie under his raincoat. He stood and faced the two men.

"You two go back to your place. I'll talk to the Iron Lake superintendent. Can't do much tonight about this field, can we?" The man was watching the two Cherry Grove fans. They reluctantly began to leave, trying to watch their team on the field and walk back to the visitor's sidelines.

"Thanks, Harry. They weren't any trouble." Tom smiled at the young man who looked so comfortable in the wet conditions on the field. It was hard to see his face, under the fedora, but Tom knew the Cherry Grove superintendent was serious about keeping his fans in line. During last year's game in Cherry Grove, several fans got into a shouting match with Iron Lake fans. The annual football game was becoming a strong rivalry.

"We should create a trophy," said Tom, "or something. It would boost our attendance and raise the level of interest in the game."

"Hey," laughed Harry. He was chuckling at the thought. He and Tom were watching the two teams line up for the next play. The Iron Lake fans were exhorting their team with 'Defense! Defense!' and 'Stop the Run.'

"It's been quite a first week for school, hasn't it?" commented Harry.

"Sure has. Any talk about a strike in your district?"

"No, but the word's out that Iron Lake will walk." Harry had heard from three different teachers who were worried that Iron Lake might have an impact on Cherry Grove.

On the field, the quarterback was looking at the Iron Lake defense. The ball was snapped and he fell back, taking three steps toward his right. Just as it looked like he was going to run the ball to the right, he handed off to his tight-end who was coming in the opposite direction. The tight-end found himself with an open field and began to angle toward the corner of the end zone. He ran directly at the spot where Tom and Harry were standing by the five-yard line. An Iron Lake defensive back was closing on the runner.

Tom saw the hit coming, in slow motion. He could see the Iron Lake player was going to hit the runner at about the eight-yard line. Tom reached out and began pulling Harry away from the sideline. But they only managed two steps back before the two players collided. The defender drove his shoulder into the runner's right arm, lifting him off the ground. Together they flew for five feet, landing and skidding through a puddle.

A blast of water and black mud hit the 'sideliners'.

Twenty feet away, the two Cherry Grove fans were yelling "Yeah! About time!" On the visitor's side, the stalwart rain-soaked fans that were still present were yelling and thumping each other on the back. On the home side, the fans were quiet. The referee took the wet ball away from the Cheery Grove runner and received a dry ball from a sideline assistant. He put it on the five yard line.

"That's first and goal," said Tom to Harry.

"It's always first and goal," remarked Harry. At this point in the game, there were six minutes remaining. Cherry Grove might not get another chance. Iron Lake was leading, 12 to 9.

"Some weeks are longer than others," laughed Tom.

"You got that right," Harry chuckled quietly. He was looking at Tom and laughing. Tom had turned away from the play, but was showered with water and mud. Harry continued to laugh while he reached into his back pocket and came out with a handkerchief. "Here, wipe your face, big guy!"

Tom looked down and realized the right side of his raincoat was plastered with black water. Tom had turned away but caught the brunt of the blast of water and mud. He felt a mess on his face. On the field, both teams were lining up for the push into the end zone. Iron Lake fans were yelling 'Defense, defense!' but some of their enthusiasm seemed to have waned.

"Tell you what, Big Guy." Harry was watching his team as the quarterback straightened up with the ball in his hands. "Let's create that trophy. We have four basketball, one wrestling match, and two hockey games coming up this winter. Most wins receives the trophy." He was watching Tom clean the dirt off his face. Tom's rain hat had black splotches on its right side.

The Cherry Grove quarterback started to run toward his right. His tight end split two defenders and angled left toward the goal line. Their quarterback couldn't find an open receiver so he flipped the ball to the tight end. An Iron Lake defensive back saw the ball coming and stuck out his hand...but he couldn't quite reach the ball. The tight end gathered in the wet, sloppy ball at the goal line and fell into the end zone.

Tom looked at the wet, dirty handkerchief he was holding. In the distance, Cherry Grove fans were yelling and screaming.

"What if Iron Lake goes out on strike?" Tom asked.

"What if?"

"Yeah, if we go out on strike, I guess we would forfeit any games we were scheduled with Cherry Grove."

"You got it, Big Guy. A forfeit is a win for us." Harry looked down at the ground. He looked at his football players who were sloshing around in the end zone, celebrating. He pushed his fedora back on his head and looked Tom in the eye. "We wouldn't be happy about it. We would prefer to play."

"Yes, I know you would."

Together, they stood shoulder to shoulder, solidarity in the face of the rain. They watched when Cherry Grove tried to kick the ball, for the point after. The kick failed. They watched Cherry Grove kick off to Iron Lake. They watched the Iron Lake player receive the ball and go down in a 'veritable hail storm' of football players. And they watched Iron Lake trying to move the ball, running on the soggy field. After two first downs, there was a minute and 30 seconds left when Iron Lake tried a pass. The ball wobbled in flight and fell into the hands of a Cherry Grove player. The game ended with Cherry Grove in possession and holding on to win 15 to 12.

Harry turned towards Tom, and smiled. "Please say Hi to your wife, for me. I see she was smart enough to stay home, tonight."

"Ahhh,...yes. The better half," Tom laughed. He put Harry's wet handkerchief in the pocket of his raincoat, planning to return it when it was clean. Without saying a word, Tom reached out and they shook hands. Tom was congratulating Harry and the Cherry Grove Raiders. Harry was wishing *Good Luck* to the Iron Lake superintendent who had to find a way to keep the teachers working.

CHAPTER SIX
Intimidation

The sun was breaking through scattered clouds, casting shadows of large school buses onto the sidewalk. Four buses were lined up, unloading the taller children first, then the smaller elementary age children. Three adults were scattered along the sidewalk, keeping an eye on the operation. Somebody's mongrel dog was loose, chasing among the children, barking and trying to play. Two small boys were trying to chase it away. One of the adults grabbed the two boys by their jackets and told them to head for their lockers inside the building. He got between them and the dog and clapping his hands, chased the dog until it went down the street.

The last boy off the last bus stopped to tie a shoe. It appeared to Mr. Harant, who was watching, that the shoe was two sizes too large for the boy. 'Probably a hand-me-down', thought Harant. The boy's backpack slid off his shoulder, making the job of tying the shoelace more difficult. Tom walked over to the boy and pulling the backpack, moved the bulky item back onto the boy's back.

"I'll hold the pack. You tie your shoe."

"Okay, meester." He was trying to remove a knot in the shoelace; it looked to Tom Harant like the lace was wet. "I'll get it…damn, damn, damn," the boy added.

The big man took a handkerchief out of his pocket. He placed it on the wet sidewalk and knelt with one knee on the handkerchief. He took his hand off the backpack and placed two fingers behind the knot in the laces. With his other hand, he located the strand of lace that needed to be pulled loose, and began pulling. The little boy watched and grabbed his backpack when it began to move. The big man quickly loosened the laces, pulled the laces tight over the boy's foot, and tied the shoe.

"There you go. Pull these laces tight, each time."

"Thanks, meester." The boy looked up with his dark brown eyes and his long black hair. He started to straighten up. He bounced his backpack with his shoulders, getting the load to balance. Looking away, he began to walk toward the door to the elementary wing. He was almost to the door when he stopped and turned. He looked at Mr. Harant, the school superintendent, and raising his right hand just slightly, almost imperceptibly, waved back at Tom.

Tom Harant smiled at the boy, knowing the boy didn't want any 'special' attention. The boy was the last elementary student to enter the building and that was a signal for the buses to depart. Tom waved at one of the drivers as she passed in her bus. The streets and sidewalks were wet from an early morning shower. The windows in the two-story brick building behind Tom were black, filled with reflections from scattered clouds. The school's Century Elm stood nearby, dripping an occasional raindrop. The two other adults waved at Tom and turned to walk into the high school. When the last of the buses was gone, silence returned to the sidewalk. Tom shook out his raincoat, scattering raindrops collected from the Century Elm.

Standing there, he must have decided that it was time for coffee. Tom started in the direction of the high school, but saw a panel truck slowing to a stop on the curb. The truck displayed the sign 'Murkiwasser Paints' on its side and it carried two ladders in a rack on its roof. Tom took three steps toward the high school, but slowed and turned toward the truck. He stopped and watched a short man...a man of about five feet six inches as he got out of the truck. The man was wearing a business suit and a look of determination on his 'bull-dog' face. The man reached into the truck and retrieved a tan fedora with a small red feather. He placed the hat on his head and walked toward Mr. Harant.

"Morning, Tom," said Arnie Murkiwasser. He seemed to be a foot shorter than the taller man. As he approached he did not look directly at Tom. Arnie was proud of his new hat and prouder still to look like a 'sharp' businessman. He looked up and down the street, making sure the street was deserted. "Can we talk?"

"It's a nice morning," answered Tom, hesitating. It was unusual for Arnie to show up at the school during the week. Arnie Murkiwasser had been elected Chairman of the Board of Directors on the basis of his 'hands-off' policy. He liked to let the principals and superintendent run the schools. Arnie knew that by showing up, he was drawing attention to himself.

"We need to talk," said Arnie. He was sure that such an expression would alert Tom to the need to discuss something in private.

"Out here on the sidewalk?"

"No!" he said abruptly. Arnie sometimes wondered if their school superintendent was deliberately obtuse when he wanted to be. Working with Tom over the past year, he had discovered their superintendent had a stubborn streak. Arnie took off his hat and holding it in one hand, smoothed his hair with the other. "In your office." He began to walk toward the middle doors, knowing that they led to the superintendent's office inside the building.

*****

Tom poured coffee into an insulated mug. It was plastic and held a picture of his daughter Corrine when she was about 10 years old. When he offered coffee to Mr. Murkiwasser, Arnie declined, claiming he already had four cups. He took his fedora off and placed it carefully on the side table, near the guest chair that faced Tom's desk. Arnie preferred the straight back guest chair because the other chair in front of Tom's desk was an old rocker, an unstable nervous type of chair.

"In the 'Cup and Saucer'?" asked Tom while he maneuvered to sit in his black leather executive chair. Arnie sat down in the guest chair. The wall with Tom's college degrees and certificates faced Arnie from behind Tom. To their right was an enormous lithograph of the Space Shuttle lifting off from Cape Kennedy. To the left of the various plaques and degrees was a front page from a 1961 newspaper, 'Astronaut Flies Into Space'.

"George Fallow called me. Wanted to meet for coffee." Tom knew that Mr. Fallow came into town just about every morning about 7:30 a.m. to conduct the daily 'gripe' session at the 'Cup and Saucer.' Several of the retired farmers in Iron Lake met to discuss the news, which meant they discussed the current prices of corn, soybeans, and hogs while passing on gossip about everybody in Iron Lake.

"So you had to run right up here?" asked Tom.

Arnie ignored the sarcasm in Tom's voice. Tom sometimes wondered if Arnie was dense or just didn't recognize sarcasm when he heard it. "There's a rumor all over town," added Arnie quickly.

"Which is?"

"Were you missing a man on the chain gang at Friday night's game?"

"Yes, we were. A parent filled in. We refunded his ticket price and paid him $15 for helping on Friday."

"Never mind him. Which man were you missing?"

"Sylvan Plant...a Fifth Grade teacher."

"That's because Mr. Plant was elsewhere and occupied."

"Where was he?" Tom asked while he wondered what Plant had done.

"Mr. Plant was seen coming out of the Laker Motel at 10:30 p.m. with a lady. The lady wasn't his wife. She was that new teacher...Lillian Harvey."

"Oh, phooey!" remarked Tom. He knew that two teachers having an affair would cause a firestorm in Iron Lake. The town wags would be burning up the telephone wires. The local pastors would get a few telephone calls demanding immediate action. The school board members would get angry calls from parents. And he would get calls demanding to know what he, the local arbiter of good behavior, was about to do about the behavior of two employees on their own time.

"Your reaction doesn't cut it," answered Arnie. "What are you going to do about their behavior? This is a small town. Every wife in town will be chastising her husband at the dinner table, and blaming Mr. Plant, who is older and ought to know better."

"There isn't anything I can do," said Tom. "It's not like they were making love in the school building, is it?"

"No, it isn't. But they are teachers *for God's sake.*"

"Yes, I know," added Tom, realizing that Arnie was about to make the argument that teachers are role models and the publicity could very well paint Iron Lake as a town of loose morals. Tom picked up his coffee mug and took a sip, while thinking about possible steps he could take. Arnie sat back in his chair and crossed his legs. In the next room, Tom heard the phone ringing. He knew his secretary Judy would tell the caller that she would pass on any messages.

"You can't just up and fire a teacher because of something he did outside of school hours."

"It wasn't outside of school hours!" said Arnie with an exclamation point.

"How so?"

"He was scheduled to work the chain gang at the football game."

Tom thought about it for a moment. Who was behind this sudden and alarming attention to a matter left quietly alone? Who had urged Arnie to bring this matter to the attention of their superintendent so quickly?

"That's a real stretch, reaching that conclusion," decided Tom after a few moments. The man's contract was to teach Fifth Grade and there was no contract for the casual workers at the games. Arnie sat up straight in his chair and stared at Tom.

"You're saying you won't do anything, aren't you?"

"I can't. Mr. Plant's conduct has to be evident and obvious during the school day. What he does on his time is his business." Tom reached up and loosened the collar of his shirt. It was unusual that a school board member, even the Chairman of the Board, should make Tom nervous so early in the day.

Tom put his coffee mug down on his desk and turned to Arnie. "I can make a note of this incident but I don't even have a witness. All you have is hearsay."

"George Fallow saw them. George was coming out of the 'Red Carpet' with his current honey, a widow from west of town. He doesn't want her name mentioned." Tom knew that the local municipal liquor store, known for its red carpet, did a booming business on weekends. Tom had heard that some men, when they wrote checks at the liquor store, made the checks out to 'MLS' so their wives wouldn't know where they were spending their money.

"I still can't do anything."

Arnie Murkiwasser was silent for a few moments. His eyebrows were jammed together and he was frowning. "We'll see about that."

Tom leaned back in his chair, wondering if Arnie would bring this matter up in a Board meeting. A public discussion could lead to a lawsuit charging defamation of character.

"There's something else I want to discuss with you," continued Arnie.

*****

Most people in Iron Lake, when they see Arnold Murkiwasser, smile at him. At five feet four or five inches, he is not seen as a threat. He is always ready to make a deal on a batch of paint or to discuss a painting job for his crew. His store has 'Murkiwasser Paints' across the front of the store in red letters one-foot high. The large windows have displays of carpet and tile samples to the left, and a small living room arrangement on the right side of the entry door. Arnie insists on getting his customers to consider 'room remodeling' and he does his best to sell complete projects. His business has grown in recent years and he purchased the next two stores for furniture showrooms. He hired the daughter of the local banker to work as an interior decorator and she has doubled his remodeling business in two years.

There are those in Iron Lake who are cautious around Arnie Murkiwasser. To many people he seems to be driven to succeed, and they wonder why he isn't working in the Twin Cities. 'How can anyone succeed by selling paint in Iron Lake?' they ask. Among those who know him, he has the nickname 'Anxious Arnie'. He believes that he can convince people that paint can cover any cracks and ugliness. And he is constantly selling something. When he sold himself for the school board, he spent two months talking to almost every voter in Iron Lake. He seemed anxious but sincere about not raising taxes and narrowly defeated an incumbent board member.

Arnie Murkiwasser, however, was still carrying a grudge against John Wilson. Mr. Wilson was the incumbent board member who told Arnie he was not going to run and then changed his mind. Privately, among his closest friends, Mr. Wilson admitted that he didn't believe that Arnie Murkiwasser could be trusted in a position of authority. Mr. Wilson's comments traveled the rumor circuit during the month before the election. *'He's a little man who wants to be bigger.'* The voters, 910 of them, voted to re-elect Wilson. After the election, Wilson was quoted as saying, *"It's a shame that 950 stupid citizens voted for the man. Can we trust him?"*

A year later, John Wilson was seen having coffee with the new superintendent of schools in the Cup and Saucer Café. Tom appreciated Mr. Wilson's concern about the future of the schools. Tom didn't realize that the gossip mill would report his meeting to Arnie Murkiwasser.

"They don't understand," Arnie once told his wife, late at night before bed. "There isn't anyone in Iron Lake who understands who I am."

She patted him on the shoulder. She was wearing her sleeping nightgown under a fluffy white robe Arnie brought home from a hardware convention in Milwaukee. "Yes, dear, I know what you mean," she mumbled while brushing her teeth. Marie knew that he tended toward paranoia late at night, when he was tired.

"And who would that be?" she mumbled, knowing the answer.

"A man who paid a lot to open a business in Iron Lake."

"Yes, dear."

"Those people in Urholt. All the inbreeding. The cousins who sleep with each other."

In his mind, Urholt was a small universe ten miles to the west of Iron Lake. A small town of German immigrants, the community of Urholt had one church, an extremely conservative chapter of the Lutheran church. It was in this small wooden church that Arnie first learned how much power one woman could hold. His mother Helmina was a stern faced matron of the church who ran the Sunday school with an iron fist. She taught the children ages six to eight their catechism. She also taught them to fear her yardstick…she was quick to dampen the spirits of her charges with a slash across the buttocks or a rap across the knuckles.

Arnie grew up in a home with a stern mother and a quiet father named Gerhardt who spent most of his days working on his small farm southwest of Urholt. When he wasn't working, Gerhardt spent time earning extra cash at the lumberyard in Urholt. At the dinner table he seldom said a word, preferring not to respond to Helmina's constant prattling and gossip. It seemed to Arnie that a truce existed, with the two men saying nothing and Helmina doing all the talking.

After high school, Arnie worked on his father's farm for two years until the day the letter arrived from the Draft Board. Gerhardt left the letter in the mailbox while Arnie drove to St. Cloud to find the Navy recruiter. When he returned to Urholt, he had signed up to serve his country. His father sent a notarized letter to the Draft Board of Spencer County informing them that Arnold J. Murkiwasser was in the Navy. Arnie sailed through 'Boot Camp' at San Diego, California despite being the butt of many short jokes. He grew to enjoy the attention. He also found that his mates would listen to him when he expressed an opinion.

After four years in the Navy, Arnie resigned. He left the Navy with the marksman's badge and the campaign medal for Southeast Asia. He served aboard the destroyer *USS Roy Warden* providing escort duty to the aircraft carriers in the China Sea. He thought he was happy to return to Minnesota.

Until the night he and two buddies drove to the Fox Lake Ballroom, just north of the Iowa border. They had heard that the women were 'frisky' and 'cuddly' at Fox Lake. There was a shortage of men in southern Minnesota, according to the rumor.

It was at Fox Lake that Arnie met Marie Jeannine Swenson, a lissome and enervated figure on the dance floor. She was a bright young woman at College of Northern Iowa and she was intent on snagging a man. After several drinks, Arnie suggested to Marie that he was going to move to Spirit Lake, Iowa and join her in college. When he reached home early the next morning, there was a patrol car waiting for him.

"I knew it was the state highway patrol," he was to tell Marie later. "Standing there in his shiny black boots, wearing the maroon uniform and the hat with the flat brim." The officer told him that Gerhardt and Helmina were dead. He told Arnie that a truck driver apparently fell asleep and drove over the centerline. Arnie's parents were killed instantly.

In the year that followed, Arnie was at a loss. He didn't want to run the farm. He rented out the farmland and lived in the home site. He wanted to do something 'bigger' as he described it. He began making trips to Spirit Lake and in the spring Marie said 'Yes' when he asked her to marry him. They moved to his farm site and 'lived in sin' until late August when they were married in the little rural Lutheran church on the south shore of Iron Lake.

The Norseland Township Lutheran church still stands on that hill, overlooking the lake. The row of tall ponderosa pines stands guard yet today next to the parking lot. The little cemetery still has an occasional flower blooming in a pot. It is a peaceful and quiet place, a white church with a spire pointing into the sky. Cornfields surround the church and cemetery. There is a solitary bell in the steeple. It was here that Arnie discovered that there are people in this world that would accept him for who he was and he enjoyed their company during the frequent 'pot luck' suppers on Sunday evenings.

The church became a habit, one that Arnie looked forward to each week. After two years of marriage, Marie presented Arnie with a daughter that they named Sharon Ann. About two years later, Arnie received the son (Matthew Mark) that he was hoping for. It was during these years that Arnie worked for a regional paint distributor and dreamed of owning his own paint and remodeling store. Then the school board in Urholt did something totally unexpected. They merged with the small school district of Warba to their west.

In the year before Sharon Ann would be old enough for Kindergarten, the rumor floated around town that Warba was talking to Urholt about merging their school districts. The elementary school in Urholt would be closed and moved to Warba. There was even some discussion of building a new school at the midpoint, about four miles between Urholt and Warba.

These discussions aggravated Arnie Murkiwasser. He wanted his daughter to attend a local school. Someone told Arnie his daughter was going to ride the bus for 45 minutes each way. He went to the next Board Meeting in Urholt and stood up and protested their plans. The board members told Arnie that Urholt was too small to survive on its own. Besides, they said, Iron Lake had rejected their overtures for consolidation talks between Iron Lake and Urholt.

Arnie Murkiwasser stood his ground and argued with the Board chairman. Then his tone of voice became threatening. The members of the public present did little to support his position. Those who were present thought a larger football team would be a plus and there might be enough good athletes to field a decent girl's basketball team. When Arnie ran out of breath, there was a pause. Behind him, Arnie heard someone say *'Serves the little twerp right,'* and he turned pale. He knew they were talking about him. He knew the people in Urholt had always considered him to be a short, stumpy joke on the rest of the civilized world.

He sat down. In that moment he decided to sell his farm and move to Iron Lake.

*****

"People in this town listen to the teachers," said Arnie to Tom. Tom was standing by his coffee pot, pouring a second cup of coffee.

"And it's time for the people to listen to the school board," added Arnie.

"What's your point, Arnie?"

"Three of the elementary teachers took personal leave last Thursday afternoon to attend a tea and bazaar at the Iron Lake Golf Club. That's not what 'Personal Leave' was intended to do."

"So, we try to negotiate a change in the definition."

"Today."

"Today? What do you mean, today? We are scheduled to meet with the negotiating teams next week."

"Cratt and Mrs. Trivic and Mrs. Fallow and myself met last night at my house. We want you to tell the union we want a tighter definition, so teachers can use 'Personal Leave' for matters that 'can only be handled during school hours', like a court appearance or closing on a house."

"I can't do it." Tom was thinking about the revelation that four board members had held a meeting at Arnie Murkiwasser's house. Such a meeting was not legal. "And you do know that four board members constitutes a meeting?"

"I misspoke," Arnie said quickly. "Mrs. Fallow only arrived when Cratt and Mrs. Trivic were on the way out the door." Tom noticed that Arnie's cheeks seemed to turn slightly pink and a bead of sweat appeared on his upper lip.

"Please be careful," Tom added, while making a mental note to record Arnie's statements in his administrative notebook. *'I'm not paranoid,'* Tom thought. He had recently attended a training session in which someone said that superintendents should keep notes about any meetings that board members attended. The school board from St. Cloud had been fined recently for holding 'an illegal meeting' in Alexandria. Arnie was sitting there looking at Tom, so he added, "I can't put 'Personal Leave' on the table."

"Yes, You can!" said Arnie to Tom, staring him in the face. Tom reached up to his tie and pulled it down an inch, allowing his neck to breathe. Arnie stood up, and backed away from Tom. When he was behind the guest chair, he leaned forward until the guest chair stopped his forward motion.

He stood with an expectant expression on his bulldog face, both hands resting on the back of the guest chair. His lips curled into the suggestion of a smile.

"We want you to tell the teacher negotiators that we are putting 'Personal Leave' on the table, as of today."

Tom started to stand up, confused. If he told the teachers, there would be two board members who were not party to the discussion *and apparent decision* by four of the members.

"I repeat...I can't do it."

"And I repeat, you will. Call me by nine o'clock tonight to report what Mr. Barnes and his cohorts have to say about 'Personal Leave'." The shorter man turned and walked out of Tom's office, if it could be called walking. Tom had a fleeting image for a moment of a diminutive majordomo goose-stepping out of his office.

*****

There are times at the end of a long day when a man, or woman for that matter, who runs a large operation will sit back and wonder what the future will bring. After supper at home and a girl's volleyball game, Tom went to his office to finish his notes about the day. Tom had called the other two board members Smith and Fitzsimmons and told them he was putting a new definition of 'Personal Leave' on the table. When he reported that the 'negotiations team' had ordered him to do it, they both told Tom not to worry. They would discuss procedures at the next closed meeting of the board.

The three teachers who 'broke' the Personal Leave rule admitted that they 'just felt like an afternoon off' and were warned that they had violated the provisions of the contract. They had become defensive and threatened to file a grievance.

For Tom's part, he failed to tell Percy or Curt about the 'instructions' he had received from the Chairman of the Board, Mr. Arnie Murkiwasser. Tom felt that private conversations with individual board members were confidential matters.

"Or, on the other hand, maybe I don't want others to know how the little dictator behaves in private?" he said out loud just before he closed his notebook.

CHAPTER SEVEN
Losing Control

"You have to try," said the man who was standing.

"And I repeat," answered Arnie Murkiwasser, "we are continuing to meet."

"Put more money on the table," said the man. He was wearing a red flannel shirt with black suspenders. His face was camouflaged behind a full beard that fell onto his chest and hair that stood out from his head. The man wore glasses with black rims and had a pencil stuck behind his left ear. His demeanor implied that he was a logger and he wasn't afraid to tell people what to do. The people seated around him were listening.

Standing behind him, with his back against the boardroom wall, was a man holding a placard that proclaimed 'It's Time to Settle.' The chairs in front of the long board table were filled. Parents were standing behind the chairs and along both sides of the room. A few teachers were scattered throughout the room. 'Bluster' Barnes was sitting to the left of the man in the flannel shirt. The door to the room was filled and perhaps five men were standing in the hall outside the room. The center of their attention was the Board of Directors, with the dapper chairman sitting in the middle. Arnie Murkiwasser was wearing a business suit and a tie with red stripes. He was prepared to fulfill the requirements of his role.

"The Board will meet," said Murkiwasser slowly, hesitating and drawing out his sentence, "as many times as necessary."

"But your teachers are going to strike," said Red Flannel.

"That's a rumor," reverberated from the end of the table when Connie Cratt jumped into the discussion. "Don't listen to rumors."

"I have it on good authority..." began the man before he was interrupted.

"They haven't taken a vote," said Connie Cratt bluntly.

"And we are still negotiating," came a high-pitched plea from Chairman Murkiwasser. He pulled out his handkerchief and ran it across his forehead.

"Will you hold school during a strike?" asked the man. He looked around the room, scanning the faces of the men and women who were watching him. Their faces mirrored his concern. He seemed to sense that he was speaking for all of them.

"I have a boy and a girl...both seniors. This is their last year and their best chance to win athletic scholarships. Don't kill their chances... please."

A full minute went by on the school clock in the back of the room. There were no words spoken. The clock mechanism moved the minute hand forward, one notch. The audience and the board were thinking about this man's plea to keep school running.

"If they strike, we will not open school with scabs," said Cratt into the silence of the room. Tom flinched when he heard the word 'scabs'. He knew Connie was 'union' and union members referred to people who crossed the picket line as 'scabs'...and worse.

The man who was standing asked the Board of Directors to keep trying. The chairman told the assembled crowd that the board would continue to meet with the teachers. A mediation session was scheduled for next week. Connie Cratt got in one last barb, reminding the teachers that the board had already 'spent' more than the district could afford. The chairman rapped his gavel and declared a recess. Many of the parents were wearing Iron Lake sweatshirts and left the room, headed for the volleyball game down in the gymnasium. The superintendent watched them leave, hoping the board could get on with its agenda.

*****

Tom Harant watched the parents and teachers and other employees file out of the boardroom. He stood up and opened two windows in the wall behind the board table. Two board members left the boardroom through his office, signaling that nothing should happen until they returned. Curt Fitzsimmons made his way behind the boardroom tables to Tom's side. Curt handed Tom a note and proceeded to leave through the superintendent's office. Tom saw the light on the wall phone turn on, and assumed that Curt was calling his wife during the break. He looked down at the note and then opened it.

'Wondering what you can do?' was scrawled in Curt's large handwriting.

Tom watched the last of the parents leave the boardroom and sat down in his chair. Patty Trivic and Percy Smith were talking to each other and ignored Tom. He seemed to sense his isolation and wrote 'How do I get control?' on the bottom of Curt's note, and folded the note in half. He wrote 'Curt F' on the outside of the note and passed the note over to Patty Trivic who put the note at Curt's place on the table.

*****

"You don't get control," said Tom's date. "You treat a person with kindness and maybe a poem or two. You take a walk in the leaves and take her out for pizza. Maybe you go to a movie." Tom's date was sitting on the couch in Tom's apartment on 'Upper Campus' at Mankato State College. She was pulling a comb through her hair, removing snarls. She and Tom had spent thirty minutes necking before she admitted she didn't want to 'go any further'.

"Control is something you don't get. You earn it, I think," she added.

Tom smiled. This young lady, who was twenty-one years old, and a recent graduate from nursing school, seemed to be wise beyond her years. Tom was watching her comb her hair and surreptitiously was watching the motion of her breasts with each motion. In a moment of extreme bravery and simpleton stupidity, he put his hand on her bare leg above her knee. He moved his hand gently up her leg for six inches and stopped. She was wearing a pleated dress in dark green wool with a white blouse. She looked down at Tom's hand.

"If she starts to like you, she'll let you know." She reached down and removed Tom's hand from her leg.

"You remind me of Patty," said Tom in wonder.

"And don't mention other girlfriends, that's another rule," said Tom's date when she turned to kiss him on the cheek. Tom was stunned and pulled back. He looked confused for a moment, while she moved to the large chair that held their coats. She began to put her coat on. "We have a staff meeting in thirty minutes."

"But you do remind me of Patty. She was always in control. I couldn't bring myself to kiss her," Tom admitted.

"You are definitely sweet," said his date while tossing him his jacket. They had twenty-five minutes to get to work at St. Joseph's Hospital where his date was a nurse and Tom was a hulking, wet-behind-the-ears orderly.

*****

At times, sitting behind the board table, Tom wondered how he managed to get himself in such a place. Was it because he had gone along with the flow without challenging his route or his goals? Is there a penalty for taking the easy route through life, when a man should step up to the plate, and take three swings, as it were? Only a few men get to hit homeruns and Tom did not fit the category of hero. When he left Marquette University, he thought he would return. He thought he would see Patty in the fall. That was the fall that he enrolled at Mankato State College...with the feeling in the pit of his stomach that he was betraying his promises.

Or, was he betraying himself? He wondered some twenty-five years later while he sat in the boardroom at Iron Lake. Was it betrayal? Or was he a naïve young man lost in the wilderness of early manhood? Going to Mankato State was a good move, he realized thinking about his wife and children.

It was a great move, the turning of a leaf, a flicker of sunlight through a glade, and firelight dancing on the face of a young lady, long forgotten. The images danced through Tom's mind while he watched the minute hand on the clock move minutely. He remembered the house next to the Newman Center, and he remembered worrying about the rent. He remembered his first car, a 1950 Ford 'flat-head V-Eight' that blew oily fumes out the exhaust pipe when he cranked it up to 110 miles per hour. They were years of frustration and anger...frustration because Tom couldn't or wouldn't settle on a goal. Anger because he felt that he had betrayed himself and settled for far less than he could have been.

After winning the Science Prize in high school, Tom had decided to follow in his uncle's footsteps in the nuclear Navy. It was the new branch, and nuclear engineers were the new kids on the pier. But Tom let himself down, first by failing to grasp calculus and then by getting suspended at Marquette. Moreover, Tom suddenly found himself taking English courses at Mankato State with the vague intention of becoming a writer.

Nevertheless, starting at Mankato was a great move, he thought years later. It was the turning of a gentle leaf and a flicker of sunlight through a hazy August afternoon. He turned a leaf when he began working at St. Joseph's Hospital as an orderly. At six foot four inches, he was easily the tallest young male in the hospital. And his height gave him an advantage when he was called upon to move a patient into or out of a hospital bed. And he suddenly noticed there were females in his world who looked up to him, and smiled, and touched his arm, and smiled. While he worked at St. Joe's he began to experiment with the opposite sex.

He gained confidence, but no conquests. He broke a few hearts after three or four dates and the nurse aides who worked on his floor adored him. Once or twice he actually got to the point of his date saying 'No' to sex, and he stopped. His third grade teacher Sister Angelica was just behind him, warning him not to cross the line with a female. He felt frustrated but he listened to 'Angelica's' voice. He was a young male, primed and ready to conquer the world of females.

"I think I have found her," he told his mother on the phone. She was named Crystal, with blond hair and blue eyes and a beautiful nose and all the 'right curves' at the right locations. He took her to a showing of *West Side Story* and they both fell in love with the sadness of the story. He took her for pizza and wrote high-flung poetry. They took long walks in the fall and studied together and played bridge together. One month to the day after their first date, Tom told Crystal that they were going to be married. She had somehow managed to convince Tom that he could be in control, some of the time. In the spring, he surprised her with a ring and in August they held a formal wedding with gowns and tuxedoes on a hot Sunday afternoon.

She had a beautiful face and soft skin and Tom loved running his hands up and down her back when she was cuddled up to him. She had soft lips and arms that wouldn't let go when they hugged. Tom was pleased with himself. After years of waffling, he found there was a purpose in his life. That purpose was Crystal. He set out to make her happy and in doing so, began to worry less and less about who had control in his life. Crystal gave him a son they named Mark in 1966, a son Carl in 1970 and three years later they produced a darling daughter, Corrine.

It was in the year that Corrine was born that Tom decided to make a difference. He was teaching English in Fairmont High School and becoming frustrated with the other English teachers. They wanted to teach the classics; Tom wanted to introduce some Twentieth Century authors. He resigned at Fairmont, packed his family into their red station wagon and moved back to Mankato State. They settled into a low-income apartment called 'Homestead Apartments' up on the hill across from the ice arena. Tom completed his Master's and Specialist degrees in fourteen months and they moved to Sherburn, a small town between Fairmont and Jackson.

The two years that followed were fun, and challenging and quite exciting. Tom supervised forty-five teachers and 450 students. The morning after Homecoming, there was an outhouse on the high school roof. Before most band concerts, the cooks prepared chili and caramel rolls that were so good...they were beyond belief. The teachers talked to each other and Tom, and they worked well together. The faculty beat the senior boys in volleyball. Crystal joined the church choir and Tom stayed home with the kids on Wednesday evenings. Carl started Kindergarten at Sherburn Elementary. The town enjoyed Tom and Crystal and their children. The two years were both ideal and idyllic.

Fifteen years later, at Iron Lake, Tom realized that he had been the happiest working as a principal, counseling and disciplining students. The two years at Sherburn were the best because they did not carry the weight of the decisions he made in later years. Sitting at the board table in Iron Lake, Tom realized that he missed the camaraderie of Sherburn and the easy graceful flow of the decisions in his first CEO job at Amboy-Good Thunder, south of Mankato. Tom knew that Amboy-Good Thunder was gone now, part of the move to create larger, more efficient school districts. A-GT was replaced by a larger district called Maple River.

His second school district was, he felt, the best experience. At Great Pine, Tom joined the local Lions Club and participated in many of their activities. The Lions raised funds for eyesight projects by selling light bulbs and running the races at the county racetrack. Great Pine people liked to see Tom involved in activities. In his sixth year, Tom was elected President of the Lions Club. The following year, he was elected President of the church council. The next year he became President of the Chamber of Commerce. Tom devoted himself to making Great Pine a better place. He came to regret leaving. When Great Pine paired with Isle, the combined boards chose the more senior superintendent. The new board asked Tom to move on.

Tom came to Iron Lake in July 1990, barely 14 months before the strike.

*****

"Cripes, think of the shame of it," said Arnie Murkiwasser.

"Ha," snorted Curt Fitzsimmons. "The only thing missing is a photograph of the two of them sneaking out of that run down motel."

"Whoa," replied Arnie. "That would be something." Arnie raised his gavel to bring the meeting of the board to order. They were meeting behind closed doors after escorting all of the public out of the boardroom. His gavel rapped on the board table.

"Will you take notes?" he asked Glacinda. Mrs. Fallow was now sitting next to Patty Trivic, with her notebook open in front of her. When Glacinda nodded at Arnie, he turned his attention to Connie Cratt.

"Connie, the meeting has been called to order."

"So go ahead," answered Connie. "I prefer to stand." Connie had put his white cowboy hat back on his head and was admiring the 'cut of his jib' in the mirror over the sink. For tonight's meeting, he wore a blue and white cowboy shirt with pearl buttons and a string tie with a chartreuse stone of verdigris at the knot. The reflection in the mirror revealed his shirt was stretched across his substantial stomach. Turned sideways, he saw his stomach. Under his hat, he saw greasy hair sticking out.

"So what's with Plant and Harvey?" demanded Connie.

"That's not on our agenda, Mr. Cratt," remarked Tom Harant. He was sitting next to Arnie, with Percy and Curt on his left. They were all watching Connie Cratt as he walked across the boardroom toward the newly opened windows.

"Wrong, Tom. When two teachers are banging each other, that is the agenda." Cratt swung around until he was facing Tom and Arnie at the middle of the table.

"This is a closed meeting to discuss negotiations strategy, Mr. Cratt," said Tom slightly slower than his first comment.

"Yeah, I know. 'Personal Leave' was a red, yes, darn it, a red what, Arnie?"

"A red herring."

"That's right. A red herring. To make the union think we are discussing 'Personal Leave' as our newest lever for mediation, next week."

"The board is allowed to discuss strategy in a closed meeting. You cannot talk about two teachers without first approving a motion." Tom felt confused. He had believed Arnie when told to put 'Personal Leave' on the agenda. And suddenly, at that point in the regular meeting, Cratt had moved to hold a closed meeting. Now here he was, watching the board members violate the law.

"I move we fire Plant and Harvey," said Cratt.

"But...we need," said Patty Trivic, somewhat flustered. No one had told her about a sudden move to fire Lillian Harvey. Patty had been part of the team that interviewed the young, vibrant English teacher.

"Second the motion," said Arnie.

"Now, wait a minute!" stammered Percy Smith, looking at Cratt and Harant. "Don't we give a warning?"

"Not this time," said Cratt. "They have violated the mores of the community and openly flaunted their affair in the face of our wives."

"Hells bells, Connie. The community wouldn't even know about it except for the gossips at the Cup and Saucer." Percy Smith was determined to keep the board from acting prematurely. He noticed that Patty Trivic was writing notes. "And we can't put any of this in the minutes."

"The minutes will say that the board discussed an employee problem as well as 'Personal Leave'. Mrs. Trivic will have Arnie approve the minutes before they go to the newspaper. OK with you?"

"No, it's not *OK* with me, nor is it 'simply agreeable' to hide the truth." Percy took his role seriously. His role as a director of the board did not include breaking the law. The minutes would obviously point to an illegal discussion.

"Mr. Harant, you are sitting there saying nothing," Connie said with hard intent to get Percy to shut up for a moment. "You're the superintendent. What will work?"

Tom Harant sat and looked at the man in the blue and white cowboy shirt with the ten-gallon hat perched on his head. He wanted to stare the man down but Connie was primed and ready. He didn't blink and he stared back at Tom. The smile on his face seemed to convey a hint of threat...a threat that someone better agree with his point of view.

"Record that the board discussed a personnel issue, Mrs. Trivic," said Tom slowly. He looked at Patty and realized he had broken the contact with Connie's eyes first. When he looked back at Connie, the man was winking at Arnie Murkiwasser.

"There's a motion on the floor," said Arnie.

"You can't fire a veteran teacher like Sylvan Plant without a hearing and due process. The new teacher is probationary...you can fire her in the spring," added Tom Harant. He was seriously worried that someone would call for a vote. Even a vote in a closed meeting had to be recorded and more importantly, carried out. The board's role was to tell the administration what to do and many times his marching orders were handed out on a split four-to-two vote.

"We'll reduce the department to one teacher. That will get rid of Plant, won't it?" asked Cratt. His eyebrows were ground together into a frown.

"Yes, it would, if that's what the board chooses to do."

"OK, we will come back to this issue when we cut positions in April," said Connie. He looked rather pleased with himself. He walked back to the sink and looked into the mirror.

"And Lillian Harvey?" asked Tom.

"You put her on the list of probationary teachers we are cutting, also in April. That's an order."

"I take orders from the board, Mr. Cratt," said Tom in reply. To which Connie Cratt replied with a show of hands. Four voted to dismiss Harvey, two voted against firing her. Cratt reminded the board of the mediation session coming up and asked for a motion to adjourn. Patty wrote the time and 'Adjourn' behind the time. The ladies closed their notebooks and began to stand. Curt Fitzsimmons and Percy Smith remained in close conversation. Tom watched Glacinda Fallow and Patty Trivic leave the boardroom, followed by Arnie and Connie. He closed his own notebook, in which he had earlier written the starting and ending times of the closed session.

When he stood up to close the two large windows, he could see four board members talking to each other under the Century Elm.

"Damn," he said under his breath. "That's illegal."

"What?" asked Curt Fitzsimmons.

"Good looking night, out there. Time for a beer in the Red Carpet, I think."

"I don't think...I know," said Percy. He punched Curt in the arm, not too gently. Tom was on his way to his office to get his jacket. While frost wasn't expected this early, Tom knew he needed his jacket to ward off the chill of a mid-September night. Inside his office, he glanced out his window and saw the four board members still standing by the Century Elm. They were backlit from a streetlight in quiet conversation. They were gesturing with their hands.

"Ah, shoot," he said to himself. He shucked his suit coat and put on his jacket. While he was pulling up the zipper, he happened to glance at the plaque from his year as Chamber President. There was a gavel mounted on the plaque, and it reminded him that from his point of view, he was losing control of the board.

CHAPTER EIGHT
Waiting on da' Big Guy

"So this guy says, 'The Big Guy' is on the 10th floor."

"And was he?" said Patty Trivic with considerable interest. Tom was telling Patty and Glacinda about dinner in the Polynesian Room at the Leamington Hotel, Minneapolis. The other men on the board were talking to Kirby Jones, the state mediator. He was telling one of his numerous stories about labor strife during the 1950's. The board and their superintendent were 'holed up' in a meeting room in the Spencer County Courthouse.

"On the 10th floor? Probably." Tom smiled at the thought. The previous year, Curt Fitzsimmons started on the 15th floor in one of the book publisher hospitality suites. Tom went there with Curt but abandoned Curt on the 12th floor after several canapés and eight drinks. It was time to join the board in the Polynesian Room. Curt never showed up for dinner. Tom remembered eating dinner with the men on the school board but remembered little about the rest of the evening.

"So I made it to the 12th floor but carried one drink between four of the hospitality rooms," added Tom quickly. Curt started on the 15th floor for the second year in a row at about 3:30 in the afternoon. If he was now on the 10th floor, there was little chance he would make it to the ground floor and the Polynesian Room. There was laughter from the four men who were listening to the state mediator. Tom glanced at them but they were not paying attention to Tom and the two women.

"Half an hour later, another man comes by and says 'The Big Guy' says to tell you he is on the 8th floor," Tom said, barely able to contain his laughter. Tom remembered sitting at a table with Smith, Cratt and Murkiwasser in the Polynesian Room. Tom had reserved a table for five thinking Curt might actually make it to the dinner. It was Thursday night during the statewide convention in Minneapolis. Thursday was the traditional night for hospitality rooms when board members rubbed elbows with the vendors who were supplying the schools.

"So, low and behold, half an hour later another man comes by and says 'The Big Guy' says he is on six. He was lying, of course, because he told me six but he was drinking beer with the salesman for Quill, the school supplies people, on the 8th floor."

"Or maybe Curt thought he was on six?"

"I doubt it."

Tom suddenly realized that Glacinda Fallow and Patty Trivic had never been to the Leamington Hotel in what was known as 'Blizzard' week. The second full week in January in Minnesota is usually the coldest and coincides with the statewide convention of school board members. Iron Lake, like many of the school districts, reserved rooms in the old hotel in order to walk to the Minneapolis Convention Center. And Thursday night was party night for many of these hard working, straight-laced farmers and their wives. The alcohol flowed freely in the hospitality rooms.

The prize, however, was dinner in the Polynesian Room, usually paid for by the superintendent. Like its name implied, the room had bamboo stalks supporting the roofs of huts made of palm leaves and grass. The tables were clear glass supported by bunches of bamboo stalks. The bartenders wore white shirts with fluorescent blue beach scenes. The waitresses wore bikini tops and extremely small skirts with fluorescent patterns that lit up when they passed underneath the 'black' light devices.

A hula band of Hawaiian transplants to Minnesota provided live entertainment.

"And the dancers had long hair that covered their breasts," Tom added, watching Glacinda's reaction. He suspected that she was a 'closet prude' but she didn't react. Patty smiled.

"The four of us are finishing dinner about 8:30 p.m. when another man comes by, recognizes Arnie Murkiwasser and says, 'The Big Guy' says to tell you he is on the 4th floor." Tom paused for a moment, remembering.

"Which produced a round of applause from the tables around us. And Arnie almost fell on the floor laughing," Tom chuckled.

When the band took a break, Connie Cratt stood up, tucked his hula shirt into his belt and began to propose a toast to 'those persons missing' the party. He gave a brief eulogy to 'large persons' who sit on school boards and sat down. Percy Smith ordered a round of brandy-cokes for the four men, just as Curt Fitzsimmons walked into the Polynesian Room. Which is to say, he tried to walk into the Polynesian Room. Someone grabbed him at the first table and pulled him into a chair. He was wearing an enormous hula shirt, 'direct from Hawaii' by mail, as he told Tom earlier. Curt was smiling ear-to-ear and laughing at something.

"So, wouldn't you know it? During a quiet spell here comes this heavy roar from Curt's table, 'you said WHAT?' in the silence, so now everybody in the place knows Curt has arrived."

Tom looked at Curt, who was aware of Tom's story. He was listening to Kirby Jones talk, but waved at Tom and said, "Tell them the rest."

"Curt stands up and staggers to the middle of the room. He looks just like he's trying to convince the crowd that he hasn't had a drink. And he says, 'Yes sir, I did it. Visited every single horsh-pitty-ality room.'"

"And the crowd exploded in laughter." Arnie was laughing, Connie was laughing and Percy Smith was hiding his laughter behind his hand. Curt lowered his 300-pound frame into a chair and started looking around, as if he knew what was about to happen.

Tom knew that as hard as Curt worked on his farm, farrowing one hundred sows and producing 800 piglets every four months, he was entitled to have some fun. With the size of his operation, it was rare that he could get away from his farm for more than a few hours. When Tom asked, Curt told him that he had special phone lines from his barns to his house. If the temperature dropped below 60 degrees in a barn, a small device would ring him at home.

Curt had two daughters in college to support. His oldest girl was studying Agronomy at Mankato State. His second oldest was in Pre-Med at the University of Minnesota. He had a son Jered who was in his senior year and played defensive tackle on the Iron Lake football team. Jered helped with the chores when he could.

"So, there he was, looking around, and I began to get nervous," Tom said to his small audience.

"You know me, the married guy, two kids at home, upstanding and stalwart. What the heck, I'm still laughing and congratulating Curt for making it to the ground floor in six hours." Tom admitted later that he was the only one in the Polynesian Room wearing a dress shirt and tie.

"Suddenly the band begins to play a soft, seductive hula, a traditional piece. When I look to my right, about ten feet away our waitress is dancing slowly and unfastening her bikini top. The crowd of men (mostly) are cheering and clapping. She pulled something out of her hair, and her soft brown hair fell just far enough. Then she removed her bikini top and threw it into my lap."

In the mediation room, the four men at the other end of the table were listening to Tom. Kirby Jones was smiling, getting a kick out of this story about the 'Big Guy' at Iron Lake. Curt was smiling, pretending he remembered this part of the story, which Tom doubted.

"So the bartender steps out from behind the bar with the biggest drink glass you have ever seen. It was as wide as a birdbath with a solid stand. He gave it to our waitress who began a slow dance over to our table. And she slithers up to me and gives the drink to me."

"And you didn't know what to do with it," said Curt laughing.

"But Tom put it on the table and asked for straws," added Arnie, looking around. "And the waitress ignored him, and danced behind him, and rubbed her breasts into the back of his head," added Arnie.

"About now, his cheeks are red and his ears are beginning to turn red," said Curt.

"True, I've seen Tom's face when he's flustered," said Glacinda, enjoying Tom's discomfort. Patty reached over and patted Tom on the arm, to encourage him to finish the story.

"And the waitress, she..."

"Was cute, and wearing only a short piece of cloth around her hips," said Arnie with relish.

"She dances around my chair," Tom said, "and plops herself into my lap, wraps her left arm around my neck and gives me a big kiss on the cheek." The men in the crowd, who have been watching, applauded and whistled. The four Iron Lake board members were laughing so hard that Percy was holding his stomach with two arms while Curt pounded the arm of his chair. Connie Cratt was smiling, but not laughing.

"Off comes the tie," said Curt.

"You rat," said Tom, then to the two ladies he added, "I found out later that Curt put her up to it."

"If you could have seen his face," laughed Arnie.

"Trying to be proper," said Curt. "When she had his tie, she squirmed around in his lap and using the tie like a small brassiere, extended the ends behind her and asked Tom to tie the ends. Which he tried to do."

"And tried," said Connie, laughing with the others.

"And tried," added Arnie.

Tom's face was flushed with the retelling of his story. Suddenly, he was snapped back from the past, into the reality of the meeting room inside the Spencer County Courthouse. There was a rap on the door and 'Bluster Barnes' stuck his head in asking for Kirby Jones. The board members and Tom watched Kirby leave, waddling as he did through the door. Kirby was in his late 50's in 1990, after a full career with the Bureau of Mediation. He was a short man, about five feet six inches tall with a pronounced beer belly, and grayish-brown hair ringing a baldhead. He had more than once been mistaken for Danny Devito, the actor in the sitcom, *Taxi*.

*****

"How much do we have to negotiate with?" asked Curt Fitzsimmons, getting the crew back on task. He was looking at Connie Cratt because Connie led the negotiating team.

Connie was wearing dark blue dress pants with a white shirt and bolo tie. The white ten-gallon was not in evidence. Connie seemed to stall, or to ponder the question. He stood up from the table and walked to the windows. The meeting room was like all the other meeting rooms in Spencer County Courthouse. Two long tables and twelve chairs sat on a gray carpet. There was one wall of windows with tattered shades. A small American flag hung listlessly in the corner. George Washington occupied one wall while Thomas Jefferson smiled sardonically down at the occupants from the opposite wall. The wall by the door held a bulletin board with notices of meetings, a 'No Smoking' sign and 'Fire Exit' directions telling the reader to go 'Out the door, turn left, proceed to stairs and exit the building'.

"Whatever we had, we spent." Connie Cratt said this slowly, with emphasis. He could see that Patty Trivic was opening her notebook, preparing for questions.

"We did what the board told us to do. We put $4200 on the table."

"That's for the two years, isn't it?" asked Curt.

"Yes."

"We went a little further in August. We were increasing the offer when they stormed out of the room." Patty was talking directly to Curt, emphasizing her points.

"To be fair, they walked out," said Connie.

"Whatever," said Curt.

There was a knock on the door and Billy Washburn looked in before entering and handing Arnie a letter. He was dressed like always: shirt, tie and a pullover sweater. Billy was the high school principal and he won the duty of delivering the letter only because of his seniority. The other two principals felt Billy wouldn't get chewed out too severely.

"The principals do not agree with the Board's position?" said Arnie in a singularly loud voice, waving the letter at Billy.

"Yes, sir, that's our statement."

"What do we do with the letter, Mr. Washburn? Mr. So-called high school principal?" asked Connie Cratt.

"We wanted to be on record, encouraging the board."

"To do what?"

"Get a contract, before it's too late." Billy Washburn looked a little peaked, and his face seemed white in the late afternoon light from outside.

"We have your letter," said Cratt.

"Any response?" asked Billy hopefully.

Connie Cratt walked across the room to where Billy stood inside the door. He looked him in the eye, almost challenging him. "We have your letter. That's our response. Now get out."

Tom was sitting at the far end of the table, beginning to stand up. "Perhaps, Mr. Cratt, you are being a little abrupt." Tom had been warned the letter might arrive during mediation.

"Abrupt, nothing," remarked Connie. He had both hands in his back pockets and reminded Tom of a drill sergeant facing a recalcitrant recruit. Billy Washburn was backing into the doorway, reluctant to leave but determined to get out of 'shooting' range. He pulled the door shut leaving Cratt facing the door.

"Abrupt my foot," said Connie one last time.

Silence fell over the room while Connie moved back to his place at the table and sat down.

"Their letter says 'working together, we can make school a better place for kids'," said Tom, after Arnie handed him the letter.

"Socialist claptrap," added Connie from his end of the table.

There was silence in the meeting room, for a moment. Tom was studying the letter before he added, "We could work with the teachers?"

"No way," stammered Connie Cratt. He looked around the table. All the five board members were looking at him. "Their demands are unrealistic."

"And we have to be realistic," said Tom. His statement of purpose was punctuated by the return of Kirby Jones, the mediator. He walked into the room with a smile on his face and a twinkle in his eye.

"I'm not about to play Santa Claus, but..." and he drew out his statement, looking at Connie Cratt, who he recognized as the leader of the Iron Lake Board. "I don't think you are going to accept their counteroffer."

"What is it?" asked Connie.

"They want me to explain to the board that they are making a major concession. Their original position was $6000 per teacher. They are at $5200 per teacher."

Two of the members groaned, audibly. Arnie rapped a knuckle on the table and said, 'that's progress, at least." Patty Trivic was busy recording the offer in her notebook. Glacinda looked at Connie for a reaction.

"Tom was telling us about the waitress who did a short lap dance in his lap. That's all it was. A lap dance. Lots of motion and a big promise, that goes no where." Connie liked to use stories because his father, a union organizer, used stories. "Big words, going nowhere."

The board members looked at each other and at Tom. Curt Fitzsimmons reached over and whacked Tom on the arm and Tom laughed.

"Just like waiting for the 'Big Guy' here. Lots of anticipation, and a grand entry, to applause."

"They are serious about their offer," said the short, bald mediator.

"Big words, going nowhere," repeated Connie Cratt. He looked around the table. The teachers could go out on strike in two weeks. Each of the board members had received calls last night, urging them to settle. "Go back and tell them we will meet with them next Wednesday if they want to negotiate a contract."

The mediator looked around the room. Several board members nodded at him. Patty Trivic was busy recording Connie's response.

"I'll tell them, but they aren't gonna be happy," said the mediator.

"We're not sitting here to make them happy," said Connie.

CHAPTER NINE
Shoelaces and Sarcasm

"Can the union demand they receive the superintendent's confidential notes about negotiations?"

"No, they can't." The speaker stood tall, looking out across the ballroom at the Madden's Meeting Center. Two hundred twenty of the state's school superintendents were sitting in front of Jim Schmidt, the 'expert' provided by the Minnesota School Boards Association. For the past twenty years Jim Schmidt had led workshops, helping school administrators to prepare for the day when the board decides that a strike is inevitable.

"In fact, if you are asked, you don't have any private notes. Do you understand what I am saying?" His right hand came up and brushed long strands of brownish hair out of his eyes.

Sitting in back, Tom Harant saw many heads nodding agreement. Behind him, in the hall, a phone rang. Several heads in his immediate area swung around, checking to see if the phone would be answered. Tom knew the registration desk was manned by Sharon and Susie, two bright young ladies who kept Tom's group on task. Thirty seconds later, Susie appeared with a phone note in her hand. She spotted the superintendent from Rockford and handed him the message. He immediately jumped to his feet and headed for the exit door.

"It was like that all day yesterday," said Phil who was sitting to Tom's right.

"I noticed. I'm nervous also," added Tom.

Phil laughed quietly. Tom chuckled to himself. Phil was one of the fortunate few superintendents who did not have to worry about a teacher strike. His district had settled, giving their teachers an eight percent increase each year of the contract. But, as Phil had explained, his district was seriously behind the statewide averages for the past four years. The increases were justified, Phil rationalized.

"No, private notes are like the work papers of an attorney. No one else has the right to demand to see those notes. They are confidential." Jim Schmidt, in the front of the room, was wrapping up his comments. Several of the men in the room were streaming toward the exits.

Tom stood up and said in a loud voice, "Thank you, Jim. Can you predict how many districts will go out?"

Schmidt stopped what he was doing. He looked across the room. A sudden hush had fallen. Two hundred faces were turned in his direction. With the exception of the five ladies in dresses, the two hundred were for the most part dressed in dark blue or dark gray suits, with ties with wide stripes. There were a few heads of white hair and a few baldheads, seen from the back.

Tom stood, waiting.

Phil nudged Tom with his elbow, as if to say, "He doesn't want to guess."

"You'll know when it happens," said Jim Schmidt. He waited through a long silence. Perhaps he expected someone to come to his aid. "Your boards will negotiate in some long, trying sessions. As of yesterday, nearly 95 districts have been served with 'Intent to Strike' notices. That's 95 districts where the teachers did what they were told…they voted to file the 'Intent to Strike' and that is unheard of in Minnesota."

He stopped for a moment, and looked down at his shoes. "The earliest they can go out is Tuesday, October 6th. And I repeat, take the threat seriously. Have your 'Strike Plans' updated. Be ready. Know what you are going to do if it happens. That's all I can tell you."

Schmidt closed his notebook. Most of the superintendents were heading back to their rooms to change clothes. The Monday session was finished. Lunch was 30 minutes away and many of the men were playing in the annual golf tournament on Madden's Classic course.

Phil and Tom were standing, while many of the men filtered past them toward the exits. "What have you heard?" asked Phil.

"They say they're going."

"You have a fund balance?" added Phil. Early reports in the Minneapolis *Star & Tribune* indicated that the teachers had filed "Intent" notices in districts with sizeable fund balances.

"Not to speak of."

"What are they thinking?" asked Phil, out of curiosity.

Tom looked him in the eye. He was a pleasant friend to see at these annual meetings. Phil was tall, with gray hair around the sides of his head. Phil and Tom had similar problems, with their hair thinning on the top. Phil always had a twinkle in his eye when he greeted Tom, grabbing his hand and pulling Tom toward himself.

"I made a mistake. I put $1800 per year into the budget. Now they think they are entitled to that $3600 and they are trying to negotiate the Board up to $5200. We had an excess of $50,000 for next year, but the Board offered all of the excess and that got the offer up to $4200 per teacher."

"Sounds like your back is against the wall."

"You could say that." Tom laughed, partly from nervous tension and partly from recognizing the truth. Iron Lake schools were going to have a strike.

"Let's go get our clothes changed," Tom added.

"Yeah, sure," said Phil. He laughed and then pulled Tom toward the exits. "You are just chomping at the bit to get onto that Par 6 hole, aren't you?"

"No, I'm not," said Tom. He thought back to last year when he sliced his drive into the long fairway next to the Par 6 hole. He used his three-wood for his second shot and sent a blast down the fairway. Four superintendents were waiting for his shot. His drive started left, then faded back into their fairway, heading for the four men. Tom saw a man crouch down to duck under Tom's ball. But his ball bounced about three feet from the man and cracked him in the right cheek.

"I can still see that man rubbing his right cheek as he walked past me going the other way."

"Well, they gave him the hard luck award, didn't they?"

"An inflated inner tube, so he could sit."

"Everybody had a good laugh," said Phil.

"At my expense," added Tom. He wanted to laugh with Phil, but it was hard. Out in the hall, another phone rang. Susie was moving to pick it up.

"Let's get out of here. I need to concentrate on golf."

"That won't help," laughed Phil. "You're in the last flight. Just don't kill someone with your wild slices."

"I fixed the slice," said Tom laughing back at Phil. "Now, as always, I have to worry about my hook."

The men left the large ballroom, heading back to their rooms in the Voyager unit. Tom was thinking about his hook. 'I wonder just how many of us are going to be hooked by strikes,' he pondered. He thought back to Jim Schmidt's historical data. After the last round of strikes, every superintendent had been replaced.

*****

A soft mist swirled around the streetlights in Cherry Grove, the county seat of Spencer County. Low gray clouds swarmed across the sky, leaving most residents of the county feeling like perhaps they should have stayed in bed. The yellow school buses had completed their rounds, the students were delivered, and school was in session all across the county. Most of the county employees were at their posts in the courthouse. A few heads turned and watched a small group of men walk toward the courthouse. Across the county, it was no secret that the Iron Lake Board of Directors had been served with an 'Intent to Strike'.

Three county employees, taking a coffee break, were stationed by the back door into the courthouse. They presented an interesting sight. They wore white shirts and ties with identical brown loafers on their feet. They looked at the four men who were approaching the rear door into the office wing. One of the loafers took a white card out of his pocket and waved it at the four men.

"We have a pool on the Iron Lake strike," said the man.

"So what?" said the biggest of the four, the heavyset man with the twinkle in his eye. Curt Fitzsimmons laughed at them and at himself. "What days do you have left?"

"October 15 and 16, and October 22, 23."

"Too bad. The winner is October 6," he said laughing. The three slouches stood and watched Curt enter the courthouse followed by Connie Cratt, Arnie Murkiwasser and Kirby Jones, the state mediator. Curt and Connie wore dark gray overcoats against the mist. Arnie wore a dark blue suit, claiming the light mist wouldn't hurt the material. Kirby Jones was wearing his usual nondescript brown suit with a flashy red and white tie that 'looked like a barber pole.' The other three men wore hats while Kirby's brown fringe was wet with small drops of water.

They met a newspaper reporter from the Cherry Grove *Journal Press* in the first floor hall. Jones told him there would be no statements and he swung around on the chairman, Arnie Murkiwasser. "That's correct, isn't it?" he asked.

"Yes," said Arnie, directly at the reporter. The four men proceeded down the hall to the meeting room. The day was Wednesday, six days before the Iron Lake teachers could strike.

*****

Inside the meeting room, the men found Percy Smith standing at the window, staring out at the mist. The streetlights were on, causing Percy to remark about the gloominess of the day.

The two women, Patty Trivic and Glacinda Fallow, were seated at the worktable, stirring creamer into their coffee. Tom Harant was at the coffee machine pouring another 'cup of hemlock' for himself. Kirby quickly took off his suit coat and stretched it across an empty chair. While the board members arranged themselves around the table, he poured himself coffee.

"We talked until 5:30 a.m. this morning. They have a counteroffer," he said quickly, to get their attention. He walked back to the table, where all heads were turned in his direction. He had dismissed the board members at 2:00 a.m. to get some sleep. He held the union negotiators until 5:30 a.m., while they worked out details of a counteroffer.

"Well, let's have it," said Connie Cratt.

"Yes, let's hear it," said Arnie, trying to retain a last vestige of the control he was supposed to have over the board.

"They want to front load it. Increase your $4200 to $5200 in the first year, and lower the second year to $4000."

"No, goddammit," said Cratt. Connie looked like an old truck, rusty on the edges with mud splattered on the fenders. There were bags under his eyes from the 'lousy' hour of sleep he crammed in before leaving his kitchen for the drive to Cherry Grove. "Even I can see that their so-called counteroffer is $9200, which is an increase over our $8400."

"We aren't going to take a strike over $800, are we?" Percy Smith was fed up with this process of continually meeting. He wanted to get 'the problem' as he called it, resolved.

"We told them last night...$8400 over two years. That's as far as we can go." Connie Cratt was firm in his answer to Percy's suggestion. Arnie Murkiwasser looked at Patty Trivic and Glacinda Fallow. They both nodded in agreement. He looked at Curt Fitzsimmons, the 'Big Guy'.

Curt felt alone in this battle. He felt that any increase to avoid a strike was acceptable. "Let's take a straw poll."

"Let's not," said Cratt loudly, with force.

"We already know where we stand, Connie. Two in favor of increasing the board's offer, four opposed. In favor, raise your right hand."

Arnie looked around the room. Curt and Percy raised their hands. The two women looked down at their notebooks, avoiding the eyes of Percy and Curt. Cratt broke the silence.

"Nothing for us to consider, Mr. Jones. No increase."

Kirby looked down at his notebook and began writing. "I'll tell them you are discussing their counteroffer. Then I'll come back and check with you, one more time."

"Sometimes, people get what they ask for," he said quietly. He looked tired, working with the Board and the teachers group for over 24 straight hours. Kirby had bags under his eyes. His baldhead reflected the lights over his head. His brown hair was neatly slicked back. He had shaved, but nicked himself near his chin. He took a sip from his coffee cup and made a face. The board members and Tom Harant sympathized with him.

"There was a time, workers at the Grain Belt plant in St. Paul wanted to get their twenty-minute coffee break into the contract. This was the twenty-minute break that usually stretched to thirty minutes while they had a leisurely beer across the street from the plant. So they insisted on negotiating it into their contract. They wanted it in writing."

"And what happened?" asked Curt Fitzsimmons.

"They got it alright. Ten minutes for coffee breaks in the morning and the afternoon. In writing. It was *what they wanted*. And the union stewards had to help enforce the new rule," added Kirby.

"Too bad," remarked Connie with a firm tone. "Our teachers ain't going to get what they want."

"My story wasn't aimed at *your* teachers." Mr. State Mediator, Kirby Jones looked a little flustered. Tom Harant saw that the skin above his collar was turning red and his face color seemed darker than two minutes earlier. In his notebook, Tom wrote '*Do we want a strike?*'

Connie Cratt stood up and walked toward the meeting room door. Percy Smith jumped to his feet, started to say something, but stopped. Kirby folded his notebook, intending to head for the employee cafeteria down in the basement. Kirby intended to let both sides 'sit and stew' as he described it. He began to follow Cratt into the hall with its gray carpet and light green 'institutional' walls.

"We know our teachers want a strike," said Mrs. Trivic to Kirby's back. "You are not telling us anything new."

"No, I guess not." Kirby turned in the doorway, intending to argue with the Iron Lake board members. Instead, in a last ditch effort to prod them into sensibility, he asked, "Do you know what you want?"

*****

"We're over a barrel," said Cratt when he returned from the men's room. "If they even guess there is a split on the board, they will try an 'Alinsky' on us, dividing the board."

"That's the third time you have mentioned this *Alinsky* without explaining," said Tom. After two hours of sleep and a quick shower, Tom was just as tired as the rest of the board. He was also frustrated with the teachers who would not recognize where they were headed.

"Alinsky…the commie union organizer down in Chicago. He taught union people how to divide the owners and how to win labor struggles. He had a lot of influence within the AFL-CIO. Steelworkers. Longshoremen."

"And your point is?" said Percy Smith with sarcasm.

"We don't divide. We stand as a group."

"That's right," said Patty Trivic.

"My neighbor says they don't give a damn what we do," added Glacinda Fallow. She knew her husband was upset about the pending strike, but there was little she could do to slow down his drinking.

"That's right," said Patty Trivic. "They don't."

"We should have taken a hard line six years ago when they went out. They didn't lose anything. They think this strike will last two, maybe three days. They get what they want and go back to work." Arnie Murkiwasser was angry. When he came home last night, he heard a message on his new answering machine. Someone, a voice he didn't recognize, accused him of overcharging his customers and overcharging the school for painting jobs. "Gonna picket my store." He said it out loud, not realizing he said it.

"We've heard these arguments and heard these arguments," said Connie. "I move" and he paused, "that if we take any votes, we tell the public the board is unanimous in its determination to settle the contract talks. All in favor?"

Mr. Tom Harant's notes recorded the vote at 4 Ayes, 0 Nays, with Smith and Fitzsimmons abstaining. Their votes meant they did not agree with the rest of the board but they would join the board in issuing 'unanimous' statements.

"Percy Smith left meeting room 9:50 am. Refused to discuss Plant and Harvey. Board wants action. Settled for verbal warning." Tom had explained to the remaining five members that the board had no *behavior* on which to base a dismissal. He would go out on a limb and explain to Sylvan Plant and Lillian Harvey what they were doing to their careers by carrying on in a small town like Iron Lake.

In the end, they waited for Kirby Jones to return from meeting with the teachers. Nothing had changed. Tom wrote a note to announce that school district buses would bring all the kids home on Tuesday morning if the pickets appeared on the sidewalks after the buses began their morning routes.

Tom's notes from the Wednesday morning session were directly under a strange note he wrote the previous night. Crystal had left him a note that read "Voice on phone says 'Settle up or get out. I knows youse causing the problem Iron Lake teachers is having.' September 31, 1990 11:10 p.m." When he asked her about it, she raised her head from her pillow and mumbled something about writing it just the way she heard it.

Low clouds out of the southwest continued to stream across the lakes and valleys west of Iron Lake. Small waves crossed the lake, kicking up white foam as they approached the northeast corner, near the town. The clouds were pushed by a high-pressure cell moving into Minnesota from South Dakota. At noon, the clouds began to dissipate, casting a mottled look across nearby fields, standing bare and brown after harvest.

The board was dismissed at 1:00 p.m. by the state mediator. Kirby Jones told both parties he would call another session, by phone, if either party wanted to negotiate. Privately, he told Tom Harant he expected the worst.

*****

Eighteen buses, fender to fender, stretched along two blocks by the Iron Lake schools. Tom was on the sidewalk at 3:10 p.m. to watch the buses load. To his left, about a block away, high school students were rushing to catch their buses. To his right, a few Elementary 'stragglers' were plodding toward their buses. Behind Tom, the school's Century Elm cast a shadow across the sidewalk.

A small boy walked up to him. The boy was wearing a blue jacket with a brown leather cap on his head. Tom could see the Kindergarten teacher Mrs. Wilson watching the boy. Tom pointed at the boy, then at Mrs. Wilson, and she nodded back at Tom.

"Hi there," he said to the boy.

The boy stood for a moment, before asking, "Are you the 'Big Cop on the Block', like my buddy Ernie says?"

"Well, I guess you could say that," replied Tom, laughing.

"My mother said if I ever needed help I should ask the cop on the block. Is that right?"

"Okay, you bet," Tom told him.

"Well, I guess," he said and extended his right foot toward Tom, "would you please tie my shoe?"

Tom laughed and began to kneel down. The boy's teacher was coming in their direction. It seemed to Tom that the boy needed to get his shoe tied and head for his bus before he missed it.

"That's not *too* big a job for our all-knowing *superintendent*, is it?" asked Mrs. Wilson.

Tom thought briefly about the tone in her voice. It was rare that anyone used sarcasm on him. "No, I like helping kids," he responded while he tied the shoelace. He watched as she grabbed the boy by the shoulder of his jacket and pulled him toward the third bus in line. The boy tried to turn back, and waved a hand at Tom. Tom smiled back while saying 'You're welcome' under his breath.

"Anonymous phone calls and little boys with shoelaces," he replied when Karen Clark asked him about his day. She had walked over to the Century Elm where he was standing, after watching him tie the boy's shoelaces.

"What's with Mrs. Wilson?" he said, while he watched the little boy get onto his bus. "She seems 'out-of-sorts' today".

"You represent the Board, don't you? She's scared of you." Karen, in her role as Principal, had been quietly advising Tom about the mood of the teachers in her building.

"Is it that simple?"

"Some of your teachers are scared, some are angry, some are desperate. One of my teachers asked if she could work, she needs the medical insurance for her daughter who has M.S."

"If they go out, they are all out. That's a board decision. No scabs, as Connie Cratt would say."

The first yellow bus in the line began to crawl away from the curb. The bus was crammed with kids, most in their seats, a few still trading seats with other students. Tom glanced at the second bus and saw the high school kids were in the last six rows, with two empty rows until the 'little kids' heads were visible. When the third bus went by, he briefly saw the brown leather cap of 'his' Kindergarten student near the front. The boy was looking at Tom.

When the buses were gone, Tom looked at Karen Clark and told her the Board was unhappy with the letter from the Principals. She told Tom they were advised to protect themselves. He told her the Board considered them disloyal and already was arguing about firing the three Principals. Mrs. Clark was looking down while she buttoned her coat against the late September chill. "I'll do what I can," he said meekly when she looked up.

He turned and walked away, expecting no response from Karen Clark. He wanted to get back to his desk, write his notes, make a few calls and close up for the day. To himself he said, "Life is one big surprise."

CHAPTER TEN
Football on a Frosty Night

Fridays were special to Tom Plaine. Friday was a day of relaxation—the week was almost finished, the kids were ready for a break and the teachers were in a good mood, looking at two days 'without' kids. In Tom's previous districts, the teachers wore sweaters and ties were forbidden on Fridays. In Iron Lake, there was an unwritten rule: casual dress was acceptable on Friday, but wear something that was red and white, the school's colors. The cheerleaders and all the athletes wore the colors on 'Fred Day' and principal Billy Washburn held a pep rally on every other Friday, last thing in the afternoon. The pep rallies always coincided with home football or basketball games. Everybody went home fired up for the weekend.

Tom enjoyed the camaraderie among the teachers on Fridays. In the Elementary wing, Jerry Ruhela would bring in a smoked fish and Karen Clark's tribe of teachers and aides would snack on fish and crackers all day. Someone usually added a chocolate pound cake and a pan of bars. Tom would walk into the faculty lounge and feel guilty. It had been months since he and Crystal had contributed to the pans of bars. One of the female teachers would cut Tom a piece of chocolate cake that he couldn't refuse. He sometimes wondered…were they worried that he wasn't eating enough or was there some other motive? They were a friendly lot, concerned that none of their own would get cut if the district eliminated teaching positions.

On this particular Friday, four days before the Iron Lake teachers could strike, Tom decided to walk into the faculty lounge at the high school.

In the hall, he glanced into the High School office through the large picture windows. The secretaries were busy finishing the attendance reports for the day. He could see that Billy Washburn was deep in conversation with his Assistant Principal Dennis DeFain. Billy told Tom earlier that three football players had skipped the first three hours of classes on Friday. Billy was probably informing Dennis that those boys had to be ineligible for Friday's game with Fillmore. Dennis, as usual, was trying to find a way to make them eligible. The annual Fillmore game was notorious for hard hits and 'lousy calls' by the referees. Fillmore was north of Iron Lake, in Redwood County and the Fillmore Flyers had been rated number two or three all year in the Class One-A Coach's polls.

Passing the high school office, Tom saw that 'Bluster Barnes' was down the hall, walking toward the faculty lounge. Mr. Barnes was wearing a sear sucker jacket that he found in a garage sale the year before. The jacket was a mass of red and white stripes that some poor fool had worn in a barbershop chorus.

As Tom approached the door, he realized that Barnes had not held the door. He had allowed the door to swing shut in Tom's face. 'Should I, or shouldn't I?' Tom asked himself, before deciding to '*Grab the lion by his whiskers*'.

He pulled the door open and saw Bluster Barnes standing by a table where Sylvan Plant was sitting. Sylvan taught Fifth grade and specialized in math and computer applications. Sylvan was part of Barnes' negotiating team because he could run the computer analysis of all the teacher salary proposals. Also sitting at the table were Wayne Williams, the Chemistry teacher and head of the English Department, Joan Kneiss.

"Sorry, Tom," said Barnes. "I didn't realize you were coming in."

"Or you hoped I wasn't," Tom laughed. Barnes was pulling out a chair at the table. "Can I join you?" Tom was somewhat surprised by himself, talking back to Barnes in such a manner. He walked to their table, pulled a chair over from the next table, and sat down. Of the four at the table, Wayne Williams was the most colorful, wearing a bright red sweatshirt with the Iron Lake Panthers logo on the left breast. Mrs. Kneiss had worn a blue jacket and slacks for Friday, but decorated the jacket with two old Panther Homecoming pins. Sylvan Plant, as usual, had worn an old blue suit. There were rumors that he wore the same suit for two weeks and then switched to his other suit for the next two.

The people Sylvan worked with were relieved when he didn't wear his light blue double-knit 'Leisure' suit. It was so ugly that students would stand around and laugh after he passed them in the halls. What nobody knew, and Tom kept a secret, was that Tom's favorite suit, never worn in Iron Lake, was his light blue dress suit. When he was in a silly mood, he would threaten to wear it. Crystal had even smuggled the suit into the pile of clothes for Goodwill, but he had stolen the suit back. Looking at Sylvan, Tom felt a little sorry for the man. He was in his late forties, having a fling with Lillian Harvey. Tom wondered what the two could see in each other. What he said directly to Sylvan was,

"Ah, the *Bluster* Trust. Planning next week?"

There was silence around the table. Joan Kneiss seemed to be biting her lip. Wayne Williams laughed out loud. Sylvan raised his hand, and began to point at Tom, but withdrew his hand. Robert Barnes sat and looked at Tom.

"You meant *Brain* Trust, did you not?" said Joan Kneiss.

"That's what I said, didn't I?"

"You said *Bluster*, Mr. Harant."

"Well, you know what I meant," said Tom. His shirt suddenly felt too tight and his armpits felt sweaty. Tom had worn his favorite Friday suit, a heavy blue job with a red vest. Tom felt the suit was jaunty because it had white piping sewn in the edges of the lapels. He reached to his rear pocket and retrieved his handkerchief, intent on stalling while he cleaned his glasses.

"It's all right, Mr. Harant. I know what people call me. I don't like that nickname because it implies that I am an actor who exaggerates."

Tom had heard it from Curt Fitzsimmons, the board member who seemed to keep up with the gossip around town. Ten years back, a much younger Robert Barnes had emphasized 'Damn the Torpedoes, full speed Ahead!' when he quoted David Farragut at the Battle of Mobile Bay in 1864. His students went around the building saying 'Damn the Torpedoes' for the next week. His friends on the faculty named him 'Bluster Be Damned' when they saw how he talked to school board negotiators. Robert Barnes was now the most senior teacher in the Social Studies department, lead negotiator for the teachers. Tom, and his principals, believed that Bluster Barnes was the lead negotiator in order to protect himself. Billy Washburn reported that complaints were filed each year about the number of worksheets that Barnes expected his students to complete.

"And you know that I don't exaggerate, right?"

"Oh, absolutely!" said Tom, laughing. "No one ever exaggerates at the bargaining table, do they?"

He realized that the other people at the table were not laughing. In fact, Joan Kneiss had an expression on her face that would have melted lead.

"We take what we are doing very seriously," Joan added.

"I'm sure you do," said Tom quietly, directly to Joan. To the table he added, "But we all do, don't we? I am certainly taking your position seriously."

"And getting ready for a strike?"

"Of course."

"But we are not going out," added Wayne Williams. "We have only filed an Intent."

"And rented a building down by the Econofoods grocery store next to the Post Office," laughed Tom. He couldn't believe they were trying to tell him they weren't going out. "At Ten this morning, someone put up a sign that says 'Strike Headquarters'. What should I make of that?"

"We aren't going out," said Wayne a second time.

To himself, Tom thought *Then come back to the bargaining table.* He kept his mouth shut, realizing that he shouldn't say a thing. The Board had elected Arnie Murkiwasser as spokesperson for the Board.

"It seems to me," said Tom, "your real bargaining leverage exists until you go on strike. After you go out, the board does not have to bargain, does not have to reach a settlement until the board is ready. You lose your leverage, do you see that?"

Joan Kneiss jumped to her feet. She walked backward, away from the table. "What do you mean, we lose?"

"You lose your leverage," said Tom quickly.

"Oh," she said slowly. Joan had backed herself almost to the door. "I thought you were threatening us."

"No threat. But a prediction," added Tom. He stood up, intent on leaving the room. *'This was a mistake,*he said to himself.

"School will be shut down. Deal with that," added Robert Barnes. "We are not going to be impressed by your last minute attempt to talk us out of it."

"I wasn't...oh, Hell and Consternation." Joan Kneiss was through the door and Tom was on her heels. She went to the left, toward the office. Tom turned right, on the spur of the moment, deciding to visit the *Cup and Saucer* downtown.

*****

As he left the high school, Tom stopped outside the entry door and watched a car park in back of the small white frame house directly across from his office. The house was painted white with black trim. The shingles held a few patches of moss and the paint was peeling off the rain gutters. The owner had failed to remove the storm windows in the spring. To Tom, it was a small house that had long ago outlived its usefulness and should have been demolished or burned in a fire training exercise.

Tom saw Connie Cratt get out of the car and haul a box into the house. A few moments later Tom heard the 'whirr' of an air conditioning motor. Tom stood and watched Connie go back out to his car and haul another box into the house.

'Strange,' thought Tom. He knew the house had been empty. Now Cratt was using it. At the curb now, he turned left and walked downtown.

*****

From the outside, the *Cup and Saucer* looked like almost any other café. A false roof of split shingles extended out over the sidewalk. Picture windows gave a view into the café. From outside, Tom could see the usual group was at the large round table, holding coffee cups with their elbows resting on the table. Parts of the Minneapolis *Star and Tribune* were scattered across the table. Percy Smith was holding forth on the Governor's proposal to cut funds from the K-12 Education budget. George Fallow, with his usual scowl, was waiting to jump into the argument. Arley Green, the former superintendent was listening. To Arley's left sat Noah Fynmore, owner of Bulrush Bay Resort, Tom's favorite place for Sunday morning coffee and rolls.

When Tom sat down, Percy stopped talking. George Fallow cussed out the governor for 'not ever knowing how to balance the state budget' and for being one of 'them damn Democrats'. Then he looked at Percy and Tom and told everybody the school board *couldn't get a settlement if it was handed to them on a silver platter.*

"The other side has to want to settle," remarked Percy sharply.

"Ah, shee-eyete," drawled George. Gossip had it that George Fallow had worked on a farm owned by James and John O'Keefe when he was in his early twenties. He had retained the O'Keefe tendency to say words slowly with a Gaelic pronunciation.

"That's the way it is, George."

"Sure, you bet!" George spit back. He sat for a moment, then asked if they knew the Carl Hanson house had been rented and by who? They didn't. Tom wasn't sure until George described the house as the white clapboard house across the street from Tom's office.

"Says he is going to write a book on the history of the labor movement in Minnesota," added George while he watched several jaws pop open in mute disbelief. "Last night, I helped him move a desk, a couch and eight chairs into that house. He set up a typewriter and an old filing cabinet he found in the back of the Goodwill store."

"When does he have time?" asked Tom, thinking about Connie's work schedule for the county. Connie worked in the metal fabricating shop of the county, put up signs and repaired the furnaces and heating systems in Spencer County buildings. He was the local President of Metal Worker's Local #313. He was brash, aggressive, somewhat intimidating and definitely the Alpha Male at his work site.

"They are still on a 'four-tens' schedule," explained George. "He gets his 40 hours in by end of the day on Thursday."

"Well, that would explain why I just saw him up at that house," said Tom.

Arley Green pulled the dice shaker from the middle of the table and the men went on to shake '6-5-4' to see who would pay for the coffee. Percy got out in the first round, rolling a total of 'ten' after his '6-5-4'. George got out, followed by Noah. Arley and Tom tied with totals of 'five' on the next round. Arley failed to qualify with '6-5-4' in the next round and lost when Tom rolled '6-5-4' with a total of 'three'. When he stood up, Tom heard George saying to nobody in particular, "Well, I hope to hell we can score more than three points tonight against Fillmore."

"So do I," added Tom.

*****

Billy Washburn was wearing his old letter jacket with the red leather arms when he picked up Tom on the way to the football game. Tom had put on a red sweatshirt with white piping that the cheerleaders sold last year. They were both wearing red and white stocking caps because they expected the temperature to hit the lower forty's by game time. They were standing inside the gate, watching the ticket takers when the Fillmore Superintendent walked by and said, as loudly as he could,

"Twenty-dollars."

To which Tom replied, while laughing, "No way. When your team came out to warm up, the field tilted."

Billy knew the two superintendents were joshing each other, but looked at Tom Harant with a quizzical expression on his face.

"No, I never have," said Tom. There had been times in his career that he wished he could bet on the local team but he knew that he might live to regret such foolishness. As a licensed superintendent, he was technically the highest-ranking official of the Iron Lake schools. If the press got hold of a story about superintendents gambling, the fallout would be nothing less than horrific. The State High School League would probably investigate. The local parents might continue to support their local school administration but their loyalty only went so far. Parents (and voters) were quick to forget what their administrators did last week for their schools.

"But I pray a lot," he added, "that no one gets seriously hurt."

"Any reason?"

"The other team, like tonight, comes out on the field. They get their biggest players toward the middle of the field while they are warming up. I know it's probably not true but Fillmore looks like it is three inches taller and 40 pounds heavier at every position."

"That's because they are," laughed Billy. The two men stopped talking and faced the far end of the field. Three sixth-grade boys, picked for their serious attitude, were raising the American flag. The stands on the visitor side were full and along the sidelines fence stood a long line of adults. On the home side, the stands were half filled, with only a few stalwart fans along the sideline fence. Both men held their hands over their hearts while the Iron Lake pep band squeaked its way through the national anthem.

While they applauded the band, the Fillmore team prepared to kick-off to the Iron Lake Panthers, standing with hands on hips in their white uniforms with the red piping on the legs.

"Doesn't get any better than this," said Tom to Billy Washburn.

"A frosty night in October. Two weeks from now..." he started to say, then stopped. "if we still have school, it will be colder, wetter and miserable." Washburn had a reputation as a realist, prognosticating the future. In the distance, the pep band was doing a lengthy drum roll that hit a crescendo when the Fillmore player put his foot into the ball. Tom watched the ball sail up, and up, and slowly down while the Iron Lake player backpedaled from the twenty-yard line, trying to get beneath the ball. He almost made it, slipped in the mud, and stretched out. The ball landed in his hands but hit the ground when he fell, the ball rolling down the ten-yard line toward the sidelines. He was almost back on his feet when Fillmore's tight end reached the ball and picked it off the grass. Iron Lake's players had no choice…they tackled the tight end and it was Fillmore's ball on the Iron Lake eight-yard line.

"The result of this game seems inevitable, doesn't it?" said Washburn.

"We can only hope, can't we?"

"Hope has been out of fashion this week, don't you know?" After twenty grueling years as a principal, Billy Washburn was tired. Some called him a realist; others knew he was a cynic.

"But it's a great night for a game!" said Tom with authority. He took a deep breath and blew out steam. "Hah!"

CHAPTER ELEVEN
An Early Skirmish

"Too many phone calls," said Cratt with true, unadulterated anger in his voice. He was sitting at the head of the board table in the unused classroom that served as a boardroom. Board members were scattered around the table and superintendent Tom Harant was sitting at the opposite end of the table. The high school principal was the only other person in the room.

Outside, on the sidewalk, teachers were walking back and forth, carrying the large signs that declared 'On Strike' and 'MEA Local #1220'. Across the street, a few children and their parents stood and watched. There was little to see at the moment. No one was entering or leaving the high school building. The teachers asked each board member not to cross the picket line, with little effect. Everyone knew the board members had to cross the line to get to a 2:00 p.m. board meeting.

"So, don't take the calls. Have your wife tell them you are at work or out of town," added Arnie Murkiwasser. He had marched proudly into the boardroom wearing a dark blue three-piece suit, complete with a gold chain for his watch, stretched across his stomach. The first thing he did after he sat down was to loosen the tie at his neck. "For that matter, for $50 you can buy an answering machine to record their comments and no one will have to answer the phone."

"I don't want to listen to more wimps telling me what an asshole I am, and they won't tell me who they are," said Connie Cratt.

"Out of the mouths of babes," said Tom Harant, laughing.

There was silence for a minute. Tom glanced at Billy Washburn, who was obviously trying hard not to laugh at *'wimps calling Connie an asshole.'* Glacinda and Patty smiled but said nothing.

"Your role is to listen to your neighbors," said Percy Smith.

"They might actually say something smart," added Curt Fitzsimmons. "But I doubt it," he said laughing.

"You were elected. *Do your job*," emphasized Percy Smith.

"My job does not include getting yelled at on the phone. One of those *bleeping* teachers told my wife to watch out." With red coloring creeping up his neck, the fair skin on Connie's face was becoming mottled and dark.

"Speaking of answering machines," broke in Curt.

"Chair recognizes Curt," added Arnie, officious to the last.

"Can we tell the people when the next negotiation session will be?" Curt was looking at Tom Harant and the board turned toward Tom.

"I can change the message. What date?"

Curt swiveled to look at Connie Cratt. Glacinda and Patty did likewise. Connie raised his right hand and squeezing his ear, pulled slowly downward, stretching his ear lobe until he ran out of ear. "Next Tuesday or Wednesday. There are 15 teacher strikes underway. Our mediator, Kirby Jones, says he is booked through Monday."

"Change the media report," said Arnie. "Say, oh, something like 'no sessions are planned at this point'. Then tell them 'listen to the Cherry Grove radio station' for further announcements." Arnie's role was 'spokesman' for the school district. By consensus, the board agreed to let him be the up-front person for dealing with the media. Any press releases, supposedly, were to be jointly agreed to by the board chairman and the head teacher negotiator.

"No sessions, *hell!*" said Connie. "We ain't ready to negotiate. Let them learn what it means to be on strike, to be on a real picket line."

"Mr. Cratt, you can't mean that, can you?" asked the superintendent.

"Oh,...yes...I can."

Outside the window a car with rust spots drove by and blew its horn several times. Several heads turned to watch the car.

"They won't be ready to negotiate for weeks. I do mean *weeks*. So what's the point of taking off from work to sit around, while they play this 'the board refused to meet' game? The television stations will eat it up. The parents will get angry. But they gain nothing."

"Some sympathy, I think," said Tom Harant.

Connie Cratt stood up and walked to the coffee pot. "Is this coffee any better? Last week it tasted like a dishrag."

Tom ignored his question. Tom looked at the rest of the board and asked, "Are you ready to negotiate?"

Arnie shook his head left and right. Glacinda said 'Nope' with firmness. Patty Trivic was writing in her notebook. Curt Fitzsimmons looked at Tom and raised an eyebrow, asking himself 'Why not?' Percy had a disgusted look on his face. Cratt turned from the coffee pot with a white mug in his hand and said, "They asked for this strike. Now they got it!"

"We're not ready," said Percy quietly, expressing the sentiment of most of the Board.

"They put a sign on their strike headquarters, today." On the street, the brown car with rust drove by a second time, honking its horn. "Hell, that ain't nobody. It's the bookkeeping teacher," said Arnie watching the car.

"Feeling good. On the street. Not at work. It's the first day of the strike. Of course, they feel good." Curt Fitzsimmons seemed to summarize how the teachers felt about their strike. He stood up, preparing to leave. "Anything else?"

"I didn't like how they stared at us when we came into the building," said Glacinda Fallow directly at Cratt. Connie put his cup down, watching Fitzsimmons move toward the door.

"Neither did I," added Patty Trivic without looking up from her notebook. She put the cap back on her ballpoint and closed her notebook. "It's quiet out on my farm. When Bill is at work, I could be attacked."

"What gave you that idea?" asked Tom.

"A man's voice, on the phone."

There was only one response from the people around the table. Tom said 'Damn' once, disappointed in the behavior of 'some people' but then he had been warned in 'strike training' that if the teachers went out, there would be some ugly incidents. He told the board members to keep a private notebook, to record any unusual calls. If they received threats of any kind, they should call the County Sheriff.

*****

Looking out the window, Tom saw a sheriff's car across the street. A deputy was standing on the far curb, listening to a man that was gesturing in the general direction of the picketers. The deputy went back to his car and used the radio to send a message.

In the boardroom, the members began to leave. Cratt was satisfied that Tom Harant had not allowed any teachers to enter the building. Billy Washburn had reported that the secretaries and custodians were on the job. Tom's secretary came in to report the sheriff's deputy wanted to talk to Tom, outside, across the street.

An hour later, Tom wrote his notes for the first day of the strike. The deputy had reported the workmen on the roof had flipped 'the bird' at the pickets on the sidewalk. Tom responded that 'Freedom of Speech' was still guaranteed by the Constitution. The deputy told Tom the workmen were guilty of disturbing the peace. Tom informed the deputy that the local school superintendent had legal jurisdiction over the actions and behavior of all the people in (or 'on top of') the school building. The deputy said he could stop the workmen tomorrow morning and issue tickets before they got onto 'your school grounds'. In the end, Tom agreed to talk to their foreman and encourage the workmen to ignore the pickets. The deputy said he would wait to see how the workmen behaved the next afternoon.

Billy Washburn came into Tom's office while Tom was writing in his notebook. Billy left a report of the names of the people who worked during the day, and noted that one custodian had refused to come to work. On the phone, the missing custodian told Billy that he *knew* the Iron Lake school superintendent was getting kickbacks from the school's suppliers.

"And how did you respond?"

"Told him I would look into it."

"Let me guess. Lance Jamsic?"

"That's a great guess."

"Not really. I know Mr. Jamsic and his delusions." Last month, Jamsic had told Tom about the Sergeant of Detectives over in Cherry Grove. According to Jamsic, the Sergeant was receiving $1000 payments each week from the man who ran the drug network in Spencer County.

"He claims the undercover agents working out of the Sheriff's office want him to be an informer," said Tom to Billy Washburn.

"You're telling me…"

"He is a little whacko," completed Tom.

"Just another day, hey?" laughed Billy. Washburn was the most senior of the Iron Lake administrators. He claimed he had seen everything. He had the ability to laugh at most situations, knowing as he put it, that nothing is a real surprise. He picked up his overcoat from the back of a chair and began to put it on.

"Heading home, are you?" asked Tom. Billy said nothing, looking at Tom's hand, where he had his pen poised over a page in his notebook.

"You were serious?...about writing down what happens?"

"Yes."

"In that case, I'll see you tomorrow. The building is secured. The night janitor will keep an eye on it."

"Custodian," said Tom quietly.

*****

The WCCO 'Six O'clock News' opened with a report from Washington. Sam Donaldson, standing in front of the White House, remarked that several of President Bush's advisors had been in consultation with the president during the day.

"Last week, Soviet Foreign Minister Eduard Shevardnadze told the UN General Assembly that 'war may break out in the gulf any day, any moment'." Behind Donaldson an insert showed Shevardnadze addressing the United Nations.

The video switched to President Bush saying, "As I said last month, the annexation of Kuwait will not be permitted to stand. Iraq's leaders should listen. It is Iraq against the world."

When the camera came back to Sam Donaldson, he added, "Observers in Washington have noticed that President Bush seems to be firm in his decision to force Iraq out of Kuwait."

The second evening report opened with shots of striking teachers, walking back and forth on the sidewalks in front of the Iron Lake schools. After thirty seconds, the camera panned right, to show parents and children standing on the opposite side of the street, watching the strikers. The camera caught a pickup truck with its horn blaring when the truck ran past the camera location.

The voice-over was Dave Moore, a venerable and respected news reporter. He was saying "the Minnesota Education Association reports 21 school districts were struck this morning, including the school at Iron Lake, out in Spencer County."

The video switched to a man wearing a 'preppy' tie with a dark blue casual blazer. He was standing behind a podium that supported six microphones. Several other men and one woman were arraigned in a line behind the man at the podium. The audio came up just as he said, "six years of salary increases that did not keep pace with inflation. Our teachers are losing ground each year. This year, our MEA locals intend to fight for adequate wage and benefit increases. The MEA local in Bloomington received salary increases of fifteen percent in year one, and ten percent in year two. That's the kind of salary increase our teachers deserve."

Dave Moore concluded the report by noting "informal reports indicate there will be more schools going out on strike in the coming month. The school boards and the parents in these districts, face a formidable challenge to get these two-year contracts settled."

"Ain't that the truth," said Tom Harant aloud. He was sitting in the breezeway just outside his kitchen. Crystal was inside, preparing supper. Tom had changed into an old pair of trousers and a sloppy golf shirt when he came home at 5:30 p.m. With his favorite pair of brown leather slippers on his feet, he was relaxed. A soft current of air meandered through the breezeway.

"Who you talkin' to?" Crystal said loudly in the kitchen.

"Nobody, I guess."

"Can I ask you a question?"

"If I know the answer."

"And if you don't know the answer?"

"I'll probably tell you what I think is possible." Tom was guessing that Crystal was going to ask how long the strike would last. When two newspaper reporters asked earlier, Tom had responded that the contract would be negotiated, and the strike would end. How long that would take, he could only guess. He switched the television set to mute, and sat there, watching Bud Kraehling give his usual weather report.

"Sun will come up," said Tom mimicking Bud Kraehling on WCCO.

"In the morning," said Crystal from the doorway into the kitchen. She laughed, looking at her husband in his sloppy clothes.

"General darkness, followed by sunshine in the morning, as the 'Hippy, Dippy' weatherman would call it," laughed Tom. He had never heard George Carlin perform live but he admired Carlin's irreverent attitude. Tom knew it was all acting, but wondered how much pot the 'Hippy, Dippy' weatherman smoked.

"Will there be sunshine?" asked Crystal.

"Hard to know. I heard some tough words today from board members who are excited about the strike, afraid of their neighbors, and angry that Iron Lake's teachers are on the sidewalks."

"What should I say if I'm asked?"

"It will be over when it's over." Tom looked up to see a man walking up his driveway. The man was backlit by the streetlight. The man raised his right arm and waved what appeared to be a whiskey bottle inside a paper sack.

"Here comes Wrecker. By the looks of it, he wants a drink."

Crystal turned back into the kitchen. Tom heard the clink of glasses and assumed she was going to fix one for herself and one for Wrecker. "He likes Cola on his brandy," said Tom, sending his words into the kitchen.

"Darn right he does," said Wrecker just outside the screen door to the breezeway. "I brought you a present." Wrecker opened the screen door and stepped in, allowing the door to swing shut. Tom took his feet off the small table that doubled as a makeshift hassock. Wrecker handed the sack to Tom. Tom felt the distinctive shape of E&J Brandy.

"Did you have to wave it around? Give the neighbors the wrong impression, why don't you?" In his mind, Tom saw an image of Wrecker laughing with abandon at one of Tom's 'lousy' jokes, during a drinking session they held back in the warm nights of July.

"Ah…who gives a damn what they think?"

"I do," said Tom. Wrecker Kline made a point of saying 'You're welcome' and plopped into the other easy chair. "Evening, Crystal," he said while admiring how fast she could mix a drink.

"Not too much, tonight, you *galoot*," Crystal said to Wrecker..

"Just enough to help him sleep," Wrecker snapped, smiling at Crystal after she sat on the arm of Tom's overstuffed easy chair.

"Enough, *my foot*!" broke in Tom.

"It ain't your foot that needs it," said Wrecker. Tom had introduced Wrecker to his favorite brandy and then discovered that they both preferred cola on top of the brandy. Wrecker served as a foil to Tom's exuberant personality, serving to keep Tom from getting an enlarged sense of his own importance.

"There's a reason," added Wrecker Kline.

"Which is?"

"Rumor from a little birdie. Birdie says the high and mighty superintendent of the Iron Lake schools has been up drinking coffee in his kitchen for the last four nights running."

"Worrying about our procedures."

"So, how did it go?"

"Just like clockwork. Buses took the kids home. I walked out to the sidewalk and told 'Bluster Barnes' to come to work. He laughed. I told him that from his actions, I had to conclude the Iron Lake teachers were on strike. He said, 'that's right.' Then the secretaries, custodians and principals worked the rest of the day. We forgot to tell the teacher aides not to report but they figured 'No students, no aides' as one of them told me on the phone."

"So, what were you worried about?"

"Nothing, I guess." Tom watched Crystal when she stood up from the arm of his chair and stepped up the two steps into the kitchen. She walked into the kitchen and took their supper off the burner of the stove. She dumped the stew into an oven-safe dish and put the dish in the oven to keep it warm.

"Half an hour," said Tom to Crystal's back.

"But how did it really go?" asked Wrecker, using the low voice of a conspirator. He knew there were things Tom would not bring up for fear of causing his wife to be stressed. He brought his drink to his lips and took a large swallow.

"Not good. Three of the board members are following Connie Cratt's lead. I don't know where Curt Fitzsimmons sits. Percy Smith seems to be the only person who wants to get the strike over."

"But they will change."

"You're right. Two, three weeks of phone calls from parents and the board will cave in."

"I'll drink to that," said Wrecker. He raised his glass and drank the bottom half of his drink. He watched while Tom brought his glass up to his eyes and seemed to be looking through the swirling liquid, as if it were a crystal ball.

"I wonder," said Tom quietly.

"Bout what?"

"The Iron Lake board members. They don't have to be in a hurry."

Tom was concerned about Cratt's challe[n]
Lake teachers learn what it meant to be

"What about your football games?"

"And volleyball. Don't forget the gir[ls]"

"What happens in a strike?"

"No games will be played. If the oth[er]
Lake will forfeit."

"That's too bad," said Wrecker. "Ha[ve]
seniors in their last year."

"They will only miss two or three gam[es]
drink out of his glass, savoring the taste of t[he]
up, intent on refilling their glasses.

Wrecker looked at Tom and smiled. "V

Tom was concerned about Cratt's challenge. Cratt wanted to let the Iron Lake teachers learn what it meant to be on strike.

"What about your football games?"

"And volleyball. Don't forget the girls!"

"What happens in a strike?"

"No games will be played. If the other school is not on strike, Iron Lake will forfeit."

"That's too bad," said Wrecker. "Hard for that to happen to your seniors in their last year."

"They will only miss two or three games," said Tom. He took a long drink out of his glass, savoring the taste of the brandy. He began to stand up, intent on refilling their glasses.

Wrecker looked at Tom and smiled. "We can only hope."

CHAPTER TWELVE
'Roll with the Punches'

"I wonder," said Tom quietly.

"...'bout what?" said Crystal. She was drying dishes in the kitchen while Tom stared at his back yard. An early October mist seemed to be clinging to the tall sentinels that lined the east edge of his property. A line of thirty-foot redwood pines stood valiant guard over Tom's back yard. Had there been no clouds the redwoods would have shaded the yard until the sun was high enough to reach the triple birch and Tom's fountain. The fountain was filled with yellow leaves from the birch and the yard needed mowing. A solitary black grackle stood in the birch, watching a gray and black cat meander through Tom's yard.

"They aren't listening."

"The board?"

"Yes," he said, watching the cat slink into his neighbor's yard. "They think they are doing the right thing."

"But it will be over in two weeks, and everything will be back to normal, won't it?"

"I don't know," he said slowly, watching the grackle land below the birch. He knew that Mr. Conifer Cratt wanted to show the rest of the state that he could bring a union to its knees, just in advance of Cratt's campaign for union president. "Cratt wants the teachers to learn about strikes the hard way."

"Like Wrecker says, 'we can hope' the strike is short." He saw a dark shadow in the bushes behind the grackle. He knew the cat was stalking the grackle; his neighbor's cat had killed three birds in the last week. Tom started toward the kitchen door, intent on scaring the bird before the cat reached it. To the left of the kitchen door, he removed a tan raincoat and put it on. He patted his pockets, checking for his keys. In the breezeway, he jangled his keys and the grackle looked up at him…just as the bird disappeared in a flash of black and gray fur.

Tom turned to leave then reached back and grabbed a tan felt hat that he puffed out and put on his head. "Too late," he said more to himself, than to Crystal. He walked through the breezeway. Standing under the red maples in his front yard, listening to the mist drip on wet leaves, Tom hunched his shoulders against the wet dew in the air. He decided to walk the three blocks up to the school.

To the maples he said, "Too late." The maples said nothing. Like trees everywhere, they stood and listened and kept their own counsel. While he was walking up the block toward school, his stomach began to churn.

'What the hell am I doing?' he wondered. *'What am I supposed to do?'* he wondered. How does a CEO learn to manage a strike? Tom was sleepless before the strike, but there were only a few problems on the first day. Still, he worried about the future.

Tom was standing across the street from the strikers, watching them walk up and down the sidewalk, when he heard the helicopter. He turned and looked up to see 'Channel Four News' painted on the side; the 'copter was aimed at the empty playground south of the Iron Lake Elementary School. *'Well,'* he thought, *'who in the hell gave them permission to land on 'our' playground? I know I didn't!'* He was about to charge across the street to challenge 'Bluster' Barnes when an image of his uncle telling him to roll with the punches came to mind.

*****

"We were naïve," said Uncle Jim. "Hell, worse than that. We were wet behind the ears, babes at sea, if you don't mind the analogy." Jim and Tom were sitting on the porch of Jim's ranch house outside Alamogordo, in the foothills looking west towards the White Sands Proving Ground and Holloman Air Base. "We didn't know what we were doing. But we had a crusty old curmudgeon of a training Sergeant back in England. He kept telling us to fear the unknown and be ready for anything."

James Fynmore Harant, otherwise known as 'Hardnose' Harant was sitting on an old kitchen chair, with his weathered boots resting on a beat-up hassock. Without moving he leaned over to open a blue cooler and remove a beer. He popped the cap off the *Corona Extra* and handed it to Tom. Off to his left, a blast of wind whipped past the corner of the house, pushing dirt and a small tumbleweed. The two men watched the tumbleweed roll toward the pinyon pines that marched down hill toward the highway. Jim reached into the cooler and grabbed himself a beer.

"You were saying, I think, that serving in the Office of Naval Intelligence was exciting, but you remember being afraid?" said Tom.

"We were too young to be afraid, I think," said Jim. "Our first mission was supposed to be a training mission. Piece of cake. 'The cat's pajamas.' You have to understand. I was just out of the Academy one year, promoted to Lieutenant (Junior Grade) when I was assigned to the Navy's Intelligence unit. ONI sent me to England to work with their 'SIS'…what we call 'Special Services, Intelligence' although they only had about forty men (and two women) in the division."

Jim reached up and pushed his hair away from his face. He had heavy gray eyebrows over a straight nose that tried to hide a bulge where it had been broken. There was a white ridge of scar above his left eyebrow and mottled skin tissue below his left eye. His hair was thinned on top, brown with errant strands of white. He wore glasses with dark brown frames. His glasses framed a pair of clear blue intense eyes that seemed sometimes to be looking beyond the visible horizon. He would stop talking for long silent moments to form an idea or to back up with an explanation.

Tom's wife Crystal was helping Jim's housekeeper. When Tom and Crystal arrived on Saturday before Easter, they had been surprised to find the housekeeper, called Holly working in the garden at 9:00 a.m. in the morning. She was apparently about the same age as Uncle Jim, thin yet 'well-preserved' in blue jeans and an old flannel shirt. Tom had chided his uncle for not giving Holly the day off, but Jim merely said she lived at the ranch house.

(This produced a quick glance from Crystal to Tom. There had been gossip among Tom's cousins, but Tom himself had only met James Fynmore Harant the previous year when Jim came to visit his brother Frank. There was no mention of the 'housekeeper' Holly who was not traveling with Jim).

"We trained, the three of us, learning marksmanship and code procedures and how to send messages at Wormwood Scrubs, an old prison, in the summer of 1938. Then we set out from Southampton aboard the *Empress of Scotland.* She was a beautiful passenger liner. Originally built in Hamburg, Germany. The ship in 1938 belonged to the Pacific and Orient steamship line. P&O was the company that operated the Trans-Canada railroad connecting Quebec City with Vancouver."

"Halfway over, some thug tried to knife Bill Emery. Bill was a little shorter than me, but a bull of a man. Bill was injured, but managed to jack-knife the thug over the stern railing of the *Empress*," he said while raising his bottle of beer.

The third member of their team was a woman cryptographer who had spent three years working at Bletchley Park and had earned her promotions to 'Leftenant, His Majesty's Royal Navy.' Jim laughed, noting how the injured Bill Emery received some very solicitous care from two Swedish nurses who were traveling to Winnipeg. He said they were competing for Bill's affections, and one managed to get into his bunk 'with Bill.' It was only a shipboard flirtation, and Jim Harant guessed that the third member of his team, Leftenant Heather Mackay didn't approve of Bill's behavior, but she said nothing.

*****

Tom Harant was in his second year at Amboy Schools when he and Crystal went to New Mexico over the Easter break at school. Tom didn't know his uncle Jim…only that Jim had served in the Navy during World War II. It was Jim who explained that the Navy assigned him to 'Counter-Intelligence' efforts in California, Arizona and New Mexico. In the late 1940's and early 1950's Jim had been part of the Security team at Holloman Air Force Base (and liaison to the Navy) when the early V-2 rocket tests were conducted. Jim said he had witnessed several A-bomb tests at Los Alamos and spent time debriefing some of the soldiers from the trenches on the site.

"It's all water over the dam, these days," Jim said, reflecting on the serious security measures they took in those early years of the Cold War. "We trained our first astronaut over there at Holloman. His name was Enos, the chimpanzee. He was launched in a Mercury-Atlas capsule that completed two orbits."

When Jim Harant died in 1988 from complications related to lung cancer, his nephew Tom Harant wondered if the radiation from the A-bomb tests could have played a part. Uncle Jim left his house and a half-million dollar annuity to his housekeeper. It was a small two-bedroom house, ranch style, at the end of a gravel road with a good view of the San Andreas Mountains off to the west.

The members of Tom's family admitted later that Uncle Jim rarely talked about his experiences in WWII. Tom filed a request under the Freedom of Information Act and he found that James Fynmore Harant was serving aboard the cruiser *North Hampton* (CV-26) escorting the carrier *Enterprise* (CV-6) when Pearl Harbor was bombed December 7, 1941. Two years later a newly promoted Lt. Commander Harant led a commando team of eight off the destroyer *Badger* (DD126) when *U191* was captured, resulting in the capture of a German Navy version of 'Enigma.' His service records carried a DSC (Distinguished Service Commendation) from the British Navy, 1938; and the Navy Cross, 1943. Harant had returned to the Office of Naval Intelligence in 1945 and was placed on special assignment in the Navy's 'Counter-Intelligence' unit.

*****

"Really smart agents we were. Traveling on the *Empress* was such a lark that we forgot about 'watching our backs' until Lt. Mackay thought she saw two men in black raincoats watching us. Their coats were a little out of season, but not totally unusual on a passenger liner at sea. It was cold at night."

"So you weren't sure..." added Tom. He watched his Uncle Jim while the older man considered how to answer Tom's question. Tom glanced at the screen door into the house, wondering if the women were going to join them on the porch. After another minute's hesitation, Jim said, "We were traveling west from Ottawa when Bill started talking about a lime green coupe that seemed to be matching our speed and staying back. Sure enough, we were being followed. We thought they were Nazi agents."

"And they were?"

"Much later, I think, about the time an unfortunate woman was tortured to death in Duluth, we were told the two men were agents of the Japanese *Kempeitai*, or Secret Police."

Off to the west, the sun was beginning to touch the tops of the San Andreas Mountains. Scattered white tendrils streamed over a peak, falling into the valley in front of Tom and Jim. In the sky above the two men, Tom could see high stratocumulus clouds catching the last rays of the sun.

"Our mission was simple. Go to the Iron Range in Minnesota, find an Irish monk named Harris, retrieve the religious artifact he was protecting, and bring it back to Ireland. It sounded *so simple* to the three of us."

He was quiet for a moment.

"Our goal was to practice sending daily reports in code; to test the communications ops on the east coast and Nova Scotia. We drove from Duluth up onto the Iron Range, couldn't find the Irish monk, and when we got back to Duluth it was in time to watch his sister Mary die, after one of the two Japanese demons had sliced off large chunks of her skin on her stomach and her legs."

"Damn, that still aggravates me. Three months on the mission, Bill was injured twice, and in the end I had to kill one of the Japanese. But we never found the *Golden Eagle* that Brother Harris hid somewhere on the Iron Range. The object was an eagle with uplifted wings, with rubies and diamonds, made for the Emir of Aleppo. Originally, it sat on a stanchion like a battle insignia. It was rumored to contain the cup Our Lord used at the Last Supper, but who could prove that?"

"You gotta' roll with the punches, Tom. You never know…" he said slowly, while his eyes wandered over the clouds streaming over the far peaks. "We were taken off the mission after we failed. I don't like failure." James Harant went on to explain that at the end of their mission he finally told Bill Emery and Heather Mackay what their admiral in England didn't want them to know. Their daily reports were used to locate and catch two German agents in Canada, and another agent who was sending decoded traffic to a German supply ship in the North Atlantic.

Crystal stepped onto the porch, holding a glass mug of soda with ice. She walked past the two men to the wooden swing. Tom watched her fanny in the tight jeans with pride. She had given him two sons and a daughter, and he was justifiably proud that she looked good for a woman of 35; she was the love of his life. She sat on the swing and smiled at Tom before asking Jim why he never married.

"Don't know, really."

"Holly says you were in love before the war."

"She wants me to admit I was in love with Leftenant Heather Mackay, the female member of my team when we came to Minnesota on 'Dragonlair,' the mission to recover a religious artifact.

"She's my housekeeper. She ought to keep her opinions to herself," Jim said laughing while he leaned forward to wink at Crystal. *'What's that about?'* Tom asked himself.

"I was infatuated. I was also the team leader. Nothing happened between us. She went back to England where she was arrested and spent ten years in prison. We knew there was a German agent, code name 'Sorly' on our tail. Turned out that Heather Mackay grew up in Hamburg. When she was a little girl she saw the American version of perpetual happiness, Shirley Temple singing and dancing in the movies. Her code name became 'Sorly'.

"I was also disappointed in her. She had fooled so many in England with her mathematical ability at Bletchley Park, where the code breakers worked."

The three of them sat quietly watching the gold in the sky turn slowly purple. The housekeeper came to the door and announced the chili and rolls would be ready in five minutes, if the oven didn't quit. "This old man refuses to buy me a decent oven."

"Yes, Holly, I know," said Jim, laughing. He turned toward her, but she was already walking back into the kitchen.

"You didn't answer my question, Jim," said Crystal.

"About Heather Mackay, the oh-so-proper British Leftenant?"

"Yes," Crystal said. She had a feeling that he was evading the issue.

"Well, she wasn't all that proper," said Jim. "Nowadays, you young folk would say she had the hots for me. Damn, that woman could look at me and my tongue tangled into knots."

"You never saw her after 1938?"

"I didn't say that," he said laughing. "There is an old Japanese proverb, that says 'Leave the cage door open so the bird may return.' And I did."

Jim explained that her prison term for espionage was 20 years. She was released in 1949 after serving ten years.

"In those years, we used code names that were close to our actual names, to help us recognize our name if someone called out our name. My code name for Project Dragonlair was John Haroldson."

"And the British Leftenant's code name was…?" said Crystal, guessing where he was going.

"I think her last name was Matthews," Jim said.

"And her first name was Holly," added Crystal.

"You don't mean?" began Tom.

"Let's go in and see if Holly's chili is any good, shall we?" said Jim.

*****

The striking teachers were marching up and down, 'demonstrating' their solidarity for the Channel Four News camera. Tom stood on the opposite sidewalk, watching while his stomach churned. He looked up at the Century Elm, a symbol of the promise of growth to be earned while in school. There must have been a break in the clouds; sunlight lit the bare branches of the elm tree.

There were streaks of wet bark running down the branches of the tree. The gray bark had stripes of black wetness meandering down its sides. *'That tree looks sadly out of place,"* thought Tom. A woman walked up to him and tugged on his raincoat, looking up.

"How long, Mr. Harant?"

"Two weeks, I think."

"Is there anything the parents can do?" she asked.

"Nothing I can think of," said Tom. He didn't feel it was his place to tell a parent to get on the phone and talk to the teachers. He crossed the street, paused for a moment looking down the sidewalk at the strikers and then entered the Elementary School doors.

Thinking back to his uncle Jim, Tom smiled at his uncle's attitude. *'Take it as it comes, boy,'* the retired Navy intelligence officer told him. *'You can't predict or forecast each day.'*

Walking down the deserted hall of the Elementary school, Tom felt alone and somewhat ill at ease. *'One day at a time, I suppose.'*

CHAPTER THIRTEEN
A Seductive Mirage

A soft drizzle fell through most of that Wednesday, during the first week of the strike. A long line of strikers carried 'On Strike' and 'No Contract' along the two-block front of the school. Five of the striking teachers were set up in the back, where they blocked the entry to the parking lot. There was little for them to do in back. The only people using the parking lot were the superintendent, two principals and the head custodian. The action was in the front, where twenty teachers stretched a long line of blue mackinaw raincoats down the sidewalk. On Wednesday, Channel Five News sent their remote truck, which made an imposing sight with its satellite dish pointed to the heavens. The on-camera reporter interviewed a few teachers. The superintendent in his brown raincoat came to the sidewalk and delivered a short press statement to Mr. Robert Barnes.

Bluster Barnes looked at the press statement for a moment and realized the Channel Five reporter was holding a microphone pointed at him.

"Ready to negotiate? The board says they are ready to negotiate. Speaking for the teachers, I can tell you…" but he was interrupted. The blast of a truck horn distracted the cameraman. His camera swung up and caught an older Ford pickup weaving its way past the high school. As it approached Barnes and Tom and the reporter, the truck swerved to its left, crossed the intersection and hit the telephone pole on the corner opposite, 'dead on' as someone later described it. The bumper folded in the middle and fell off the truck. Fortunately, for the driver, he was only moving at about twenty miles per hour. The truck bounced back from the pole and stopped. The driver side door opened and George Fallow climbed out. Dressed in a red flannel hunting shirt and dark trousers with suspenders, he walked, somewhat unsteadily, toward the Channel Five reporter.

When he was ten feet from the reporter, Tom Harant raised a hand to tell George to stop. Fallow stopped and looked around. He seemed intent on trying to remember something.

"You guys gotta know something," he said slowly. The reporter had moved his microphone toward George. Several of the striking teachers were moving toward George, also. They formed a small knot of people around George, anxious for what he had to say.

"We approved some extra money for the schools. Last summer. Now the teachers want that extra money to go for salaries. Lord knows they are already paid more than any other employee in town, with the exception of the SOB who runs the bank." He laughed at his description and pulled a glass whiskey pint out of his back pocket. He stared at the bottle, and then raised it skyward. It dawned on him that the bottle was empty. He flung the bottle over his shoulder. The cameraman followed the bottle's flight, up for a moment, then down toward the curb, where it shattered.

"Just like that bottle. Lotta empty threats from these here teachers."

"George, what *are* you talking about?" asked Barnes.

"Empty threats," said George again. "You tell 'em to stop calling. I ain't listening."

"All right, George. I will." George, however, was not listening. He had turned away from the reporter and Barnes and Harant. He began to walk, albeit unsteadily, back toward downtown Iron Lake.

From behind the cameraman, someone said 'Go on, George. Go find another bottle. That'll help.'

Tom yelled at him, "George, what about your truck?" George stopped, looked at the truck and began walking across the intersection. Someone shouted, 'Can you drive?' He climbed into his truck, slammed the door, backed up and drove away.

When the reporter asked who the man was, several teachers responded in unison, "George Fallow." When the reporter asked Barnes if he had any reaction, Bluster responded with a 'No Comment'. When the reporter looked at Tom, Mr. Harant pointed at the press statement that the reporter was holding in his hand. Tom turned and made his way through the blue raincoats around him and walked back into the school building.

Behind him, he heard the reporter listening to Bluster Barnes expound on the failure of the school board to negotiate. Tom started to chuckle, wondering what would make the evening news, Barnes or George driving his truck into the light pole.

*****

Back in his office, Tom found Billy Washburn looking out the window, watching the small knot of people clustered around Barnes and the Channel Five reporter. Washburn was thinner than Tom and wore his suits with an understated elegance. He had a rough, but pleasant face and always carried the look of a consummate professional around the office. William Washburn was long in experience, a principal who had seen all there was to see.

"I asked your secretary to call Glacinda at home…tell her that George is probably in the 'Red Carpet' downtown."

"Thanks," said Tom. "He looked like he could use a little direction."

"From what I hear, he isn't living at home."

"What did you hear?"

"Just a rumor. His truck was parked at the Laker Motel the last two days."

"That's too bad."

Tom thought about his recent encounters with George Fallow. George was definitely not the 'Mellow Fallow' that Tom first met two years ago. George had become bitter, caustic and sharp tongued. "Something is bothering him."

"It might be something to do with Connie Cratt."

"Oh…really?"

"Word uptown is, George made threats against Cratt two nights ago. But then, he often makes useless threats."

Tom said nothing, remembering George standing on his front lawn, late on the night of the referendum.

"I told Lance Jamsic to come in for a conference."

"What time?"

"Two-thirty." Washburn was still looking at the pickets gathered on the sidewalk when he added, "Jamsic is crossing the street. Be here in a few minutes."

"It's crazy. We barely know what is going on," said Tom.

"In a strike, the administrators are usually the last to know," said

Washburn. He laughed. He turned around and sat in one of Tom's office chairs, crossing one leg over the other. He watched Tom loosen the collar of his shirt. They both heard Jamsic talking to Tom's secretary in the outer office. Tom pulled out a pack of cigarettes and lit one. He took a long drag, enjoying the sensation and blew smoke toward the ceiling.

"We barely know," said Tom a second time.

"There's an old saying, 'They keep us in the dark,' added Washburn.

"And feed us manure," finished Tom as Judy, his secretary knocked on his door jamb and told Tom that Lance Jamsic was here for an appointment. When Jamsic was seated in the other office chair, he stared at Billy Washburn for a moment. Then he turned to Tom and said,

"Here I am."

Tom looked at him for a long minute. Jamsic began to fidget, crossing his leg and then uncrossing it.

"Mr. Jamsic, I had a call about noon from the head of the Custodian's Union in Minneapolis. You were in his office this morning."

"Yes, I was."

"Claiming that I and the former superintendent Arley Green have been receiving kickbacks from our suppliers."

"Yes, you have."

"No, I haven't. I don't know about Mr. Green, however." Tom brought his cigarette to his mouth and took a long pull, enjoying the distraction.

"Last time the floor wax man was here, he threw an envelope into your car when he walked past it. You had just paid him $15,400 for the year's supply of floor stripper and floor sealer."

"And then what?"

"I saw you open the envelope when you got into your car." Jamsic was sitting straight up but leaned back and crossed his leg again. Tom pushed the end of his cigarette against his ashtray, twirling the end to peel off the ash.

"I'm going to move next week. The drug dealers in Cherry Grove are watching me. They must have figured out that I'm a snitch for the drug task force guys in the courthouse."

"Geez," said Washburn slowly.

Tom ignored Washburn and looked at Jamsic. "Did you take a pistol with you and wave it around in your union office?"

"Is that what he called about?"

"Yes. Said you were agitated. Rambling about drugs and kickbacks and custodians that waste their time watching volleyball games." Tom seemed nervous. With his right hand, he wiped a small amount of sweat off his upper lip. He looked at his cigarette, estimating there were four more puffs.

Tom glanced at Washburn. Billy looked like he was not about to say anything helpful. Tom looked at Jamsic, pondering.

"Do you have medical insurance?" asked Tom.

"Yes"

"Is the school district paying for it?"

"Yes."

"Then I am ordering you to go to Golden Valley and get a psychiatric evaluation. The medical insurance will pay for it."

"Say what?"

"You are directed to get a full psychiatric evaluation. I am suspending you with pay. You will return to work when I see a statement that says you are not angry with your fellow workers."

"Well...hell. Is that what you want?" When Tom said 'Yes,' Jamsic asked, "And did Mr. Washburn put you up to this?"

Tom laughed, and felt just like a man in a swamp with a circling bevy of alligators. He saw where Jamsic was going and swore that the decision was his alone. "After all, I am the superintendent here and not Mr. Washburn."

"Like hell you are." Jamsic stood up, and backed toward the door to Tom's office. "You're just a crook who takes orders from the school board." When he reached the door, Jamsic told the two men that he wasn't going to the clinic in Golden Valley. He turned quickly and left the room. Ten seconds later, Tom and Billy heard the outer door slam.

Washburn looked at Tom and said, "Whew." Tom sucked on his cigarette and then expelled smoke.

"That's how I feel. How *did* I get into this?" He put his cigarette out, tamping the angry end into his ashtray. It was the cut glass ashtray, a present from his journalism students. Tom wondered, briefly, why he felt he had to become an administrator.

"Why should I go through this?" he asked aloud.

"Don't you feel like a mushroom, sometimes? Kept in the dark and fed manure?" Billy Washburn knew some questions came with no answers. The phone rang in the outer office. Ten seconds later the phone rang on Tom's desk. Washburn watched Tom while he talked. Tom's hand came up to his collar and he pulled his tie down. Billy glanced at the three college diplomas that hung on the wall behind Tom. He looked at the framed picture of a ceremony, Tom holding the cut glass ashtray. Tom had told him about the Journalism students in Prescott, Arizona. How he helped them to name 'Badger Mountain' and to produce an award winning newspaper.

"It's your job," said Billy when Tom hung up the phone.

"I guess it is," said Tom laughing. He grabbed his cigarettes and lit one.

"Good news?" asked Billy, referring to the phone.

"No. It was Barnes. Said he wanted to tell me what he told the reporter."

"That's generous of him," snickered Billy.

"Said he wanted to tell me the truth." Tom went on to relate how Barnes tried to tell him 'the truth' as Barnes described it. The truth, according to Barnes, was that the teachers would not settle the strike for less than $5200 per teacher.

"He was real nice about it," added Tom, watching for a reaction. Tom took a second puff on his new cigarette. He stood up and walked around Billy to the window. While he opened the window, he saw the Channel Five crew was packing up their gear. The number of strikers on the long two-block sidewalk was down to four.

"I'm glad he was nice," said Billy, standing to leave Tom's office. "I think I should warn you, however. If Barnes is nice, it's time to be careful." Tom started to laugh, protesting that Barnes was an advocate. Billy looked at Tom with a stern expression. Then he said, "Nice is a seductive mirage on the rocky desert of truth."

*****

Tom took what he called a 'walking tour' of the Iron Lake school building late in the afternoon. He wanted to make sure all the doors were locked. He knew from past experience that employees leaving the public school rarely checked the door when it closed behind them. He knew that Iron Lake employees were comfortable listening for the 'click' of the lock that they would hear if the door was locked or unlocked. The night shift of two custodians shared the job of making sure the building was secured.

In the Elementary wing, Tom passed the classroom in which Maria was pushing a dust mop to clean the tile floor in a Sixth grade classroom. He paused a moment and waved. She waved back. Her radio was playing 'Pretty Woman' by Roy Orbison. At the door to the boiler room, he opened the door briefly and found Henry, the other custodian, sitting at a table smoking a cigarette.

Tom was on the backside of the building, walking toward the Science wing when he saw a classroom door that was ajar. There was a light on in the Chemistry lab. He began to walk with lighter feet, wanting to come up to the door as quietly as possible. He stopped ten feet from the door when he heard the metal door of a cabinet 'clang' shut. Raising his voice, he said 'Good afternoon' because he didn't want to surprise whoever was in the Chemistry Lab. When he turned into the lab, he found Connie Cratt picking up a briefcase from the floor.

Tom looked at Cratt, then at the briefcase, then at the dark blue work clothes that Connie was wearing. They stared at each other for a moment.

"Checking the building," said Cratt, with a quick explanation.

"So am I," said Tom.

"That door was unlocked," said Cratt. "So I thought, why not check the cabinets. They are all locked."

"Well, that's good," said Tom. From his work clothes, Tom guessed that Cratt came to the school on the way home from work. Cratt passed by Tom near the door to the lab and walked into the hall. He moved down the hall, while Tom pulled the 'Chem Lab' door shut. "Be sure the outside door is shut when you leave."

"Yes, I will," said Cratt while he waved his empty hand. Cratt walked ahead of Tom. When he reached the west side exit, he turned left and exited through the door. It never occurred to Tom to wonder why Cratt had parked near that particular exit.

Ten minutes later, Tom sat down in his office to write his notes for the day. He recorded his action with the paranoid custodian and a note about Barnes demand for $5200 per teacher. He sat there for a moment, thinking about finding Cratt in the Chemistry Lab. 'Strange' he thought to himself. In his log book Tom wrote '5:40 p.m. Cratt in Chemistry Lab. All secure.'

*****

Crystal told Tom about the 6:00 p.m. news on Channel Four when he arrived at 6:15 p.m. The first news item was Sam Donaldson, reporting from the White House. "Something about Israel distributing gas masks to all of its four million citizens. And they showed Army Special Forces boarding a C-130 transport, bound for somewhere in the Middle East."

In the second news item, a video of Iron Lake teachers (from Tuesday) was rerun. Dave Moore reported that St. Cloud Schools had been struck on Wednesday, bringing to 22 the number of schools with strikes.

When Tom asked about the Channel Five news, Crystal said she didn't know. She suggested he watch Channel Five at 10:00 pm. Tom walked to the liquor cabinet and removed the brandy. After filling a glass with brandy and coke, he walked to the kitchen table and sat down.

"It's all a seductive mirage," he said.

"What is?"

"This whole thing. As if I could do anything to stop it."

CHAPTER FOURTEEN
Flames Across the Street

An old Chevy pickup, rusting at the sideboards, spattered with dried mud, slowly drove into the alley in the block across from the Iron Lake schools. After the truck passed the first house and the second, it turned left into the backyard of the third house. This was the older white house, with the aging clapboard siding and the rusty gutters. The truck engine was turned off. A man got out of the truck and walked to the back door. He let himself into the rear hall, near the kitchen. He walked through the house and checked the front door, making sure it was locked.

Turning right, he walked into the living room and looked down at the card table that held a typewriter and a stack of papers, some typed, and others blank. He took the bottom half of a five-inch artillery shell off the card table and looked at the hundreds of cigarette butts that filled the shell. He smiled and set the cartridge on the floor near the table. With his foot, he kicked the shell, scattering cigarette butts across the ratty carpet that covered the floor. The shell came to rest against the metal folding chair, with some of the butts still inside.

He walked back into the kitchen and opened the cupboard under the sink. He removed a red can that said 'Flammable' on one side and walked back into the living room. Starting near the spilled cartridge ashtray, the man dribbled gasoline onto the carpet, making a wide swath of gasoline in the general direction of the spilled cigarette butts. Then he took the red can to the second floor. He poured more fluid onto a pile of rags that were sitting in an empty room. Taking the can, he went down the stairs and to the back, where he found the stairs to the basement. In the basement, he picked up a pile of rags that were sitting on a couch. He moved to the floor directly below the bathroom sink, which he located from two water pipes that ran over to the water heater. He threw the rags on the floor and soaked them in gasoline.

Back on the first floor, he put the empty can near the back door.

Going to the kitchen sink again, he removed a plastic one-gallon milk container, two brown glass jars and a white plastic funnel. Standing at the counter, he took out a knife and cut the milk container in half, but not quite. He folded the top half of the container back onto itself. He took the first glass jar and looked at it. A warning label read 'Magnesium Shavings –eight ounces'. He poured the magnesium into the milk container. He then opened the other jar, which read 'Potassium Permanganate (KmnO4)'. This he poured into the milk container. He gently swirled the contents until they formed a small nest in the middle of the container. Next he pulled a small blue paper container from his pocket. It read 'KmnO4 Fine Ground' on the side. He slowly poured half of the fine Permanganate into the middle of the nest. He looked at it and decided half the fine ground Permanganate was enough. Then he refolded the milk container and using masking tape from his pocket, taped the container together. He placed the funnel into the top of the milk container and taped it into place.

The man moved to the bathroom, opposite of the kitchen and put the milk container gently, underneath the sink. Returning to the kitchen, he lifted a plastic juice container from under the sink. The container held a solid material, to a depth of five inches. The man cut the bottom out of the container, revealing a gray paraffin wax. Then he shaved the wax from the inside edge of the bottom, forming an inverted 'V' around the edge. From practice, he knew the container would fit onto the top of the funnel. Turning the container over, he cut off the top of the container and shaped the wax into a shallow funnel.

Using the end of his thumb to the first knuckle, he made sure there were four inches of wax from the bottom of the paraffin funnel to the bottom of the juice container. Satisfied, he took the paraffin and placed it, ever so gently, onto the white plastic funnel in the bathroom.

He studied his handiwork for a few moments. Then he returned to the kitchen and found the box of trash bags under the sink. He threw the masking tape, the bottom of the juice jug, the top half of the jug, and the two brown glass jars into the trash bag. He removed the paper container with 'KmnO4 Fine Ground' from his pocket, and placed it inside the bag. At the back door, he added the red 'flammable' can. He checked the kitchen again and closed the door under the sink.

The man looked at his watch. It read 4:30 p.m. and he smiled. He knew the glycerin in his pocket would eat through four inches of paraffin in three hours. He returned to the bathroom and removed the stopper from a four-ounce bottle of glycerin. He carefully poured the glycerin into the center of the paraffin funnel, capped the bottle, and put it into his left shirt pocket.

Outside the back door, he quickly moved to the truck and threw the plastic trash bag onto the passenger side floor. He climbed into the truck and lit a cigarette and stared at the glowing ember. He started the engine and looked up and down the deserted alley.

Without thinking about it, the man took the glycerin bottle out of his shirt pocket, opened the trash bag and threw in the glycerin. He did not hear the bottle crack against a brown glass jar. "That's the way to do it," he said aloud.

It did not occur to the man from Chicago that the blue paper container still contained a dangerous amount of fine ground Permanganate. Going down the freeway north of Chicago, the chemicals created a fire of 5000 degrees and burned a hole in the floorboard. The truck was engulfed in flames when it hit the overpass.

*****

Off to the west, clouds were reflecting the pink of the setting sun. A brown pickup truck without a front bumper turned into the alley of the block across from the Iron Lake School. The truck drove down the alley and turned onto the grass behind the third house. The driver stopped the truck and turned off the engine. He looked at the house to his left. He could not see across the street to where a striker manned the 'picket' line. He looked at the house to his right. The side of the house blocked a clear view of the street.

"Good," he said to himself. He pulled a whiskey bottle out of his back pocket. After removing the cork, he tipped it up to his mouth. He drank a long swallow, grimacing while he drank. "They can't see me." The small bottle was quickly empty and George tossed it onto the floorboard, where it joined two other empty bottles.

George Fallow opened the driver side door and turned to his left. His feet seemed to find the ground of their own volition. He pulled his baseball jacket around himself and felt the comforting weight of his .38 caliber Smith & Wesson pistol in his right hand pocket. George reached behind and grabbed a full quart of Harmony Canadian from the seat. He tried to stand up and stumbled against the door. His feet slipped and he reached for the door handle. With his left hand, he kept the bottle away from the hard metal of the door.

He straightened up and looked around. Two houses away he could see a woman in her kitchen but she seemed to be busy. The alley was empty. He turned and walked to the back door. He grabbed the doorknob and pulled upward. The door opened inward and he stepped into the kitchen.

"Ha, didn't know I knew about that lock, did you?" he said loudly into the silence of the house. The house, for its part, refused to answer George. He walked through the kitchen on kitten feet, expecting at any moment to be challenged. He bumped into the doorjamb in the hall and turned toward the living room. There were no lights showing. He looked into a bleak room, where weak light from outside pierced the rips in an old window shade and silhouetted a metal folding chair near a card table.

"Well, damn. He's usually here at this hour." George peered at his wristwatch. The watch told George that the hour was 6:15 p.m. The lights were on at 6:00 p.m. when George drove by on Tuesday and Wednesday night.

"Did I miss him?"

The house did not answer.

He moved to the folding metal chair next to the typewriter and sat down. Taking the quart bottle, he twisted the top until the paper broke and the plastic stopper turned. George poured a little whiskey on the typewriter, laughed and took a long, satisfying drink from his Harmony Canadian.

"Book, my foot." He picked up a sheet of paper and tried to read in the weak light of the room.

Minutes passed. George's head went south, toward his chest. He jerked once, and looked around the dark room.

"What the pluperfect blazes am I doing here?" he asked, laughing. The afternoon had been wasted with a salesman from Willmar, the two of them buying each other drinks. "Hell, I am pluperfect tired of waiting." He laughed again, and took another swig from the bottle and tossed the stopper at a mirror on the wall.

Standing up, he staggered back into the hall that led from the backdoor to the front door. He walked to the backdoor and pushed it shut. He heard the latch click and tested the door. It was closed. Then he turned to his right, where steps led to the basement. Holding his bottle under his arm, he retrieved a pack of matches, removed one, and lit it. The match lit up the steps. There was a candle lying on its side on a shelf to his left. He picked up the candle and lit it. Holding the candle in his left hand, he then grabbed the bottle with the same hand. With his right hand, he grabbed the wooden railing and started down.

At the bottom, he smiled to himself. The old couch was still there, with two musty blankets stretched across it. He walked to the couch and sat down.

"I'll just wait for you," he said to the house. With his right hand, he pulled one of the musty blankets up over his right shoulder. He set the bottle of Harmony Canadian onto the floor. He looked at the candle, casting its yellow light into the black gloom. He could see streetlight coming through two small windows. There was a crack in the floor near his left foot. The crack was slightly smaller than the base of the candle. He pushed the candle into the crack, wedging it tightly. Then he picked up the bottle and savored the taste of the Canadian.

George Fallow, in what was to be one of his last coherent thoughts, looked at his watch again and thought, *'I'll hear him when he comes in.'*

George sat, watching the flame of the candle. The flame rotated in a slow gyration, much like a rotund belly dancer in a cheap hashish house. The flame seemed to mesmerize George and slowly his eyelids fell. He slumped to his left and his head came down on the arm of the old couch. He knew he was holding the bottle and tried to set it upright on the floor. After three minutes, his hand loosened and the bottle tipped, making a gurgle as it rolled away.

The escaping whiskey made a wet spot on the floor, reflecting the solitary flame of a stalwart candle that stood watch over the tired, angry man.

※※※※※

A fifty-gallon drum was standing on the inside of the sidewalk, at the midpoint of the two-block expanse. Three picket signs leaned against the drum while their owners clustered around a hibachi grill. The three men, wearing nondescript coats with blaze orange hunting caps, were sitting on lawn chairs in a circle around the grill. One man was trying to warm his hands over the glowing coals while the second was grilling two hot dogs and keeping an eye on a pot of Irish mulligan stew. He laughed and told the other two the stew was bubbling.

"Fire burn, and cauldron bubble," said the third man, who was looking toward the lighted windows in the center of the high school. He was hoping the school board meeting would adjourn so he could go home.

"Unless I'm mistaken, the king in that play got the knife in the back. Is that right?"

"Yes," said the third man. The three men were two houses up the street from the white clapboard house with the rusty gutters. From where they sat, they couldn't see the yellow and red flames inside the rear of the house. Yellow flames flickered on the torn window shades in the front, like flickering neon lights above a 1950's Hamburger Haven.

"We are like the three witches," said the second man.

"If you can foretell the future in yonder stew," said the third, laughing.

"I can," said the first. "I predict that through yonder doors of the castle, the inimitable Bluster Barnes shall shortly appear and talk to his minions." He had been watching the window of the boardroom and saw Barnes leaving.

Barnes, however, walked south and came out the Elementary wing doors. Seeing the three men, he turned left and walked up the sidewalk. Halfway to the men, something caused him to turn his head. He looked for a moment, then ran over and rapped on the boardroom window. He shouted 'Fire, fire' twice and then turned around. He ran across the street and stood in front of the house.

It was evident to Barnes that most of the house was engulfed. The window shades in the front were burning and flames were shooting up the old chimney. The upstairs rooms were flowing with the red and yellow flickers of growing flame. When the three men joined him, one started for the front door, and stopped. He backed up when a front window blew out and the quiet fire became a roar of sound.

The fire siren erupted, sending its wail across the town, summoning the thirty men of the volunteer fire department. The four men stood transfixed until the fire reached out for them, sending a tendril halfway to the sidewalk. They quickly retreated to the other side of the street.

While they walked backward, facing the fire, Percy Smith came racing across the street, shouting 'Anybody in there?' at the top of his lungs. He was almost up to the house before he heard Connie Cratt yell 'No, its empty.' Smith backed up when he felt the heat of the fire. He turned and walked over to Cratt.

"How do you know?"

"It's empty?"

"Yes," he insisted. "How do you know?"

"There is only one person using the house," said Cratt. He looked around. A knot of teachers was standing up the street, about thirty feet away. Arnie Murkiwasser and Glacinda Fallow were standing nearby. They were watching him.

"I rented the house," he said loudly. From downtown, the two fire trucks could be seen turning the corner, racing for the fire.

The trucks rumbled up to the house. Firemen were suddenly running in every direction, stretching hose toward the water hydrants at the two opposite street corners. A blast of flame burst through the roof of the house, sending sparks high into the sky. A rumble of noise was heard through the front room window and sparks flew out toward the firemen. Someone standing near Tom Harant and Connie Cratt shouted that the second floor just fell in. A fireman with a bullhorn was shouting at his men to put water on the two neighboring houses. The fire hoses suddenly came to life, bulging up and turning stiff with the pressure of water. A stream of water hit the house to the left, where a curl of steam was rising from the shingles nearest to the burning house.

The spectators stood and watched. A second stream of water hit the other house for about fifteen seconds and then turned to the burning house. At the same moment, the first floor gave way and fell into the basement, sending another burst of flames into the sky. The Fire Chief came over to the group and asked if anyone was inside. Cratt shouted back that the house was empty. The Chief raised his bullhorn and told the men to turn off the water, let it burn, and watch the neighboring houses.

Patty Trivic walked over to stand next to Cratt. Her face betrayed her concern. "Did you have insurance?"

"Wasn't my house. I rented it." He was smiling.

"What on earth for?"

"A place for the school board to meet. Before I heard that we could use the big dining room out at Bulrush Bay Resort." Cratt smiled, almost from ear to ear. Then he reached up and pulled at his chin, diminishing his smile. He glanced at Patty Trivic. Mrs. Trivic seemed to be hanging on his every word.

"That's not what you told me," she said to Cratt.

"Never mind now," he answered. He was suddenly aware of all the pairs of ears that surrounded him. "I'm heading for the Red Carpet."

Mrs. Fallow and Arnie turned to follow Cratt toward their cars, parked on the south end of the street. Patty Trivic seemed content to stand and watch the fire and the firemen. Curt Fitzsimmons and Percy Smith left her standing alone and walked over to where Tom stood with Billy Washburn. They both had questions on their faces.

"Did you know?" Curt asked.

"I heard a rumor," said Tom. "Come to think of it, back in July, I heard he was writing a book."

"Well, I'll be damned," said Curt. Curt turned away, heading for his car. Percy smiled at Tom. Then he turned to follow Curt. Billy Washburn took two steps closer to Tom and nudged Tom with his elbow.

"You heard a rumor," said Billy. "You know what he was using that house for, don't you?"

"No."

"Are you dense, or just obtuse?"

There were more spectators, now. A gathering of men, women and children lined the sidewalk. A pair of tourists from Iowa had seen the flames and turned south when they reached the middle of Iron Lake. A reporter from the Cherry Grove *Journal* came running with his camera around his neck.

The sidewalls fell in, first. Then the rear wall, unsupported, fell into the basement with a shower of sparks. The front wall stubbornly resisted the fire, but did fall backward, providing spectators and firemen with a credibly beautiful blaze of bright yellow light as it crashed. The fire continued to burn and the Chief came over to tell everybody to go home. The strikers picked up their signs and walked away. Patty Trivic and Mr. Washburn left, heading for home. Tom walked back to the building and using his Allen wrench, turned the lock in the front door from open to locked.

IRON LAKE BURNING

Tom stepped outside. He heard the door click. He glanced at the burning remains of the house as he walked around the building, back to his car. He wondered about the house that Connie Cratt rented. However, Cratt said he had no insurance, which made sense if he was renting, and Tom put the question out of his mind.

*****

"Your chairman Cratt..." said the voice on Tom's phone. "He's been trained to break that teacher union."

"Who is this?" asked Tom.

"Doesn't matter. Cratt went to training last June. Said he was definitely going to break the 'phony union' of teachers in Iron Lake."

"How do you know this?" said Tom, without sparing the sarcasm. During the first week of the strike, Tom learned there were people who would try to damage the reputation of other people out of, what? Spite? Jealousy? Revenge?

The man on the phone was quiet for ten seconds. Tom asked him again, "How do you know this?"

"If I answer that question..." There was silence on the phone. "I'm a member of his union. I have relatives among the teachers. That's all I'm going to say."

"You're a member? So what?"

"Some of the union officials from Chicago were there. Last June. Dark shirts, black ties, $5 cigars. They encouraged him. I heard them promise he would have help. Those people are dangerous."

"Are you serious?"

"Mr. Harant, you need to get your head out of the clouds." The phone went dead and dial tone followed. Tom put the phone back in its cradle.

Crystal, sitting on the small rust colored sofa on the breezeway, was reading a lady's magazine. "Serious about what?" she asked.

"Oh, nothing much. Trying to poison me against Cratt." Tom went to the back door, looking out on his yard. He opened the door and walked onto the patio. A full moon was throwing beams through the Norway pines that lined his property. The moonlight fell on the fountain and the empty rose bed next to it. He remembered his father standing there with Mark, Carl and Corrine. Cookie graduated from Mankato

State the same weekend that Crystal and Tom moved to Iron Lake, in August 1990. Tom remembered his father laughing when Cookie told him she had been offered the Art position at Iron Lake High School. "She was always the apple of his eye," said Tom to Crystal. "My dad got to see our kids grow up."

"He's coming home from Rochester next week. Your Mom called tonight." There was a hesitation. "There's a letter from Mark. I read it."

*****

On the kitchen table, Tom found an envelope that carried no stamp but had Mark's AFP address in the upper left corner. Mark was aboard the *USS George Philip,* a guided missile frigate, that Tom presumed was in the Indian Ocean. He looked up at Crystal. She stood in the doorway.

She smiled. It was a silent message that their son was well, neither injured nor ill. "Something about training."

In Mark's letter, Tom found the usual comments about life aboard a ship. Mark said a company of Marines had recently joined the ship. Unexplainably, the 'grunts' were praising the shipboard chow as 'a damn sight better' than Parris Island chow. Mark went on to describe an amphibious operation. A petty officer brought an LST alongside the *George Philip* and Mark went aboard as an observing officer and delivered thirty Marines to a beach on the Saudi shore. He added "all the men" were debriefed and told they could talk about the training mission.

His letter was dated 1 October 1990. Mark Harant already knew he was part of *Operation Camel Sand,* an attempt to convince the Iraqis that amphibious forces would attack the shores of Kuwait south of Kuwait City.

CHAPTER FIFTEEN
In the Swamp

Heavy gray clouds slowly lumbered into town from the west. Patches of sunlight lit the water on the lake, alternating with dark shadows from dark clouds that seemed to presage the early arrival of winter. In the fields outside town, the combines were almost finished with the soybean harvest. A few tractors were already pulling choppers, digging up and chopping this year's corn stalks. Cars and pickups lined the streets of Iron Lake for two blocks on each side of Red's Pizza. The striking teachers were holding a meeting in 'Strike Headquarters'. Directly across from Red's Pizza, in the municipal parking lot, six pickups were parked in front of the municipal liquor store, also known as the 'Red Carpet'. Each of the six pickups had a placard in their front window that read 'Get It Over With! Now!'

Arnie Murkiwasser, Chairman of the Iron Lake Board, stood resolutely in front of the municipal liquor store. A taller man, in a yellow windbreaker was leaning over Arnie, telling him something. An observer said the man was telling Arnie where to go, from the way he was waving a huge finger on a large hand in Arnie's face. A second man, also wearing a yellow windbreaker, left the liquor store and walked to the first pickup truck, opened the door and grabbed the 'Get It Over' sign. He waved the sign at Arnie and then he faced the 'Strike Headquarters' across the street and yelled, 'Get It Over, Now!' He put the sign back in the window of his pickup and walked over to Arnie and the first man.

One block away, Tom Harant in a long brown raincoat came out of the Reliable Drug Store and glanced up and down the street. He spotted Arnie Murkiwasser and began walking toward the liquor store. The two men standing near Arnie saw Harant approaching and they turned and walked into the Red Carpet.

"End of another week," shouted Arnie as Tom approached. At least, Mr. Harant was a friendly face and would not attack. After two and a half weeks of strike, the town of Iron Lake had reached the MEA break, that annual convention in the Minneapolis Convention Center. Arnie Murkiwasser was beginning to worry about the angry phone calls he was receiving. Statewide, through the third week, there had been 25 teacher strikes. Twelve of the strikes had been resolved and Arnie's neighbors were beginning to wonder why Iron Lake was not yet settled.

"I was trying to get you on the phone, Mr. Murkiwasser." In public, Tom Harant was formal when he talked to Iron Lake board members.

"More bad news, I suppose," said Arnie walking toward the middle of the parking lot. "What is it?"

"The kind we don't need in public," said Tom. 'Another alligator' he said to himself. "We need to keep it quiet."

Arnie stopped in the middle of the lot with a question on his face. He nervously ran his hand through his hair. He straightened his tie, pulling his tan coat around himself. He looked up at Tom Harant.

"One of our custodians moved a filing cabinet this morning. In back he found four cancelled payroll checks made out to Mavis Malloy." Tom looked across the street to where he saw a teacher watching them.

"Mavis retired three years ago."

"They were forged."

"Are you sure?"

"My secretary, who knows everything about this school district, knew where the cancelled checks from three years ago were. She retrieved five samples of Mavis' handwriting." Tom knew instantly that the checks were forged. They were written in March, April, May and June of last fiscal year. The checks, quite noticeably, were cashed in August and September of this fiscal year. Which did not make sense unless someone was trying to get the school's auditors to overlook these checks. Tom confronted the Payroll Clerk, Linda Hummel, and she admitted the forgeries. She started to cry and told Tom about her husband leaving her with three children under eight-years-old.

Arnie looked at the forgeries and put the checks back in their envelope. "What do you want to do, Tom?"

"I think, we write a private statement, in which she admits her guilt. We get a county judge to issue an order requiring restitution. It's the only way we get some of the money back. Assign my secretary to monitor each payroll."

"That keeps it quiet?"

"I hope so."

Off to the west, there was a visible end to the gray clouds. A clear blue sky would arrive in Iron Lake in about thirty minutes, bringing the warmth of the sun back to a town that sorely needed a little cheer.

*****

Television coverage of the teacher strikes in Minnesota diminished but did not disappear. In the first two weeks, the twenty-five teacher strikes had drawn enormous coverage in the media. Every other day there would be a report in which a 'local president' was quoted asking the school board to come back to the bargaining table. There were settlements but the 'out-state' districts did not warrant much coverage. WCCO Evening News carried a daily report and noted that twelve of the striking schools had successfully reached agreements. Their teachers were back at work.

There were reports that reached Tom Harant by telephone and by word of mouth. The Chairman of the St. Cloud Board of Education reported that he had received five calls threatening to 'gang-bang' his daughter if he didn't get the board moving toward settlement. St. Cloud police reported that three board members had picture windows blown out by shotgun blasts. During a board meeting in quiet and sedate Sauk Centre, also known for the play *Our Town,* six cars had their tires slashed. In Willmar, to the north of Iron Lake, an unknown number of farmers drove their manure spreaders into town and dumped their loads on the front lawn of the Willmar High School. This occurred during a dark night. When the superintendent claimed he had ordered the extra fertilizer for the front lawn, no one took him seriously.

Charges of Unfair Labor Practices were lodged against the Forest Lake and Anoka-Hennepin school districts. Attorneys for the teachers were using the threat of federal intervention to increase pressure on the school board. Teachers in Warba and Urholt, to the west of Iron Lake, sent a bag of dimes to the Iron Lake teachers. Once again they had insulted their peers. The WCCO Channel Four traffic helicopter landed at Iron Lake two more times, getting video of teachers walking the picket line. Tom Harant noticed that when WCCO cameras arrived, there seemed to be twice as many teachers on the picket line as the hour before the cameras arrived.

Tom's peers cared. At least he thought so. During the second full week of the strike, an administrator called Tom to offer his support. Tom, however, was dealing with daily brush fires. Six months later he remembered the phone call, but had no idea who to thank.

The Iron Lake Board held a closed meeting to discuss negotiation strategy during the second full (MEA) week of the strike. During this meeting, Connie Cratt explained to the board that the district was saving about $10,000 per day by not paying the teachers. Curt Fitzsimmons argued that many of the days lost would be made up. Cratt rejected this idea. He spent an hour giving the board reasons why the strike should go on, with the strongest being the teachers did not want to settle. He also pointed out that before the strike, the teachers had leverage by their threat to strike. Now that the strike was underway, the board had the leverage to tell the teachers what terms they could take.

In the end, the Board told their negotiators (Cratt and Fallow) to lower the board's offer to their position before the teachers stomped out of the session in August. The Board agreed, knowing that a lower position would be a position of strength if Iron Lake went to arbitration to get a resolution.

"Are you with me?" Cratt asked at the end of the meeting.

Three members (Murkiwasser, Fallow and Trivic) said they were. Percy Smith and Curt Fitzsimmons both said they were not with Cratt. They were with the children of the district. In Tom's notebook, he wrote 'Board split, 4-2.' These were to be prophetic words, but Tom didn't know it.

*****

Percy Smith served on a 'Riverine' patrol boat in the Mekong Delta during the Vietnam War, serving his term in 1967 and part of 1968. Percy, who believed he was unlucky, arrived back in the states one month before the Democratic National Convention in Chicago. He heard reports of the deaths of Martin Luther King and Robert Kennedy on Armed Forces Radio, while in Vietnam. Leaving 'Country' in a Boeing 727 jet in mid-June, Percy looked forward to returning to a country that revered its soldiers and sailors. He wore his uniform with pride.

It was drizzling in San Francisco on the day he arrived from Hawaii. In Hawaii, orientation officers told the men returning to the states to expect to be ignored. Waiting in line for a plane to Chicago, a pretty, long legged brunette in a mini-skirt and a chartreuse jacket spit on him He watched her walk away; with those long legs and that certain sashay in her hips and wondered why he went. Was Vietnam so repulsive that its fighting men should be spit on?

In Cedar Rapids, Percy went to his father's American Legion Club, expecting to have a few old soldiers buy him a drink for returning from Vietnam. To his chagrin, he was ignored. He bought himself a few drinks in memory of Bill Johnson and Peter Flores and Kenny Braun, friends who did not return.

A month later, when he still had not found work, he packed camping gear into a used Volkswagen bus, loaded in four cases of beer and drove to Chicago. He heard that the war protestors were going to camp in a park near the site of the Democratic Party convention. Percy wanted to join the veterans and Young Conservatives who were planning to defend the convention hall. He arrived on the second day of the convention, just in time to be chased out of the area by a police squadron on horseback. In a bar, he saw the evening news. He couldn't believe that policemen were using truncheons and tear gas on protestors. What had they done, he asked a neighbor at the bar, to be treated like criminals? The neighbor responded by pointing out that this convention was Mayor Daley's party, and Daley 'don't brook no dissenting opinions about nothing'.

Percy returned to Cedar Rapids, wanting to find a job and a spot to settle down. He couldn't find work and drove north to Faribault in Minnesota. A man in the unemployment office, which was now called a manpower office, helped him get a job making pool tables in LeCenter. After six months of boring, mindless work with an electric drill, he quit and moved to Madelia. He took a job at the Tony Downs plant, making 'Bully Beef' for the Army and Navy. He heard the stories about 'Bully Beef' making the Rough Riders sick during the Spanish-American war in 1898. The joke around the plant was that the 'Bully Beef' they were putting in the cans was the same beef from 1898, reconstituted and repacked.

In six months, Percy was ready for a new challenge. He moved to Mankato in Minnesota, intending to use his G.I. benefits to get a college degree. It was while he was in Mankato that he met and fell in love with a 'gorgeous, stunning' brunette, Rebecca Grossman, a native of New

Ulm. She was in her junior year at Mankato State, intending to become a teacher of Physics and Chemistry. When he thought about Miss Grossman, he saw a bright whirlwind unlike any other person he had ever encountered. She moved into his apartment on north Sixth street at the end of her Junior year, intending to marry Percy the following January when she finished her Student Teaching. They had six beautiful months together, making love, drinking beer, going on picnics until the weather turned cold. Percy worked at Mettler's Bar on Front Street, attended classes that fall and absolutely adored 'Becca'.

In early December, on her way up Minnesota 14 to New Ulm, during a heavy snowstorm, her car crossed the centerline and hit a Tow Brothers delivery truck on its way back to Mankato. Rebecca was killed instantly. During her funeral, her father came over to Percy, patted him on the shoulder and said he was sorry.

For the next three days, he sat in Mettler's Bar and grieved, in his fashion. It was here that he made the acquaintance of Tom Harant, a young man who was similarly engaged, except his young lady was a 'long-legged blonde.' Percy and Tom worked behind the bar and Tom occasionally, at six foot four inches, was called upon to check ID cards or to act as a bouncer. They listened to 'Old John' when the bar's veteran employee talked about Mankato in the years during the 'Great Depression' and Roosevelt's four terms. Percy listened to the story of Old John's life and wondered how God could throw so much heartache and sorrow at one person.

They became bookends, Percy and Tom. Old John liked to describe the two young men as 'Mutt and Jeff'. While Tom was an optimist, Percy was a pessimist. Where Tom found the goodness in people, Percy believed that it was dangerous to have any hopes for a relationship with another person. Tom's girl Crystal organized blind dates for Percy with girls from Crystal's dormitory. Later, she admitted defeat, saying that Percy was not soon going to get over losing 'Becca.

A year later, Percy's cousin in Cherry Grove recommended Percy for a sales job with Sandstrom Distributing in Iron Lake. The owner, David Sandstrom was convinced that Percy would make an excellent 'Outside' sales person, making deliveries in a four county area. Eight years later, when Percy ran for the school board, five of his good customers wrote letters of support and Percy won in a small landslide. When Arley Green announced his retirement, Perseus Smith, board member, immediately thought of Tom Harant who was now a school superintendent in a different small school district.

*****

Reliable Drugs of Iron Lake is a long, narrow store with decorative tin, painted white, covering the ceiling. There are shelves of greeting cards and knick-knacks immediately inside the door. A long black soda fountain runs toward the back, where the prescription counter protects shelves of drugs. To the right of the soda counter are four booths, used by customers for coffee and a roll or to play dice in those endless games of '6-5-4'. The owner, and pharmacist, John Snard keeps an eagle eye on everything that happens in his store. His doors and windows are barred, and he was the first in town to install burglar alarms wired into a satellite service.

When Tom and Percy walked into the drug store, the store was deserted. John Snard was inside his drug counter, making up prescriptions. His clerk, Mary Beth was in back, cooking beef for sandwiches. They poured coffee for themselves and found a booth. Tom pulled an ashtray off the counter by the black cash register, took it to his booth, and lit a cigarette. Percy watched him inhale and hold the smoke, then exhale.

Tom noticed Percy's attention. "I know. Not good for me."

"Shorten your life span."

"So will stress." He laughed. In all the years he had known Perseus Smith, he could not remember a time when Percy was completely satisfied with the world around him.

"Percy, you are too much the realist."

"You told me that back in Mankato. Do you remember?"

Tom could see Percy, muscles bulging in his arms, hauling three cases of beer in glass bottles up from the basement in Mettler's Bar. He could see Percy laughing with Old John, after they finished sweeping up the bar. He remembered the three of them enjoying a nightcap, as John called a short whiskey with a spritz of seltzer. Tom also could see Percy in the year after Rebecca died, turning sour and cynical and morose.

"You are the realist. How long will the strike last?"

"Too long, I fear." Percy looked around the drug store, checking for eyes and ears of watchers. He picked up a spoon and added sugar to his coffee. In a low voice he added, "The teachers are being manipulated by their headquarters in St. Paul. They don't know it."

"And Cratt isn't?" Tom was reacting to phone calls that hinted Cratt was taking orders from the Amalgamated Iron Workers.

"You're the idealist, Tom. You tell me."

"I can't." Tom looked at his friend. He wanted to tell Percy that he believed some events went beyond the control of the rational persons in a community. He wanted Percy to know that he was losing faith in his mission. He blamed himself for not doing enough to stop the strike before it happened. He felt just like a fireman who waits for the alarm. You can't plan for the next fire. All you can do is react.

"I think I believed once that men working together..." Tom paused to collect his thoughts. "Could make a better world."

"I know better. What happens, happens," said Percy.

"You are the realist, Percy. I am somewhere in between. I believe I can't afford the luxury of idealism. Not today. Not last week. Not tomorrow. I have to find a way out of this quagmire, this strike."

"That could be," said Percy as the County Sheriff walked into the store, spotted Tom and walked over. The Sheriff explained that the news would be all over the county in about an hour. The men working to excavate the burned out house found a body in the basement. The truck parked in back of the house belonged to George Fallow and nobody had seen George for a week.

"Couple a times I saw him, he was pretty drunk last week," said Percy without hesitating.

"That's so, Sheriff," said Tom. "I saw him drive into a power pole across from the school."

"Mr. Harant, do you know why his behavior changed in the last month?"

Tom considered the question. To answer truthfully, he would have to demur and claim ignorance. On the other hand, he could tell the Sheriff about the rumors.

"No, Sir, I don't." Tom picked up his cup and sipped at the lukewarm coffee. The Sheriff asked him to call if he heard anything and turned toward the pharmacy counter.

"Speak not ill of the dead," said Percy in low tones.

"Say the truth, only. Leave rumors for the gossips and backstabbers."

"There will be plenty of those, I am sure," added Percy as he stood up. He left, heading for the pay phone on the sidewalk, to call his wife. Tom dropped fifty cents on the table and headed back to his office.

*****

Tom was sitting in his office when he heard mumbling voices through the wall between his office and the boardroom. He stood up and reached for the door handle. He was opening the door when he heard Arnie Murkiwasser say "…Hummel forged the checks. She was planning to put the cancelled checks into last year's cancelled checks. No one would have been the wiser."

Murkiwasser took off his tan overcoat and sat down on one of the black leatherette chairs. Connie Cratt stood and looked at Tom. He was wearing his white cowboy hat, with his blue Future Farmers jacket. Three patches from the 1971, 1972 and 1973 annual conventions in Kansas City were sewn on and surrounded the FFA emblem. *'Trying to tell us that he's a farmer,'* thought Tom to himself. He heard the clacking of women's shoes on the hard surface of the hall. Then Patty Trivic entered the boardroom, followed by Curt Fitzsimmons.

Tom looked at the four board members. They seemed intent on holding a meeting. There was, and this was a big item with Tom Harant, no legal notice posted of the meeting. Percy Smith and Glacinda Fallow were not present. He looked at Curt and asked if he was going to attend an illegal meeting. When Curt said yes, Tom turned and left the boardroom.

"Damn," Tom said when he reached his desk. He reached for his notebook, and began to write a record of the meeting. There was a knock on the door and Curt stuck his head in.

"If we have any questions, we will send someone to ask you."

"Thank you, I think."

Curt pulled the door shut. Tom sat there staring at the page in his notebook. Twenty seconds later, Percy Smith walked into Tom's office, entering from the outer office where Tom's secretary had her office. He walked to the coffee pot and poured a cup of day-old coffee.

"The meeting is next door," said Tom quietly.

"Ain't going. Period. End of Report," countered Percy.

"Well, I have to admit I'm surprised."

"I asked Curt to attend. He will tell me if they are up to no good."

"But the meeting is illegal."

"Sure it is." Percy smiled at Tom. "They want to discuss Plant and Harvey."

Tom groaned. He had hoped that the affair between Sylvan Plant and Lillian Harvey would be ignored, in the heat of the strike. Tom stood up to get a cup of coffee. Percy told him the coffee tasted old. Tom sat back down. He felt the stress that comes with too many issues and not enough time.

"There are times, Percy. Times."

Percy said nothing. He watched the administrator he had helped to hire about sixteen months earlier. Percy had confidence in Tom's abilities. He knew that all the administrators were working under pressure. It was understood.

"It's hard to remember that my original purpose was to drain the swamp, when I'm up to my ass in alligators."

Percy laughed, loud and with gusto. "Yes, alligators."

The door to the boardroom opened. Connie Cratt stuck his head in and looked at Percy. Percy told Connie that he was refusing to attend what was an illegal meeting. Connie pulled the door shut.

"Different kinds of alligators. Right?"

"Absolutely." Tom laughed to himself. He realized that in the last two weeks, he had begun to use the word 'absolutely' entirely with too much abandon.

Percy started laughing. "And you really feel, *absolutely*, that some of these alligators are really crockagators, don't you?"

CHAPTER SIXTEEN
Iron Circle

"He's a real mean bastard," said Patty Trivic, right to Glacinda Fallow's face. They were at a table in the Central Café. "He's mean and he enjoys his power."

The owner's wife was working in back, cleaning her griddle and washing dishes. A lone man was sitting at the counter, nursing a hot mug of soup. The café was nearly empty but three board members and Tom Harant sat at a table near the front door. Outside, snow fell on Central Avenue, coating the downtown of Iron Lake with a white powder. Gray light filtered through the dingy, unwashed front windows of the café.

"It's not the power," said Arnie, one of the inner core of the Iron Lake Board. "The union turned him mean…ruined his father. Connie has been trying to prove himself to the union bosses for years."

Silence surrounded the three while the owner's wife brought the coffee pot. Glacinda stared at her cup, then moved it for a refill. Arnie broke a donut in half, ignoring the waitress. Patty watched the street outside where the snowfall almost seemed to be a joyous expression of nature's love for mankind. The gray light and the soft snow, however, did little to lift the spirits of Iron Lake.

Central Café was largely disserted at 4:30 p.m. in mid-November. The booths were empty. Carmen, the owner's wife began to clean glass on the pie cabinet. The four adults sat quietly sipping coffee, preparing to leave for a meeting in the school.

A few moments passed before Glacinda raised her eyes from her coffee cup. She looked out the grimy plate glass window into the gray, blustery day. The day seemed to mirror how she felt. The interminable strike was six weeks old and she could barely remember life without the strike. She could barely remember George's face, three weeks dead. She watched a truck drive by, turning south toward the school.

"I always thought he hated teachers," Glacinda said, "for what they are and what he isn't."

In the background, the fuel oil furnace of the run-down café churned out heat. An acrid aroma gave the café the smell of decayed incense. Glacinda, called 'Glacial Linda' by the Iron Lake teachers, looked in her purse for a tissue. She found one and blew her nose. She was wearing a dark blue sweater with blue slacks. In the eyes of the two men at the table she was a good looking woman...despite years of raising children and holding down a part-time job as a bookkeeper. Her light brown hair framed a face with brown, but determined eyes.

"Connie is right. And you know it," she said to Mr. Harant, looking him almost in the eye.

"Connie hates all teachers," said Tom Harant. "He always has. He wants to keep them right where they are...on the picket line."

Tom was uncomfortable with this discussion of Connie Cratt. Harant was a large man; his button-down bluish shirt squeezed into a well-worn three-piece suit. He ran a finger around the inside of his shirt collar. When he reached the knot of his tie, he unbuttoned the collar and loosened the tie.

"You have to know...his union trained him to break the teachers." Tom said this quietly, keeping his comments within the four. "Now he wants to open school with replacement teachers," said Mr. Harant slowly. He looked across the street at the Municipal Liquor Store. A bartender was pushing a snow scoop along the sidewalk.

Tom looked at the three board members. Glacinda Fallow, who always followed Connie Cratt's lead. Patty Trivic, the eight-year veteran on the board who argued about the smallest details in the minutes. Arnold Murkiwasser, the owner of Murkiwasser Paints, a remodeling business. Arnie was a 'vertically challenged' person who lacked the courage to say 'No' to Connie Cratt.

"You don't mean replacement teachers, you mean scabs," said Mrs. Fallow, in an accusatory tone of voice. Glacinda wasn't quite sure where she stood.

"No, I mean licensed teachers," said Tom while he picked at a mole near his hairline. "What Cratt wants is to hire a whole new staff. Fire the strikers and hire an entire staff. Since the teachers went on strike, he has the power...his ironfisted attitude is pushing the rest of the board, including especially you three...and you know it."

Tom held his breath. These were unusually blunt words for him. He expected one of the three to take exception to his words. The teachers were on strike and the board was trying to present a unified front, though insiders knew the board was split four-two. There was an emotional maelstrom swirling around the Board. The majority of four refused to meet the demands of the teachers. Behind the scenes, Connie Cratt held the small cabal of four in line.

There was no reaction. The three board members sat and looked at Tom Harant. "When are you going to think for yourself?" asked the superintendent. He noticed a dark green pickup truck as it slowed and turned left, south toward the school. He rose slowly, looking at Glacinda.

"Are you going to talk to Connie?" he asked.

"No," she said.

"Well, that's it then," he said to himself, not expecting an answer. He threw fifty cents on the table. He turned, pulling on his overcoat and walked to the door. Behind him, Mrs. Fallow said, "Stop working against the Board, Mr. Harant." Tom looked back at the three board members and then opened the heavy door.

*****

He pulled up in front of the school in time to see Connie Cratt parking next to the sidewalk. Two strikers stood picket duty about fifty feet away. Cratt was wearing a brown topcoat over a white shirt and tie. Tom watched him stomp his boots on the sidewalk. Tom looked down at the packed snow and saw Cratt was wearing clean cowboy boots, boots with fancy scrollwork.

"I see you're dressed."

"Yes," said Cratt. It was not unusual for Connie Cratt to arrive with traces of manure clinging to his work boots, having jumped off his tractor at the last minute to make the meeting. Cratt also worked for Spencer County as a mechanic. "Meeting still at six?"

"In about ten minutes," answered Harant, seeing two more cars pull up behind his used Lincoln. Snow crunched under their feet. The sun had gone down to the west, leaving the school in a gray twilight. Cratt kicked a chunk of compacted snow. The missile skipped up the sidewalk, slid to the right and hit one of the striking teachers on the foot. *"That's typical,"* thought Tom.

Cratt and Harant passed the two striking teachers silently. The teachers stared back. At this point, after six weeks, the picket line was manned daily by a token force of two, on rotating shifts of two hours.

"Abandon hope," Tom said while he tried to insert a key into the Kelly green door of the school. "...all ye who enter," he added while holding the door for Cratt.

"What's that?" demanded Cratt.

"It's a line from a poem about an inferno," answered Tom.

Cratt passed through the door. He looked at Harant with one eyebrow raised, and added, "Yeah, we could use a little heat around here."

They walked down the quiet hall and entered the boardroom where Curt Fitzsimmons and a reporter were waiting. The boardroom wasn't fancy. The room and its blackboards had once been a classroom. Carpet muffled any extra sounds. A Simpson school clock clanked the passage of a minute. Seven black leather chairs were pulled up to a long table, which stood in front of thirty folding chairs. The chairs stood in mute accusation of the absent public who would fail to appear at the meeting. Three teachers entered the room, followed by two men in yellow windbreakers.

Mrs. Trivic, Mrs. Fallow and Arnie were heard stamping snow off their shoes in the building entry. Half a minute later they entered the boardroom. They threw their overcoats across the backs of folding chairs. Board members and the superintendent moved toward the black chairs. The lone reporter sat down, just as the high school principal William Washburn entered and sat down. The Board Chairman Arnie Murkiwasser declared it was six o'clock and called the meeting to order.

Tom Harant sat at one end of the long table. At the other end, Connie Cratt stood silently until all eyes were on him. "It's been six weeks. It's time we got on with educating kids. I feel it is time to open school with substitutes," said Cratt.

"You can't do that," said one of the teachers, loudly. One of the men in yellow windbreakers stood up, said nothing, and then sat down.

Curt Fitzsimmons raised an objection. Perseus Smith was absent, deer hunting in the Grand Rapids area. Harant explained the board could pass a motion to waive the three-day notice, but Perseus Smith *could argue* the meeting was illegal because he had not received the proper notice.

The chairman ignored his comments and asked for a motion to waive the three-day notice. The motion was quickly passed without discussion.

"You could go back to the bargaining table," said the teacher, sharply. He looked at Cratt. Connie stared back. The rest of the board fiddled with the notepads in front of them. The reporter suddenly remembered his tape recorder and turned it on.

"Your union says you won't come back to work for less than $5200 on the salary schedule," said Cratt deliberately. He waited a few moments "…or until hell freezes over."

"And we can't afford $5200 per teacher," echoed Glacinda Fallow, smiling at the teacher. The teacher and his two neighbors sat and looked at Glacinda, then at Cratt. Connie tried to smile back but one lip refused and he produced what looked like a sneer.

"What you really mean Connie…is you have the teachers on the street…and you intend to keep them there," said Tom Harant firmly.

Connie Cratt sat down, leaned back in his chair and looked at Harant. An observer might have wondered if Cratt was going to respond. He finally turned to look at the three teachers and said, "I'm just one member. Decisions are made by a majority of the board." Three of the board members nodded their heads, agreeing with Cratt.

*****

Arnie Murkiwasser called the closed session to order, after the three teachers, two men in yellow and the reporter left the boardroom. The observers could wait in the hall while the board met in closed session. Tom Harant started the tape recorder and spoke the names of the board members and Billy Washburn, Principal. He noted that Perseus Smith was absent, deer hunting at the Jack Pine Savage Resort north of Grand Rapids.

Cratt was still looking at Tom and gradually he looked at the rest of the board. "Mr. Harant really wants to get this strike over, doesn't he?" He looked at Patty Trivic. She winked at him. Cratt glanced down the table at Arnie. Glacinda nudged Arnie and whispered in his ear.

"I move we advertise for substitute teachers and open school in two weeks," said Cratt. "And I want a board member to come in every day to receive a report on progress from the superintendent."

"I second the motion," echoed Patty Trivic.

"Mr. Cratt...dammit...what do you want?" said Tom Harant in a monotone. "You want a board member here everyday...to watch me, don't you? Why don't you have the board cancel my contract and appoint you to my job?"

"You'd like that...*wouldn't you Mr. Harant?*" said Connie deliberately. He leaned back and put his feet on the board table. "You'd like anything that would get this strike over, *wouldn't you?*"

"Yes, I want to get the strike over," said Tom. "Our kids need to be working on their reading and math, they need a daily schedule, *again*. Opening with subs will prolong the strike. Our teachers need to get back to work...they've got bills to pay. Christmas is five weeks from tomorrow."

In the silence that followed, Cratt finally asked for a show of hands. Three members voted with Cratt to open school. Curt Fitzsimmons voted against the motion to open, but agreed to abstain in the public vote.

"And now, for that other issue. Plant and Harvey."

"I object," said Tom Harant quickly. "You can't discuss a personnel matter when you called this closed meeting for negotiations strategy."

"As I said, Plant and Harvey." Cratt was determined to bring this issue to a vote. "I want the superintendent to begin steps to fire these two."

"On what grounds?"

"Moral Turpitude," said Connie Cratt.

Fitzsimmons started to laugh. "Where did you hear that term, Connie? Are you working with a bunch of coffee house lawyers?"

"Moral Turpitude. It means depravity. Plant and Harvey are having an affair and flaunting it in front of everybody. They can be fired for not holding to the community's moral standards."

"That may be," said Curt.

"May be," added Tom slowly, "But..."

He waited until he had their attention. Patty Trivic had been writing in her notebook and she looked up. Glacinda blew her nose, once again. When they were looking at him Tom said, "How do I prove they are shacking up?"

"I have a witness who has recorded the dates and times of their visits to the Laker Motel," noted Arnie Murkiwasser. Cratt suddenly choked on his coffee, sputtering and spitting coffee. He looked sideways, briefly at Glacinda before he began to wipe the coffee off the table in front of him.

"I can't fire them. They're on strike, for crying out loud. And if I did, that would be an unfair labor practice." Tom paused for a moment, gathering his thoughts. "The union would claim the action was in retaliation for the strike."

The board members looked thoughtful. The scratching of Patty's pen in her notebook filled the void. Billy Washburn stood up and walked to the coffee pot. Cratt stared at Arnie, waiting for his chairman to act. After two long minutes, in which Washburn returned to his chair, and Patty stopped her writing, Arnie called for a motion. Cratt moved the superintendent discipline Plant and Harvey when the teachers come back to work. Arnie seconded the motion and it passed.

"It may be that I will choose to issue a written warning about their behavior," said Tom stiffly. He looked around the room. Washburn smiled at him. Tom avoided looking at Connie Cratt.

"Whatever," said Cratt.

*****

When Patty Trivic reopened the door to the hall, about fifty persons filed back into the boardroom. The chairs quickly filled and some of the men stood along the sides of the room. One of the farmers in a yellow windbreaker told Tom Harant that 'word is all over town.' Robert 'Bluster' Barnes at the last moment asked to address the board and sat in the front row. Connie Cratt made sure that all who wanted space were in the boardroom. Arnie Murkiwasser rapped the table with his gavel and the room became quiet.

In the silence that followed, the whirr of the reporter's tape recorder could be heard. The clock on the wall notched another minute. Mr. Harant pulled an ashtray toward himself while lighting a cigarette. The other board members looked at Connie Cratt. He smiled back.

"I'm only one vote. After six weeks with no progress, the board feels it is time to open school with substitutes."

"Scabs," said someone in the crowded room. "Yeah, *GD scabs*," said someone else.

Tom Harant stood up. He looked around the room, trying to get their attention while the muttering and grumbling died down.

"Replacement teachers, we want. We will hire licensed teachers," said Tom.

"It's only a word, Mr. Harant," said Barnes. He went on to tell the board that opening school with replacement teachers was tantamount to declaring war on the entire teaching faculty. When Connie Cratt asked him if the teachers were willing to discuss $4400 per teacher, Barnes said the teachers were firm in their need for $5200 per teacher. They went out on strike to get $5200 and they were going to get it.

Cratt thanked Barnes for his forthright answer. "It's what I have been telling the board in mediation. $5200 or until hell freezes over."

"I'm only one vote on this board. But this board is going to vote to open school in two weeks." He made the motion directing the administration to hire substitutes at $105 per day. This was a surprise to the audience because Iron Lake paid its substitutes $65 per day. $105 was unheard of. Someone yelled, *'that's unfair'* from the back of the room. Glacinda looked at the wall behind Cratt. Patty smiled at him. Arnie doodled on a notepad.

Patty quietly said, "Aye?" just before Glacinda added her "Aye!"

Arnie added his stubborn, "Aye!"

When it was Cratt's turn to vote, he looked at Mr. Harant and smiled. "And I vote aye," he said. Harant looked down at the notepad where he was recording the vote. Curt Fitzsimmons, the remaining member, abstained. The abstention was counted with the yes votes. Someone in the crowd said, "You can't do that," to which Cratt replied, "We just did." The teachers began to file out of the room. One of the farmers in a yellow windbreaker stood up and told the board that there were people in Iron Lake who supported the school board. Arnie thanked him for his comment. As they filed out, Tom saw two or three teachers look at him with expressions that said, 'Can't you do something?'

*****

Two or three people were standing in the hall chatting with Arnie and Curt, when Curt turned and walked back into the boardroom. Tom was still writing the minutes of the meeting that would go to Judy in the morning.

"There's a rumor," said Curt. He waited until Tom lifted his head.

"That fire three weeks ago? Some of George Fallow's neighbors have been asked some pointed questions about George. Was he depressed? Was he in trouble with the bank? Problems at home?"

"Sounds like routine to me," noted Tom when he closed his notebook.

"Maybe," said Curt. Mr. Fitzsimmons was proud of his ability to recognize malicious gossip when he heard it. He was in no hurry to spread the rumor that Glacinda Fallow was secretly meeting Connie Cratt twice a week. Curt instinctively knew there were people in Iron Lake who were enjoying the daily drama of the strike, people who would think nothing of damaging the reputation of a school board member.

"Yet, how many people knew that house was rented by Connie Cratt?"

"I did," answered Tom. "Connie told me."

"Well, could be there's nothing to the rumor. George was drunk and dropped a cigarette and started a fire. Word is, they found a loaded pistol near George." Tom jerked upright, and stood up. He took his notebook next door into his office. Curt followed him, adding, "It was an accident, probably. Bartender at the Red Carpet reports George was 'very drunk' when he left the bar that Thursday afternoon."

"Yes," added Tom. The coffee curmudgeons who played '6-5-4' each day in Reliable Drugs had decided the fire was an accident. Word of mouth spread their decision to the far reaches of Spencer County. The matter was closed.

*****

On the 10:00 o'clock news there was no mention of the on-going teacher strikes in Minnesota. Dave Moore promised to review the football players who were named to the 'All State' team. The situation in the Middle East led the newscast.

The video showed Soviet President Mikhail Gorbachev while a commentator added that 'Gorbachev has again stated that the Iraqi government may be 'reconsidering' its position on whether to withdraw from Kuwait.' When the video switched to a government official, the commentator said, "There is large-scale skepticism throughout the area. Iraqi Information Minister Latif Nassim Jassim told reporters "Kuwait is province No. 19" and "Americans must leave the region."

When the video switched to Sam Donaldson, he was standing

with 'Big Ben' in London behind him, over his left shoulder. Sam told the American people that President Bush was on the first leg of a nine-day trip to Europe and to visit American troops in the Persian Gulf for Thanksgiving. The video switched to a chart reading 'Center for Defense Information' while Donaldson informed the viewer that the Center's report showed the United States could suffer from 2,000 to 12,000 military deaths if war breaks out in the Persian Gulf.

"Why should they think we are serious?" asked Tom. In his mind, he saw Saddam Hussein sitting with his feet up in Baghdad, watching CNN News. "We tell him what we are doing and then we argue about it in Congress."

"That's right," said Crystal in the kitchen.

"President Bush announced two days ago that we are sending three Army divisions, three aircraft carriers and their task forces, and a second battleship to the Persian Gulf. Hussein has to think Bush is bluffing."

"That's right," said Crystal. She turned and brought a new letter from their son, Mark. There was an APO address in the upper left corner. Tom knew that Mark's ship was somewhere near Saudi Arabia. In his letter, Mark told his parents that they were continuing to train for amphibious landings.

"The death toll in *Operation Desert Shield* is 42. Anyway you put it, 42 boys won't ever hug their mothers again." She turned her back and walked back to the sink.

Tom looked at Crystal. She leaned against the kitchen sink, watching him. He could see the fear in her eyes.

CHAPTER SEVENTEEN
Drawing the Line

It had been a week of events. The administrators welcomed 110 substitute teachers who had crossed the picket lines. Many of them admitted they needed the $105 per day that Iron Lake promised. Two of the replacement teachers said they thought that subbing would help get the strike over.

Two, possibly three hundred teachers were holding a rally in the parking lot north of the Iron Lake High School. 'On Strike' signs and banners calling for a settlement waved and flapped in the cold wind. A few yellow balloons silently took wing, wafting across the trees to the north. A vendor on the outside of the rally was selling helium filled balloons. The streets both east and west from the high school were jammed with parked cars. Today was 'Rally Day' and teachers from a hundred schools had driven to Iron Lake in a show of solidarity with their 'brothers' on the Iron Lake picket line.

The atmosphere in the north parking lot was electric. A leader with a bullhorn would lead a cheer, followed by a general blast of gusto yelling, and then another cheer would erupt. Iron Lake owned the alley that ran for one hundred feet before it emptied into the parking lot. Standing at the terminus of the alley, Robert 'Bluster' Barnes took up the bullhorn and explained how Harley Bellows, the District Court judge in Cherry Grove had ordered the union and the superintendent to draw a line in the alley.

*****

The headlines screamed 'Sheriff increases Deputies in Iron Lake' and 'ILEA Demands a TRO'. The lead article reported the Spencer County Sheriff commenting about threats of violence on the sidewalks in Iron Lake. Sheriff Curt Larson admitted his men were relatively helpless to prevent violence if someone was determined to start a fight with a picketing teacher. His public announcement was intended to assure the citizens of Iron Lake that he was not going to tolerate any troublemakers interfering with a legal strike. The press release announced there would be a sheriff's deputy on station near the high school at all hours of the day.

The second article for the Wednesday before Thanksgiving week described the legal maneuvering by attorneys for the Minnesota Education Association. MEA, on behalf of the Iron Lake Education Association had filed a request for a Temporary Restraining Order, seeking to stop the Iron Lake schools from paying $105 per day to substitute teachers. The request for a TRO would be heard in Judge Harley Bellows court in Cherry Grove. It was an unfortunate coincidence that approximately 200 school districts were not holding school that Friday. Their teachers held Parent-Teacher conferences on Tuesday and Thursday evening and were rewarded with a Friday off.

Most of the state's teachers took Friday as a day to rest, do the last minute yard chores before winter, or to go shopping or to close up their cabins in northern Minnesota. It was Iron Lake's bad luck that 250 teachers decided to bring themselves to a rally in Iron Lake.

When Judge Harley Bellows walked into his courtroom, he was carrying a copy of the Wednesday *Journal-Gazette*...the newspaper with the 'Violence' and 'TRO' stories printed on the front, and the salaries of all the Iron Lake teachers printed in a full page ad placed by the superintendent.

*****

Tom Harant, wearing his favorite blue suit and Arnie Murkiwasser were seated to the left side of the courtroom. 'Bluster' Barnes and Sylvan Plant, accompanied by three attorneys for the MEA were seated to the right side. A few of the striking teachers were sitting in the back, as far away from Judge Bellows as possible. It was a typical courtroom. Light tan maple panels covered the walls. Fluorescent lights lit the room. Four rows of benches stood behind a divider wall. At the head of the room, behind a court clerk and a bailiff, a raised bench stood in front of the American flag. 'His Honor' put the newspaper on his desk and folded it until the page of teacher salaries was exposed. He raised his newspaper and waved it at the people in the courtroom.

Bellows scanned the attorneys to his left and gradually seemed to

IRON LAKE BURNING

concentrate on the two men sitting to his right. Arnie and Tom were wearing three-piece suits, with dark blue ties. Neither man felt especially joyous, having to appear in District Court. Tom's right leg was bouncing in nervous anticipation of the Judge's words. Arnie seemed to be enjoying himself.

"Are you Tom Harant?" the judge demanded.

"Yes, your honor," answered Tom.

"And you are?" he asked, looking at Arnie.

"Murkiwasser. Arnold J. Murkiwasser. Board Chairman."

"Well, good for you, Mr. Muddiwater." The judge stopped to look at the newspaper. "I'll come back to you two…"

He looked to his left, at the attorneys. When he asked who represented the teachers, a middle-aged man with a soft paunch below his vest, stood and responded. When Bellows had determined that the Iron Lake teachers were properly represented, he turned back to Arnie Murkiwasser.

"Uh, uh, what was it? Muddi…?"

"*Mr.* Murkiwasser," said Arnie with defiance.

"You are not a mister in my courtroom, unless I decide you are," the judge declared with a slightly louder tenor. "Is that clear?"

"My name is Murkiwasser, sir."

"So be it. Are you responsible for this ad?"

"The school district paid for the ad," said Arnie, and then added "Your Honor."

"Well, what in the blue blazes possessed you to put such an inflammatory piece of material in the newspaper. Are you deliberately trying to get the teachers, and everybody else, angry with you?"

"We are not, your honor," said Tom jumping into defense of Arnie.

"Well, what then?"

"Many people have asked us to publish what is, after all, public information. The list of salaries is public." Tom didn't want to tell the judge that Step 27 in the Strike Plan called for publishing salaries, to let the citizens see for themselves. Ninety-five percent of the people living in Iron Lake and the surrounding farms were making less than the teachers. Step 27 was deliberately designed to weaken the striker's argument that they were underpaid.

"So, you always do what your citizens ask, Mr. Harant?"

"The strikers are sending newsletters directly to every home in the district. The school board has the same right, your honor."

The judge was silent. He declared a recess and ordered both parties into his chambers.

*****

"He said, 'If you open school, there will be blood on the sidewalk,' your honor."

"Is that true, Mr. Barnes?"

"Not in exactly those words, your honor." Barnes was sitting directly in front of the judge's desk in his private office. The judge had put Tom Harant in the other chair directly in front of his desk. The attorneys and Arnie Murkiwasser and Sylvan Plant had settled for two large couches above which the Judge had hung plaques and pictures of his political friends. His office sported a large wall map of Minnesota, with several stickpins on northern lakes. Venetian blinds were partially closed and protected by voluminous dark green drapes. Judge Bellows pulled his tie down and turned on his desk lamp before proceeding.

"In what words, then?" asked the judge.

"Near as I can remember, 'There will probably be blood,' but you know that I was not predicting the teachers would resort to violence." For the first time since the strike began, 'Bluster' Barnes was looking a little unsure of himself.

"You are sure he said 'If you open', Mr. Harant?"

"Yes, your honor," replied Tom.

"You attorneys want to add anything?" Judge Bellows was leaning into his desk and his face was just above the edge of the light from the desk lamp. From where the attorneys sat, he looked diabolical and sinister. None of the three attorneys reacted, although their feet seemed to have an itch to move toward the door.

The judge went on to tell Robert Barnes and his attorneys that no one was going to have any further comments about the threats of violence. He asked Harant to explain how he came up with $105 per day for paying teachers. Tom explained that if you took the starting teacher wage on a per hour basis and added the Social Security and Teacher's Retirement and cost of fringe benefits the replacement teachers would not get, the total was $106.35. Judge Bellows then told Tom to explain that answer in open court, when they resumed the public hearing.

Tom remarked that the teachers were having a difficult time staying off the parking lot owned by the school district. No one seemed to know where the city's alley ended and the school district property began. Bellows ordered Barnes and Tom Harant to get the City Clerk to show them. For safety reasons, he wanted the teachers to stay off school district property while they were striking.

Back in the courtroom, Judge Bellows told the court that he was satisfied there would be no further comments about violence, by either side in the dispute. He listened to Tom's explanation of how he calculated the daily salary for replacement teachers and denied the MEA-ILEA request for a Temporary Restraining Order. Then he entered an order directing the school superintendent to resolve the "Great Alley Controversy" before the end of the day.

When Arnie stood up and asked the judge what happens if they could not resolve the problem, Judge Bellows laughed, for the first time.

"Why then, Mr. Muddiwater, I get to put you in jail for contempt of court. Is that clear?"

*****

Standing on the sidewalk near the north edge of the high school, Tom looked over the 'circus' in front of him. The parking lot itself was at a lower elevation than the sidewalk. There were 250 teachers circled around 'Bluster' Barnes who was talking to them with a bullhorn. Something he said produced a cheer and the balloon vendor released three-dozen balloons. Tom could hear Barnes saying that the balloons represent hopes of the community for a quick settlement of the strike.

"Quick settlement, my foot!" said Arnie. He reached up with both hands and pulled down on his coat lapels.

"Trying to look taller, maybe?" Tom asked himself. He was struggling to figure what motivated a man like Arnie Murkiwasser. Arnie seemed to enjoy the celebrity of his position. He didn't look like he was ready to wade into the large crowd in the parking lot.

"I'll leave it up to you."

"To decide where the end of the alley is?"

"Yes." Both men were looking to their left where Tom's secretary Judy was walking down the sidewalk, obviously with a message. She was holding a pink message slip in her hand, the winds of November ruffling her skirt. In Tom's estimation, Judy was an efficient secretary and the height of discretion. Her brown hair was waving past her face while she tried to hold her hair with her hand.

"Two messages," she said, handing the message slip to Tom.

"And they are?"

"Someone called from the Strike Headquarters, downtown. They saw His Honor the Mayor leaving town on his motorcycle. He heard you wanted help from the city and he ducked out."

"That's typical of him. He's my cousin," added Arnie. "Never had a lick of sense or an ounce of courage." Tom laughed and hit Arnie on the shoulder. In Tom's mind, he was congratulating Arnie on his characterization of the 'gutless wonder' of Iron Lake.

"And I called the City Clerk," said Judy. After pausing to catch her breath, she told Tom that the City Clerk was on vacation.

"How convenient," said Arnie with obvious distaste.

"But the City Attorney is the person you want."

"And?" said Tom quietly, beginning to suspect that he was going to have to decide where the alley ended without any help from his neighbor, the City Attorney.

"Jerry Mohler says the plat maps do not show an alley. He can't help."

"I'm not surprised," noted Tom.

"That's OK," added Arnie. "Mr. Harant, here, is…uh? Going to solve the problem. Someone has to tell those strikers where they can stand and picket when cars try to enter the parking lot."

Arnie patted Tom on the arm. "Right, Tom?"

Tom looked back at the 250 teachers. Still more people were arriving from the side streets. Two men unfurled a big banner on poles. It read, 'No Scabs! Negotiate!'

Judy turned to walk back to her office when Tom thanked her. Arnie as quickly, turned, leaving Tom to deal with 'Bluster Barnes.' From the east, Tom heard the 'ruff-ruff-ruff' of an approaching helicopter. He looked up and saw the WCCO Skycam helicopter passing overhead, descending toward the Elementary school playground.

"Well, what the hell?" He started walking slowly toward the crowd and 'Bluster Barnes'. *'Another media event, another soundbite. What else can happen today, I wonder?'*

IRON LAKE BURNING

He stopped at the edge of the crowd. Barnes saw Tom was not moving and shouted 'make a hole' to the crowd. The mass parted, allowing Moses the school superintendent to sedately walk into the 'recorded and videotaped' history of the Iron Lake strike.

*****

"Your people are on school property," Tom yelled at 'Bluster' Barnes over the roar of the crowd. Half the crowd was yelling 'No scabs' and waiting while the western half shouted 'Settle now!'

"They are parents and teachers from all over the state," shouted Barnes.

"Yeah, I guess," said Tom.

"They support our efforts to get a fair settlement."

"Bullshit," said Tom, looking Barnes in the eye.

"Isn't this fun?" shouted Barnes. He was laughing at the big man, at Tom's discomfort. "Do you always swear when you don't like something I say?"

"I can see your point but I still think you're full of it! This is all bull-own-nay!" said Tom loudly, waving his right arm in a circle, indicating the parking lot and the protesting teachers with their 'Local 157 Supports ILEA' and 'Urholt Teachers Say Settle'.

"What do you mean?" asked Barnes.

"A lot of *sturm und drang*," said Tom. "You know, 'fire and thunder, signifying nothing' and getting us nowhere, no how, no contract." From his left, on the hill toward the sidewalk, Tom could see the video crew from WCCO Channel Four was filming the crowd.

"Your audience is here," added Tom.

"Isn't this fun?"

"If you think so?" added Tom. "Hell, this is a riot. I must be having fun." He had jammed his hands into his trouser pockets, but didn't allow for the age of the suit. Tom's dark blue three-piece once belonged to his father-in-law who gave his used suits to Tom. When Tom looked down, he realized the pants leg had split from just under the pocket nearly to the knee. Tom, unfortunately, was wearing briefs instead of jockey shorts. To an observer, it might have looked like Tom was wearing no underwear.

"Two grown men," said Barnes. "Here we are, two grown men."

"Hey," laughed Tom. "This isn't the first time. You drew a line when you said you wouldn't come in for less than $5200 per teacher."

"We won't," answered 'Bluster' to the satisfaction of those teachers standing around him who could hear what he said.

"OK, so you and I have to decide where the city property ends. You don't have to put pickets in this alley, you know."

"Oh, ah…ha! Ha, ha!" said Barnes, not really laughing. "We don't have to be nice to *your* scabs, do we?"

"We are hiring licensed teachers," replied Tom quickly, which raised a chorus of disgruntled 'boo's' from those standing nearby. Tom could see the TV camera working its way from the back of the crowd.

Just as the camera arrived, Tom took the bullhorn and thanked the protestors for coming to Iron Lake. He then told the crowd that Judge Bellows had ordered him to settle the 'Great Alley Dispute.' Tom started laughing, wondering how this situation became so ludicrous.

He continued to laugh. Some of the teachers around him began to laugh. Their laughter was spontaneous. The TV crew was recording it. 'Bluster Barnes' took Tom by the arm and pulled him up the alley for fifty feet.

"Is this a good spot?" said Barnes, trying to keep a smirk off his face.

"Guess so," said Tom.

Barnes took his shoe and made a mark in the dirt. Tom used the side of his black dress shoe to draw a longer line. Someone handed Barnes a small stick and he pushed it into the ground and tied a small rag. Taking the bullhorn back from Tom, Barnes announced that the picketers could go no further south in the alley.

A general round of 'boo's' greeted Barnes' announcement. The western end of the crowd took up the 'No Scabs' chant and the eastern end, near Tom and 'Bluster' took up the 'Settle Now' chant.

"Goes to prove," said 'Bluster' Barnes.

"Prove what?" shouted Tom.

"That I can't always be the hero," answered 'Bluster'.

"We're just human, doing what we can," said Tom. When Barnes held his hand out, Tom took it and shook it. There was a small cheer from the people around Tom. He now had his left hand by his side, holding the cloth of his trousers together. As he passed through the crowd, the reporter for WCCO Channel Four pulled Tom to one side to ask if this action represented a new stage in the strike.

Tom laughed. He shook his head from left to right. "The spokesperson for the board is Mr. Arnie Murkiwasser. You know that, I believe." Tom walked away, holding his trousers together. *'I can't believe that. I told Barnes he was full of it, and he didn't react. No matter what anyone says...I did not give up an inch to Mr. Barnes.'*

CHAPTER EIGHTEEN
To Love Controversy

When Tom Harant turned the corner, he saw cars and people and flashing red lights and yellow windbreakers. Lights were reflecting off an early snow that left three inches of new white crystals on the grass. The sidewalks were wet where the snow had melted. 'Yes,' he said to himself. 'It was a good idea to walk up to school.' The area was jammed with parked cars in all directions.

On the south end of Ninth Street, an Iron Lake police car blocked the street. Two blocks north, a second police cruiser blocked the street, with its red light flashing. Up on the north end, two sheriff's cars were parked to the side, conspicuous by their presence. On the sidewalk in front of the high school, at least twenty strikers were carrying signs that read 'Iron Lake Refused to Meet'. In the street, directly in front of the strikers, four sheriff's deputies and four local policemen were drawn up in a makeshift line, parallel to the strikers. Across the street, a blur of yellow windbreakers were waving signs that said 'Meet Now' and 'Take the Offer'. Approximately twenty pickup trucks, many with men in yellow windbreakers, were parked across the street.

There was a shock to Tom's normally quiet attitude toward what happened at school. From half a block away Tom realized that the men in yellow windbreakers were yelling and swearing at the striking teachers on the other side of the street. The men seemed to be angry, vociferous and agitated, Tom thought. One particularly large man, carrying a sign that said 'No Interference' on one side and 'Let them Play' on the other, walked out to the middle of the street and paraded past the strikers. From Tom's perspective, the man looked to be six feet with an additional six inches. 'Large enough to take on anybody,' thought Tom.

A sheriff's deputy walked out to the man and took him by the arm and turned him toward his side of the street. When the man resisted, the deputy spoke to him. Both men separated and returned to their respective sides of the street.

Tom reached the middle of the line of deputies in time to hear the deputy say something like, 'I could arrest him for drunk and disorderly. Wouldn't be the first time, not for him'.

"That's Noah Fynmore's cousin, isn't it?" asked a deputy.

"That's him," said another. "Six peas short of a salad, if you ask me."

The crowd behind the 'Yellow' line seemed to be enormous. It was hard to tell in the early evening darkness of early December. The streetlights and police lights seemed to be lighting the center of the street. Away from the sidewalks, it was difficult to see how many people were standing behind the 'Yellow' jacket line of farmers and fathers. Tom estimated that perhaps three hundred people were stretched along that side of the sidewalk.

Behind the striking teachers, there were only a few persons standing on school property. When Tom turned to go into the school, a striking teacher said 'How long, Mr. Harant, you going to let this go on?'

Tom said nothing, looking to the north where a school bus was turning the corner to come south. There was a sheriff's car with a flashing red light in front of the bus. In front of the sheriff's car a large group of students and parents were unfurling a twelve-foot banner that read 'Iron Lake Welcomes Cherry Grove.' The student group was forming into a parade, with the deputy's car and the bus behind them.

Inside the high school, Tom found Billy Washburn and the replacement Physical Education teacher, Gordon James. Mr. James, from Texas, would be coaching the Boy's Basketball Team, if the players showed up for the game.

"We have four basketball games and one wrestling match with Cherry Grove in the next month," said Billy Washburn quietly. He was referring to the Spencer County Trophy. Iron Lake had lost their football game with Cherry Grove and forfeited two volleyball games in October. Iron Lake was 'Down Three' but the two basketball teams swore they were going to win the trophy.

"Trophy is in my office," added Tom, "in case you want to show the boys what they are playing for."

"No thanks, Tom."

Tom Harant stood there, looking through the glass of the front doors on the high school. Outside, he could see students running to join the crowd in front of the bus. The sheriff's car left room for the bus to stop even with the front doors. Between the bus and Tom stood six striking teachers, each holding a sign. It did not look like they intended to move aside for the Cherry Grove students.

*****

At 8:30 a.m., an anonymous voice on the phone told Tom Harant that there would be violence before tonight's basketball game. When Tom asked from whom, the man hung up.

At 8:45 a.m., one of 'Tom's' teachers called to tell him he had heard rumors that a large group of farmers was going to meet at the 'Red Carpet' at about 3:00 o'clock. They were angry and looking for a way to get the teachers to agree to a settlement of the strike. Tom promised to report the rumor without divulging the name of the teacher who called.

At 8:50 a.m., Robert 'Bluster' Barnes called to inform Tom that he had heard the farmer's group was going to meet. A 'reliable person' had told him, that the farmers were bringing their baseball bats.

At 9:05 a.m., Tom received the call he was half expecting to receive. Harry Hagen, the superintendent at Cherry Grove, called to report his coach had heard rumors about violence in Iron Lake. Apparently, some farmers were going to keep the teachers from blocking the sidewalk. Tom assured Mr. Hagen that there would be no interference; the students and people from Cherry Grove had no reason to worry.

At 9:15 a.m., after considering his options, Tom was about to call the County Sheriff when Judy buzzed his phone and told him the Sheriff was on line two.

Sheriff Curt Larson told Tom that he had talked to Mr. Robert Barnes this morning. The teachers were not going to block the sidewalk. The teachers would stand by quietly while the students entered the high school.

Tom told the Sheriff the rumor about the baseball bats and the Sheriff said he would have extra deputies in the area, as a presence to forestall trouble.

At 9:25 a.m., Arnie Murkiwasser called. Someone had left a message on his answering machine this morning while he was in the shower. The message was 'We are going to make sure those damn teachers don't interfere with tonight's game'. Tom told Arnie about their preparations for the game.

At 10:30 a.m., Holly Johnson, the Cheerleading Captain, called to ask if it was okay for a group of students to meet the bus when it arrived in Iron Lake. Tom told her it would be a good idea, but to be careful. When he asked where she was calling from, she told him she was using the phone outside the High School Office. Tom thanked her for being in school.

At 11:15 a.m., the high school principal, Mr. Billy Washburn, came in to report that three students had complained about the Social Studies teacher in Room 214. He was drinking between classes and had a bottle of whiskey in his desk.

Tom told Billy to call for a new replacement. If they could get a teacher during the day, they would both go up and confront the man today.

At 11:41 a.m., a lady calling herself *Mrs.* Gordon James called from Texas. She asked if her husband was teaching at Iron Lake. When Tom's secretary refused to answer the question, Tom took the call and discovered she was trying to find out where he was. Apparently, members of the teacher's union had called her in Texas to ask her to dissuade her husband from working as a 'scab' at Iron Lake.

Tom asked how they got her phone number. She said the first person that called her admitted they got her address and phone number from the Department of Motor Vehicles in Texas. Tom reported her husband was working and would be coaching the basketball team. She asked Tom to tell her husband to call home.

Tom wondered, 'Does that mean she will try to talk her husband into quitting, or will she support him?'

At 12:20 p.m., Billy Washburn reported they had a replacement teacher lined up for Room 214. Tom and Billy walked upstairs and into the classroom. Tom walked over to the man's desk. The room was empty. Fifth hour would not start for another twenty minutes. Tom leaned into the man and smelled his breath.

"Have you been drinking today?"

"Yes, sir."

"How much?"

"Don't know. But I sure do enjoy it."

"In a classroom?" asked Billy Washburn, with disbelief in his eyes.

"But I don't take a drink in front of my students."

"In a classroom?" asked Billy a second time.

Tom and Billy were silent. Tom looked around the classroom. To Tom's eye, the man had done nothing or very little to make the room more attractive. The Iron Lake teachers had stripped their rooms the last day they worked.

"Do you have a bottle in your desk?"

The man opened the bottom drawer on the left side of his desk, nearly hitting Tom's leg with the drawer. He pulled out a bottle of Canadian Club in which two inches of whiskey remained.

"Do you have anything to say for yourself?"

"Never in front of my students."

"They aren't your students. No longer."

Billy Washburn was standing to Tom's left, watching the man. He and Tom didn't know how the man would react. He was a licensed teacher who taught last year in Wisconsin, unemployed until he showed up at Iron Lake. The man ran his hand through his red hair and then scratched under his chin. "You mean I'm fired, don't you?"

"Pick up your stuff, right now." Tom waited while the man collected his personal items and then gave Tom his key to the building. Tom walked him out of the building. Billy Washburn went down to his office, to prep the replacement teacher who would be the 'new' replacement teacher in Room 214.

*****

The day that Iron Lake opened school with replacement teachers, Tom was standing on the sidewalk, watching the buses arrive. Tom and Barnes had agreed that all the buses would stop at the center doors and all the children would exit their buses and go straight into the school building. The striking teachers would leave the sidewalk empty where the children had to cross the picket line.

A man in a yellow windbreaker walked up to Tom and thanked him for having school 'Six weeks was about five weeks too long with no school', the man said to Tom. Tom didn't respond. The man added he had eight children and only the school could keep eight children occupied. He smiled and gave Tom a friendly pat on the shoulder.

The little boy with the big brown eyes got off his bus and seeing Tom said, "Hey, there, Mr. Helper Man."

Tom smiled at the boy. The boy smiled back while shifting his backpack. "You see my shoes? Tied 'em myself."

Tom bent over to get to the boy's level. He patted the boy on the arm and said, "You should be proud of yourself. That's important, to tie your shoes." The boy looked at him, smiled and began to walk toward the elementary wing. Out of the corner of his eye, Tom saw the Channel Four cameraman had his camera trained on Tom and the boy. Tom waved a hand, telling the cameraman to get off the little boy.

When the reporter with a microphone walked up to him, Tom put his hand over the microphone and said, "Cameras will not be allowed on school property, for any reason."

"And that means inside the school?"

"Especially inside the school. Cameras are a disruptive influence. I don't want our students 'performing' for your cameras. They have serious work to do."

"Is this a policy?"

"Always has been, with me. Even more so, now. No cameras inside the buildings." Tom was not about to tell this nosy reporter with the cute eyes and the business woman's suit that the policy was Item 7 in the Strike Plan.

She smiled up at Tom. Tom looked at her, then away, scanning the street, watching a bus pull up to the center door. "But you can't stop us from taking pictures of the kids on the playground, right?"

"Stay off the playground. You can shoot from the sidewalk."

"My boss is not going to like this," she said. She turned with a shrug toward her cameraman.

"Off the playground or I *will* have you arrested," added Tom with emphasis on the 'will'.

He was watching her walk away, her hips sashaying slightly. Her cameraman was ahead of her, walking toward their van. She stopped in her tracks and turned toward Tom.

"I don't know if you meant that. I would be careful if I were you. The Press has First Amendment rights and I will discuss this policy with our attorney."

"Go ahead," said Tom trying to smile. In times of stress, Tom found it was very difficult to do anything more than stand with a blank face, with no emotion. He knew that in Minnesota, the school administration had the right to bar any person from the school if that person was likely to cause a disruption to the educational process. The Minnesota Education Association had charged in recent press releases that the children in Iron Lake would not be receiving a real education. Tom, following the Strike Plan, knew all about Sensationalism. Tom had taught journalism in Prescott, Arizona and Fairmont, Minnesota and was extremely familiar with the old rule, 'Don't get caught in a stinking contest with a skunk, the skunk will win.' He knew the reporter had to find something unusual to report on. If all they could shoot was children playing, there might not be a story.

"While you're at it, ask him if I can stop your helicopter from landing on the south athletic field. That happens to be school property, also."

*****

'That's the way it will be,' thought Tom after the reporter left. There is a certain risk to following the Strike Plan. In the end any of the 'policy decisions' could be detrimental and could backfire.

In the past six weeks, many of Tom's decisions were debated and argued downtown. The coffee table quarterbacks in the Reliable Drug store debated every issue. Unofficial word was they agreed with the superintendent's decisions.

The strikers did not like the idea of paying 'scabs' $105 per day when the normal substitute rate was $65 per day. Judge Harley Bellows, however, had refused to issue a Temporary Restraining Order. Tom had designated which doors the 'new' employees could enter and exit from, in an attempt to control the union's access to those teachers. The north parking lot had pickets at the entry point and Tom heard the replacement teachers were having no difficulty driving across the picket line.

Tom's administrative team, comprised of the three principals and Arley Green, the former superintendent, had decided there would be two weeks of conditioning before their boys and girls resumed competition. This decision raised a stink around Iron Lake. Some people could see the point, others wanted the teams to go right back into competition. The two basketball teams forfeited four games each during those two weeks. The wrestling team forfeited two matches. The hockey team was practicing under the supervision of two parents while Billy Washburn tried to find a licensed coach.

Hockey became another controversy. Tom's administrative team was divided: Billy and Dennis wanted the team to resume competition with any parent who wanted to be a coach. Karen and Arley Green were opposed. Tom decided to err on the side of safety. He broke the deadlock by deciding that if there was no licensed coach, the hockey team would continue to practice but no games would be held.

There was a point in the weeks after the board's decision to open school when Tom felt just like the 'nutso' Air Force General in *Dr. Strangelove*. Tom would be sitting at a table, listening to other people talk, and he would see an image of the general expounding on how the Commies were poisoning our drinking water with fluoride, how the preservatives in our foods were sapping the strength out of the common soldier. Tom sensed his 'school' was surrounded by enemies and the Commies might attack at any moment.

"We bring the kids in, they are in the building all day, and then we let them out. We have the doors locked to keep adults (and troublemakers) and television cameras out of the building. Is there anything we are not doing to protect our children?"

The question found no answers. There was no response from the principals or the one board member who was observing the meeting.

"This is all about *How I Learned to Stop Worrying and to Love Controversy,* isn't it?" he asked the three principals.

"What do you mean?" asked Dennis DeFain, with his voice challenging Tom's statement.

"The other title of *Dr. Strangelove*, the movie," said Tom. He could see that they did not understand.

"What is that title?" asked Karen, the Elementary Principal.

"How I Learned to Stop Worrying and Love the Bomb," said Tom. For one fleeting moment Tom thought about explaining *Dr. Strangelove* and how the movie drew a vicious picture of 'generals' who thought a massive attack with nuclear tipped missiles would catch the 'Russkies' with their pants down. Then he considered explaining how he felt, after nine weeks of crossing the picket line to go to work. He chose a shorter statement.

"There is no other way to say it. When you are under siege, you begin to think about escape. I have learned to love controversy."

*****

That Friday afternoon, the day of the 'big' game with Cherry Grove, a detective from the Spencer County Sheriff's Office walked into Tom's office and flashed his badge. He introduced himself as Sam Johnson and told Tom he was there because of some irregular questions about the death of George Fallow. He was wearing a dark blue suit with a nondescript blue tie, and he looked, *to Tom*, to be the image of authority and the law in Spencer County. The man had a plain face, and months afterward, when Tom tried to picture the man, he couldn't.

Sam Johnson sat down in the black leatherette chair in front of Tom's desk. After he was comfortable, he pulled a small notebook from the inside of his suit jacket and flipped it open. Tom had a strange thought, 'just like a reporter' but let the thought pass.

Johnson began by explaining that his questions were routine.

"You said they were 'irregular' if I remember correctly."

"Well, let's say unusual, shall we?"

"I guess," answered Tom.

"The house that burned. Did you know that Conifer Cratt was renting that house?"

"Yes, I did. He told me."

"Did you ever see him go into or out of the house?"

"No, I never did. I saw his truck parked in back, several times."

"Did he use the house?"

"I saw lights on the ground floor. Assumed it was him."

"Did you ever see anyone else enter or leave the house?"

"Can't say that I did."

"You weren't watching?"

"Why would I be watching?"

"There is a rumor that some members of your board of directors met several times in Cratt's rented house, 'across the street' I was told by an anonymous caller."

"I couldn't see the side of the house that showed the backyard from my office windows, from this point of view, you understand."

Mr. Johnson stood up and looked out the nearest window. "Oh, I see." He looked at his notebook for a moment.

"So, you wouldn't know if Mr. Cratt and Mrs. Fallow met in that house, would you?"

Tom was stunned. He thought this detective was asking about the school board using Cratt's house, which Tom thought was very unlikely. Cratt had more than once reminded the board that four members constituted a quorum and they must be careful not to be seen together.

"As I said, I didn't see anyone go in or out of that house. Have you asked some of the striking teachers?"

"They told me they pull their pickets off the 'line' as they call it at 5:30 p.m. in the afternoon."

"I see," said Tom. He was, however, not clear on the question about Mrs. Fallow. "Do these questions have anything to do with our strike?"

"Ah, actually...no." Sam Johnson looked at Tom and paused to frame an answer. He stood up and put his notebook away. Johnson reached for Tom's hand and they shook.

"Thank you for your time. As I said, routine questions. An insurance company raised a question about a claim that Mr. Cratt filed. Seems he had a manuscript he was writing in that house and had it insured for $135,000. His claim wouldn't raise eyebrows except that the insurance agent was Mrs. Glacinda Fallow."

With that, Sam Johnson turned and left Tom's office.

*****

When the school bus stopped in front of Iron Lake High School, a large cheer went up from the students who were gathered in front of the bus. They began to form a double line of students, making an alleyway for the Cherry Grove Boy's Basketball Team.

The first person off the bus proved to be Harry Hagen, the Cherry Grove superintendent. He walked directly at the six teachers lined up on the sidewalk and stopped in front of them. The six strikers split into two groups and left the sidewalk empty. Harry Hagen walked into the school, looked around, and then turned to look out at the scene outside. The student 'alley' was festooned with inflated balloons and small signs of 'Welcome' and 'Iron Lake Says Hi!'

Harry Hagen went back outside to the school bus and said something into the bus. Cherry Grove athletes, dressed in white shirts and ties under their Blue and Gold letter jackets, began to exit from the bus. Spontaneous applause broke out from the students and from across the street, many parents were cheering. Hagen walked back into the building with the athletes. Stopping in front of Tom, he said,

"Good luck, tonight."

"And just what did you say to the teachers out there on the sidewalk?" asked Tom, curiously. He barely heard Harry Hagen's 'Good luck, tonight.' Tom was still watching the parents and farmers and 'yellow-jackets' across the street.

"What I said was, 'You have made your point'. The short one in the middle, wearing the rug on his head…"

"Ha," snorted Tom. "That's Sylvan Plant. What'd he say?"

"Something like, I guess so."

"Well, good for him. They probably realize those men across the street are waiting for an incident."

"Thanks for the reception, Tom. And good luck, tonight."

In the end, luck swung the tide. Down by two points at 54-52, the Iron Lake guard swatted the ball away from a Cherry Grove player, moved the ball down the court and cut hard left through two defenders to make a lay up. The ball dropped and he was fouled in the process. With 23 seconds left on the clock, he made the free throw putting Iron Lake ahead at 54-55. Cherry Grove took time out, came back from the break and stalled, trying for the winner when the clock ran down. Their hottest shooting guard got the ball deep in the right corner, took his shot over the hands of a defender, and hit the rim. The ball bounced outward and was recovered by a Cherry Grove player, who began to flex his arms, preparing to shoot. The buzzer went off before he could shoot and he stopped, holding the ball.

To a man, the Iron Lake players and cheerleaders lined up to thank the Cherry Grove athletes for their courageous appearance on the Iron Lake floor. To some of the parents in the bleachers, it looked like the Cherry Grove players were laughing and saying, 'Next time it's our floor'.

CHAPTER NINETEEN
Crossing the Line

Standing in his kitchen, Tom Harant stared out the picture window in his kitchen, mesmerized by the split birch tree in his back yard. The three trunks of the tree slashed skyward, each bending away from its neighbor. For some reason, the early fall snows had failed to dislodge the yellow leaves, leaving three white slashes surrounded by yellow, standing against the dull gray of his neighbor's ash and elm trees, gray slashes in the background. Last week's snow melted over two days, leaving a wet, soggy yard between the house and the flower garden. To Tom, the yard looked like any other yard in winter, a pile of dirt where the flower garden had been and wet grass turning brown.

Behind him, the teakettle screeched. Tom turned away from the window, pondering the split birch and the struggle between the Iron Lake teachers and their board of education. *'The teachers, the board and the students, each pulling in three directions'* said Tom under his breath. He walked over to the stove and lifted the teakettle, pouring water into a waiting cup. When he returned to the picture window, he could see a bluebird sitting among the yellow leaves of the split birch.

"Better head south," he intoned quietly in the direction of the bird. "It gets brutal in this country," he added out loud.

Tom put the coffee cup with its teabag and hot water on the kitchen table. He stared at the teabag for a minute, then back at the split birch. The bluebird was gone, vanished. *'That's good,'* thought Tom as he picked up the teabag and a spoon. He put the teabag onto the spoon and wrapped the string around the spoon. When he pulled the string tight, he squeezed the extra water out of the bag into the cup. *'It's always good to pay attention to the details,'* said Tom to himself.

He thought about the bluebird and wondered if it could reach warmer climates before winter became bitter. Tom lifted the cup and blew across the surface of the tea, sending a small cloud of steam toward the cold, damp surface of the picture window. He carefully took a sip, burning the surface of his lower lip. With his other hand, he reached out to the picture window and tried to wipe away the small circle of steam. A bird flashed into the split birch, landing on almost the same branch. It was the bluebird.

'Well, perhaps not,' thought Tom. 'Even the bluebird has the right to be ignorant of the weather in Minnesota.'

*****

"What is this, the ninth week?" asked Crystal when she came into the kitchen. She was wearing a pair of light tan slacks with a dark blue blazer. A corsage of red and white plastic flowers was attached to her blazer, over her heart. She was pulling a hairbrush through her hair while she removed a cup from the cupboard.

"It's Tuesday, start of the ninth week," said Tom, and put his cup down on the table. He walked over to the cupboard to the right of the sink and grabbed the instant coffee. He pulled a spoon from the dish drain and proceeded to dump a heaping teaspoon of instant coffee into Crystal's cup. She put the cup down on the counter and Tom poured hot water into the cup.

Crystal took the spoon from his hand and stirred her coffee. She put her hairbrush on the counter and picked up the cup of coffee.

"Are you okay?" she asked.

"Hope so," he answered.

Crystal stood there, looking at her husband in his three-piece blue suit. He looked like a comfortable administrator but she knew the strike was eating at his stomach. For the past three nights, he had barely slept. Tom slipped out of bed in the dead of night and spent hours at the kitchen table or in the breezeway, smoking cigarettes and sipping a cola. When she asked him how he slept, he lied each morning. He had taken to hitting the shower before she got up, presumably to wake up and look alert when she headed for her morning shower.

When Tom said, *'Hope so'* he felt like he was ready for another day, but he wasn't exactly sure of himself. Lately, he had taken to writing long notes in his notebook at school, trying to explain what happened.

"You sound as if you are blaming yourself," said Crystal.

"I am, I guess."

"For what? You said yourself that the strike was inevitable," she said.

"No one could have stopped either party from their 'headlong rush' as you described it to Wrecker, just after the strike began."

"I feel...ah, just like...uh, yes. It's getting out of control." He said this while he turned his back on Crystal and walked back to his cup of tea on the table. Looking at the split birch, he saw the bluebird was gone. He lifted his tea and took a long sip, enjoying the sharp taste of the Oolong Green tea. He put the cup down and walked to the coat rack near the door. Lifting his tan raincoat, he added,

"Three of our teachers want to cross the picket line, today. I tried to talk them out of it. They need our medical insurance and they can't go any longer without it."

"And you're worried *for them,* I suppose?"

Two of the teachers were married to each other. They had a daughter who required a medical aide for part of her day, to drain her lungs and administer her medications. These teachers could not afford to go any longer without medical insurance. The third teacher was openly opposed to the strike and was known to be swearing at the leadership at every union meeting. To add to the pressure, 'Bluster' Barnes had called Tom on Monday to inform him that any 'scabs' that crossed the line would face retaliation when the strike was over.

*****

"Knee-ice day, isn't it?" said Tom when he approached Joan Kneiss on the sidewalk.

She grunted, which was for her, a snort of derision. Mrs. Kneiss was head of the English Department, a twenty-year veteran of the Iron Lake schools. Her husband taught History at the Community College in Cherry Grove and their son was enrolled in 'Pre-law' at William Mitchell College of Law in St. Paul. In those twenty years of teaching, she believed she had heard every possible variation of the jokes about 'Kneiss Granite' and 'Nice Day' and even 'Nice Lay' from some of the men.

Joan Kneiss was not the kind of person to make jokes with because she saw every contact with an administrator as a possible confrontation and challenge to her role as the head of the 'Most Important' department, the group of teachers who taught reading and writing to the ignorant children of the farmers and immigrants in and around Iron Lake. Her grunt was a snort of derision, laughing at Tom's twist of the word 'Knee-ice' and his general manner.

"Mr. Harant," she began, "this is neither the place nor the time for you to be making jokes. Too many days out here. We were happy to be leading the state when we came out in October. But now I'm in no mood to be trading barbs with my superintendent."

"Some of the regulars on this picket line haven't been here in a while."

"It's not what you think, Mr. Harant. They are teaching." She smiled when she said this, thinking the dumb superintendent had not heard how the Iron Lake teachers had opened two schools for their own kids and any other children who didn't want to cross the picket line.

"I know about the schools," Tom said. "I was about to ask about your daughter, the one who is a senior."

"Jennifer. We transferred her to Cherry Grove. Gerald drives her to school on his way to work. It's working well. She doesn't like it but at least she is not attending *your excuse* for a school."

"Our teachers are licensed. They wanted to work."

"Big deal," said Joan, in a flat tone.

Tom was about to say something when Joan Kneiss whirled and walked away, toward the line of demarcation behind the sidewalk. A snow fence had been put up to separate 'Striker's Land' from the parking lot the replacement teachers were using. She walked up to the fence and stopped. Joan watched while four lady teachers got out of a brown Chevy, intent on entering the high school by the parking lot door. Suddenly she began screaming, 'You're taking my job; you're taking my job! Do you have a conscience?'

The teachers looked at her briefly, walked to the north door and disappeared into Iron Lake High School. Joan continued to stand by the fence, holding onto a slat of the fence in each hand. The other three teachers on the sidewalk were watching but none were moving to join her. Tom walked over to stand next to her. She looked at her boss and asked why the strike had to happen.

Tom told her he didn't know. They stood there watching another two cars crossing the picket line on the north edge of the parking lot.

Across the parking lot to the west, a solid elm tree rose to a height of fifty feet. The tree's owner thought it was at least 100 years old. Among the highest branches, a crow cackled and laughed…two times, then three.

'Laughing at me, isn't he?' said Tom to himself.

*****

In the Persian Gulf, troops of several nations continued to build base camps in Saudi Arabia. President Bush pushed for a meeting between U.S. Secretary of State Baker and the Iraqi Foreign Secretary, Hafiz Aziz. President Saddam Hussein rejected several dates late in December and was immediately accused of stalling to delay the talks.

On the 27th of November, several Kuwaiti refugees testified before the UN Security Council that Iraqi troops had raped and pillaged their country. Two days later, the UN Security Council voted 12-2 to authorize the use of military force to shove the Iraqi Army out of Kuwait.

Australia and Turkey decided to send troops to Saudi Arabia to help the coalition effort. Twenty-three Americans classified as 'hostages' were flown out of Baghdad on a chartered jet.

Lt.(jg) Mark Harant wrote home, telling his parents about the Thanksgiving dinner they were served aboard the *USS George Philip*, a guided missile frigate. The turkey and yams were great and they had pumpkin pie with real ice cream. He couldn't get over how the Marines loved ice cream.

Mark also reported that the Marines were upbeat and his ship would be providing cover for the amphibious landing ship, *USS Iwo Jima*. He couldn't tell his parents much about *Operation Camel Sand*, due to security. He had, however, been granted permission to explain that he would be in charge of a landing craft ferrying Marines to the beach. This next exercise would be held less than 25 miles from the Kuwait-Saudi border.

Tom laughed, and then chuckled. When Crystal looked at him, he explained that a so-called 'expert' on CNN had opined that the amphibious training was a ruse, to fool the Iraqis into believing the Americans would attack Kuwait from the sea.

To which she replied, "Can't those damn experts keep their mouths shut? Or don't they realize that the Middle East watches CNN News?"

CHAPTER TWENTY
Hand of a Friend

Standing in the hall outside the main gymnasium, Tom was nervous. He could see there were 600 to 700 people in the west bleachers. The new bleachers, installed after the 1977 fire, were designed to hold 1100 people. Tom could see the seats were at least half full, if not three quarters full. In front of the bleachers, stood two long tables covered with a white tablecloth. A set of seven chairs stood behind the tables. A podium with a microphone stood beyond the table; a second microphone stood on a stand in front of the crowd.

The Iron Lake Board of Education was about to hold a regular board meeting. They had been warned to expect an enormous crowd. From the top of the stairs that led down to the gymnasium, Tom could see the six members of the board lining up. The two women entered first, taking the first two chairs. The four men, with Cratt and Murkiwasser coming last, took the next four chairs. Murkiwasser left the last chair for Tom Harant, their superintendent of schools.

'Is this what Hell feels like?' thought Tom to himself. He floated down the stairs and did not touch the railing. Outside the door to the gymnasium, he stopped floating and stood still. Looking down he saw his friend Wrecker and the local doctor, Kenworth Clark, looking up at him. Wrecker said something. The words garbled and mashed and broke upon his head, crashing with the impact of a car hitting an embankment, shooting upward into the night then crashing down onto the train tracks north of town. Ken Clark said something and reached up to pat Tom on the shoulder. Tom saw his mouth move, but heard no words.

He was sitting at the board table, in front of 700 people. He did not remember walking over, nor sitting down. Some of the parents were shouting at Arnie. The board chair was gesturing, pointing at the microphone in front of the bleachers. Tom couldn't understand what he was saying. Murkiwasser sat down and rapped the table with his gavel. Tom saw the scene from a distance, from behind the line of seven people sitting at the two tables in front of the bleachers. He was sitting in the east bleachers, the only person sitting on this side of the gymnasium. He could see the top of the head of the man in the dark blue three-piece suit. His hair was thinning at the crown. What he saw was neither good nor bad, seeing that man sitting in the chair next to Murkiwasser. It was himself, he knew. He felt nothing watching himself.

His stomach churned. He looked down and saw his left hand was wrapped around his right wrist. He was turning his wrist inside his left hand. Looking up at the board table, he could see the board was going through the 'Consent Agenda' items. The board minutes were approved quickly, as were the bills. The chair, Mr. Murkiwasser turned to the man on the end of the table and said something. Tom could see his lips moving. Tom could see Connie Cratt's white hat on the table. At the other end, Patty Trivic had her notebook open and was writing. Arnie reached out and grabbed Tom's arm above the elbow. It hurt,

"…any other important additions?" he heard Arnie Murkiwasser say. Tom shook his head side to side, and then said "No" leaning toward the microphone. Arnie then announced an 'Open Microphone'. Several parents got up and urged the Board to return to the negotiating table. After a long, emotional tirade by one parent, Connie Cratt stood up and walked to the podium. Standing as straight as he could with his bulging stomach, Cratt proceeded to explain that the board wanted to meet, but the mediator kept refusing, saying the teachers were not agreeing to change their last position.

Tom could see these people talking. But the words were beyond him. He saw Cratt turn toward Arnie and make a gesture that said, 'See, I told you. You can't reason with these people.' When Cratt abandoned the podium, a large man in a flannel shirt walked down four steps and picked up the microphone. He walked back up four steps and turned toward the board.

"Can't do this, can't do that. When are you people going to do something about the teacher in Iron Lake Elementary who is obviously pregnant? She is sitting right there!" With these words he pointed at a teacher who had a raincoat wrapped around a bulging stomach.

"And so?" asked Arnie, sitting next to Tom. Tom was suddenly at the table, Arnie to his left, the podium to his right, and the man in flannel straight ahead of him, standing in the aisle of the bleachers.

"She's not married, you idiot!" shouted the man. From behind him, several people said 'Hear, hear,' agreeing with the man. "Is this any kind of example to be setting for our children?" asked the flannel shirt.

Off to Tom's left, he could see Cratt leaning forward to grab the microphone that sat in front of Arnie. Tom wanted to say something; these accusations were unfair. He was the only person in the gym that knew she was married. He saw dark blue, dark black and global gray pictures across the horizon of his mind. He saw Cratt's hand wrapping around the base of the microphone. Tom wanted to stop Cratt. This question had nothing to do with the strike, did it?

The microphone approached Cratt's mouth. Tom could see a spittle of foam at the corner of his mouth. Cratt waited until the murmur of voices slowed. The microphone came up to his mouth.

"The Iron Lake Board of Education does not condone such lewd behavior. Any teacher who is living in sin, obviously, does not set a good example for our children. She should be fired." Cratt paused for a moment, looking around the crowd in front of him. "I am, of course, only one vote on this board."

There was dead silence, broken by a woman's sobbing. The Kindergarten teacher, Mrs. Wilson was sobbing, with her hands over her face. Sitting next to her was Corrine Harant, Tom's daughter. 'Cookie' was looking at Tom, and Tom saw her eyes as if there was a deep gorge filled with fog standing between her and him.

Something made a noise in the hall outside the gymnasium. He could see Wrecker and Dr. Clark. What was it they told him before the meeting?

*****

"What is this about?" he asked on Tuesday evening when Patty Trivic and Glacinda Fallow showed up at his house. They were polite enough, but for two board members to come to his house was very unusual, 'to say the least'. They showed up in his breezeway, dressed in their coats, each holding a purse. After Crystal insisted they come into the kitchen, Tom again asked what this visit was about.

"Thursday night. That's what. Our next board meeting," said Mrs. Trivic, running a hand through her hair, trying to smooth it. She was aware that Tom's wife was standing near the sink, just behind Tom.

"Cratt is angry that you allowed the union to put your comments about the budget into their *'so-called God-damned newsletter'* as he called it," added Glacinda. She was smiling, just like a Great White shark bearing down on a victim.

"I said, 'working together, the community can build a plan for the future.' What is inflammatory about that?"

Patty put her purse on the kitchen table. She straightened her dress and looked at Crystal, then Tom. "Your words make it look like you do not support the Board."

The teakettle intervened, screeching. Crystal reached over and lifted the kettle off the burner. The screeching stopped. When she asked, both ladies said they would prefer coffee to tea.

"We are here with one question," said Patty.

"Yes," added Glacinda. "Do you support the Board, or don't you?"

Crystal was putting freeze-dried instant into the coffee cups. Tom stood and watched her actions, frozen in place. His mind was a blank, his face looked like the face of a cigar-store Indian…wooden and flat. When Crystal finished stirring the water into the cups, she took both cups over to the table. Tom poured himself a cup of water, forgetting to put in coffee.

"Do you support the board?" asked Glacinda a second time.

"It's not that simple," said Tom. He knew he was conflicted over this issue. On the one hand, he was an *ex officio* member of the board, the person who implemented their decisions. He had drawn up the *Strike Plan* and he was firmly convinced that to win a strike, once the strike begins, the administrator must have no feelings of pity for the strikers. Like a general, the superintendent's role had to be to attack and get the strike over as quickly as possible.

The fact that this strike was still going on was due to the hard line attitudes of the negotiators on both sides.

On the other hand, Tom had a plaque on the wall, called 'The Code of Ethics for School Superintendents', adopted by the American Association of School Administrators in 1973. The first line said 'the superintendent shall make no decisions without considering the impact upon the students' of his school. Tom never read beyond that first line, knowing that *every* decision he would ever make had an impact upon all the children of his school district. When he thought the strike would last two weeks, he felt good about his role. In the fifth week, he knew that this strike was getting out of hand. Both sides had drawn lines cast in concrete. In the sixth week, when the board decided to open with replacements, Tom knew that Cratt hated the teachers and wanted to hold them under his thumb.

To Tom, the board's decision was unethical, as well as being illegal. Jim Schmidt in the School Board's Association had advised Tom to implement the board's decisions, without fail. Tom's role was not to 'second-guess' the board he worked for.

When Glacinda asked if he would support the board, it became evident that the board members must be concerned that Tom did not support the board. For Tom, the question had no answer. He saw things as they were but could not support the board and their maniacal leader, Cratt. Curt Fitzsimmons and Percy Smith both tried to bolster Tom's morale but they were on the outside of the 'core group' that Connie Cratt was leading. Tom knew, at heart, that anything he did now to support the board could needlessly extend the strike.

"Do you support the board?" asked Glacinda a third time.

"It's not that simple," said Tom weakly.

"Yes, it is," she said in flat tones.

"I don't know," he finally admitted.

"You either support the board or you support the teachers."

"I don't know," he said, in a voice growing weaker.

"Should we tell them you don't support the board?"

"I don't know," he said, barely above a whisper. He was sitting closest to the window and he turned to look out the window, into the empty blackness. He could barely see a suggestion of his split birch in the corner of the yard. Glacinda waited for two minutes and then asked to use the phone. Crystal pointed her to the phone in the dining room, just off the kitchen.

Tom continued to stare out the window, ignoring the two ladies. He heard Crystal tell them that he had not slept in five or six days, he was drinking far too much coffee. Reflected in the blackness of the window, Tom saw Patty Trivic turn toward him.

On the phone, Tom heard Glacinda talking to Connie Cratt, telling him that Tom was ill. He heard her say it a second time, 'He's ill, I tell you' and then she hung up.

Glacinda came into the kitchen and picked up her purse. Patty Trivic followed suit. On the way to the door, Glacinda asked Tom if he thought he could keep his mouth shut during Thursday's meeting. He said he didn't know, to which she replied, 'Don't know much, do you?' in that sarcastic tone of voice usually reserved for a prostitute who wants you to work a little faster so she can get dressed and escape from the seedy motel room that her 'John' paid for.

Patty said little and followed Glacinda onto the breezeway. After they left, Crystal sat down at the table across from Tom. Looking at her reflection in the black window, Tom saw that she was looking at him. He almost said to her, 'What could I say?' but he remained mute, unwilling to burden her with his turmoil.

*****

"You are talking at 240 words a minute, Tom" said Harry Hagen, "and you look like death warmed over." Harry had arrived to pick up the Spencer County trophy. By agreement, the trophy would be on display for two weeks before the next game, scheduled for Cherry Grove. He was perhaps curious, which might explain his good-natured insistence on talking to Tom. Perhaps Judy, Tom's secretary, asked him to talk to Tom.

"Are you sick?" asked Harry.

"No, I am working under a lot of stress, I guess. My wife says I'm not sleeping. Hell, I'm not even sure of when I last had two hours of sleep.

"Looks to me like you are extremely wound up, Tom. You need to see a doctor. I mean, like today."

Tom thanked Harry for his solicitous advice and gave the trophy to Harry. Harry left, again telling Tom that he was talking extremely fast.

*****

'Kee-rye-st,' thought Tom. 'Did I just see him try to get me to take another tranquilizer?' Tom was sitting in Dr. Kenworth Clark's office, following a simple exam. Tom's blood pressure was extremely elevated (240 over 100) and his heart rate was slightly faster than normal. 'Dr. Ken' had given Tom a tranquilizer and told him to sit quietly. While the chemical was taking effect, the two men talked about the strike and its impact upon the people of Iron Lake.

Tom looked at the two diplomas on the wall behind the doctor. He saw the license to practice medicine hanging to the right of the diplomas. When he looked back at 'Dr. Ken', there was a second tranquilizer sitting on the desk in front of Tom.

"I thought it was one pill every six hours."

"It is. That is what I told you," said Clark.

"What's that?" said Tom, nodding toward the pill. The motion that followed was so swift that for years afterward Tom wondered if he had actually seen it. Clark's right hand swept across the desk with a tissue and the pill disappeared. Tom looked at the doctor for a good minute trying to digest what had happened.

"Did you just try to get me to take a second pill?"

"No."

"What did you just take away? It was right there?" he said, pointing at the front edge of the desk. "I know what I saw."

"No, I don't think you do."

"I know..."

"No, you don't," said Clark with emphasis.

Tom stood up to leave. Clark told him if he didn't feel better in two hours, to give him a call at home. Clark and his wife lived a block from Tom and Crystal. Tom told 'good, old Dr. Clark' that he knew what he saw. Clark said 'Yes, I know, Tom' with that particularly patronizing tone an educated man sometimes uses on a child. Tom didn't like the tone and pulled away from Clark's hand. Tom knew the man was trying to poison him and keep him from attending the board meeting.

*****

Walking back into his office, Tom found a young lady sitting at his desk. She had short brown hair and was wearing a red and white Iron Lake Panthers embroidered sweater with a short skirt. She smiled at him when she knew she was caught and stood quickly. She opened the door to the boardroom. When Tom asked what she wanted, she smiled and said 'I'm going'. He watched her exit through the boardroom.

When he looked down at his desk, he realized that his coffee mug had been moved to the center of his desk. It was the plastic mug, with the cute picture of his daughter, age 5, in Kindergarten. He remembered pouring a cup of coffee before he went to ask his secretary to run off copies of the board agenda. He was gone, what? Five minutes? Why would someone move his coffee mug?

Tom picked up the mug and took a long drink of the black coffee. He remembered that he hadn't told Judy to replace the coffee in the boardroom with decaffeinated coffee. His board members seemed to be feisty and jittery during meetings. Perhaps decaffeinated coffee would help?

At 5:30 p.m. that afternoon, Tom Harant stretched out on his bed at home, trying to get his heart to slow down. Crystal was on the phone talking to Dr. Clark. Tom had a weird sensation that he knew what the young girl in his office did to his coffee. He knew she put Lysergic Acid, called LSD, in his coffee. And he, like the 'stupid gobshite' that he was, drank it, 'good to the last drop' and he couldn't get his heart to slow down.

*****

Fifteen minutes later, Dr. Clark injected a form of a tranquilizer to slow down Tom's heart. Tom's blood pressure was 240 over 110 and Dr. Clark was seriously worried. His eyebrows were furrowed and he was watching Tom, listening to his heart by stethoscope every five minutes.

"You don't have to go to this meeting, do you?"

"Yes, I do." Tom was looking at Crystal, wondering how to explain the compulsion he felt, a compulsion to be at tonight's board meeting. Tom had known, since the meeting with the School Board Association attorney, that his role would be to support the board at this month's board meeting. The meeting was 'the talk of the town' and everyone he met on the street said they were coming. After all, he was not hired to go somewhere and hide when the @#** hit the fan. The school board would expect him to be present. The parents would expect him to be present. Glacinda Fallow would expect him to be present, with his mouth shut. The board members would do all the talking.

"You are under enormous stress," added Dr. Clark. Out in the kitchen, Dr. Clark told Crystal that Tom was exhibiting the classic symptoms of a soldier under fire. The stress he was under was creating fear for himself and for his family and Tom's fear was pushing his blood pressure up while his heart raced.

Dr. Clark used his stethoscope to listen to Tom's heart, once again.

"I'm going to give you a sleeping pill, Sinocain, to put you to sleep after you get home from the meeting."

"Will the pill knock him out?" Crystal asked. She was sitting on the edge of the bed, ready to go to the meeting. Dr. Clark told her the pill would slow him down and his own mechanisms would put him into a deep sleep. He told Crystal not to attend the meeting, that her presence would add to Tom's distress. Dr. Clark added that he would stand in the hall at the high school and watch Tom. If there were any trouble, he would take Tom directly to the hospital. Crystal asked Tom if he had to be at the meeting.

"I have to be there," Tom said with finality.

He was looking at Crystal when Dr. Clark said something that pushed Tom right to the edge of the cliff. He could feel his heart beating faster but he willed his heart to slow down, while he lay on the bed breathing slowly and deeply. For some reason, he knew that Dr. Clark was worried about a heart attack. When Dr. Clark and Crystal left the room, Tom lay as still as possible, willing his breathing to be slow, requiring his heart to slow down, demanding that his system become calm. In fifteen minutes, he was ready to head for the high school and the largest crowd at a board meeting in his memory.

*****

Noah Fynmore, the owner of the Bulrush Bay Resort, was waiting for Tom near the door to his office, when Tom arrived about 6:15 p.m. Noah had never attended a meeting of the school board in Tom's memory. The fact that he had put on a shirt and tie was impressive. The fact that he was waiting for Tom was unnerving.

Tom said good evening and was opening the door to his office before Mr. Fynmore said anything. Tom's secretary Judy was leaving, hauling a small box of fliers that told people how to behave at a public board meeting. She smiled at Fynmore and went down the hall toward the gymnasium. Noah closed the door behind himself, which further alerted Tom to Noah's concern.

Tom thought about Bulrush Bay Resort and wondered if the resort had been hit hard by the strike. He was about to ask when Noah said,

"Did you hear about Cratt's insurance claim?"

"What claim is that?" responded Tom. He wasn't sure he wanted to be violating Connie Cratt's privacy.

"The claim for his book. Had it insured for $135,000. Claims two publishers were interested."

"And the book was in the house?"

"On the table in the living room."

"Well, I'll be hornswoggled," was all that Tom could think to say. He had heard his grandfather use the term 'hornswoggled' when he was fishing with his grandson, describing a fishing line that was hung up on the bottom of the lake.

"But that's not why I'm here," said Noah, with determination.

Tom had spent many Sunday mornings out at Bulrush, trading barbs with Noah and the other Sunday pundits, discussing the Vikings and the luckless Twins and the North Stars, the 'Minnesota' hockey team. He had never heard Noah talk with so few words.

"What is it, then?" asked Tom, anxious to head for the gymnasium.

"Last Tuesday. I'm across the bay, getting gas for my boat motor, when I see that Arnie Murkiwasser's place has six cars parked, all six are sitting on the south side of Arnie's hedge of lilacs. That's strange, says I to myself, unless they were trying not to be noticed. I see Arnie's Ford Galaxy in the driveway. So who are the other five, I get to wonderin' and have you heard the rumors?"

"Which rumors?"

"About illegal meetings of the school board?"

"What did you see?" Tom was becoming increasingly anxious. He picked up his notebook and prepared to walk to the gymnasium. The noise from that direction indicated a large crowd must be present.

"Well, you know rumors. I get to thinking it's my duty to find out…"

"And what did you see?"

"Went over to Fred's place, next door south. Sat on Fred's deck and had a cigarette. Then two more cigarettes. Along about 10:30 p.m. here comes Connie Cratt, Patty Trivic and Glacinda Fallow. About a minute behind them, two men in suits, they both got into large cars and drove away. Cratt, Trivic and Glacinda stood by Cratt's truck talking. Out comes Arnie, he joins them. Twenty minutes they talk. I sit quietly, they don't know I'm there. I could hear some of the words, but not much."

"Noah, I must get to the meeting."

"What should I do?" he said, with an expression on his face that made him look like a little boy who was caught stealing apples.

"Talk to the County Attorney. He can decide how to proceed." Tom was out the door, waiting for Noah. Noah turned left and left the building. Tom saw him later, coming into the gymnasium.

*****

Tom was sitting at his desk, early in the afternoon, when the only funny thing to occur that day, happened. Billy Washburn came in with a list. He said it might cheer Tom up. It was a list of *"Things to Say in Negotiations"* drawn up by someone in the BMS, the Bureau of Mediation Services. Tom closed his notebook and lit a cigarette, taking a break. Billy said that a person wouldn't dare to use these lines unless he was already anticipating the need to get the other side angry:

1. I can see your point, but you're still full of it.
2. I'm easy to get along with; once you learn to see it my way.
3. It sounds like English, but what are you saying?
4. Ahhh...I see the screwup Fairy has visited us again.
5. I'm already visualizing the duct tape over your mouth.
6. What am I? Flypaper for freaks?
7. I'm not being rude. You're just insignificant.
8. I'm trying to imagine you with a personality.

Tom started laughing before he finished reading the first line. He was visualizing the face of 'Bluster' Barnes on the other side of the table while Tom said what he was really thinking. Washburn laughed with Tom, telling him to enjoy the lines.

"These lines remind me of Alice in a wind tunnel. We go forward to a negotiations session and spend two hours running forward while the union blows hot air at us and we finish where we started."

"There is a line I just read in a newsletter," said Washburn. He laughed, and then stopped. "Perhaps I shouldn't tell you," he added. "It's from Eugene O'Neill, who abused drugs when he had the money." He was pulling a single sheet of paper out of his jacket. "And here it is: There is no present nor future, only the past which we are condemned to live over and over."

"Oh, really?" said Tom, laughing. "You sure know how to cheer a guy up."

*****

In the hall outside the gymnasium, Tom walked over to Wrecker and Dr. Clark. The three men stood and watched the 'good citizens' stream out of the gymnasium, heading for their homes.

"Did you notice? No one stood up to tell the teachers to get real."

"We weren't really listening," said Wrecker. He reached out with his right hand and the two men swung their hands together, trying to make a 'Pop' sound. Tom, the taller man, laughed.

Tom looked at his good friend, a friend he could count on, and said, "What did you tell me before the meeting?"

"A line from your grandmother's Irish blessing. 'May the hand of a friend, Always be near you,' to remind you that I was here. Hell, I promised Crystal that I would be here."

Tom smiled, or tried to smile at Wrecker. He noticed a few gray hairs were showing above Wrecker's left ear. He looked at Dr. Clark who was buttoning his overcoat, preparing to leave.

"I remember walking to the landing up there and watching the board members go into the gym. I don't remember coming down here. You said something to me, I think. Next I know, Arnie squeezed my arm and it hurt."

"You looked like a zombie in there," said Dr. Kenworth Clark.

"Tom, go on home, now." Wrecker was ready to drive him if needed.

"But what was it you said, Doctor?" The doctor picked up his medical bag from the floor and stood facing Tom.

"Something like, if your heart starts racing, tell us. *If you collapse* there are four volunteer firemen in the crowd.

*****

The following morning, at 9:00 a.m. precisely, Billy Washburn and Wrecker Kline showed up at Tom's house with one mission in mind. They had talked to Crystal last night and knew how worried she was. Billy had suggested that Wrecker and himself should convince Tom to go into a hospital, if they could find a hospital where Tom would be out of the limelight, with no access to the press.

Tom was groggy. The sleeping pill he took didn't allow him to spring to life and jump out of bed. He seemed depressed. Billy, on the other hand, was forceful and determined. He explained to Tom that they were taking him to the Golden Valley Center, a rehabilitation center for alcoholic young men. GVC would not admit that Tom was on their grounds and he would be protected. In Wrecker's view, Tom was due and he should treat his stay like a short vacation, all meals provided.

Tom was concerned. How would this look in the community of Iron Lake? Billy said that they would announce this afternoon that Tom had been hospitalized for stress.

Tom sat in the passenger seat in Billy's Chevy wagon, with Wrecker behind him. Crystal leaned in and gave him a squeeze on the arm. He tried to smile at her.

On the short drive out of Iron Lake, Tom suddenly came to life. He started laughing and told a few of his favorite Irish jokes. When Billy turned onto Highway 30 to head east into Minneapolis, Tom was smiling ear to ear, claiming that for the first time in months, he felt relieved of an enormous weight off his shoulders.

At Golden Valley, Tom convinced the nurses to take a blood sample. He wanted his blood tested for any unusual chemicals. The results were negative and someone told Tom the sample should have been taken inside the first twelve hours.

During his stay at Golden Valley Center, one board member took the time to call him. It was Patty Trivic. She wanted him to know the pastors in Iron Lake were holding prayer vigils, each night in a different church, praying that both sides would end the strike.

The man, as Wrecker told him later, needed three or four weeks of recuperation from the stress. Tom was not a person to stay away for weeks, when there were people hurting back in Iron Lake. He knew there had to be something he could do. Perhaps he needed to ask for help from the state. At the very moment when Tom should have been listening to Crystal telling him to stay, Tom signed himself out of Golden Valley Center. He had been there for six days.

CHAPTER TWENTY-ONE
Iron Lake Board Guilty!

Guilty is what he said, after listening to testimony from two teachers who were watching Arnie Murkiwasser's house. He found the entire board guilty and fined all six members $100.00 each. Guilty of holding an illegal meeting." The Commissioner was holding a copy of the Minneapolis *Tribune* in which the news made the front page.

Tom Harant and Karen Clark, the Iron Lake Elementary Principal, were sitting in the walnut paneled office of the Commissioner of Education, Mr. Shane Cleveland. The Commissioner had summoned them to report on the condition of the strike in Iron Lake, a strike that to Tom's way of thinking was getting far too much publicity.

"Apparently only four members of the board were guilty. I'm told two members have never met with the core group," said Tom, by way of explanation.

"And this 'core group' that you refer to, is responsible for the strike continuing week after week?" asked the Commissioner.

"Absolutely," said Tom. "There are rumors that Connie Cratt is being coached by some 'tough guys' from a union office in Chicago. But who knows where these stories get started."

"And he is the leader?" asked the Commissioner. He was on his feet, and walking around his office on the Eighth Floor of 550 Cedar Street, St. Paul, also known as the Education Building. The office featured four over-stuffed leather chairs in a semicircle in front of the Commissioner's desk, gray carpet and dark blue drapes on the windows. The walls held paintings framed in black and chrome. The Commissioner said the paintings were winners in the State Arts Contest held annually in August.

"He's not the chair. He's just one board member, as he likes to point out," said Tom while Karen Clark nodded her head. "He talks, they listen. The 'core group' of four tell the other two members how they are going to vote once the board gets out of a strategy session. In the public sessions, the board is now voting four-two on most issues."

"And why are you here, Mr. Harant?"

Tom paused, considering how much he should tell the Commissioner. Tom knew that he had no proof that Connie Cratt was being coached in how to handle the strike. There were many rumors circulating about the board members. Tom was reluctant to violate the sanctity of the closed sessions of the Board. The Board relied on its superintendent to be the CEO of the district and he held their trust so long as he didn't discuss what went on in closed meetings.

"I can tell you from observations, that Mr. Cratt has the teachers where he wants them, inside his fist, and he is not about to let them go, unless he is forced to settle the strike."

Commissioner Cleveland looked at Tom, 'asking' if this was true. He looked at Karen Clark, and she nodded.

"Then along comes the MEA, filing an Unfair Labor Practice, backing the Iron Lake Board into a corner. Now the entire board is angry."

"Well, my attorney tells me the Unfair Labor charge could be dropped as part of the strike settlement," said the Commissioner. "Tell me why you are here, Tom."

"It's out of control. There is nothing I can do. It's almost Christmas break, and no progress is being made. There are people in Iron Lake who have been praying, hoping for a settlement before Christmas. Yesterday, the Board Chairman—that's Mr. Murkiwasser—informed me that mediation will be held on Wednesday before Christmas. He is positive nothing will come of it."

"And you feel responsible? Mr. Harant?"

"Yes, I do, Commissioner."

*****

Christmas break arrived. On the last day before break, someone delivered hot buttered rum to the men on the picket line. Mr. Harant ignored this violation of rules about alcohol in a public school. There was nothing to be gained, he figured, by making an issue out of it.

The business owners of Iron Lake delivered hams to each of the striking teachers' families during the last week before the break. The striker's newsletter continued to charge the board with vindictive behavior...

> "Why are certain members of the board unwilling to have the whole board and the board chairman involved in the negotiations process? Why don't the board negotiators want the <u>entire board</u> at the mediation sessions?
> Instead of sitting down at the bargaining table and negotiating until a settlement is reached, the board continues to let vindictiveness control their thinking."

The Replacement teachers, on board now for seven weeks, all brought dishes for a potluck and had a feast in the Iron Lake boardroom. They were happy to be reaching the Christmas break, pleased to be teaching 'real classes' and using real support materials, giving real tests and 'real grades'. In another two weeks, they would complete the second quarter of the school year.

There was a little apprehension about the Christmas break. All the Replacement teachers had been contacted at home by union members three and four times. A few had defected; 90 percent were still on the job. Tom Harant reassured these teachers that they would be expected on January 4, the first day of school after New Year's. Then he left for the mediation session going on in the courthouse in Cherry Grove.

During the week, the board negotiators, Connie Cratt and Patty Trivic, had been meeting in private with the teacher negotiators, 'Bluster' Barnes and Sylvan Plant. The mediator called a mediation session for two o'clock on Wednesday, the last day of school before Christmas, and the teacher newsletter announced the mediation session, but no details. Behind the scenes, Tom's secretarial staff and the janitors and the bus drivers were smiling, expecting a settlement.

At 6:00 p.m., the negotiators for both sides shook hands on a tentative deal. The Iron Lake Board of Directors was present for the four-hour session. The teachers left with smiles on their faces, knowing that a settlement was imminent. The mediator asked the Board to wait until the teachers approved the deal, then meet.

On Saturday afternoon, the Board of Directors met in the boardroom. They passed a motion waiving the 'three-day' notice and then passed a motion for a closed session. They were in 'Closed Session' for one hour and then resumed an Open Session. Cratt made a motion to reject the tentative offer and it passed, 6-0. The Iron Lake teachers met and passed the proposed settlement, 48-10.

Two days later, Judge Harley Bellows refused a second time to issue a Temporary Restraining Order to stop Iron Lake from running school with 'substitutes'. In his order, he declared that the Iron Lake board had "a duty to and is required to engage in good-faith negotiations." The Iron Lake Board responded by taking the position that they could not meet in closed session because Judge Bellows had found them guilty of violating the 'Open Meeting Law.' The Board declared they were unable to meet again until January 7.

*****

Tom and Crystal spent a quiet Christmas at home, decorating the house, watching the news from Saudi Arabia, baking banana bread and sending presents in the mail to Carl, who was working in Denver, and to Mark aboard the *USS George Philip* in the Persian Gulf.

Corrine came over twice, to cheer up her father. She didn't seem overly cheerful herself, with the strike weighing on her mind. She admitted she was tutoring some of her students, quietly, without the union knowing about it. She also told her father she didn't believe the school board was negotiating in good faith.

On the national scene, there was daily television coverage of Army units loading into C-130 transports, beginning the long journey to Saudi Arabia. Occasionally, a reporter would note the sailing of a transport ship with heavy mechanized units (tanks and armored personnel carriers) sent to the Middle East.

President George H.W. Bush announced that Iraq must agree to talks no later than January 3. Iraq announced that due to the dispute over dates, any such meetings 'are postponed indefinitely'.

Moreover, in Iron Lake, Minnesota, their school superintendent in a cynical frame of mind said to himself, *'that sounds familiar. No talks anywhere.'*

On December 22nd, a ferry carrying more than 100 sailors from Haifa in Israel to the *USS Saratoga* capsized, killing 19 men and raising the death toll in *Operation Desert Shield* to 73. On December 28th a 17-ship flotilla, led by the aircraft carriers *USS America* and *USS Theodore Roosevelt* left Virginia, headed for the Persian Gulf.

In Iron Lake, Tom Harant reviewed his notebook, and found a note to himself that read *'It will be over next week.'* He did not smile.

*****

"Is the coffee hot?" said a voice Tom didn't recognize.

"Yes, I guess it is," Tom said, wondering who he was talking to.

"This is Curt Larson, Spencer County sheriff. Two of us want to drop in on you, for some questions. Do you mind?"

"No, I'm here anyway."

"Oh, really? I thought you would be at home or on vacation?"

"Most people think that," said Tom. "I work year round." Tom wondered for a moment why he was defensive about his job. Administrators worked 240 days in each year. He certainly didn't need to apologize for working between Christmas and New Years. Judy was in the outer office working on a 'staffing' report for the Department of Education.

The day was Wednesday and tomorrow was New Year's Eve day. Tom had finished his mail and was reviewing the Accounts Payable when he heard two men introducing themselves to Judy in the outer office. Getting up, he walked to the coffee maker where a pleasant aroma was filling the air. He took three mugs from the small mug rack and set them on the table. After filling the three mugs, Tom turned and saw Curt Larson at the open door of his office.

Larson stepped into the office, bringing with him a second man, dressed similarly. Both men wore dark blue suits, with dark ties over white shirts. The second man's suit had a small white stripe, and seemed, to Tom's eye, to be a little newer. Larson introduced him as John Smith, an investigator with the Minnesota Bureau of Criminal Apprehension. Tom laughed, adding,

"Yeah, sure…and John Smith is your real name?"

The man had dark hair and a dark complexion, with sparkling blue eyes. He laughed with Tom and started to reach for his documents. Tom stopped him. Tom reached for a mug of coffee, lifted one and turned for his desk. "The coffee is poured, instant cream in the jar, grab a chair."

"What can I do for you?" he added.

The other man, Smith, was looking at Tom's three diplomas from Mankato State and his State of Minnesota license. He sat down in front of Tom's desk and pulled an ashtray toward himself. Tom watched Smith pull out a small bag of tobacco and a package of cigarette papers. Larson and Tom watched the man roll himself a cigarette.

"Actually, it wasn't. Smith, I mean. My name was John Running Scared. I grew up on the Red Lake reservation, in the 1950's, when the BIA ran the reservation and we 'poor Indian trash' didn't have much to say. A lot has changed. We have casinos, and smoke shops and gas stations and hotels. Our people are working, and so are many other folks."

Tom smiled, remembering the visit Crystal made to Jackpot Junction in Morton. She went with a girlfriend and they played the 'Red-White-and-Blue' slots all night. Every time they won a pot, they cashed in their chips. Crystal and her friend came home with $1800 a piece. 'Beginner's luck,' he called it.

"You're not here about the school board, are you?"

"No, sir. Not today," said Larson. He blew on his coffee, cooling it. Curt always believed in being straight forward with potential witnesses. "John has some questions about the fire back in October."

"That's good, because I'm tired of answering questions about board meetings and mediation sessions and contract details and how much does the board have on the table."

"Good," said Smith. He brought his cigarette to his mouth and the end glowed for a moment. He seemed pensive, considering his question, while he blew smoke at the ceiling.

"Did you know Conifer Cratt had rented the house?"

"He told me he did," said Tom.

"Did he tell you why?"

"Said he was writing a book on the advancement of the AFL-CIO inside Minnesota unions, their history and advancement, something like that."

"That's what he told the insurance company."

Tom didn't say a word. He had heard rumors.

"Did you have an occasion to see the book?"

"No, I was never invited to cross the street."

"Why is that, do you think?"

"I saw the lights, mostly late at night, when I was on the way home. Many nights I was involved with parent meetings or sports events here at school. There wouldn't have been many opportunities for him to invite me."

"Well, it doesn't matter," said John Smith. He smiled and added, "Mr. Murkiwasser and Mrs. Trivic both say they saw parts of the book on the table in the living room."

Tom watched Curt Larson light a cigarette. Tom wondered if the sheriff had heard these questions before, then realized that Larson was intensely watching John Smith. It was Larson, Tom suddenly realized, who had made the initial statements to the press, describing the death of George Fallow in 'accidental' terms.

Smith brought Tom's attention back to himself. "Did you ever see Mrs. Glacinda Fallow entering or leaving the house at 815 South Ninth Street, across the street?"

"No, I never did?"

"Did you ever see her leave a school board meeting with Conifer Cratt and get into his car?"

"Can't say I did." Tom was beginning to wonder why Smith was asking about Glacinda Fallow.

"What can you tell me about their relationship?"

"Not much, only what I may have noticed."

"Which was what, precisely?" asked the BCA investigator.

"She watches," Tom began to say and then stopped. He thought for a moment before adding, "She listens to Cratt during board meetings. She always seems to know how he wants her to vote. When I first met her, I was aware that she adores power and people with power."

"Have you heard any rumors about the two of them that would imply there is something going on between them?"

"I've heard rumors and gossip since last July. Then again, there are people out there 'ready willing and able' to spit on the reputation of persons who live in the public eye. I tend to ignore gossip. It doesn't amount to much."

"But you heard a rumor about Cratt and Mrs. Fallow?"

"Rumors about her trips to the Radisson in Minneapolis, last summer. Then late in September, there were rumors that George Fallow was drinking heavy...or should I say, *heavier* than usual. Someone put two and two together, I think."

"But you don't know anything definite, do you?"

"No, I don't. I hope it's not true."

"That's an interesting attitude," said Larson as he stood up and went to the coffee maker. He poured another cup and brought it back to his chair. He put the cup down, stretched his back muscles and then scratched his chin. "Do you mind explaining why you hope it's not true?"

"Two board members 'in bed together' *feels* like Cratt wielding more power than he is entitled to." Larson sat down and looked at Smith.

The eyebrows above Smith's brown eyes seemed to pull together while he tried to get his mind around Tom's statement. Larson chuckled, but quietly.

"So, if I summarize," added Smith, "you absolutely do not know if Mrs. Fallow and Mr. Cratt were carrying on, as someone described them?"

"No, I do not," said Tom. He looked from Smith to Larson then back to Smith. "But," he started. Then he looked at the county sheriff, sitting in his chair, drinking his coffee. "The fire was an accident, wasn't it?"

"Yes and no," said the sheriff. Larson was reluctant to acknowledge what they knew, but trusted Tom to keep it to himself.

"Which was it?" asked Tom, anxiously.

"The fire was arson. It was not an accident," said Mr. Smith finally. Tom looked at Smith, puzzled.

"How can it be arson? At least, we all assumed George Fallow was drunk and started the fire in the basement?"

"It may be, he did start the fire. But it was arson." Smith was pulling the zipper around his flat document briefcase. He opened it briefly and pulled out a sheet of paper with horizontal lines and 'peak' lines indicated by color marks on the paper. The upper left corner read 'Ion Chromatogram' and 'December 21, 1990' and just under the date were the words 'BCA130709-George Fallow'.

"Whenever there is a fatality in a fire, we secure samples of body fluids and body tissues before we release the body to the mortuary. The forensics lab was backlogged...that sounds familiar, doesn't it?" Smith said, laughing at the sheriff. Sheriff Larson returned a weak smile.

"These colored marks are 'peaks' and indicate the presence of hydrocarbons. Peak #1, with my 'star' in black ink, is for 'methyl-tert-butyl-ether, also known as MTBE. Peak #2 is benzene, #3 is toluene, and number 4 tells us ethyl benzene was present in the fire. Peaks #5 and #6 are the two peaks for xylene."

"Are all these chemicals used to start fires, or, I mean, flammable?" Tom could see that Smith and the BCA must have overwhelming evidence.

"The benzene, toluene, ethyl benzene and xylene are flammable. Then again, we usually find evidence of them in most house fires today."

"Tom," said Curt Larson, "what would you find under most sinks in most houses, today?"

Tom thought for a moment. "Cleaners, disinfectants, window sprays, cleaning gloves, jugs of concentrated cleaner."

"Plastics," said Mr. Smith. "When a house burns, all the plastics in the house produce hydrocarbons that produce these peaks in the gas chromatograph. Gasoline produces the same peaks. So these peaks can't be used to indicate an accelerant."

"Except for Peak number one," added Sheriff Larson.

"That's right. We would expect to see peaks #2 through #6 in the tissues of a fire victim, unless they lived in a house, say,...oh, maybe in a third world country where their containers are clay pots," added Smith.

"And the 'MTBE' peak is unique, isn't it?" said Sheriff Larson.

"MTBE is an additive in gasoline. It is not formed when plastics are burned. It was present in George Fallow's brain. He was exposed to gasoline either before or during the fire that killed him."

"Is that definitive proof?" asked Tom, trying to appear intelligent and allowing the BCA investigator to run with his 'story' of the arson.

"Here's the chemist's statement, from the written conclusion," he said while flipping to a page attached to the graph.

"And I quote, *'The results of the chromatograph analysis of subject Fallow's brain tissue indicate that he was exposed to gasoline shortly before the fire. Fire investigators and eyewitnesses have said the fire rapidly and totally ruined the house in which this victim subsequently died. It is my conclusion then, the fire probably generated very high temperatures and owing to the low boiling point (55.2 degrees Celsius), MTBE was not found in the fire debris submitted for analysis. The gas chromatograph data, that contains evidence of MTBE present in the victim's brain tissue, clearly indicates that arson contributed to the cause of this fire',*"

"That's really sad, that a man could do that to himself," said Tom.

"That's what we think," said Curt Larson.

"Fallow's pistol was found near his body," said the BCA agent, "and a whiskey bottle was inside the burned frame of a couch. I think Fallow intended to kill Cratt and then burn the house. He had the house doused and ready to go, fell asleep on the couch and, probably a burning cigarette lit gasoline fumes in the basement."

"So why the questions about Cratt and Mrs. Fallow?"

"He stands to receive a sizeable check from the insurance company and Mrs. Fallow was the agent who wrote the policy."

"So you have to know who committed the arson, is that 'on the mark' as my son would say?"

"Yes, we do. I should add, for your peace of mind, one thing. We have absolutely no evidence tying Conifer Cratt or Glacinda Fallow to the arson."

*****

When Tom walked into his mother's kitchen on Victoria Street in Fairmont, he knew right away that his Dad's condition must have worsened. His mother was sitting at the table, smoking a cigarette, writing phone numbers on a list. She explained that she wanted the numbers ready for the day she needed them.

"He is lucid, some of the time. He sleeps, then wakes up screaming from the pain. The cancer is all across his hip bones; he can hardy lie still when he sleeps."

Tom stood in the door to his father's bedroom. A hospital bed had been rented to keep his father from twisting himself off the bed. White cotton strips were tied to the railings, holding his father's wrists. The dresser was covered with flowers, cards and small gifts from Frank's cousins. A large bouquet of roses was centered on the dresser, from Frank's mother in Northumberland, Pennsylvania.

Tom looked down at his father and wanted to cry. Here was a man who made false teeth most of his life and then changed careers and worked on the 'Echo' satellite produced by Scheldahl in Northfield. Frank's cheeks were sunken, his eye sockets were dark. His arms looked like the sticks used to hold bean plants in Frank's garden.

"His mother sent the flowers. They tried to talk but he mostly cried while she was on the phone. At her age, she doesn't feel she can make the trip."

Tom put his arm around his mother's shoulder. She was five foot six inches tall, and he was looking down at her hair, which had somehow turned gray. *'When did that happen?'* he asked himself. *'When did we all move into our own lives?'* he wondered. On the bed, his father was twisting, turning his hips, and trying to relieve the pain.

"He's going to be in pain when he wakes up but he wants to tell you he loves you," said Tom's mother.

"We've never said that to each other," said Tom. He remembered the day his father took him squirrel hunting. He saw the shotgun and the butt of the gun against his shoulder and his father helping him aim the gun into the high branches where a nest made a perfect target. He felt the kick and the blast of the gun, and his stomach churning, and the squirrel falling in slow motion out of the tree. His father walked over and picked up the dead squirrel. When his father asked him how he felt, he lied. He said he felt nothing. No thrill from shooting a squirrel. What he felt was disgust. Disgust with himself for doing something he didn't want to do in the first place.

"He knows I love him," said Tom.

'But I've never said it,' said Tom to himself. He was such an ornery cuss, quick with his temper. "The one time I defied his authority, I stood up to him when he wanted help with the storm windows. He walked over to me and flattened me with a punch. I was sitting on the steps by the kitchen door when you came out the side door. We both lied, told you that I slipped on the bottom step."

"He told me about it, years later. You were thirteen or fourteen years old. He was proud of the way you didn't blame him for punching you."

"What about the morphine?" Tom asked.

"It works quick, relieves his pain. You and I have to decide something. You're the oldest. It's your place."

"We have to decide *what?*"

"He is almost constantly in pain these days. His doctor has given me a prescription for a morphine drip. It would keep him constantly drugged."

"And take all the pain away, wouldn't it?"

"He's suffered enough, through this year. The chemo and the revisits to the Mayo Clinic." She looked at her son, standing close to his father's bed. She held his arm and stood looking at her husband. What was there to say?

"Then that's our decision. I will explain it to my sisters." Tom knew the morphine would keep his father in a state of perpetual dreaming. He guessed that the pain and the stress on his father's body was wearing the man down. He must be approaching the point where he hoped to be permanently relieved of the pain.

On the bed, Frank turned and opened an eye toward Tom and his mother.

"Tom's here, dear. He has something to say."

Tom bent over the bed, looking down into his father's eyes. His father raised his right wrist but couldn't reach Tom's hand. Tom quickly untied the strap holding Frank's right arm and his father grabbed Tom's wrist. The strength of his grip was a surprise until Tom guessed his father was transferring some of his pain into his hand. Tom bent down to his father's ear and said 'I love you, Dad.'

When he straightened up, he saw tears in his father's eyes.

"Wipe my eyes, darn it," said Frank. "I can't see you." He was looking around the room. "Where's my card?"

Tom's mother walked to the dresser and picked up four cards. She found the card with Tom's name on it and gave it to Frank, explaining that Frank wrote these cards back in November. He wanted his kids to have them.

Frank pulled on Tom's wrist, indicating that he should bend over the bed. Tom looked into Frank's eyes and the frail man said, "I love you." He suddenly stiffened, the muscles in his arms bulging as he pulled against the railings of his bed. The bed shook with the vibration of his pain. In a moment, the shaking subsided. He reached up and gave the card to Tom. Tom's mother was inserting a needle into Frank's arm, administering morphine. Frank's body began to relax. His eyelids started to droop.

"Sleep now, my dear," said Tom's mother, patting her husband on the shoulder. Tom could see the pain while she watched her husband drift away, on gray clouds across a dark sky with lazy dreams.

On the 3x5 card, written in Frank's tortured scrawl were the words,

'May God fill your heart,

With gladness to cheer you'.

CHAPTER TWENTY-TWO
'Hell doth Freeze Over'

The room was small, measuring twelve feet wide and twenty-four feet long. Down the center of the room, a mahogany conference table dominated the room, surrounded by twelve high-backed, padded chairs. In the corner, a wet bar provided liquid medicine for the restless, coffee on top and sodas in a small refrigerator. On the walls, enlargements told the story of labor unrest in Minnesota. Under the single window, a wall ventilation unit struggled to remove the tar dispelled by the five people who were smoking. A stack of legal pads lay in the center of the table. Only one notebook was open. Mrs. Trivic was writing a note.

The Iron Lake Board had been ordered by BMS Director Lane Tuttlesworth to appear for a mediation session, beginning at 9:00 a.m. on Friday, January 8. Mr. Tuttlesworth made it clear that nobody was going home until there was a tentative settlement. It was the same mediation room the Iron Lake Board used in early December when an aborted settlement was rejected 6-0 by the Board. The view out the single window, if a person looked hard left, included part of the State Capitol dome with the gilded horses on the third floor roof.

No one was looking out the window. All six persons were turned toward the door, expecting Connie Cratt to return at any moment. They had been startled at 9:30 a.m. when the BMS Director stepped in, introduced himself and asked Cratt to join him out in the hall. At 10:00 a.m., Arnie Murkiwasser, nervous as always, looked into the hall. The hall was empty.

Tom Harant put out his cigarette and stood up to stretch. Murkiwasser returned to his seat with a worried expression on his face. Glacinda Fallow put out her cigarette and lit another one, passing her *Marlboros* to Curt Fitzsimmons who took one and passed the pack to Percy Smith who also took another cigarette, checking to see which end had the filter.

"You're sure we hired the right attorneys?" asked Percy, for the second time.

"Yes," said Tom.

"They're tough. No fooling around," said Arnie.

"If you could have been there with us," said Tom. "Arnie and I are sitting in these large leather chairs, two of six chairs in front of Popovich's desk. He stands up and growls at us, 'Well, God dammit, it's about time you showed up' and then he comes around his desk. He opens a humidor…you know, a heavy wooden thing for cigars, and he offers Arnie and me a cigar. We both said 'No, thanks'. Then he takes one, pulls a snipper device from his pocket and trims one end off a cigar. He brings a wooden kitchen match out of his pocket, scratches the match on the base of a marble statue of an eagle that sits on his desk, and lights the cigar. He takes one hellacious pull on the cigar and the entire end is bright red, like its about to burst into flame. Then he breathes out a cloud of cigar smoke that damn near fills the room. I can tell you, I was impressed."

"Then he starts to walk around the room," adds Arnie. "He talks about strikes in Minnesota and how he has been watching the Iron Lake strike. Then he switches to talking about an attorney, a real hotshot that stood up to some union strike leaders out in Montana and backed them down."

"Speaking of which…" said the man standing in the doorway. He was ordinary in height, almost six feet tall. He had a pleasant face on a standard frame. Tom introduced Mr. B.G. Sharpe to the rest of the board while the attorney set his briefcase on the table and proceeded to open it. He looked up and told the Board to call him 'Ben' or call him 'Big Gun' if he earned the title.

"Our firm represents the Minnesota School Boards Association and about 90 public school districts. We know the law, and we know the bargaining law," he said by way of introduction. He took out a legal pad, noted the day in the corner, and set the pad down and then locked his briefcase.

"I've been meeting with Mr. Cratt. That is, Lane Tuttlesworth and I have been meeting with him. Do you people want this strike to end?"

There was silence around the room. Tom watched Arnie and Glacinda and Patty squirm. He knew what was coming. Sharpe had warned Tom they were going to separate Cratt from the rest of the board. Tom and Jim Schmitt from the MSBA had the job of keeping the Board in line. Tuttlesworth had Cratt. The mediator, Kirby Jones had worked with the Iron Lake case since last July. Jones had the Iron Lake teachers group. Ben Sharpe added that it was possible that the State President of the Minnesota Education Association might be across the hall, working to convince the teachers to settle.

"Do you people want it to be over?" he said a second time.

Percy Smith and Curt Fitzsimmons both said 'Yes' loud enough that the room and Mr. Sharpe heard them. Patty Trivic nodded her head. Glacinda and Arnie didn't move. *'Wondering what is happening?'* Tom said to himself while he watched Arnie. The little man seemed to have shrunk in the last minute. Glacinda watched Ben Sharpe like a fisherwoman gutting a fish, pulling the filet knife upward through the stomach and vital organs.

"We're going to get it over. Be patient. This is going to take some time. Mr. Jim Schmitt, who met Tom and Connie Cratt back in December, will look in on you and bring you updates." With this, he picked up his pad and left the room.

Arnie immediately turned to Tom and said, "What the hell is going on?"

To which Tom said, "I don't know."

*****

Sitting and wondering would describe the rest of the day. At 1:30 p.m., Jim Schmitt of the MSBA entered the room and explained the progress to date on fringe benefits and language items. The teachers had agreed to pro-ration for this year, and would lose 25% of the normal contribution, representing the time they were out on strike. On the Personal Leave issue, the board would agree to leave the language unchanged although the contract was far too permissive.

Schmitt sent them to lunch shortly after 1:40 p.m., telling them to return at 3:30 p.m. They found a gray world outside, with the temperature hovering around zero. A sharp wind forced the Board to turn their backs to the wind while they entered Tom's Lincoln Town Car. He drove them to the restaurant in the Excelsior Hotel where they watched the traffic on I35-E while they ate Reuben sandwiches with French fries. Cratt and

Tuttlesworth and Ben Sharpe ate lunch in the employee cafeteria in the BMS building.

When they returned, Schmitt reported that the teachers and Connie Cratt had tentatively agreed to language guaranteeing that all eligible students would graduate on time even if school ran into June. At 7:30, Jim Schmitt told them to get supper somewhere nearby and return at 9:30 p.m. At the Excelsior again, they ate larger meals. Curt Fitzsimmons and Patty Trivic had several drinks, claiming it was cold outside and they needed the 'anti-freeze'.

At 9:30 p.m., they found Jim Schmitt making a pot of coffee in the mediation room. He reported that the teachers wanted to make up all the days, to which Arnie and Curt and Percy all said, 'No way' simultaneously. Schmitt said that was the message being delivered by Ben Sharpe.

"No one, absolutely no one, is going to send their children to school for 58 days in the summer," said Tom.

"Like I said," Schmitt added, while rapping Tom on the shoulder, "no one is going to agree to make up the days you've lost." He went on to tell the Board that he had talked to the Commissioner of Education who had agreed there would be no penalty for falling short of 170 days of school.

At 11:30 p.m., Jim Schmitt returned with three empty coffee cups and filled two. On his way out the door, he reported that Cratt was coming back to their meeting room.

When Connie Cratt entered the room, the members present watched him pour himself a cup of coffee. He asked them how they were holding up and they said they had enjoyed a good meal.

"You set this up, didn't you?" he said looking at Tom Harant.

Tom didn't answer him. When Arnie asked Cratt what he meant, Connie said they had kept him separated in a room all day. He had met with the teacher negotiators twice but Ben Sharpe was doing all of the talking, pushing and cajoling the teachers, threatening to formally hire the replacement teachers and go to court to settle the issues.

"You should see them...they're scared of Ben Sharpe," added Cratt. "But he knows what he is doing, what he can give and what he can't. Somebody set this up. I think I know who."

Tom's stomach turned over. He felt like a deer caught in the headlights of an eighteen-wheeler bearing down with tires singing, late at night on a lonely road.

"I don't know what you mean," said Tom while he looked at the door, hoping somebody would come in and distract Connie Cratt.

"Anyway. Here's the deal we want to offer. $4750 per teacher over two years. They lose 58 days, so the first year cost is minimal."

"You're kidding, aren't you?" Tom said with vehemence. "You and this board said not a penny over $4200 per teacher. Hell, let me think." Tom did some quick arithmetic on a yellow pad. "That's probably an increase of $60,000, reduced to $20,000 for lost time, and with increments, an increase of $80,000 in the second year, for a total of $100,000 over the balanced budget. We'll have to reduce teacher salaries by $120,000 to break even."

"That's the ball park that Mr. Schmitt came up with, also," said Cratt.

"We can't do that," said Arnie.

"Lay off teachers. I vote 'No' and I mean it," said Percy Smith.

"We went through this strike, all this grief, and now we're going to give them more than we can afford, and then turn around and lay off teachers?" said Curt Fitzsimmons. He raised his right hand and told the rest of the board to veto such a preposterous idea. Cratt sat down, smiling. He spent the next thirty minutes telling the board why they couldn't agree to give more than $4200 per teacher. "Remember, our superintendent has told us more than once that we have put all of the available money on the table. Haven't we, Mr. Harant?"

Tom felt that same lump of lead in his stomach. He tried to look at Cratt but couldn't. Was it simply because he was surprised? He didn't know. He had thought that this board would never agree to give more than $4200 per teacher and now here they were considering it. He was surprised. Perhaps Cratt knew that the state's longest teacher strike had to come to an end.

Ben Sharpe returned at that point. He sent Cratt down the hall to find Lane Tuttlesworth and report on the board's reaction to $4750. After Cratt left, Mr. Sharpe explained the situation to the board.

"Here's how it's going to go. We are going to allow ourselves to be negotiated upward, to about $4800. In return, they are going to agree to lose 53 days of salary. We are going to agree to five makeup days. They are going to insist on 'no reprisals' in return for dropping all lawsuits. Can you live with that?"

Curt Fitzsimmons immediately told Ben Sharpe that $4800 meant they would have to lay off teachers in the spring. Mr. Sharpe pointed out that sometimes school boards spent more than they could afford. The state average, through December 20th was over $5400 per teacher, so the Board could claim they gave less than the state average increase in salary. "The teachers were going to bite the bullet and settle for less than $5000, and you people told me they said they would never settle for less than $5200," said Sharpe.

"Or hell would freeze over first," added Percy Smith, laughing.

Sharpe had a blank look on his face.

"That's what Robert Barnes told the judge out in Spencer County," explained Tom. The line was a motto inside Iron Lake.

"Whatever," said Sharpe. He left the room and they sat discussing the proposed settlement. Tom worked through the figures, a second time. He told the board they would have to reduce spending by $120,000.

Nobody laughed.

*****

Tom turned his Lincoln Town Car southwest at Shakopee, heading down Minnesota Hwy 169. Sitting in the passenger seat was Connie Cratt. In the back, Arnie sat between Patty and Glacinda. At 1:30 a.m., after 16 hours of mediation in the BMS building, they were told to go home, get some sleep and return to the BMS building at 3:00 p.m. in the afternoon. The attorneys were drawing up documents. The teachers were still demanding that they make up all the days lost in the strike. Ben Sharpe was still threatening to hire all the replacement teachers.

Patty and Arnie left their cars in St. Paul. The temperature was 22 degrees below Zero and they were too tired to drive. Tom, being the superintendent, volunteered to drive them home. He had faith in his Town Car...a heavy car with good traction and a good heater. They were out in the country, driving into a southwest wind of 15 mph when it happened. The speedometer started to scream, and continued to scream while the needle buried itself at 120 mph.

One of the ladies asked what was wrong and he explained that the cold had frozen the speedometer cable. He pulled the car over onto the shoulder of the road and stopped. He sat there, thinking. Then he laughed.

"You know, don't you, that 'Bluster' Barnes always said they wouldn't come back in for less than $5200 or until Hell froze. Well, folks, I think Hell finally froze. This is a Lincoln. These things don't happen on a Lincoln."

In the backseat, Arnie laughed, more from fatigue than from enjoying Tom's joke. Glacinda mumbled something about 'Not funny'. Cratt was holding Tom's flashlight, shining it under the dash. Patty, in the back said something about 'What am I going to tell my husband?' while she tried to straighten her hair.

Tom was reaching around under the dashboard, locating the speedometer cable. When he found it, he squeezed the connector and twisted and slowly it loosened. With the cable disconnected, Tom put the car in gear and resumed the drive toward Iron Lake. "You tell anyone that Iron Lake settled for less than the average of all the increases in the state." Tom said that, and felt the bitter taste of bile in his esophagus, *'and then we fired some employees, because that's the process'.*

*****

On Sunday at noon, the Iron Lake Board held a meeting in the Iron Lake High School Library, in front of four television cameras and perhaps twenty reporters and part of the teaching faculty. After the meeting was called to order, Chairman Murkiwasser announced the Iron Lake Education Association had ratified the new contract on Saturday night. He asked for a motion to approve the contract. Member Fitzsimmons moved the approval, seconded by Member Smith. On the motion, all members voted 'Aye' and the Chairman announced the new contract was ratified, and the students would return to school on Tuesday.

Superintendent of Schools Tom Harant stood up, picked up his chair and slammed it down on the platform. He turned to Arnie Murkiwasser and said, "Mr. Chairman, I have nothing to say." On the way out of the Library, his secretary Judy handed him a note that read, 'Call Fairmont immediately'.

*****

On the front page of the Fairmont *Sentinel* on Monday, January 11, there was a headline,

Iron Lake Teacher Strike Finally Ends.

IRON LAKE, Minn. (AP) The longest strike of public school teachers in Minnesota history ended Sunday with a 6-0 ratification by the Iron Lake School Board of a two-year pact.

Members of the local education association had approved the contract 47-14 Saturday night. Teacher spokesmen said the agreement provides for an average $4,803 more in pay and fringe benefits for 69 teachers in the 1100-student school system located in Spencer County, some 90 miles southwest of Minneapolis-St. Paul.

Superintendent Tom Harant said teachers would report to work Monday and that classes would begin Tuesday.

"We're glad the strike is over and hope the school returns to normal," said Harant.

On page two of the Fairmont *Sentinel* on Monday, January 11 was the obituary notice for Frank Harant of 929 Victoria Street, Fairmont. The notice announced the funeral services would be held on Wednesday at St. John Vianney Church with burial at the Calvary Cemetery in Blue Earth.

Following the gravesite services on Wednesday, Tom Harant's Lincoln Town Car refused to start. He bundled his mother and Crystal into the car and used the car phone to call for a tow truck.

"What's this make, now?" he asked. "Six straight days of minus-twenty below zero?"

Tom started to laugh. His wife looked at him with a question on her face. "He's laughing at me, big deal school superintendent, with a big deal car, a fancy Lincoln Town Car unlike anything he could ever afford, and I can't get my own mother home from her husband's funeral." To himself he thought, *'I don't like the stone that is turning in my stomach.'*

"As I said last Friday night..." and he felt the stone rumbling, "and Hell doth freeze over, at least once every century."

CHAPTER TWENTY-THREE
Retaliation

"I have a teacher who is very nervous about meeting with you," said Billy Washburn, standing behind the counter in the high school office. He was wearing a three-piece suit that had seen better days. His tie was pulled down. He brushed his hair back with his right hand. Tom Harant, standing at the counter, glanced into Washburn's office, but it was empty. Washburn saw the glance, and added, "He's still in class."

The central office at Iron Lake High School was like a thousand others, staffed with work desks, large activity calendars and a small American flag mounted on one wall. The principal's secretary and two clerical assistants had desks behind the counter. At the moment, only Washburn's secretary was present, talking on the phone.

Tom glanced at the large clock mounted on the outside of the clock/alarm unit. The final bell for the day was about to ring and 1100 children would be rushing to get to their buses. Through the windows, Tom saw the long line of yellow buses, standing curbside, and smaller children already loading. Three of the school's paraprofessionals were on the sidewalk, supervising. Tom knew the final bell would signal a mass exodus of high school students. Most would flow toward the east doors and their buses. A few would exit from the west doors, heading for their cars. A few would head for the locker rooms and team practice.

"Tell your teacher to bring a union steward," answered Tom. The minute hand on the clock/alarm unit clanked, marking the passage of another school day in Iron Lake. Alarm bells rang. A student burst through the office doors, ran around the counter, dropped two pieces of paper on a desk, and ran out of the office. A young man, hauling a backpack and two books, entered and stood at the counter. Behind him came two girls in cheerleader outfits carrying a banner on white paper. One of the cheerleaders picked up the earpiece on the counter phone and began dialing. The other girl went behind the counter and opened a drawer, where she found scissors and masking tape.

"Too busy, right now," said Mr. Washburn.

"How about ten minutes?" said Tom.

"My office in ten minutes, Mr. Harant," said Billy Washburn. With students present, the two administrators always spoke formally to each other. They expected all the adults to show similar courtesy in front of their students.

Tom walked into Washburn's office and stood by the window, watching the buses loading. He saw a boy of about twelve squeeze between two buses and then stop in the street, waiting for a parent who was picking him up. Tom took out a notebook and wrote a note. He would insist, again, that parents be told to pick-up children on the south sidewalks. The area was away from the buses with plenty of room for cars to pull over and stop.

He closed the 'pocket' notes that he carried with him, putting the notebook into an inside pocket in his tan plaid jacket. In the outer office, he saw Billy Washburn approaching, with Wayne Williams and 'Bluster' Barnes behind him. If there had been time, Tom would have groaned at the thought of another meeting with Barnes, but Washburn was already in the office. Billy moved around his desk and sat down in his executive chair. When he indicated the three padded chairs in front of his desk, Tom took the chair by the window. He pulled his chair back and turned it sideways so the chair faced Barnes and Williams.

"Not too close, huh?" asked Barnes.

"I thought I should face you, Mr. Barnes."

"That takes guts, doesn't it?" said Barnes. The two men had been barely cordial to each other; during the first three weeks after the Iron Lake teachers came back to work. Barnes had been quoted laying the blame for the length of the strike on Tom Harant. Mr. Harant, for his part, knew that Barnes had convinced the Iron Lake teachers they could get $5600 per teacher if they held out long enough. Both men wanted to 'survive' by avoiding contact with each other.

"It's like the buses out there," said Tom. "If they get too close, the exhaust from the bus in front can be a problem."

"Lead dog gets the best view? The other dogs see another dog's rear end?"

"That's not what I meant," Tom said quickly. He glanced at Williams and then back at Barnes, who was busy loosening his tie.

Wayne Williams seemed to be nervously scratching the arm of his chair. "A little distance is safer."

"What? You are safer if you keep a distance from me?"

"Not what I meant," said Tom.

"Whatever," responded Barnes.

Out of the corner of his eye, Tom saw Billy Washburn looking at a cigarette. He didn't light it. Tom didn't like the way Barnes dismissed his comment. Tom believed that all adults had a zone of comfort around their person and he wanted to respect that zone without crowding Barnes.

"We are here with a problem," said Barnes.

"So I understand," responded Tom with a formal coolness in his voice.

"Mr. Williams wants to tell you something."

"Yes, I guessed as much," said Tom. In previous meetings with the union reps, Mr. Barnes always took an attack attitude, telling the superintendent that one of his principals was violating the contract and the union expected the superintendent to resolve the problem, or they would file a grievance. In some cases, Tom would get the facts from both sides, consider the issue, and then correct the error. In most of the cases, however, the union was 'stirring the pot' and trying to get the Iron Lake superintendent to change a managerial practice, giving away a management right and making the union 'stronger' in the eyes of its members. Mr. Harant would reject the union's demand. He knew that half the issues would show up in the next round of negotiations.

"Is this a contract issue?" asked Tom.

"Only in the sense that Mr. Williams failed to do something."

"And what was that?" asked Tom, looking at Wayne Williams. Tom's voice may have sounded harsh. Williams seemed to cringe away from Tom, or it could have been Tom's imagination. It was Barnes, however, who said,

"Forgot to send the hazardous chemicals to the disposal site in Willmar."

"Well, that's not the end of the world," said Tom. He felt a sense of relief. As far as he knew, no one had been harmed. No chemicals had been spilled. "Or is it?"

Wayne Williams cleared his throat and uncrossed his legs. His right hand came up and he scratched his forehead above his right eyebrow, while looking at Mr. Harant.

"Christ, spit it out man!" said Barnes.

"Those chemicals I told you about, that could be used to make Lysergic Acid, that's LSD, you know, are missing."

"Things happen," said Tom. He meant that in a strike, strange things do happen. Tools disappear. Some food had been stolen. Four of his teachers reported missing textbooks. The two-foot boa constrictor from the Natural History lab was still missing, out catching mice under the building, was the common joke.

"Yes, but I'm responsible," said Williams.

"That's true," added Billy Washburn. He went on to explain to Tom and Barnes that he had reported the theft to the county sheriff and ordered Mr. Williams to conduct a complete inventory of all the chemicals.

"Let's hope there is nothing else missing." Tom did not feel compelled to discipline Mr. Williams. This teacher was twenty-five years old, in his third year with the district. Washburn described Wayne Williams as a caring, concerned teacher who spent many hours of his own time helping students with chemistry experiments and tutoring the 'less gifted' students in his classes.

Tom told Washburn to file a written report of the theft after the inventory was completed. He told Williams to be careful in the future and dismissed the meeting.

When Williams asked, "That's it?" his union rep responded, "That's it."

What Tom Harant did not know was that a bottle of magnesium shavings and a bottle of potassium permanganate had been taken from the 'Hazardous Chemicals' cabinet, and later replaced.

*****

A month for retaliation was how Tom Harant described the month following the Iron Lake teacher's strike. On January 12th, Congress voted to go to war against Iraq. Syrian President Hafez al-Assad appealed to Saddam Hussein to withdraw from Kuwait before the Americans attacked. Four days later, President Bush issued the order for an air attack on Iraqi positions.

In the first attack, *AH-64 Apache* helicopters crippled Iraq's radar installations. *F-117A Stealth* fighters attacked military bases around

Baghdad. Americans turned their television sets to CNN's Bernard Shaw, who described the incredible scene across Baghdad in the early hours January 17. Shaw, and a few others, described the waves of attacks by *F-117A Stealth* fighters. Americans saw streams of tracer shells stitching the night sky and they collectively and *silently* said prayers that the Iraqi guns could not reach the Stealth fighters.

Patriot missile batteries were sent to Israel, for defense against Scud missile attacks. Rumor had it that Hussein would not hesitate to use chemical weapons in his Scud missiles. Two days later, 37 Patriot missiles were fired to intercept ten different Scud missiles fired at Riyadh and Dhahran in Saudi Arabia. A single Scud slammed into a suburb of Tel Aviv, killing three and wounding 96. Scud missiles continued to attack targets in Israel and Saudi Arabia but were largely inefficient. In his State of the Union message, President George Bush told the American people, "Iraq stalled and delayed but American pilots are delivering the retaliation we promised."

Inevitably, the Iraqi tank forces attacked Coalition forces at al-Khafji, inside Saudi Arabia, killing 12 US Marines in the first ground skirmish of the war. The next day, forces led by Saudi troops announced the recapture of al-Khafji. Iraqi forces in southern Kuwait were brutally assaulted by American *B-52* bombers. The air campaign was known as Operation Desert Shield. Secretary of State Dick Cheney, after a tour of Saudi Arabia, announced that the air war must continue. No one doubted the United States and Coalition forces intended to attack Iraq's Republican Guard inside Kuwait.

On February 15, Saddam Hussein reported on 'Iraq's readiness' to deal with an 'acceptable political solution that included withdrawal' from Kuwait. The United States rejected the overture. On the same day, the Iron Lake Board of Directors met in what their superintendent later called the 'Retaliation' meeting.

> "I attribute the small number of distinguished men in political life to the ever-increasing despotism of the majority in the United States."
> Alexis DeTocqueville (*Democracy in America*, 1835)

On the third Thursday of the month, which happened to be the first night of the Girl's State Basketball Tournament, the Iron Lake Board of Directors held their regular board meeting. The High School Principal, Mr. Washburn asked for a change of date, but the Board Chair, Arnie Murkiwasser replied that he didn't care that the Iron Lake Lady Panthers were playing in the state tournament. The Board had business to conduct and it would definitely hold a meeting and Mr. Washburn had better 'be there' to discuss reductions in the teaching faculty.

The room was warm, almost as warm as August. The windows were shut and outside, light flurries swirled around the cone of light from the street lamp. 'Almost everybody' in Iron Lake was gone, heading for the St. Paul Civic Center. In a very real sense, Tom felt deserted. He felt the people who cared about education in Iron Lake were gone to the Girl's Basketball tourney. They probably expected to see him and Billy Washburn at Thursday night's game. That did not change the feeling that Tom would have no friends except Washburn and Clark at the meeting.

When Tom Harant entered the boardroom, he found all six members of the Board present. The men wore white shirts, ties and jackets; the two women wore flowered dresses. There were only two observers, Billy Washburn and Karen Clark, the Elementary Principal. The Middle School Principal, Dennis DeFain was absent, *as usual*. Mr. DeFain had explained to Tom that he did not trust the members of the board and he felt his monthly report was a waste of time. "They're going to do what they feel like doing, *come hell or high water*, and they will ignore most of what you say." DeFain's description of a totally recalcitrant Board left Tom feeling deserted by DeFain. This was the principal that had been bad-mouthed by his teaching staff before the strike. Faculty members at the Middle School continued to criticize DeFain for requiring that they arrive on time, while leaving his building at the earliest possible moment after 3:00 p.m.

Tom removed his jacket and hung it over the back of his chair. He said aloud to Arnie, 'Does DeFain even care about his role as principal?' to which Arnie replied, 'Don't ask me. He's your problem. You straighten him out before next month's meeting'. Tom barely had time to write a note about DeFain before Connie Cratt jumped in with a question about Plant and Harvey.

Tom reported that he had personally seen them working together in the Industrial Arts shop. The shop had a picture window that faced the parking lot. At least half a dozen parents, during the basketball game that night, asked Tom if he saw Sylvan Plant with his arm around Lillian Harvey. Tom told the board he had issued written warnings, to which Cratt replied,

"I move the Board fire Sylvan Plant and Lillian Harvey for conduct 'unbecoming a teacher which materially impairs the teacher's educational effectiveness'." When Cratt finished reading this from a piece of paper, he put it into his pocket. He was smiling like the Cheshire cat in Alice in Wonderland. He reached out and touched the brim of the white hat on the table in front of him. He looked at Arnie Murkiwasser, probably expecting support from Arnie.

"That's the law, isn't it?" asked Cratt, when nobody seconded the motion.

"Same statute you asked about two days ago, Mr. Cratt," said Tom. He went on to tell the board the statute said *'Conduct unbecoming'* which implied that the teacher's behavior inside the school was *morally indecent.* Tom said that dropping notes on each other's desk did not rise to the level of immoral conduct.

"The Hell it doesn't," said Cratt quickly. He glared at Tom before turning his attention to Patty Trivic, almost as if he knew he needed to persuade Mrs. Trivic to join his side. "Their actions impair their effectiveness, don't they?"

"What kind of actions would fit the definition?" asked Patty Trivic.

Tom stopped for a moment, considering his answer. "Immoral conduct on the grounds of the school building," said Tom.

"You mean shacking up, don't you?"

"Yes."

"Well then..."

"We don't know anything about that kind of behavior," added Tom.

"I renew my motion," said Cratt. Arnie called for a vote and the motion failed, three to three, with Trivic joining Percy Smith and Curt Fitzsimmons in voting down the motion.

Cratt's reaction was instantaneous. He tore the first sheet of paper off the board agenda lying in front of him, wadded the paper into a ball, and threw it over his shoulder. The paper bounced on the counter behind him. Patty Trivic reached over and patted him on the arm, as if to say 'That's all right, big fella'. He did not return her smile, but waved at Arnie, indicating another issue.

"What about Miss Wilson?"

"I sent a card and flowers to her room," said Tom.

"Did she have the baby?" asked Glacinda Fallow, suddenly coming to life.

"It was a girl, seven pounds and nine ounces, to be christened Vermilion Veronica," said Tom.

"That's really nice," said Glacinda.

"Huhhnh!" broke in Connie Cratt. "That's not what I meant!"

"Well, what exactly did you mean?" asked Arnie.

"Like I promised during the strike. The board should fire her."

"For what reason?"

"Because she is not married. Having a baby out of wedlock is a clear case of immoral behavior."

"Who said she is not married?" asked Tom, from the fringes of the discussion. He knew that he couldn't reveal what he knew, unless the board was meeting in a closed session to discuss the performance of a teacher. To admit what he knew in a public session was definitely, no question about it, a violation of the Employee Data Privacy Act of Minnesota.

"Well, that man in the flannel shirt at the December board meeting." Cratt calmly reached up and twirled the end of his collar. "Several parents have asked me what we are going to do about Miss Wilson."

"That man was Herman Fynmore," said Curt from the opposite end of the board table. "Everyone knows he is four peas short of a salad."

"I'll word my question in a different manner," Tom forced into the conversation. "Who says Miss Wilson is not married?"

"Are you trying to tell us something?" spit Cratt. "Is she married?"

"I can't answer that question."

"You can't or you won't?" said Connie; in subtle, slinking tones like a slithering cobra about to strike. He glared at Tom. Harant, for his part, found it hard to look at Cratt and glanced instead at Karen Clark. Mrs. Clark had that smile on her face that says, *'You don't know everything, you idiot'* when she turned to Tom and winked at him.

"Mr. Cratt, are you aware that Mrs. Wilson's husband is in Saudi Arabia, at one of the support bases?"

Cratt stopped, with an expression that reminded Tom of a deer caught in the headlights of a fast moving truck. He sat back in his chair and his shoulders seemed to slump. He looked deflated, as Billy Washburn described him later.

"Thank you, Karen. I had forgotten that point," said Tom.

"Which means what?" growled Cratt.

"That if you persist in attacking Miss Wilson, the board will wind up with egg on its face and lawyers at every meeting, trying to defend your behavior." He said this, looking directly at Connie Cratt, knowing that this man would probably try to fire their superintendent with his next breath.

*****

In Tom's mind, he saw his predecessor Arley Green at a similar board meeting, when this same man, Connie Cratt made a motion that effectively fired Arley. Only the fact that Green was about to retire kept him from being fired.

"Lawyers," said Cratt. "All they do is obfuscate and delay."

To which Arnie Murkiwasser replied by asking if Cratt didn't have another issue for this board meeting.

Two hours later, over doubles of Bushmills on ice, Billy Washburn suddenly commented that it had looked like Arnie Murkiwasser knew that Cratt had another issue.

*****

Connie was pulling out his cigarettes. The board waited while he lit a dark brown Manicetti from Italy. He sucked in one full lungful and then exhaled slowly.

"We have an issue that could decide the future of the Iron Lake schools. We all know that we went over budget with the teacher settlement. Mr. Harant has suggested we may be cutting $500,000 out of next year's budget. I have a proposal."

There was silence in the room. Tom was lighting a cigarette. Patty Trivic was carrying her cup toward the coffee pot. Percy Smith and Curt Fitzsimmons were watching Cratt, like two hounds pointing at quail.

"Is it true," Cratt asked Tom, "that in college, many of the classes are taught in large lecture halls, with 100 or 150 students present?"

"Yes," said Tom. His stomach felt like a mass of lead and he began to reach for his antacid tablets.

"Do those professors have helpers?"

"Assistants, usually upperclassmen. People to take attendance, grade papers and tests, provide mentoring when needed." Tom wasn't looking at Cratt. He grabbed a quick glance at Washburn and Clark. They both looked like two large Doberman Pinschers, ready to attack but reluctant to growl. Tom turned his chair until he was facing Connie Cratt.

"Is there any reason?" Cratt asked, while Trivic was returning to her chair.

"Is there any reason you can think of that one teacher in each department can't teach all the students in a theater setting?"

"What do the students do when they aren't in class?" asked Tom.

"They use the library, study in the cafeteria, and we have an open campus."

"Whoa, back up there, Connie." Arnie suddenly was involved. "Did you ask any of the owners downtown about this?"

"Several said they can use the increase in business."

"But changing to an open campus?" said Curt Fitzsimmons.

"An open campus gets them out of our building, makes the building quieter." Cratt had that look of determination on his face, knowing he was leading the board toward his view of the future.

"No, on the Open Campus," said Percy Smith. "Emphatically, no."

"Wait a minute, Percy," stammered Cratt.

"I don't have to wait a minute. You told me on the phone. You want to lay off all the teachers, except the most senior teacher in English, Social Studies, Math, Science, Spanish, Industrial Arts and Home Economics. That's a reduction of fifteen teaching positions, isn't it, Mr. Harant?"

"I would have to check the seniority list," said Tom from inside the fog swirling around in his brain.

"And twelve positions would save us $600,000 and give us a surplus next year of nearly $200,000, wouldn't it? Mr. Harant?" Cratt was insistent, demanding that the superintendent make an estimate.

Tom looked at the numbers he was writing. '$600,000' stood next to the number '15'. He stood up, taking his coffee cup with him. He moved to the coffee pot and poured himself a cup. He stood with his back to the board, trying to think. *'Keeryeest,'* he thought. *'Fifteen teachers?'*

"Most of the least senior teachers are the youngest, with the smaller salaries. So the estimate of $600,000 may be too high." These words were spoken slowly, from the front row of the visitor seats. Billy Washburn was staring at Cratt while he spoke.

"So, we don't know? We can still layoff all those teachers and retain one in each department, give them extra planning time during the week, hire some teacher aides to help." Cratt was adamant, demanding adherence to his plan, just like the boisterous and commanding leader of the Green Bay Packers, Vince Lombardi.

"Seems reasonable to me," added Glacinda Fallow. *'You would follow his lead'* thought Tom.

"You make it sound so simple," said Curt Fitzsimmons.

*****

The sun was setting on the Pacific while Tom and Crystal sat on a cement barrier on Wakiki Beach, Honolulu. Tom brought his wife to Hawaii to celebrate their 25th Anniversary, which occurred, as luck would have it, the August after the Iron Lake teacher's strike. Tom and Crystal delayed their trip for three years, until after Tom left Iron Lake.

There were a few scattered couples walking along the beach, admiring the crimson of the sun as it sank into the sea. Crystal reached over and put her hand on Tom's. He looked up and admired his wife, and smiled at the red sheens and highlights that were reflected in her blond hair. Looking out at the sun, Tom realized that the stand he made at the 'Retaliation' meeting was the start of the end. That was the night he faced a decision…he could have allowed Connie Cratt to go forward with his plan to layoff fifteen teachers. The public backlash would have ruined them all. Instead he fought Cratt to a draw.

"Strange, the twists and turns we take," he said quietly to his wife. To the west, the last red edge of the sun was slipping below the placid waves of the ocean.

*****

"You are rather transparent," said Tom loudly, directly at Connie Cratt. "You came in last week and I gave you a copy of the seniority list."

"So what? You don't vote," Cratt said, "do you?"

"No, I don't. But the board should know that it is transparent, what you want to do." Tom lit another cigarette, while his stomach churned. Percy Smith stood up and moved to the far end of the boardroom and stood by the door. He admitted later that he was afraid that Cratt was going to come after Tom and Percy wanted to be where he could put himself between Tom and Cratt.

"Damned stubborn, obstinate, dragging his feet," said Cratt to the rest of the board.

"You know I will implement whatever the board decides," said Tom while glancing at the entire board.

"No, you want to stop us from laying off fifteen teachers, don't you?"

"Yes, I do."

"Why?" said Arnie.

"You know why he wants to layoff these teachers?" said Tom to the board. "If you layoff all but one teacher, you will be laying off 'Bluster Barnes, Sylvan Plant, and two other negotiators."

"But we will be laying off fifteen and organizing to provide the same classroom programs with less teachers," said Glacinda, trying to stand up for the idea that Connie Cratt probably hatched with those two friends of his from Chicago.

"This will be seen as *retaliation*, plain and simple," argued Tom, with all the determination he could muster despite feeling part of the board was absolutely opposed to his leadership. "Retaliation, which you agreed not to do."

"He's right," said Percy Smith. "This smells like retaliation."

In the discussion that followed, the board members argued the pros and cons. There was no clear majority on the issue. No decision was made. Tom argued that teaching classes in large groups would probably destroy the reputation of the Iron Lake schools. If the parents became unhappy, it would take very little coaxing before they took their children to the neighboring school districts of Cherry Grove, Urholt or Fillmore.

In the end, Cratt, Trivic, Fallow and Murkiwasser were convinced that Tom Harant was the kind of person who became obstinate and would argue with the board about any issue. This was far from the truth but they failed to see the truth while Connie Cratt was leading.

The Lady Panthers lost their first game in the State Tournament and finished second in the 'Consolation' round. The parents and sports boosters were excited and satisfied with their performance at state. The minutes of the February 15, 1991 Iron Lake Board of Education meeting show that the board discussed some alternative methods of classroom instruction.

*****

The ground war (G-Day) began on February 24th. Resistance was light when Coalition forces stormed north across the Saudi-Kuwaiti border. In less than twenty-four hours, Saddam Hussein announced that Iraqi troops would withdraw from Kuwait. On the 26th, it was evident that Iraqi troops were in full withdrawal from Kuwait. U.S. and Coalition forces slashed west and then northeast, flanking the elite Republican Guard tank units. The demoralized Iraqi troops surrendered in the thousands. On February 27, President Bush announced Kuwait had been liberated and the war would end at midnight.

In the military hospital ship, *USS Relief,* the young naval lieutenant called 'Harpoon' by some of his men, regained consciousness after a second operation on his leg. On February 24th, Lieutenant Mark Harant had competently delivered his first load of US Marines to the beach fifteen miles south of Kuwait City. He and his coxswain, Seaman 1st Class Griffith, had turned their LST seaward when the small ship was hit by a five-inch shell from an Iraqi battery, positioned three-miles inland. Lt. Harant had turned to watch the action on shore when shrapnel hit him in the back of his right leg. His boatswain received superficial wounds in one arm. The actual war was over in less than 100 hours.

In the southern Iraqi desert on March 3rd, television cameras showed the Coalition Generals Schwarzkopf, de la Billiere (British), Roquejoffre (French), and Prince Khalid bin Sultan, head of Saudi forces, when they met with Iraqi generals to discuss a permanent ceasefire. They met at the captured Iraqi airfield of Safwan, three miles north of the Kuwait-Iraq border. On the same day, Mrs. Thomas Harant of Iron Lake, Minnesota received a scrawled letter from her son in which he 'matter of factly' told his parents he had been wounded rather severely and the doctors were hoping to save his leg. He proudly announced he had won the Purple Heart. His mother sat down at her kitchen table and cried.

CHAPTER TWENTY-FOUR
Little John and Robin

Reduce the supplies budget by 10 percent—$35,000"

"Reduce heating fuel budget by 10 percent—$8,000"

"Eliminate three teacher aides—$24,000"

"Cut one bus route—$16,000" The four administrators were reviewing a pile of cards, each with a budget reduction item. They had been at it for two hours. Through the open window came the voices of boys on the baseball field.

'Hey, batter, batter!'

'No hitter, no Hitler, no swinger!'

'Over the plate, Tommy.'

Occasionally, a 'plank!' or a 'plink' would interrupt the chatter on the field. Then there would be a few moments of quiet until either a few of the players clapped for a play at first base, or someone groused that the runner was not safe at first.

"Increase the fee for home games by $1—$25,000"

"Increase the lunch fees by twenty-five cents—$25,000"

"Eliminate one section of grade Three—increase the average to 26 students."

"Eliminate the Music teacher, savings of $32,000."

"Well, hell," said Karen Clark.

"I know," said Billy Washburn, sitting next to her. His forehead was shiny with dew, the result of not removing his suit jacket. He brushed his upper lip with a finger to remove a small amount of sweat. Karen looked at Billy and then she closed the notebook that was sitting in front of her.

"Tom, I can't do this," she stated bluntly. "We can't be expected to prioritize these cuts. These are our people that we are talking about." Her face betrayed a soft determination, a single-minded desire to succeed with this 'reduction' project. In her light tan business suit, Karen looked every bit the professional adherent for her elementary school.

She looked directly at her boss. Tom was sitting back in his chair, holding a glass with RC Cola on ice, chewing on the ice. He listened to Karen, saw that Billy Washburn was nodding in agreement, and turned to Dennis DeFain. Dennis was sitting to Tom's right. The four of them had started at 2:30 p.m. to review all of the ideas that Tom had placed on 3x5 cards. It was 4:30 p.m. and they looked a little bummed out. DeFain looked disgusted.

"You can't expect us to absorb 20 more kids into four sections of grade five. That makes four sections of 30 students each. Hell, Sylvan Plant will have a coronary."

"Sir Sylvan," said Billy Washburn.

"And Black Bart," added Karen Clark. She realized that Tom had a blank look on his face, and added, "There is a drawing going around. It shows a fat friar with a fringe of hair, sitting on a jousting horse, aiming his lance at another rider. His opponent has armor and is charging his trusty stead toward the friar. Someone wrote 'Friar Tuck' under the friar, and 'Black Bart' under the knight. At the bottom is scrawled 'Iron Lake Schools'.

"And Black Bart is..."

"Of course, it's 'Bluster Barnes' and his slick sidekick, Sir Sylvan."

"And Friar Tuck is..." Tom was reluctant to ask, but he thought he might just as well go along with the joke.

"Friar Tuck is you, Tom."

"Oh, really?" he said laughing. He was puzzled about the hair. Dennis DeFain opened his notebook and brought out a copy of the drawing. The friar did indeed have a fringe of hair.

"But I don't look like that, do I?"

Karen Clark laughed, and nudged Billy to her left. "You tell him," she said laughing.

Billy Washburn chuckled, and then raised an eyebrow. His facial expression seemed to say, 'Should I tell him?' He sat up straight, like a soldier doing his duty no matter how distasteful.

"Your hair, Tom. On top. It's thin. When you bend over, all we see is scalp with a fringe of hair around the outside."

"Oh, for crying out loud," Tom snorted.

"What did it was when you walked around the building with 'Little John *Whasshisname?* My secretary said, there goes Friar Tuck and Little

John," said DeFain with a smile. Dennis seemed pleased with himself, implying that his boss stepped out of a 12th century story of knights and knaves.

"Little John…that's a good name for him. He has always been Little John around the state. A good man." Tom Harant did not need to add that Little John was an employee of Minnesota School Boards Association, a consultant hired to review Tom's list of budget cuts. Tom was unsure of how to handle Little John. And the board was expecting a report from Little John at the public meeting tomorrow.

"Jousting and clashing. I can see it now." DeFain laughed, and laughed, and stood up to walk to the window. He pulled the window shut, cutting off the noise from the baseball battlefield.

"Black Barnes and his faithful sidekick, Sir Sylvan, leading the charge into the board meeting, at the head of thirty teachers who want the board to back down on making cuts."

"But the board cannot back down," said Tom.

"And there sits the Sheriff of Nottingham, with his bulging stomach jammed against the table, turning red in the face. His trusty cohorts arranged on both sides, with Sir Arnie the Groveler sitting to his right and Glacial Linda to his left."

"He Maid Marion," said Billy Washburn, suddenly.

"Who?" said Tom.

"The Sheriff. He *made* Marion."

"Oh, really, Billy" said Karen Clark. "You're terrible."

"That naughty sheriff," mimicked Billy. "He had his house maid upside down."

DeFain's laugh turned into a guffaw. Tom, in spite of himself, began laughing, and then he added, "Wasn't the sheriff always trying to get Maid Marion into his bed?"

"True," said Billy. "But in our version, the Maid ain't no more. And the sheriff wants to send the 'Merry Men' to the unemployment line."

"And where is Robin in all this?" asked Tom.

"Down in St. Paul, robbing the rich to pay our humble salaries," said Karen getting into the spirit. "You know what they say. Neither man nor beast is safe while the State Legislature is in session."

"No help from those quarters," said Tom with terse urgency. "Governor Carlson has pledged to build a 'rainy day fund' of $650 million."

"It's raining in Sherwood Forest," said Karen quietly.

"Too bad. Robin is away on a crusade," added Tom.

"Ha," added Dennis DeFain. "Who is going to protect Maid Marion? Not the Sheriff, surely?"

"Maybe Black *Barnes* will come to her aid?" said Tom, smiling at Karen.

"No, I think not," answered DeFain.

There was a quiet moment. Billy glanced at the clock, where the hour hand was crawling past Five. He looked at Tom, then Dennis, and then he glanced out the window. He could see a boy rounding the bases while a player in the outfield chased a ball to the wall.

"It's your call, Tom." Billy Washburn decided that Karen was right. They couldn't prioritize the cuts. The superintendent would have to do it.

*****

With a little imagination, DeFain's vision of a jousting match happened the next evening. The spectators filled the boardroom with signs and balloons. The atmosphere was neither festive nor forlorn. The teachers were corralled in the band room until the board members were seated. Then in came Black Barnes with his sidekick, Sir Sylvan, leading the pack. Once all the teachers were in, standing along the back of the room, Barnes demanded that the Board not make any cuts that affect the classroom programs. He waved the list of cuts proposed by the superintendent and began asking questions.

The Sheriff of Nottingham sat quietly, smiling at Barnes. When he said they were considering all their options, Sir Arnie said, 'Yes, indeed.'

Glacial Linda patted 'Sheriff Cratt' on the arm, at one point.

In the end, Little John stood at the end of the board table and faced the teachers and parents. He set his briefcase on the table, opened it, and removed a printed report that he distributed to everyone present. He said, in his opinion, the superintendent had used *a scalpel* to trim expenses from next year's budget. Faculty cuts included an English teacher, a science teacher, two Middle School teachers, one Elementary classroom teacher and the Elementary Music teacher.

The superintendent, Tom Harant, stood to thank Little John for his work on behalf of the Iron Lake schools. From the back of the room, someone snickered. Billy said later that from his point of view, the two men did look like Friar Tuck and Little John.

"But in our version," added Tom, "there is no King Richard the Lion Hearted to rescue us from the evil sheriff."

"I guess not," laughed Washburn as he walked down the hall.

*****

"John Smith is here," announced Judy.

"That man with the nondescript name? Send him in," Tom said with enough force to be heard in the outer office.

"I'll only be a couple of minutes," said Smith, apologizing to Tom's secretary for interrupting her routine.

Tom stood up to greet the shorter man from the BCA. Smith had brown hair, in a shade of mahogany brown, thin on top. Tom noticed the man's hair was thin on top when Smith bent over while sitting down.

"You and I," said Tom. "Thinning on top."

"Comes with the territory," said Smith. "At least your hair isn't gray."

"Thank you."

"I wanted to follow up on something your Chemistry teacher mentioned. You asked him to conduct an inventory after the strike?"

"Yes, that's correct."

"And before school started, back in August?"

"Correct again. Mr. Williams filed both inventories."

"Anything out of the ordinary?"

"He told you about the missing chemicals, I suppose?"

"Yes, he did. Williams was embarrassed." Smith leaned back and crossed his legs. He began to pull out a pack of cigarettes but decided he didn't have time.

"Can you get me the names of all your replacement teachers?"

"I could. Good luck finding them."

"What do you mean?" asked Smith.

"About a third were from other states."

Smith thought about that for a long minute, while Tom waited. He heard a noise and looked at the open door to the boardroom. He was sure someone was in the room.

"Did you get a chance to review your notebook?"

"Yes, I did," he said while moving toward the open door. Tom took the door handle and began to pull the door shut.

"Anything unusual?"

"No, I looked through my copy. It's right there on my desk." He glanced into the boardroom and saw Connie Cratt standing at the near end of the board table, waiting. Tom finished closing the door.

"You said *your copy?*"

"My secretary is a little paranoid, or cautious, I guess. She made a copy and filed the original in the school safe."

"That never hurts," said John Smith standing up.

After Smith left, Tom opened the door to find Cratt sitting in a boardroom chair, waiting. Cratt asked if Tom had considered laying off the Elementary Art teacher and covering her sections with teacher aides. Tom said that he hadn't. He felt that cutting two teachers at each level seemed to balance the impact. Cratt said that he realized Tom couldn't just put his daughter's position on the list.

Tom must have looked a little startled. Connie said he didn't want to surprise him at the April meeting, and Tom should know that Connie was going to add Corrine Harant's position to the cuts list at the April meeting.

'How long have you been thinking about this, you great big son of a bitch?' Tom said to himself. He could feel his ears turning red. To Cratt he said,

"Is this necessary? She didn't do *anything*! She didn't even stand on the picket line out front? She kept her nose clean and didn't draw any attention to herself. Darn it, Connie!"

"Nope. Nothing to do with the strike, Tom. We have to have a Physical Education teacher in the Elementary school. The art sections, on the other hand, can be covered by a teacher's aide."

"So you think it is appropriate to layoff my daughter?"

"It's nothing personal, Tom."

"Well, now, Mr. Cratt. Do you think I am going to believe that piece of horse pucky?"

"Don't get angry, Tom."

Tom stood. An observer would have seen the color in his cheeks. He watched Cratt leave through the boardroom.

He smiled to himself, thinking about the Irish prayer that our enemies turn their ankles so we'll know them by their limping. 'Don't get angry!' said Tom quietly under his breath. He wanted to laugh. It seemed so ludicrous that Iron Lake could hire a good Art teacher and then fire her because her father was the superintendent. 'Hell, no, don't get angry!' he said again.

When Judy stuck her head into his office, she saw Tom closing the windows. He was preparing to leave for the day. "What was it you said?" she asked.

Tom stood and looked at her. She always acted so competent, so polite and so forgiving of the men who worked around her. Tom's ears were still red. He felt like a professional wrestler, ready to crush and maim the next thing he touched. Instead he tried to smile at Judy and said,

'Don't get angry, get even."

CHAPTER TWENTY-FIVE
We will Know Them by Their Limping

Crystal Harant stood in the door of the hospital room in the Bethesda Naval Hospital, with Tom behind her. The hospital room was flying a blue banner with yellow trim that declared the occupant was a crewmember of the USS *George Philip,* the guided missile frigate, still on station in the Persian Gulf. She was looking at her son Mark in a hospital bed, with his right leg elevated in a truss. Mark looked healthy enough, considering his leg was wrapped in foam and Ace bandages, from the hip down to his ankle. Crystal sighed once and reached back for Tom's hand. She assumed the girl was Mark's 'special' person that he had only hinted at in letters home.

Mark's left hand was raised and the girl was holding it with both hands. Her brown hair was pulled back into a ponytail, tied with a leather strap and she wore a band of yellow cloth around the crown of her head. A large, white hibiscus was held behind her left ear by the yellow band. She wore a knee-length blue skirt with a scalloped-neck blouse that highlighted a necklace of seashells against her dark skin.

"She's very pretty," said Tom admiring her face. He noticed the girl had a slightly flattened nose, giving her a Polynesian appearance that went well with the hot pink lipstick she was wearing.

The girl picked up a thin hairbrush and began to comb Mark's hair. In the doorway, Crystal cleared her throat. Mark saw her first, and said "Mom!"

The girl stood up and backed away from Mark, leaving room for Crystal to make a dash to the bed. His mother nearly threw herself onto Mark, burying her face against his neck, surrounding him with her arms. Tom and the girl heard Crystal's sobs, muffled by Mark's neck. Crystal turned and kissed him on the cheek, looked him in the eyes, and whacked him on the right shoulder.

"Hey! Mom!" he said in her ear. "I'm okay."

"You could have told us more details," she said.

"I lost some muscle mass between my hip and the knee. Doctor says I won't play tennis any day soon."

"Ha," snorted his father. "You didn't play anyway." Tom was straightening his clothes, a nervous habit from his teaching days. He reached out and touched Mark's right leg gently. Looking at Mark, Tom said, "I'm glad you're okay."

"I am Dad, really."

"You haven't met Mara, yet. Dad, and Mom, this is Aymara Leeann Hanawaki, from Honolulu. That's a mouthful, isn't it?" The girl to his left was standing with her hands behind her, smiling at Mark's parents.

Crystal turned toward Mara and held out both her hands. The young lady slowly placed both of her hands in Crystal's. Mark's mother leaned forward and kissed Mara on the cheek. "Are you his special girl?"

"Mom!" protested Mark.

"Well, is she? You men don't tell me enough!"

"We set the date this morning. Third Saturday in October, on the patio facing the ocean at the Sheraton on Waikiki Beach."

"Oh, Mark," gushed Crystal as she leaned forward to kiss Mara again, with moisture forming in her eyes. Then she turned to Mark and hit him on the shoulder again. "You can't keep me in the dark, like this."

"My executive officer on the *George Philip* filed my transfer papers. I put in for Pearl Harbor. He thinks I'll get 'Recuperation' duty for at least a year, before returning to the *Philip*."

*****

In Iron Lake after the quick trip to Maryland, Tom found the same tensions floating around the school. The older teachers in the high school were angry, vociferous and irritable. They felt they had failed to accomplish anything by their three months on the picket line. The younger teachers seemed to be upbeat, trying to be optimistic although six of their number were about to be laid off. The elementary faculty was ecstatic to be working with their children.

The three teachers who crossed the picket line were being harassed. They were receiving 'nasty' notes, about once each week accusing them of disloyalty. Among the citizens of Iron Lake, the word was 'Don't talk to the teachers'. Many of the residents who supported the school board knew the teachers were angry with the business community. Gossip had it that eight homeowners had filed for building permits for backyard fences. Dr. Kenworth Clark, the only doctor in town, reported stitching up five sets of busted lips in recent weeks.

The pastors at the Evangelical Lutheran Church, the Hoch Deutsch Lutheran Church and the Catholic Church gave sermons in March and early April, extolling their parishioners to practice charity toward those who were recently 'swept up in the emotional maelstrom of the strike'. Rumor had it that the church council at Hoch Deutsch passed a resolution asking the Iron Lake teachers to resign and move on to other towns. Tom's secretary Judy remarked that she was glad she lived in another town...Iron Lake seemed to be turned toward vengeance and retribution.

Karen Clark reported that four families with nine children had moved out of Iron Lake. Billy Washburn said his attendance clerk noted there were at least ten students who told the High School Counselor they were moving after school was out.

The high school's Student Council told Washburn they were looking for ways to accentuate the positive. Tom Harant found a report on his desk when he returned. Connie Cratt and Sylvan Plant apparently started shoving each other in the hall at the Middle School before Dennis DeFain could separate them. There was also a written complaint about DeFain's behavior.

Tom decided not to order DeFain to appear at his office. Instead, he went to DeFain's office so Dennis would not feel defensive. Tom's effort failed. In the end, Dennis failed to be honest. "Patting a young lady on the butt is what it says."

"Was there a witness?"

"According to this report, there was. An adult. And this time was not the first. I talked to the girl's mother. She claims you have special girls that you are very cozy with, when the girls are doing work around the office complex.

Tom hated this kind of situation. He had to act; he could not ignore the accusation. Even if it was not true, he knew he would have a hard time trusting DeFain again. After Tom told DeFain he was suspended pending an investigation, Tom left DeFain's office, saying nothing to DeFain's veteran secretary.

'*Some days,*' said Tom when he was back inside the CEO's office building.

"What?" asked Judy when Tom walked past her desk.

"Make hay," he answered and picked up the log he kept from October 6 to January 10. He flicked through the pages, back to front. Near the front, the page for October 8 was missing. When he asked Judy, she said the new Xerox machine sometimes stuck two pages together and one didn't get copied. She walked into his office and picked up his copy of the log, intending to insert the page for October 8. Five minutes later she came back into his office, with a puzzled look on her face.

"Did you pull this log apart, for some reason?"

"There's no reason why I would. Why?"

"Look at the front." She showed him the front of the log, pointing at the staple in the corner. The staple appeared normal. Then she turned it over. On the back, the staple was crimped, as it should be. But there was an extra set of holes next to the bent staple. "The original staple has been removed and a second staple inserted, but it did not hit the original hole all the way through the log."

"Why are you telling me this?" asked Tom, wondering where she was going with this staple business.

"I heard that BCA man, that Mr. Smith, tell you to take good care of your log. That's why I put the original of your log in the safe."

"Thank you," he mumbled, "for that."

"Here's a copy of the October 8 page," she said handing him the page. '*So someone removed this page from what they thought was my log,*' he said with hesitation to himself.

Tom reached up and pulled his blue tie with green shamrocks down an inch. He unbuttoned his collar. It had been a busy day, culminating with his conference with Dennis DeFain. He watched Judy leave his office, thankful once again that an experienced secretary is the best safeguard for an efficient office. He sat and read the daily log, remembering that first week of the strike, the long days and difficult decisions. Toward the bottom of the sheet, he saw an entry that read 'Cratt in building. Checking security in Chem lab.' An image popped into his head…an image of Connie Cratt bending over to pick up a briefcase off the floor of the Chemistry lab, just in front of the Hazardous Materials locker.

But of course, he thought, there was nothing to worry about. Mr.

Williams had removed all the hazardous chemicals before the strike. Or so he thought, while he watched Cratt leaving the Chemistry lab, walking down the hall and turning left to leave the building on the west side.

'*Damn,*' thought Tom. 'Why didn't I see it when it happened?'

*****

"Mr. Williams, what does this mean?" asked Tom. He was holding the inventory that Wayne Williams completed in January, after the strike. Mr. Williams, embarrassed, had pointed out the ethylene and acetone chemicals that were missing, the chemicals that were the main components of LSD.

Mr. Williams took a pencil out of a coffee cup full of pencils on his desk and walked to the pencil sharpener in the corner, near the door. He sharpened the pencil and gave it to a student who was working on a makeup test. Then he turned to look at the inventory Mr. Harant was holding. Behind the item 'Potassium Permanganate' was a one, indicating one bottle, and a note that said, 'No dust, full.'

"That's what I found. No dust on the bottle."

"Is that strange?"

"Top shelf in the locked cabinet. Most of those items haven't been used in years. Should have been destroyed long ago. Lots of dust on that shelf."

"You mean you found an item with no dust?"

"Exactly. One full bottle of Potassium Permanganate."

"You wrote down, 'full'. Why?"

"If you scan back about four columns, there is my note from last August, where I entered '3/4'. The bottle was three-quarters full."

"Show me this bottle."

Williams unlocked the cabinet and pointed at the bottle. It stood toward the back of the shelf, next to another bottle with no dust; a bottle marked 'Magnesium Shavings'. When Williams looked at the inventory, he found Magnesium on the previous page. It was also marked '3/4' in the August inventory. Today, the bottle was full. Both bottles had the little paper labels on their sides, with the price of the contents. All the labels of all the chemicals on the top shelf were marked with Reliable Drug labels. But the two bottles with no dust had tan labels while the remainder of the items on the shelf carried white labels, with some of the labels decidedly older and grungier.

"It looks strange. Why would someone take two bottles from the cabinet and then replace them? If that is what happened? Did our replacement Chemistry teacher do the experiment that produces the volcano?" When Mr. Williams said he didn't know, Tom asked him to keep the cabinet locked and thanked him for his help.

The next morning, the *Cherry Grove Journal* carried a story about a hearing held in Spencer County District Court.

> **Cherry Grove [AP]** Hearing was held Tuesday, April 16 before Judge Harley Bellows in Spencer County District Court. The Farmers and Mechanics Insurance Company filed suit against Mr. Conifer Cratt of rural Iron Lake, asking that Mr. Cratt show cause why the insurance company should not disallow an insurance claim filed by Mr. Cratt.
>
> Stan Stevens, an Assistant State Fire Marshal, read from his report, in which he cited evidence that the fire was arson. Spencer County Sheriff Curt Larson testified that it was the conclusion of his investigators that the fire was arson, probably started by accident by George Fallow. Fallow died as a result of the fire that rapidly consumed the house at 1006 South Ninth Street in Iron Lake.
>
> Owner of the house, Noah Fynmore, who runs the Bulrush Bay Resort on Iron Lake, reported that Cratt rented the house in June 1990 for the purpose of creating an office. Judge Bellows took the case under advisement, and will report his decision in 90 days.

Tom Harant did not see the article. On Friday night, following a baseball game between the Iron Lake Panthers and Warba Wolverines, Tom was sitting in his breezeway when Wrecker Kline plopped into the easy chair next to the porch swing and said, "Did you see the insurance company sued *Conifer* Cratt? I guess they don't want to pay him for his lost manuscript."

"No, I didn't see that."

The next morning, Tom called the County Attorney and scheduled a private conference. A sheriff's deputy came to Iron Lake late that afternoon and collected the two bottles. He put them in separate containers, surrounded by asbestos foam.

*****

"The County Attorney didn't say why you suspected Mr. Cratt." The County Sheriff, Mr. Curt Larson was standing, hands on hips, looking at the burned out house and the yellow 'Police Line' tape.

"It was something I didn't see until just the other day," said Tom watching a leaf fall from the roof of the high school. "Mr. Cratt always parked right here, on this curb, almost as if he owned the school. I saw him park here, especially during the strike, mostly to aggravate the pickets. But that Thursday afternoon, in the first week, he parked on the west side of the building. If I hadn't been checking the door locks, I would never have seen him. He left the Chem lab, walked down the hall, and turned left, going directly out of the building."

"So you assume he was parked on the west side."

"Yes. I think he was. What did you find out about our *chemicals?*"

"We traced the Potassium Perglandinate," said Curt Larson, the Sheriff.

"You mean Permanganate, I think," said Tom.

"Yes, sir. Per–mangl–nate," said Larson.

"What did you find out?" Tom was standing on the sidewalk, the former site of the charcoal burner the strikers used to keep warm. The sun was trying to break through light clouds while a 10 mph wind blew from the west. The wind blew an occasional brown leaf off the roof. A few leaves ran a marathon race down the gutter past Tom's feet. The gutters and streets in Iron Lake were clean, recently swept by the street 'engineer'.

Larson zipped his jacket against the cold air while he considered how to answer the question. The Iron Lake superintendent was not an employee of the sheriff's office but Larson felt he could trust Harant to keep his mouth shut. It was Larson's experience that when someone took the risk that Tom Harant was taking by divulging the information he brought to the County Attorney that Harant deserved to know that the information had been worth something.

"Any useable fingerprints were smudged by your Mr. Williams."

He stood there and smiled.

"Except for one fingerprint."

"It was Cratt, wasn't it?"

"Surprisingly, no. She was fingerprinted when she filed for her CLU Insurance license. It was Mrs. Glacinda Fallow. She purchased the Potassium and Magnesium at Reliable Drug the week after the fire destroyed that house." He was looking across the street where an empty hole remained of the house at 1006 South Ninth Street. Yellow warning tape was stretched between the two small ash trees in the front yard, running to posts in the backyard.

"Too bad, really," said Larson.

"I didn't know Fallow well, except for one night he showed up in my yard, had been drinking, tried to tell me not to get too big for my suits, I think." Tom felt sad for the man who drank and couldn't seem to get his life organized.

"Well, anyway. The reason I came over here today." He paused, letting Tom hear his words. "Do you have any evidence that puts Mrs. Fallow in your building, perhaps replacing those bottles?"

"No, I don't."

"Like I said, it's too bad, really."

*****

"We'll know them by their limping, won't we?" he said with a chuckle.

"Yes, we will," said Corrine, in the hall outside the boardroom. It was an old saying, one that she had heard her father use many a time when drinking. He would have both feet up on a hassock, a glass in one hand after handing a similar glass to his old friend Wrecker. The two of them would look at each other and say 'Consternation' and laugh. She could never decide if they were laughing about a recent calamity or cursing someone who had the misfortune of being on her father's 'list'.

She did know that when the Bushmills was on the counter, the two men were likely to be engaged in serious grown-up talk. She was twelve or thirteen before she mustered the courage. When she asked Wrecker about 'Consternation,' he explained that the rest of the curse was 'to our enemies' and said it was a friendly warning not to tread too heavily on Tom or his friends.

Wrecker and her father were heavily into a bottle of brandy one evening when she heard the clink of glasses. They were toasting Tom's version of the ancient Irish prayer,

May we cherish those who love us,
And ignore those who fail to love us.
May God turn their hearts; for if
He cannot turn their hearts,
May He turn their ankles
So we shall know them by
Their perpetual limping.1

Tom had one complaint about his version. "I can't make up my mind," he said when he went to the kitchen to refill his glass, "whether it should say 'their perpetual limping' when I think it should say 'their perpetual griping'."

That was the night her father, Tom Harant, the slightly inebriated school superintendent explained to her, half laughing and half serious, that there are always unpleasant people who believe their role in life is to tear down their neighbors. These people are, most times, friendly when talking to you but unpleasant and critical behind your back. To know if they are truly an enemy, he said laughing, look to see if they are limping.

Corrine was the youngest, born after Mark and Carl, who were always the oldest and the fastest and the best in school. They looked out for their little sister and protected her from hurtful people. She sailed through high school, made the Dean's List four times in college at Mankato State, did her student teaching at Janesville Elementary and received her teaching license when she was barely twenty-two years old. She was hired to teach Elementary Art exactly one month before the Iron Lake board hired her father. She was proud of her father and worried that he worked too hard. During the strike, she ignored the spiteful people who couldn't understand what a superintendent did.

Tom, for his part, was proud of his daughter and fond of walking by her classroom to see what her children were doing, weaving with colored paper or finger-painting or exploring art in some other fashion.

When Cratt said he wanted to cut Elementary Art, Tom debated about warning his daughter. After two sleepless nights, he warned her that the board might cut her position during the meeting at the end of April.

There she stood, in a sweatshirt and jeans, with the words 'Art for All Children' across her chest. Farther up the hall, three elementary parents were standing, ready to go to bat for Corrine. She looked a little scared, until her father, dressed as always in a blue business suit, said

"Well, Cookie, we'll know them…"

"By their limping," she said, smiling at the man who rarely smiled.

*****

The second meeting in April was nearly 'pro forma' as her father described it. He presented the final list of budget reductions and briefly explained the teacher cuts and how the schools would compensate. When he finished, there were several questions. A farmer from west of town, the same man in flannel from the early December meeting, the boisterous mouth with the scratchy voice, asked if the proposed cuts would create a balanced budget for next year.

Tom said the Iron Lake schools would have a projected surplus around $20,000.

The same man asked if the surplus was large enough.

Tom said it could be larger. There was no 'rainy day' fund and from month to month, he never knew if there would be enough cash to pay the bills.

The same man hooked one thumb in a belt loop and looked at the chairman, Mr. Murkiwasser. He then asked the chairman if the board had considered cutting Elementary Art.

Tom felt like a swimmer in shark-infested waters. What could he say? The board chair told the man they had not considered cutting Elementary Art. Mr. Conifer Cratt stepped up to the plate at this point and asked the school superintendent if the Art position could be handled in the same manner as the Music position, with teacher aides supervising the art sections.

From within the fog, Tom said 'Yes, with teacher aides.' He saw Corrine standing with her back against the storage closet, next to a parent who held a sign, 'We want Art'. He saw that parent talking to Mr. Cratt but was unaware of what was being said. When Percy Smith asked,

Tom said 'No,' he didn't recommend that Elementary Art be eliminated, even for one or two years.

He heard the motion by Cratt to add Elementary Art to the list of cuts. Mrs. Fallow seconded the motion. Mrs. Trivic talked briefly about the responsibility of the board to have a balanced budget and to look forward to future years. The motion passed four to two, with Percy Smith and Curt Fitzsimmons voting against it.

On the larger motion to adopt the list of cuts and send notices to the teachers who were cut, the vote was identical, with Percy Smith protesting that adding to the list at the last moment was against their 'rules' and should not be tolerated. In the front row, the reporter for the *Cherry Grove Journal* was writing furiously. Tom looked at Corrine, his daughter. He saw the disappointment in her face, and an attempt at a smile.

After the meeting, the reporter asked Tom why the issue of Elementary Art had not been raised earlier. Tom told him to ask the members of the board who voted to eliminate Elementary Art. Then he added, "I know them by their limping."

CHAPTER TWENTY-SIX
Graduation Day

When Percy Smith asked Tom to do something, Tom generally listened to Percy and then did what Percy asked. The towns' folk recognized Percy's place in Iron Lake society and accorded him some respect for being a school board member. And Percy, for his part, listened to the comments at the coffee table in Reliable Drug and if an issue had merit, he would take the issue to the superintendent.

In this case, however, Tom was, to put it bluntly, afraid that the request might be both inappropriate and unethical. Tom was the CEO, the *ex officio* member of the board. Was it appropriate for Tom to ask an elected official to excuse himself from the year's graduation ceremony? Was it ethical to tell Connie Cratt that several townspeople felt he should excuse himself from graduation, that many residents did not want an embezzler on the stage. Tom was unsure of himself but drove out to Cratt's farm at 6:30 p.m. in the evening, two weeks before graduation.

When Cratt came bursting out of his house and down the three steps to the yard, Tom immediately thought he must have driven over something in the yard. He quickly scanned the area but saw nothing. He turned around and Cratt was standing within two feet. When Cratt asked him what he wanted, Tom told him.

"You'd love that, wouldn't you?"

"It's not my place to have a preference, is it?" answered Tom, trying to smile. The brow ridges above Cratt's brown eyes were furrowed, burned together.

"You'd like to get rid of me, wouldn't you?"

"It's still not my place to have a preference."

"You ain't...getting rid of me. Period. End of sentence."

"Mr. Cratt, there are people who believe you committed a fraud by pretending to make an office and, wasn't it convenient? Your manuscript burned up in the fire?"

"My attorney tells me that Judge Bellows has recused himself.

The new judge has set a trial date for May 24th. That's five days before graduation. You can't ask me to step down as a board member until I am guilty of a felony."

"Yeah, *I guess…*that's right," mumbled Tom.

"You understand, don't you? No one's gonna *push me* around."

*****

The reporter covering the trial for the *Cherry Grove Journal* included an interview with Curt Larson, the Sheriff of Spencer County, in his first story. Larson was quoted as mentioning that the gun found in the basement had been traced to George Fallow. His detectives decided based on the ownership of the gun that Fallow had broken into the house with the intention of lying in wait for Connie Cratt.

'That's why Mr. Cratt was not charged with Second or Third degree murder', added the Sheriff.

The same story explained that Mr. Conifer Cratt of rural Iron Lake was charged with 'Conspiracy to commit arson'. The indictment charged that Cratt hired 'person or persons unknown' to use stolen chemicals to torch the house on the evening of Thursday, November 5th. The arson expert from St. Paul was on the stand for three hours on Wednesday afternoon, explaining his findings of arson. At the bottom of the article, the story noted that Judge Harley Bellows, in Spencer County District Court had issued an order directing the insurance company to pay the claim filed by Mr. Conifer Cratt.

On Thursday morning, the BCA detective, Mr. John Smith presented his findings, largely that the gun belonged to George Fallow and there was a whisky bottle found inside the springs of the burned out couch. He noted that George Fallow died of asphyxiation and his blood alcohol measured .21, or two times the legal limit. When Cratt's attorney asked him if there was any evidence connecting his client to the arson, Mr. Smith reported that Mr. Cratt had been seen in the Chemistry lab at the high school, and that incendiary chemicals had been removed and later replaced. When Cratt's attorney pressed on, Mr. Smith admitted there was no evidence proving definitively that Connie Cratt had removed or replaced those chemicals.

Cratt's attorney asked for a dismissal of the case and the attorneys for both sides went into a conference with the judge. An hour later, the judge came back to the courtroom and dismissed the jury for the rest of the day.

At 5:00 p.m. the court clerk and bailiffs were called back to the courtroom. Cratt's attorney entered a plea of guilty of culpable negligence. While Cratt sat and listened, Mr. Noah Fynmore testified that the back door locks on the house had been broken twice in the month before Connie Cratt rented the house. Fynmore added that he was present when George Fallow helped Cratt move furniture into the house.

The Spencer County Attorney stood, and said that in view of this evidence, the County would dismiss the conspiracy charge and agree to a plea of guilty of culpable negligence, for failure to adequately protect the house, for both men. The judge fined Fynmore and Cratt $100 a piece. Then he remarked that the County Attorney could refile the arson case if new evidence turned up.

*****

The Iron Lake graduating class of 1991, dressed in crimson red robes with white caps, was lined up in two lines, out in the hall, waiting to begin. The bleachers inside the gymnasium were full as were the 300 seats on the crowded floor. Programs were flapping, vainly moving small amounts of air past perspiring parents. The high school custodians were turning on large room fans, also trying to move the air. From where he was sitting, Tom could see four Junior Attendants giving the graduates small cups of water. When he nodded to the band director, the man raised his baton, paused, and began to swing his baton in the 4/4 beat rhythm of the *Graduation March.*

For Tom, graduation was a culminating event, the last *big event* of the school year. The seniors were about to complete twelve years of school. These were the boys and young ladies who had played in hundreds of games, performed in band and choir, won trophies in debate and theater, and earned scholarships to help with college and vocational school. In Tom's view, each of these graduates was special, even the boys who barely qualified to graduate. They were all special and their parents were special for supporting them through their high school years.

He was surprised when he looked up and saw Mrs. Trivic, in the hall, waving to him. He wondered what was wrong but stood and weaved his way up the aisle, avoiding the graduates in their red robes. He found the Iron Lake Board clustered around Patty Trivic. Mr. Cratt stood a little way back, with florid color in his cheeks. It was obvious to Tom that Cratt was angry.

Mrs. Trivic informed him that Smith and Fitzsimmons were claiming that Cratt was no longer a member of the school board.

"Based on what?"

"On Thursday afternoon, Connie pled guilty to 'culpable negligence' in the fire that led to the death of George Fallow," said Percy from behind Mrs. Trivic.

"Is 'negligence' a felony, Percy?"

When Percy didn't answer, Tom answered for him, explaining that negligence was a gross misdemeanor but it was not a felony. "And you can't remove a board member for committing a misdemeanor."

"Ha!" snorted Connie Cratt, with a large smile on his face. He sucked in his stomach, pulled both sides of his suit jacket around his stomach, and buttoned the jacket. His white shirt looked like it was newly pressed and his bright red tie seemed to be in fashion for graduation. He stood in line, behind his fellow board members, and together they followed the graduates, with Cratt and Tom at the tail end.

Tom didn't sit. He moved onto the stage, where he welcomed parents and relatives to the 89th graduation from Iron Lake. An observer would have noted the color in Tom's cheeks, indicating that his blood pressure was up.

In a departure from normal, Tom reminded those present that the school year had been somewhat contentious. He asked all the Iron Lake residents to put the past behind them, look to the future and find ways 'that we can make the world a better place'. He told them the Iron Lake teachers were professionals who took their jobs with equal amounts of seriousness and dedication.

When Tom returned to his chair, he could see that Mr. Cratt didn't like his remarks to the audience. Tom sat down and the high school choir began to sing a melodic interpretation of 'Under His Wings'. Cratt turned to him and said, "That's all horse pucky and you know it."

"What is?" said Tom.

"That bit about our teachers being professionals."

"It's time to forget the past, Mr. Cratt."

"To hell with that," said Cratt. Cratt turned away from Tom and crossed one leg over the other. When he did, his jacket fell open. Tom could see an oil stain on Cratt's white shirt, at the waist. Tom guessed that Cratt had been on his tractor after he dressed to come to graduation.

By tradition, one half of the school board took turns handing out the diplomas. This year, the rotation fell to Cratt, Fallow and Fitzsimmons. Tom knew that Cratt was not about to excuse himself.

Billy Washburn stood up and announced that the members of the class of 1991 had met the requirements for graduation. The class stood and prepared to move in single file to the stage. Cratt, Fallow and Fitzsimmons stood up and walked over to the stage platform, a small stage raised two feet above the gymnasium floor.

Connie Cratt must have been enjoying the moment. He put his left foot on the first riser to the stage and from somewhere in the bleachers, a 'boo' was heard. When he reached the platform of the stage, he looked in the direction of the 'boo' for a moment and then turned to stand by the table with the 110 flat packets holding the diplomas. From the opposite direction, a 'boo' followed by a 'get off' were shouted across the stifling cavern of the gymnasium.

The crowd was silent. From both of the bleachers, a sound of shushing could be heard. Some of the parents wanted no further shouts from the two or three protestors. There were no further shouts. The three board members delivered diplomas and rotated, so that Curt handed a diploma to his son Jered, Mrs. Fallow handed a diploma to her niece Karen McNeil, and Connie Cratt handed a diploma to his daughter Alice. When they were finished, there was a round of applause while the three board members returned to their seats.

"Do you see, Tom?" asked Cratt when he sat down. "The number of people who were upset with my leadership of the board has dwindled down to almost nothing."

"You can believe what you want," answered Tom. He tried to smile but his lip turned up on one side and he produced a sneer. The processional started, and Tom watched the 'grads' file out, in haste to get rid of the hot gowns, no doubt. He stood back, and watched the board file out through the crowd. A man about ten feet away stuck his hand out toward Connie Cratt and shook Cratt's hand. Further on, a second man did the same. Cratt received several pats on his shoulder and four more men shook his hand.

"Are you watching?" said Billy Washburn from behind Tom. Mr. Washburn had served the Iron Lake schools for twenty-four years. He knew the Hoch Deutsch Lutheran Church tried to run the town, despite the efforts of the ELCA church to mend fences and be good neighbors.

"Three of those men are on the Church Council. One of them told me, once, that Cratt's family name was Rattzenkreuzer back in Germany. They wanted an American name. Just like a few others in that church. That's a conservative group. They think the teachers got what they deserved. To some of them, Cratt is a hero."

*****

Tom went home, pensive. After he hung up his suit and put on shorts and an old golf shirt, he walked into the kitchen. He opened the liquor cabinet and pulled down the half-empty bottle of E&J Brandy. Into a tall drinking glass, he added three ice cubes, a double shot of brandy and then he filled the glass with diet cola. His friend Wrecker hated to see Tom ruining good brandy; to Tom the drink was like ginger and scotch...medicinal but easy to drink.

He was at the bottom of his first drink when Crystal came in from the breezeway to get more iced tea. She was quietly celebrating the end of her school year at Urholt Elementary.

"Is he feeling guilty?" she asked.

"What, Cratt? He never feels guilt. About anything."

"How did the crowd react?"

"A couple of 'boos'. Afterward, he got half a dozen pats on the back."

"Well, honey," she said turning to Tom where he leaned against the counter in the kitchen. She put her hand on Tom's arm. "He grew up here, didn't he?"

"Don't know. I guess so,"

"And that means what?" she asked.

Tom thought about her question. Cratt would have some school friends in the community. There were people inside his church who probably trusted him. The news articles, this week, hinted at fraud but stopped short of accusing Connie of fraud. Everything taken together, Cratt was in good shape and a hero to boot for standing up to the teachers.

He reached for the brandy bottle and poured the glass half full. After he added another three ice cubes, he took his glass of brandy and the diet cola bottle out to the breezeway. He sat down and put his feet up on the hassock. "You're telling me he will stay in power for the immediate future."

"Power is the operative word," she added as she resumed her seat in the recliner, putting her feet up as well.

"How many parties do we have tomorrow afternoon?"

"Only seven." It was a custom that if you knew the superintendent from drinking coffee with him, or lifting a stiff one in the Red Carpet, or helping with the chains during a football game, or helping him make popcorn, that you sent an invitation to your graduation party.

"Maybe we'll run into the blowhard?" said Crystal.

"Lord, I hope not."

In Tom's world, the towers were white ivory covered with climbing vines. In Crystal's world, the towers were old granite with weeds growing up around the base. She said it without thinking. "Cratt will try to get rid of you."

*****

Tom sat at his desk, quietly writing three checks for $1000.00 each. His desk sat in a corner of their living room in Iron Lake. This was the room barely used, a room of protection for two 'stately' French provincial couches, Crystal's upright piano, and a built-in bookcase. Tom's desk was actually an old library table with three-inch thick legs and a two-inch thick top. He finished addressing three envelopes just as Crystal entered the living room and came up behind him, looking over his shoulder.

"What are you sending to Carl, Mark and Corrine?"

"A check, and a note."

"For how much?" she asked with curiosity.

"One-thousand dollars each."

"Why?"

"It's hard to explain. Feeling sorry, I guess. I don't know if I'm feeling sorry for myself, or not. What I feel is a sense of loss. I was so deeply involved in the strike, and then my Dad died, then the girl's team went to the State Tournament, and then the school board laid off Cookie. I realized today, during graduation, when I look back, I can't see any images of our kids when they were growing up. I see basketball games, and football games and board meetings and faculty meetings."

"Where was I when our kids were growing up?"

"You were right here."

"Sure I was. Taking pictures, watching that boy pin a corsage on Cookie before her Junior Prom. Getting Carl out of trouble when he tore down that fence. Watching Carl survive his broken arm. My job was to drive Mark to Minneapolis for his first interview for Annapolis. Taking you and Corrine and Carl to Baltimore and Annapolis four years later."

"Do you want to know what I remember?"

"What is that?" she said, touching his arm. There was moisture in her eyes, but he couldn't see it. He was looking out the window at the two maples in his front yard.

"I remember...waking up in the Banff National Forest. Do you remember? Carl and I were camping in that beautiful tent. You and Cookie were in our van. She must have been, what? About eight years old? Carl was twelve. When I unzipped the tent, we were under about three inches of wet, sticky snow. What I remember, vividly, is Carl and I cooked bacon, scrambled eggs and made toast on the burners of our Coleman stove. We delivered breakfast to our two girls, snuggled as they were inside the van."

"That was a fun trip, watching you and Carl prepare our meals while we lounged in the nice, dry warm van."

"I remember so little," he said while a robin hopped across his lawn, seeking worms or an insect.

"I wasn't there enough for Carl. I have never really shared with Cookie. Mark I patted on the back, and said 'Well done' while he went off to serve in the Navy." Tom looked at the three checks he had written. "How am I going to explain how I feel? I feel I cheated them, paying so much attention to my school and my job."

"Talk to them. Tell them how you feel."

"And if I do?"

"They'll tell you that you were there. Always have been." She bent over Tom's back, and wrapped her arms across his chest. Crystal kissed his cheek and patted his chest with one hand.

"And what about me? Do I get a check?"

"Heck, no. I'm taking you on a cruise of the Hawaiian Islands."

*****

The long building stretches from a two-story wing on the north, to a one-story Elementary wing on the south. At night, the building stands quiet, waiting with infinite patience for the children to return. Along the south wing, all the windows are black, shuttered with window shades against summer's heat. On the east, a white light flows down the tan brick and across black asphalt until it illuminates the base of a large tree. The Century Elm stretches upward into the black dome of the sky, its massive branches and leaves backlit by a million pinpoints of light. A bat flits by the tree, silent on nightly rounds. Tucked into the white light, caught by a huge root, a forgotten program lists the names of 110 of Iron Lake's children.

Farther to the north, the high school office is a large, dark cavern. Three red lights blink on the Simplex master clock. The device is busy with its nightly routine, urging the clocks to find 11:55 p.m. In about five minutes, the internal date monitor will declare that Friday is gone while Saturday has begun. On a desk beneath the clock, a box marked '1990-91' holds the record books, daily logs and grade sheets that have been computerized. The box will be placed in a storage room where it will collect dust for twelve years and then be thrown away.

Those who were honored were candles on the cake. In ankle length red robes, they were topped with flaming white caps. They walked across a stage and were given a piece of paper on which an emblem of the Iron Lake High School had been engraved. They were congratulated, and praised, and words of hope were spoken over their comatose visages. These candles, with vibrant enthusiasm, then rushed out the doors, to stand patiently for pictures. They formed a line across the windows of the high school office. For a few, the pictures will be returned from processing with faces of relatives and friends reflected in the late afternoon mirrors that were the high school windows.

The candles, their parents, and their friends, are gone. They were in a hurry to leave the sheltering influence of Iron Lake, feeling an urgency to get on with life. They have turned in their robes and caps, said farewell to the principal's secretary for the last time, and smiled to themselves as they left the building.

Behind where they stood, a row of trimmed bushes lines the front of the building. A program has been impaled by someone's spiked heel. Red and white plastic confetti sparkles in the dim light, retrieved from a paper supply store by a proud grandfather. Overhead, inside the edge of the roof, two of the white candle flames have been thrown and deserted. They are no longer white after soaking in muddy gutter water.

Inside one of the bushes, a tassel has been lost. It is snarled in the small branches near the base. Next fall, a custodian will find the tassel while raking leaves. He will cut the tassel out, wonder about its owner and throw it into a pile of trash.

CHAPTER TWENTY-SEVEN
Consequences

Bidding for remodeling and improvement jobs at public schools in Minnesota is conducted by a strict set of rules. Bids are sealed and guaranteed by the bidder, who includes a 'bid bond' that guarantees the bidder will enter into a contract.

It came as a surprise, in June of that year, when Arnie Murkiwasser submitted a bid of $455,700 for the total remodeling of the south wing of the school building. His company, Murkiwasser Paints, had never competed with the large contractors like Bullworth Buildings or Rene Johns Remodeling. When the bids were opened, his bid was $5005 less than the bid from Bullworth and $8100 less than the Rene Johns bid. When the bid review committee of Tom Harant and Billy Washburn began to review the subcontractor's bids, they realized that Murkiwasser Paints' total for their sub-contractors on this bid was $36,000 more than their total bid. Allowing for a small profit, Murkiwasser's cost was bound to be $57,500 more than his bid.

The bid bond for the project was a company check for $25,000, slightly more than the five percent required. It fell to Tom Harant to call Arnie and point out to him that his subcontractors totaled more than his total bid. Murkiwasser then informed Tom that his company could not be expected to enter into a contract where they would lose money. Mr. Harant informed Mr. Murkiwasser that his company would enter into the contract or the bid bond would be forfeited. Murkiwasser hung up on Tom without responding.

Attorneys exchanged letters. The contract was not issued. Tom started the legal process to enforce the Murkiwasser bid. And three weeks later, a full page ad appeared in the *Cherry Grove Journal*. It featured General Norman Schwarzkopf next to the words, 'The Mother of all Sales'. The complete sale of all the Murkiwasser stock of paint, carpet, paneling and lights was announced. The ad announced the purchase of Murkiwasser Paints by Lymon's Lights of Urholt.

"He got what he wanted, according to the guys downtown," said Tom, responding to Crystal's question. "No debt, and a lot of cash."

"What will he do?" she asked.

"Arnie is only 52 years old. He has enough cash to retire to Mexico, hire a house servant and a cook, and live like a 'don' in a seaside villa."

"You're kidding?" she said. "Aren't you?"

"No, I wish I was." Tom hesitated to tell her the rest. One of the men at the coffee table was present in someone's house when Mrs. Janet Murkiwasser was talking about their plans. It sounded like Arnie was going to Acapulco to buy a villa. They were going to spend three months in Mexico, then two months in Iron Lake. To Tom, it sounded like Murkiwasser was going to be present for two months out of five. The board could not declare his position vacant as long as he owned property out on Iron Lake.

"The bad news is, it sounds like he is going to stay on the board."

That is how it happened that Arnie Murkiwasser stayed on the Iron Lake Board of Directors over the next three years, while missing three board meetings in a row, then showing up for the next two.

*****

The following year did contain some good news and some 'just so' news. Sylvan Plant and Lillian Harvey resigned and moved away. Sylvan took a job teaching Social Studies in Bechyn High School, south of Willmar. His wife filed for divorce and moved back to Iron Lake where she had many friends. Lillian Harvey moved to the southeast where she found a job teaching at Rochester and found a steady boyfriend among the young farmers in Chatfield.

Tom received a personal call from Harry Hagen, the superintendent at Cherry Grove. Harry wanted Tom to know that Corrine Harant had just signed a contract for Elementary Art, replacing their veteran teacher who retired in June. The next day, Tom heard that the Athletic Coach from Texas, a teacher during the strike, would be teaching Physical Education and coaching the Urholt Raiders.

The incident with Linda Hummel continued to irk Arnie Murkiwasser. Linda was the Payroll Clerk who forged payroll checks after keeping a retired teacher on the payroll. Arnie swore that he was going to sanction Tom Harant for allowing her to make restitution. The

Spencer County attorney, meanwhile, had Judge Harley Bellows sign an order, putting her on probation as long as she continued to make timely payments on her debt. When the matter came up at a board meeting, the remainder of the board, including Connie Cratt, told Arnie to 'shut up' because the matter was handled.

Dennis DeFain, the Middle School principal, was suspended by Tom until a hearing could be held. The hearing officer, a retired judge, listened to the investigator. He ordered DeFain to be reinstated to his job, with a warning. Tom Harant, meanwhile, told DeFain that he could no longer trust him. Tom suspected that DeFain would work to create doubt about Tom's abilities, in retaliation for being suspended.

Patty Trivic continued to pester the superintendent about every comma and semi-colon in the board minutes, making sure, as she said, 'the minutes are exactly correct to the last period'.

Percy Smith and Curt Fitzsimmons remained just the same…always ready to support a program if it was good for kids.

Glacinda Fallow continued to work in her insurance office, although there were rumors about a lot of business going elsewhere. The County Attorney, some time in October that year, decided not to pursue charges against Mrs. Fallow. There just wasn't enough evidence that she aided 'an arson after the fact'.

Her office secretary, it was said, had 'the straight skinny' but wouldn't say much. According to gossip, the Farmers and Mechanics Insurance Company had filed papers to remove her as an agent. Mrs. Fallow filed a counter-suit alleging employment discrimination and vindictive prosecution. According to her secretary, the company backed off and was trying to persuade her to move to a town where she was less well known. Mrs. Fallow, however, took the position that she knew her customers and she was not about to move away.

'Bluster Barnes' went on a long vacation to Montana. Tom laughed while he said he hoped 'Bluster' would stick his foot in a prairie dog hole and break his leg. When Crystal immediately whacked Tom on the arm, he said he wasn't serious.

*****

Tom volunteered to be a substitute teacher for a day when the district was short of subs. While reviewing a class assignment, he found this quote inside the play *Julius Caesar*,

"The abuse of power is when it separates Remorse from power."
            Brutus in *Julius Caesar* (Act II.1.18)

*****

Karen Cratt moved out of their house and into town, sometime in August. She was quoted as saying 'Connie is still fighting the strike'. Towards the end of September, she moved back. Tom was having a beer with Billy Washburn when he heard she moved back and he said, "You never know about some people." What he didn't say aloud was, "I can't believe a person could live with that much anger."

There was nothing Tom could do about Cratt. The man no longer talked to him and was barely civil during the monthly board meetings when they were forced to be in the same room. Gossip came back to Tom, indicating that Cratt said this or Cratt said that. Tom ignored the gossip. He believed as he always did, that if Cratt had a problem with Tom, Connie would come and talk to him about it.

Tom believed that Connie Cratt was sure of himself and was not about to 'undermine' Tom behind his back. In *this estimation*, Tom was naïve and did not realize that Conifer Cratt would bide his time until the board could be convinced to fire their superintendent.

Tom laughed when he received a card from his friend in Inver Grove Heights. The card showed a 'boss' behind a big desk, saying to an employee, "Yes, I'm an agent of Satan but my duties are largely ceremonial."

"That's me," he said when he showed the card to Washburn. "I carry out the ceremonial duties around here but I really want to be an agent of Satan."

Billy laughed.

Tom added that there were people in the school district who thought *he was* an agent of the devil. Tom felt he needed to be a little 'standoffish' around some of his detractors. That's why he was shy about going to Urholt to play golf.

Tom assumed that many people were afraid of him or didn't like him. He tried to smile when he was in crowds but the strike year seemed to leach his enthusiasm for smiling and 'being polite' to people who would just as soon that he resigned.

Crystal had her job at Urholt where she taught vocal music in grades

K-12. It was an exhausting job but she loved it. Many nights, Tom and Crystal would collapse into their easy chairs and fall asleep with the television running. Tom had his work, also, planning the schedules, writing an occasional policy and trying to balance the budget. In the next three years, he was forced to trim another $300,000 out of the Iron Lake budget.

As Tom liked to say, he had his work, and it consumed his time.

CHAPTER TWENTY-EIGHT
A Little Awareness, Almost No Change

"What we came to realize, much too late, was that the state's teacher organization had targeted Iron Lake. We were close enough to WCCO Television that they could get good video of the strike...making the evening news. That was of benefit to all the groups that went out on strike. However, when the Iron Lake teachers wanted to settle, the board said no and ordered me to open the school with replacement teachers."
(Supt. Tom Harant, in front of the Iron Lake Century Elm, on the WCCO Evening News, January 10, 1992)

They were sitting on the breezeway, enjoying brandy and cokes. Their wives were not yet back from a shopping trip to Willmar. Wrecker was sitting with his feet up, admiring the scorecard from the day's 'Quick Nine' on the cow pasture at Urholt. Tom was in the dumps, after losing five balls to errant shots, his score soared to a 59.

"I did what I could, you know."

"About what?"

"The aftereffects, the anger, the animosities, the strange way people treat each other when one side loses."

"Who lost?" asked Wrecker. He was fairly certain of Tom's answer but wanted to hear Tom's opinion.

"The school district. We lost six good teachers after the strike."

"You told me the teachers lost, when I asked you last year."

"Yes. They also lost. They lost the support of a large number of people who live in Iron Lake. Some people believe the teachers committed a mortal sin."

"Tom, you have got to let go of it."

"No one won," Tom said. He watched a car turning the corner, heading for his driveway, knowing the two women were safely home.

When Crystal opened the back door of her car, he saw her pull four large sacks out of the backseat.

"Looks like we had a successful trip," he said smiling.

*****

"You want me to forget the strike. I can't. Nor can I forget my father and his pain. Or the pain of some of the people here in Iron Lake." Tom drank from his brandy...at first, a sip...then a swallow. Tom stood up and stepped back from the table. He looked at 'the Ramblin' Wreck from Bechyn Tech' and watched while his buddy Wreck raised his glass in a salute. No words passed between them.

Crystal came up beside Tom and placed her hand under his arm. She squeezed his arm. Tom raised his glass to Wreck and said,

"May the sun always shine

Upon your window pane," before his friend Wreck added,

"May a rainbow, *dammit*,

Follow each rain."

The two men laughed. To Crystal, they seemed maudlin. She was used to their behavior but bothered by Tom's dedication to his school district. She knew he was carrying a large amount of guilt for the strike and for not visiting his father who was dying with bone cancer that fall.

"I have this dream, Wreck. Can you see this?" Tom walked to the table and sat down. "I'm in a field of wheat, running, trying to reach a small grove of trees. It's night, with no moon. Someone is chasing me. I can't see who it is, and I don't know why I'm running. I burst into the trees, and circle around to my right. Through the dark I see three men...they are carrying shotguns."

"We've heard this dream, before," said Wreck.

"I can't see the faces of the three men".

"It's a dream, Tom."

"Yes, it is. But why am I running?"

Wreck didn't answer. Tom wanted to look at his wife but knew if he did, she would know something was wrong. He knew that she would see the hurt in his eyes if he so much as looked at her.

"In the dream, I feel a conflict. I am proud that I am out front, but wary of the shotguns."

"Is that all bad?" asked his friend Wrecker.

"No…it's not all bad. There must be an end to Iron Lake. It would feel good to get rid of the bastards and leave."

There was a small gasp at his shoulder. He turned to look into Crystal's face. He could see the worry and the fear, deep inside her blue eyes. "I don't want to tell you this…but," and he stopped. Both her hands circled his arm, squeezing.

"There was a rumor," said Wreck.

"And you didn't tell me?" stated Crystal with a glare at Tom.

"Would it have made any difference?"

"No."

"What did they do?" asked the Wreck, urging Tom to tell them what they *both knew* they didn't want to hear.

"They voted Four to Two to ask me to resign." Tom turned and put his left hand over Crystal's hands. He could see tears welling up into her eyes. A drop of water squeezed out of her left eye and ran toward her chin. *'At least our kids are out of high school,'* he thought to himself.

"Which four?" asked Wreck.

"Cratt, Trivic, Arnie and Glacial Linda. She always follows Cratt's lead."

"Can the vote be reversed?"

"One of the four of them would have to move to rescind the original motion. Or Percy or Fitzsimmons would have to move to rescind and hope no one remembers Robert's Rules."

"Even then, it would require two of the original four to vote to rescind and rehire you," said the Wreck, helpfully.

"Not likely," Tom said quietly. He was still looking into Crystal's eyes. He could see the pain. They had invested so much of themselves in church choir, the local Lions Club, the Chamber of Commerce and Sunday morning coffees at Bulrush Bay Resort.

*****

"We hang by a slender thread, with the flames of divine wrath flashing about the thread, ready to burn it asunder," he said.

"You're quoting someone, aren't you, Tom?" asked Crystal.

"Jonathon Edwards, a Puritan pastor." He pulled the 5x7 card out of his pocket, to check the quote. He missed a few words but said nothing. The four of them were sitting on the breezeway, Mary Jo and Crystal on the swing, Wreck and Tom in the chairs.

"His unyielding leadership style made some parishioners uncomfortable. They eventually booted him out. He became the first President of Princeton University."

"There's no comparison," said Crystal. "You did your job."

"Consternation," added Wrecker Kline.

"*To our enemies*," said Tom and Crystal in one breath.

*****

During the fall of 1990, the teachers in 35 school districts went out on strike. In 34 of those districts, the teachers were allowed to make up days lost and were paid their regular salary. In one district, the teachers lost 53 days of salary. They also lost the good faith and trust of the parents and residents of Iron Lake.

What the union leaders don't tell the rank and file is this: there are no winners in a strike. The union has the upper hand when the Intent to Strike is filed. But the moment the members step onto the sidewalk with signs in their hands, the moment they strike, that is the moment when the leverage shifts. From that moment on, the employer has the leverage. The employer can stall, delay, obfuscate and in extreme cases, lock out the strikers. In Iron Lake, the employer hired replacement teachers. In the end, there were no winners. Both sides lost.

The State Legislature reacted by passing a bill requiring school districts to finish their contract negotiations by January 15, or pay a hefty fine. This seemed to speed up the process but the teachers retained much of the 'leverage', using the deadline to wrest large increases out of Minnesota's school boards.

Tom Harant went to a state meeting wearing a button that said, 'No Contract, No School' but he was largely ignored. He had seen, first hand, the animosity and anger among teachers who were trying to teach while their contract was not settled, trying to keep the stress out of the classroom. He believed that if the contract isn't settled by August 20, the district should delay school. He also realized that 'No Contract, No School' would put pressure on the board to settle while the teachers ran the risk of losing days of pay.

When discussing the reform of the teacher's bargaining bill, Tom Harant found that many school superintendents did not relish the thought of taking on the unions. Their role, as always, was to see that the children of the school district received the best possible education. The role of the school superintendent, Tom came to believe, was not to promote a change in how contracts with the unions are negotiated.

*****

Standing in his kitchen, *three years later,* Tom saw gentle tears in his wife's eyes. He knew she was feeling bad for him, for all they had been through during and after the strike, dealing with *the shadow* of Connie Cratt that cast a pall across their lives and the lives of Iron Lake teachers. Now, to have the board ask for his resignation…in what amounted to a betrayal.

"We should tell this story…who would believe it?" he said to himself, ten years after the strike. Tom and Crystal were in Fairmont, his third school district. His kids were grown. Cookie married a young man she started dating in high school. Carl was working in Denver. Mark was now a Lt. Commander in 'Today's Navy.'

"There will always be incidents that hang heavy on my heart. Standing at the fence hearing despair in the voice of a young teacher. Our pregnant teacher when she rushed out of the community meeting. My daughter's face when she knew she had been fired. Several of our mothers describing the hurt they feel when their neighbor won't speak to them."

"Standing on the stage at graduation, watching the faces of our graduates, smiling and hopeful and expectant. They go back to their chairs and then they sit down. They hold their diploma case quietly in their laps. When they figure no one is looking, they sneak a peak and then they *really smile.* The diploma is really inside the case. They made it. They are done. Somehow, in a quiet way, that makes it all worthwhile."

When Tom thought about Iron Lake, he saw the strikers on the sidewalk, the WCCO helicopter, and the flames inside the house across the street. But above all else, he saw Conifer Cratt winning the confidence of three members of the board. He saw Conifer Cratt daring 'Bluster Barnes' to lead his people out. He saw Cratt smiling from inside his determination to bring down *'that group. They ain't a real union.'*

That was how Tom described the story. Crystal knew that Tom, more than anyone else, still carried guilt about the strike, still thought there was more he should have done during that tumultuous year in Iron Lake.

"It's your guilt, isn't it?" she said one day when she mustered the courage to ask him. He was sitting on the breezeway among the packing boxes, listening to his trees. In the background, she heard Abba singing, *Thank you for the Music.* Tom didn't respond. He was looking out the window at a rain cloud approaching from the southwest...it was raining in that corner of Iron Lake. He knew the storm would blow over in about twenty minutes, leaving the corn and soybean fields damp with the rain they needed. The farmers called these storms 'million dollar rains' for the value they added.

Afterward, he would sit in his breezeway and listen to the final drops of rain dripping onto the patio stones. He would probably stare at the fountain, blaming himself for never fixing it properly. He would look in the direction of the retreating storm, and marvel at the crystal clarity of a blue sky. Crystal would watch over him, and take care of him. On some days, when she felt blue, she would wonder if it would ever be Tom's turn to feel the joy of a rainbow.

An Author's Footnote:

In 2003 the Minnesota State Legislature considered a major reform to the Public Employees Labor Relations Act, unhappily referred to as PELRA. The reform proposed that if the two-year contract was not settled by the first day of school after the contract expired, then school could not be held. The reform was, in essence, "No Contract, No School," and penalized both sides for not getting the contract settled.

The liberals within the Legislature could not bring themselves to support a proposal that was seen as 'anti-union' and PELRA reform was not adopted.

ENDNOTE

[1] **An Ancient Irish Prayer,** in the revised version by Thomas Harant in Goudy Old Style font, © September, 2002.

ABOUT THE AUTHOR...

Marty Duncan taught English and Journalism in Fairmont, Minnesota before becoming a high school principal in Sherburn, Minnesota. He then served as school superintendent in Amboy, then Howard Lake, then Olivia. His most recent posting was at Greenway, on Minnesota's Iron Range. *Iron Lake Burning* was written as catharsis, an act of reliving and relieving past guilt for actions not taken, for words not spoken. The book is a singular tribute to teachers for those small acts of compassion and caring that occur daily between 'our' teachers and their most precious cargo.

Mr. Duncan currently writes *O'magadh*® a weekly column of satire and current commentary. Marty is a Vietnam Era Veteran and regrets not serving in Vietnam. A member of Lions Clubs International and American Legion, Marty and Carolynn live and work in southern Minnesota.

You are invited to visit Marty's website at **www.omagadh.com**

Another Novel by Marty Duncan...

Gold...then Iron

A golden artifact disappears, hidden among the Irish miners in northern Minnesota. James Harant (U.S. Navy) sets out to recover the *Golden Eagle*. His team encounters two Japanese Army officers who will commit any atrocity. Harant's efforts go awry; a friend dies rather than reveal its location.

On a routine training mission for British Intelligence, three young naval officers are bursting with naïve enthusiasm until a series of deadly incidents challenge their loyalties. Lt. Harant almost discovers love... before fate hands him a shocking surprise! Harant's team left Minnesota believing that Godfrey's letters (contained in the Appendix) would tell what Godfrey meant by 'safe and dry'. Readers are encouraged to find the solution to the mystery.

Copies (of Gold ...then Iron) are available at:
PageFreePublishing.com, Amazon.com,
Half.com and Marty's site
www.omagadh.com

Kelsey: a Civil War Tale

An Irish lass discovers she can overcome her fear of men while waiting for Patrick Harant to return from the Civil War. *'Kelsey'* is the third in the Harant family series; set against the early Civil War in Louisiana, the Dakota Indian Uprising in Minnesota and the bloody battlefields of the Civil War.

(*'Kelsey'* will be published in 2004).